Waiting for the Perfect Dawn

To
my dear Zeynep
Best wishes now and
always
Annu Subramanian

Waiting for the Perfect Dawn

A Novel

Annu Subramanian

iUniverse, Inc.
New York Bloomington Shanghai

Waiting for the Perfect Dawn

iUniverse books may be ordered through booksellers or by contacting:

iUniverse
1663 Liberty Drive
Bloomington, IN 47403
www.iuniverse.com
1-800-Authors (1-800-288-4677)

ISBN: 978-0-595-42752-9 (pbk)
ISBN: 978-0-595-68141-9 (cloth)
ISBN: 978-0-595-87082-0 (ebk)

Printed in the United States of America

To

My father, Ramaswami, who taught me the joy of reading
My mother, Vijaya, whose life exemplifies the ideals of 'a woman of a different world'
My husband, PR, and my children, Darshan and Krisha, for their patience

Ellen Loughney, for her constant encouragement and support
Melissa Bruno, Sister Judith Dever, and Maureen Gokey,
for their valuable suggestions

PART I

She is getting married

A breezy afternoon in the autumn years of the eighteen nineties

Buvana walked across the stately hall and dutifully did her obeisance. He was sitting on a silk mat in the middle of a cluster of faces and a babble of voices. He had come with his family to assess her for matrimony. Buvana was displayed at her best. Dressed in silks and decked in jewelry, she looked every inch a money-minting, baby-making machine at the tender age of fourteen. The assessment commenced from head to toe.

Her eyes were focused on the floor. She was modest.

She spoke. She was not mute.

She looked up when someone spoke to her. She was not blind or deaf.

She was able to walk across the hall. She was not crippled.

She was the only child of a wealthy landlord. She would fetch a grand dowry.

To crown these attributes, she had a beautiful face.

Buvana passed the test in the marriage market. The visitors were pleased. This girl would make a perfect bride for their dutiful son, Sethu. With the assurance of a favorable letter, the groom's family left. The exhibition was over.

"Murthy, Saroja, your daughter is getting married. Finally, at the age of fourteen!" exclaimed a relative.

Murthy smiled in pride. Saroja hugged her daughter.

Still … there was one question that nagged Buvana's neighbors: "If Sethu is a great match, why is he still in the marriage market?"

And this ONE question gave birth to several ancillary queries:

"How old is he? Is he twenty-nine, twenty-eight?"

"Well, isn't that too late for marriage, especially the first time?"

"This is his first marriage, isn't it?"

"Are there wishy-washy health issues in his family?"

"Sethu is about twenty-eight. This is his first marriage," said Swami, Kanyakoil's matchmaker. "His family has been waiting for the right girl. Buvana's horoscope matches Sethu's perfectly—a heavenly match, you see?"

The letter arrived. Sethu's family was eager to choose a date for the wedding. Buvana's parents wondered if she liked him.

"I'm not even fifteen. Why don't I get married after a few years?" Buvana's apprehension found a voice.

The elders didn't understand her apprehension. Did she like him? Was this meant to happen? This was the first time her horoscope matched a boy's, or in this case, a man's. She was born under an unlucky star. A blemish, registered at the time of her birth, dictated her destiny!

Buvana wondered what Sethu and his family thought of her. She couldn't have heard his family's assessment of her dense, raven-colored hair that was kept together in a snake-like braid. She didn't hear one of Sethu's cousins speak of her eyes as a set of brilliant stones, smothered by velvet eyelashes. She didn't realize how her perfectly shaped lips quivered in her present apprehension of her future happiness. How could she have any clue that her wavy hair, skirting her face, accentuated her translucent skin?

Murthy and Saroja were still waiting for their daughter's reply.

"What does Buvana know about these matters? This is her future. She is fourteen. The elders know best," said an elderly neighbor, proclaiming her wisdom.

Such impertinence didn't wound Buvana's feelings. She was used to officious neighbors. She also appreciated her parents' consideration because it was a luxury. They respected her opinion! Most brides didn't see their grooms' faces until the wedding day. Buvana relieved the suspense. Yes, she would marry him.

Brinda, the ancestral home of Murthy's family, enjoyed Mother Nature's benevolence with great pride. Situated on the banks of *Cauvery* in the southeast regions, it cherished prosperity and privacy on the lap of pregnant orchards and brimming streams. Murthy did a lot to enhance the estates that enveloped Kanyakoil, the dainty village that was presently glowing in seasonal glory.

While sitting on the lowest branch of the crooked banyan tree, Buvana looked at the land around her. This was the world she knew, dappled with transient clouds and moist earth. This was her sanctuary that soothed her when she had to search her heart. Lately, that telltale heart was mute.

She opened the bag. Out came a box that sheltered a few things she valued most in her life. Her fingers landed on a few shells, a pair of glass bangles, a brooch, and a delicate porcelain box. She cherished these simple objects beyond anything she valued in her young life—not of any monetary value, nevertheless, precious. These treasures wouldn't be included in the long list of dowry that was piling high and deep in the hall. She placed the things she had brought with her inside the box. She wrote a note that included her name, the date, and the reason that warranted this safekeeping. She opened the secret compartment inside the swollen branch of the banyan tree and deposited her priceless property. This was her safe-deposit box, her one and only safe-deposit box, her precious secret.

The clouds played hide-and-seek in perfect rhythm, matching the lethargic strokes of her pen. Buvana found peace when she wrote. It brought a conclusion to her nights and birth to her mornings. She was disappointed that her family didn't think much of her writing. Well, her father was an exception. Would Sethu share her feelings? Buvana saw her mother waving to her from the veranda. She did that often when she wanted her daughter to return indoors.

"You must stop writing, Buvana. I don't know what you keep scribbling all day," said her mother. "You have to learn to be serious about things, dear. You're soon going to be a married woman with many responsibilities."

Buvana had no desire to be responsible or to be married. She was fourteen and wanted to write. She was a child and wished to remain so for a while.

Oh, what a beautiful dawn! The misty air, mingled with the jasmine-filled earth, welcomed another day. How many mornings had Buvana woken up to hear the dancing of the wind? Far too many to count! She ran to the window to breathe in the dawn. It was her routine to follow the sunlight's saffron streaks on the bountiful river. The sound of the river, sloshing on the mossy rocks, reached her through the windswept windows. These would soon be past moments.

She heard the routine sounds of the morning. Her stomach reminded her of her hunger and she raced downstairs. She should be happy. Why wasn't she? If only she knew that he liked her, that he felt something for her. He was a stranger. Would he really be kind to her?

Saroja understood her daughter's concern. "It's natural, Buvana," Saroja smiled gently, handing her daughter a cup of steaming coffee.

"Is it?"

"Yes, just the kind of anxiety every bride feels. I had the same apprehensions. Look how happy I am. I have a perfect husband, don't you think?"

Buvana tried to engrave a permanent image of her mother in her mind—her dense, wavy hair, her bashful smile that Buvana had inherited, and her dazzling eyes. Her father was sitting on his chair, taking a big pinch of the scented powder from his snuffbox. Buvana sat by him. Murthy's kind face, hiding the anxiety of the imminent separation from his only child, displayed his customary smile. His broad forehead and silver-tinted hair surprisingly accentuated a childish expression. She held his hand that had helped her through her first walk. She picked up the jewel-studded snuffbox. When she was little, her father had taught her the primary colors by guiding her fingers on the stones.

"Is this my last breakfast here, Amma?" asked Buvana, relishing the cotton-soft idli and coconut chutney. "What'll I do if I need you in their house?"

"Last? Nonsense! You're just getting married, my dear. You'll visit us many times. Don't forget that we'll come to see you."

"Amma, can I take you with me? The matchmaker said that they have a big house. I don't want to leave you."

"Oh, you're so silly, my dear," said Saroja, hugging her daughter. "You want to take me with you! You're about to enter the most important part of your life. Being a wife is a privilege and becoming a mother is a blessing, my dear. Just wait and see how beautifully you manage everything. You're going to be so happy and busy that you won't have much time to think of Brinda!" Although Saroja rallied her spirits casually, she could hardly hide her sad sighs in her spirited speech. Sending one's child away was not an easy task.

"How about a cup of coffee for me?" asked Kitta, Saroja's brother.

"Kitta Mama!" shouted Buvana. She ran to her uncle.

Swami waved goodbye to Murthy once again before closing the iron gates behind him. Murthy's daughter was to be married soon, and he had played a major part to facilitate the event. Murthy had already paid him a handsome sum. Generous Murthy! Finally, after months of mismatched horoscopes, Sethu's matched perfectly with Buvana's! Swami stopped at the corner store to purchase some provisions.

"Swami, how are you?"

Janaki! She was the most notorious busybody in Kanyakoil. It was her business to know about every inhabitant of the village—from the revered priest to the lowly sweeper. Most people were afraid of her sharp tongue. Swami was no exception.

"Swami, which girl's destiny is in your grip at the present time?" asked Janaki.

Swami told her about Buvana's marriage arrangement. She ran to the nearest friend to disclose the latest news. Within a few hours, without the town crier's assistance, the entire village echoed the good news; Murthy's daughter is getting married.

Buvana took a long look at the river and stepped gingerly on the weed-covered path that crept to her home. The solitude didn't give her the usual pleasure. The stillness somehow made her uneasy. Strange! The bloodshot clouds at sunset drew a lot of noisy birds to the trees on the spacious banks, but Buvana heard nothing. Her spirits were hard of hearing.

Premonition! She remembered reading about it in one of the English novels her father brought from the city. A young girl had a similar feeling of foreboding before walking into a disaster. Buvana felt a little silly. Her mother was right!

Buvana's imagination had a tendency to take flight at the slightest encouragement or at the mildest apprehension.

Darkness crawled into the orange clouds. Buvana could already see the silhouettes in her home through the kitchen window. She used to be afraid of these shadows when she was little. She thought they were trespassers! Wasn't it Thangam Athai who asked Buvana to imagine that the shadows were dancers behind the oil lamps? By the way, where was Thangam Athai? The parched leaves announced the arrival of someone! Her mother was probably coming to scold her for wandering along the banks after sunset. When Buvana turned to face her mother, she was surprised to see her aunt. She ran to her and embraced one of the dearest people in her life and felt the warmth reciprocated in her aunt's smile and hug.

"Athai, I lost all hopes of seeing you," said Buvana. "What happened to you?"

"Would I miss my Buvana's big day?" Thangam asked. "Would I miss my brother's only daughter's wedding? I just got delayed a little, that's all!" Thangam adored little Buvana. A warm affection and sincere regard subsisted between the aunt and the niece. "Are you ready for the most important day of your life, Buvana?" asked Thangam.

"Athai, I'm scared to leave all of you," Buvana replied nervously. "I don't know anybody in their house."

Thangam took her niece's hand and began to walk in the direction of her brother's home. "My dearest child," said Thangam. "Never think that marriage is going to take you away from Brinda and your family. You're the most important part of our lives. You'll surely bring your children here, and they'll run on the sand just like you do!"

Buvana smiled. "Will you visit me, Athai?"

"We'll visit you to see how majestically you live in your in-law's home. Do believe me." Thangam acknowledged Buvana's brave smile with a comforting embrace.

Thangam's encouraging words didn't really alleviate Buvana's apprehension. The wedding day was getting nearer. Her hope of future happiness shouldn't be tainted with doubt. She was afraid of this feeling, percolating through her veins, shredding her peace of mind a little at a time. But she felt better after reviewing Thangam's latest advice.

"Buvana, a typical husband doesn't like to humor his wife in the presence of his mother or sisters. When you feel the need to question your husband's authority, simply take a deep breath, act as though you agree with him, and do exactly what you want to do," said Thangam, winking at the end of this very interesting advice. "He'll never know."

Buvana found her mother on the balcony.

"Amma," said Buvana.

"What is it, my dear?" asked Saroja. "Are you still worried about the wedding?"

"Not really. I've been thinking about Thangam Athai. I feel terrible that she … she tries to sit away from the crowd in every function."

"I know, dear. Why are you thinking about it now?" asked Saroja.

"Well, what happened to her? All I know is that her husband died. You told me that I could ask you these questions one day. Tell me," insisted Buvana.

"Today? Now? What's the hurry?"

"I won't get another chance. I'm leaving in a few days, remember?" asked Buvana.

"All right. Well, Thangam became a widow when she was eighteen," began Saroja. "When her husband died, she continued to live with her mother-in-law. She also made frequent and long visits to Brinda to please her mother. You know, Thangam was responsible for bringing your father and me together. And to this day, we owe our thanks to her for a lifetime of happiness."

"I know. Thangam Athai is precious."

"Yes, she is. After our marriage, your father and I tried to convince Thangam to make Brinda her home. Thangam was seriously thinking of living alone. A young woman shouldn't live alone, defying customs and traditions."

"Live alone?" asked Buvana. "Did she?"

"No. To everybody's relief, Thangam made Brinda her home, but she never really lived with us for a lengthy period of time," replied Saroja. "She was here and there, helping relatives and friends around the villages. Anybody in need of consolation sought her assistance. Her presence was essential at births, deaths, weddings, and naming ceremonies—especially during the pre-ceremonial preparations. Her widowed status made her vulnerable. She was not to bring good luck on auspicious occasions, you see? As a result of this phobia, she stayed away from the crowd during the actual ceremonies—after working like a horse to make the ceremonial occasions possible."

"But she still hides behind a pillar or something! Amma, our family doesn't care about insensitive customs and superstitions. Then … why does Thangam Athai follow the same nonsense during our functions?" asked Buvana.

"Habit," explained Saroja. "She is stubborn. She doesn't listen to anybody. Even I can't change her mind."

True! Thangam learned at a very young age to take what life granted with a pinch of salt. There were a few people, such as Saroja and Murthy, who didn't agree with the way their society treated her. She was thankful for those few. Such was life! Thangam laughed at the sympathy and went about her business. Over time, she learned the art of dealing with her misery—Thangam buried her tears in her smiles.

Today, during the auspicious pre-wedding ceremony of her dearest niece, Thangam stood behind one of the pillars. Thangam forgot how to look good after she became a widow. Her society would never forgive her if she looked beautiful when there was no husband to impress. Her white, cotton sari—a widow's uniform—concealed her graceful figure. Her coarsely cut hair made her soft features appear plain.

Thangam proudly looked at Buvana. Her meager frame seemed to manage the burden of silk sari and jewelry. Her demure eyes were focused on the floor. Her sensitive lips wouldn't break into laughter. The young bride still didn't show her delighted smile. But she was young and her nervousness was understandable. Thangam felt that fourteen was probably a little too early for marriage these days! Buvana was almost fifteen, wasn't she? Marriage was a terminal commitment. It was not wise to postpone it!

◆ ◆ ◆

Brinda dazzled in the wedding decorations. The silver and gold vessels gleamed against the rainbow of flower garlands. The fragrance of the incense was in constant competition with the flavors from the kitchen. The wedding of Murthy's daughter was not an ordinary occasion. Assisted by substantial glitter, it resembled a royal function. Murthy paid extraordinary wages to invite musicians, performers, and decorators to make his daughter's wedding unique and spectacular.

Sethu sat by her and repeated the mantra after the priest. His sticky hand was holding Buvana's from the dawn of the wedding ceremonies. Buvana glanced at Sethu's profile to notice his acknowledgment of her presence. She could see nothing except his mechanical response to the priest.

While the ceremony seemed to be steadily progressing, an unexpected commotion began to test the integrity of the wedding parties. The in-laws were assessing Buvana's dowry. Unexpectedly, their calculation fell short of a sovereign or two of gold. Sethu's mother was angry.

"The wedding chain doesn't go on the bride's neck until every gram of gold and silver is accounted for," Sethu's mother shouted at the priest. "Do you understand?"

The priest retreated in fear. The guests stared at her in awe. What a formidable temper!

"Make sure you count everything now," Ponni, the mother-in-law's cousin, whispered in her ear. "Nice or nasty, Murthy is a businessman. It's in his blood, you know. He'll always try to save every rupee."

"I know, cousin. Stand by the silver display. I'll get hold of that Murthy."

Sethu's mother questioned the family's integrity in no mild terms. Her stocky physique and cold eyes supported her redoubtable personality. Murthy whispered, pleaded, and struggled to make peace in the electrified atmosphere.

Janaki, who cherished any wrinkle in a happy situation, waited with whetted curiosity for the outcome of the angry in-law's outburst. She had not earned the title of the town's most notorious busybody by simple means. Her friends joined hands to add spice to the already smoldering conversation.

"Will they stop the marriage? Did Murthy really cheat? Oh, what will happen to Buvana now?" Janaki and a few inquisitive matrons voiced their concerns.

"Thangam, what shall we do?" Saroja asked her sister-in-law. "How did this happen? Didn't we measure everything properly?"

"Don't worry, Saroja. I'm here," Thangam said confidently.

"Kitta, we can't stop the marriage now, can we?" Murthy asked his brother-in-law, afraid of the in-law's temper.

"Let's wait and see, Murthy. Don't worry," assured Kitta.

Such eruptions were common in most weddings. Shameful, but such was society! It was highly unconventional to stop a wedding ceremony at this point. Undoubtedly, a bride from a suspended ceremony would never see another marriage proposal. On the bright side, such wrinkles in a wedding ritual didn't necessarily mean prolonged misery for a bride in her new home—if the wrinkles were fixed immediately.

Everything was appraised and measured—from the grand silver bowls to the puny bronze lamps—for size, shape, and quality. Each gram of gold and silver was weighed and checked for authenticity. Buvana, although thoroughly ashamed, managed to raise her head. What was her father doing?

"Please accept this snuffbox. It should certainly add a few extra ounces of gold," Murthy said, giving the heirloom to Sethu's mother.

Buvana cringed. This antique box had seen several generations of Murthy's family. Now it was used in this distasteful bartering. She felt bitter, but she was lost in the requirements of a very confusing ceremony. Her outrage, though justified, would carry no voice in such a situation. The dowry measured up to the in-law's expectations. The only thing that fell short of calculation was the questionable integrity of one family against the temperance and good breeding of the other.

Sethu's mother displayed an angelic smile. "These miscalculations happen in quite a few weddings, you know, I'm not in the least upset," she said to Saroja. "I hope you understand!"

Saroja tried to smile. Her face was red with shame. Her heart was heavy with embarrassment.

Sethu's hand felt like a noose when he clasped the wedding chain. They were husband and wife! The couple walked around the holy fire. They promised each other everlasting love. They made a pact to rejoice in each other's happiness, share tears of sorrow, and sustain eternal commitment. They made a vow to share their strengths, to be of one mind, and to observe the vows together. Buvana still didn't feel comfortable in his company. She felt an inexplicable urge to disappear into the dense trees by the river.

The guests threw flowers and yellow rice on the bride and the groom. He walked here, he walked there, and he simpered and smiled at the guests. She followed him, lost in the rustling folds of her silk sari, weighed down by the jewelry. Music burst. Laughter broke. Greetings filled the big hall that was richly decorated from ceiling to floor with fragrant, vibrant flowers. The young bride mechanically followed her groom when he moved among the guests. The entire village had assembled for the wedding. Some had come to check if Buvana's wedding display matched her status. Some had arrived to bless the daughter of a generous benefactor and friend. The bride, unfortunately, was not in the state of mind to relish the tasty feast or the spicy conversation. Her husband, however, appeared to be at ease. Why wouldn't he say something to her?

Buvana prayed nervously. If only the sun never set. But that coward hid behind the amber clouds.

When she entered the bridal room, a thousand knots churned her stomach. Sethu was waiting for her. She saw him sitting on the bed, rather lounging on the pillows, chewing tobacco. While she stood there, immersed in apprehension and despair, he opened the snuffbox and enjoyed a luxurious pinch of the expensive mix.

That snuffbox had belonged to her dear father until that morning.

He took her hand and made her sit by him. If veins could explode, hers were ready to let her down. She looked around—anywhere but at his intimidating figure—and she greedily breathed in the cool breeze that rushed from the river. The wick on the oil lamp was wheezing in the breeze. He relieved the wick of its misery. Now Buvana's heart was wheezing from his touch. He possessed her, even as the burnt smoke, oozing from the wick, permeated the dark surroundings. He turned to the other side to snore away his victory. She moved to hide her pain. It wouldn't go away.

Somewhere down a few yards, the tiny waves crawled to the banks to convey their sympathy. Their Buvana was crying.

A long cavalcade of carriages was waiting on the gravel driveway to take the bride, the groom, and his family to Sethu's ancestral home. Buvana followed her husband into the first carriage, and his mother's generous proportions crushed Buvana's delicate silk when she squeezed in. The procession began to move. Buvana glanced at her father's kind face. He was smiling bravely. Her mother's face was half-hidden in the fringe of her sari. She was crying. The lonely bride had a glimpse of her aunt's face in the background. Thangam had a cheerful smile, shadowed just a little by her goodbye. Kitta's short, thin frame was hiding behind one of the pillars.

Buvana was not prepared for the desolate departure. She couldn't digest the blurred image of Brinda, readily merging with the distant horizon. Misery! Would her husband say something to comfort her? She hopefully glanced at his face. His severe expression matched his mother's. What an introduction to a new chapter in her life! Where was the promised happiness? Was Sethu reluctant to speak because of his mother's presence? That didn't make sense to her. What about his silence during the previous night? Why the silence?

Buvana's in-laws lived in Chinnoor, a busy market town. The new bride glanced at the ancestral home. It certainly was not another Brinda, but it had a dominating presence. The cluster of coconut trees, drooping over the stone patio, made her think of something words couldn't describe. It felt like a dangerous creature was lurking in the shadows. Her mother was right. Buvana did let her imagination run wild—what with her fancy for writing!

The crowd amazed Buvana. As she stepped out of the carriage, she was splashed with red water and yellow rice. She stepped into the house with her right foot in, turmeric-soaked and slippery. While the men measured her from a distance, the ladies directly stared at her.

"Hope she has a male child and many more after that," said the elderly ladies.

"She's educated, you know?" said one of the amazed ladies, admiring the little bride. "Hasn't she finished high school?"

"What's she going to do with reading and writing?" asked an envious woman, trying to make a point. "She's here to keep her husband happy in bed, cook a little, and push babies out like the rest of us."

Buvana forgot her humiliation momentarily due to her hunger pangs. Would her mother-in-law give her something to eat? Should she ask her? No, she was too shy to ask for food! Thankfully, Buvana remembered her mother's instructions. Men had to eat before women sat down for a meal—at least in most orthodox households. The in-laws would expect Buvana to remember this womanly etiquette in her new home. Buvana's mother, while teaching her daughter this protocol, didn't really expect the mother-in-law to follow the rule! Being a compassionate and considerate human being, Saroja had envisioned Sethu's mother with similar, gentle feelings.

Where was Sethu? He didn't come into the dining hall for another hour. In the mean time, Buvana drank several cups of water to fill the void. By the time the ladies sat down for lunch, it was late afternoon.

The bride's painful first day in her new home crawled slowly. Was there no end in sight? She was weary of making empty smiles and half-hearted conversations with people she hardly knew. On the other hand, she didn't want the day to sink into darkness. Unfortunately, the day did sink into darkness. Buvana's heart thudded in apprehension. She hated to be alone with him. Her head ached due to the journey, which had only increased with the noisy guests. Further, the fear of sharing his bed exacerbated her existing pain. But he was waiting. He took her again, as barbarically as before, never meeting her eye, never uttering a word. He was not the man to let her feel his kind touch, hear his soft words, and sense his gentle gestures. The young girl felt used and discarded.

The morning brought more misery. A crowd of family and friends arrived to welcome the bride once again. The women assessed Buvana. Dozens of eyes stared at her. Strange, unwelcome hands touched her to find imperfections. Secret voices whispered about her. The women evaluated her skin color, nose, hair, and her talents.

"She's fair, but isn't she thin?"

"Look at her hair. Looks like rain cloud!"

"Her nose is too long. She could smile a little. She's not going to lose her father's money for that."

"Have you seen her needlework? Beautiful."

"Let's see if she can get Sethu a son. Her waist is too thin to bear a child. She should gain some weight."

"She has a rich father? She's a bag of bones, isn't she? They haven't been feeding her well?"

"That woman is surely jealous of the bride," whispered another guest. "Remember, she has three unmarried daughters!"

Buvana was in agony. She saw her husband strutting among the wedding acquisitions: cattle, clothes, and money to boast! His features were etched in her mind by now, steeped in fear and disgust. His bloodshot eyes, thick hair, heavy mustache, and muscular stature complemented his rough manners. By this time, Buvana was sadly aware of Sethu's favorite hobby—his fondness for arrack. He was in the habit of chewing tobacco from dawn to dusk. One of his pockets stored a pouch of chewing tobacco and a box of snuff. The other securely held a flask of arrack. At times, as his mother proudly announced, Sethu played with expensive brandy.

The men loudly estimated the land the young bride brought with the alliance and wondered if the bulk of it was arable. "Hope she produces a son within the year," said the women. Buvana wanted to know how Sethu reacted to the guests' blessings. He wasn't there. Where was he?

The crowd was here for a luncheon that was arranged for a few family members and friends. They had missed the famous wedding! The guests were eager to appraise and criticize Buvana's dowry. A good portion of the hall was allocated for this ornate display. The women touched the expensive silk saris and scrutinized the gold and silver. One of the mother-in-law's friends picked up Buvana's gold waistband in her hands and declared that it felt quite light. It couldn't be as heavy as it appeared.

"The jewelers are getting slick," commented the lady. "They manage to use less gold to accommodate parents' purses. But the bride's father doesn't have to resort to such goldsmiths, does he? Isn't he supposed to be rich?"

"Rich? He owns a lot of property in Kanyakoil. The good part of all this is," her friend lowered her voice, "Sethu would get everything one day through his little wife. What do you think of that?"

Buvana ran to the backyard to escape from prying eyes and awkward criticism. She sat gingerly on the washing stone. It was a dense garden, sprinkled with mango and neem trees, a few jasmine bushes, and a huge vegetable patch. A well, filled to the rim with water, was situated in the middle of the yard. A brick fence ran along the perimeter of the garden, which was home to a dense growth of thorny tendrils that cleverly concealed the weathered fence.

Buvana saw Sethu. He was standing by the gate, holding a woman's hand. They were talking animatedly. Who was she? Buvana didn't remember seeing her either at the wedding or in the crowd that had gathered for the feast that afternoon. The woman seemed to be on very familiar terms with Sethu and appeared much older than Buvana. Her dress and her movements were coarse. After she left, Sethu was about to come into the garden. Was Buvana sitting in the wrong place, at the wrong time, seeing something that she was not supposed to? She nervously tried to move away. It was too late. Although Sethu saw Buvana, he didn't acknowledge her presence when he walked into the garden. It was as though she blended with the trees and the shrubs. She didn't exist.

◆ ◆ ◆

Buvana realized that she had not written to her parents after leaving Brinda. She wrote a lengthy letter and carefully avoided disapproving comments about her husband and his mother. She didn't want her parents to worry unnecessarily. Who knows? She might understand her in-laws once she knew them better. She might even like her husband in the future, although such affection seemed impossible at the present time!

While Buvana was looking for a servant to take her letter to the post office, Humsa waved to her from the cowshed. Humsa's exceptionally dark skin and oil-coated, black hair accentuated her dazzling, white smile. Buvana and Humsa had become friends instantly, ever since the young, shy bride saw the busy maid on the day she arrived. Humsa's smile was the first and only sign of undiluted acceptance and warm reception in the in-law's home. Humsa never missed an opportunity to chat with Buvana outside the house. As her father was a butcher, she wasn't allowed inside Sethu's house. Her untouchable status in the community made her unfit to gain entrance into upper-caste residences. But Humsa didn't seem bothered by such discriminations. A carefree, unassuming vein in her prompted her to ignore the idiosyncrasies of the upper caste. She displayed a remarkable sense of maturity and confidence. Buvana, although senior to the servant girl by age, began to look at Humsa as a reliable older friend.

"Humsa, will you post this letter?" asked Buvana.

"Yes, Akka, I'll be glad to."

Akka! Buvana, who was an only child, was somewhat glad to be adopted as an older sister, and this new status made the lonely, young bride happy.

Sethu and his mother intercepted the letter. While the mother lectured Humsa in her droning fashion, the son dragged Buvana away from the cowshed. He stopped only when they reached the terrace. He shoved her on the floor and thundered at her.

"You'll never write to your home without my permission. Do you hear me?" Sethu shouted.

She couldn't utter a word.

He pulled her up by her hair. "You understand me well now, all right?" he screamed, throwing her again on the cold, stone floor.

She said nothing.

"How dare you write a letter to your family without my permission?" asked Sethu. "Now you belong to me, you belong to this family until you die. Understand? If you repeat what you did today, you'll be very sorry. Don't leave the terrace until you hear from me."

His eyes, scarlet and menacing, chilled her bones. This was the first time he spoke to her. He took a big pinch of snuff from the box and glared at her disheveled form on the floor. This was the same snuffbox that was given to him by her father as a bribe to appease his family's greed during the wedding ceremony. He locked the terrace door on his way out! Imprisoned like a criminal! He left her sobbing, lonely, and terrified.

Buvana woke up when she sensed a movement by her side. Humsa had brought supper for her. The frightened rich girl and the compassionate servant looked at each other. Humsa gingerly rested her hand on Buvana's shoulder and smiled. The prisoner was embarrassed. What must this servant think of Buvana's situation?

"It's all right, it's not your fault," said Humsa. "We know what he's like. Don't worry."

Humsa was throwing furtive glances every now and then, a little afraid that someone might overhear her comforting words. Humsa's kind gesture, while soothing Buvana, brought a flood of tears.

Buvana winced. The nasty bruise throbbed when she moved her head. Humsa tore a piece of rag she had brought with the tray and dampened it with a sprinkle of water from the small, clay pot. She moved closer and pressed it tenderly on the sore spot.

"Here, won't you eat something?" Humsa asked kindly.

Buvana ate a little to please her friend.

"Buvana Akka, your husband and his mother decided to let me spend the night on the terrace. They don't want you to be alone. I'll stay with you, Akka. Don't worry."

"They don't want me to be alone?" asked Buvana, wondering about the sudden gesture of kindness. This was quite unnatural under the circumstances. "Humsa, what's going on? They're so bad and ..."

"Hush, Akka, not so loud," Humsa whispered. "There's a reason for this sudden act of charity."

"What do you mean, Humsa?"

"Akka, your husband and his mother are acting out of suspicion," whispered Humsa. "My visit now has nothing to do with their consideration. Your wicked mother-in-law doesn't want you to engage in any stealthy action. Moreover, she gave me a lecture on loyalty and deception. I'm supposed to guard you!"

That explained the situation quite well. Humsa fell asleep. Buvana, however, was not so fortunate. She thought about the severity of her punishment for writing a letter to her parents. What would Sethu do if she defied him? Her family had hoped that she would do well in her husband's home. How sad and disappointed Buvana's family would be to discover her miserable condition. She wanted to go home. This marriage was a mistake.

Buvana was allowed to enter the house after a couple of days. He visited her again at night. He needed a son. Now Buvana was convinced that she would rather face another punishment and return to the terrace. She hated his closeness.

"This is what usually happens in a rich household," declared Sethu's mother, offering Buvana a verbose lecture on the deficiency in her upbringing. "Your parents neglected to teach you to respect elders and your husband! Sethu and I wished to choose a girl from a modest family, but your parents, especially your appa, begged me to accept you as my daughter-in-law. Now we face the consequence!"

The mother-in-law's imagination and lies knew no boundaries. What an unprincipled woman she was! What uncultured people they were! Sethu's mother let her tongue run loose, especially when Ponni, her cousin, visited. Whenever the wicked mother-in-law was too busy to exercise her authority and perform jailor duties, Ponni had Buvana under her eagle eyes. Buvana was imprisoned—physically and emotionally—day and night. She had to relate the family's unjust treatment to someone, but who would listen to her? Buvana was not allowed to talk to anybody unless Sethu, or his mother, or one of the in-law's intimate relatives supervised her every move. She was under scrutiny every minute of the day. The society around Chinnoor was not to know of Buvana's predicament under any circumstance. The family did everything possible to retain the situation within the perimeters of the home.

Buvana utilized her freedom from Sethu whenever she was subjected to life-on-the-terrace. She pushed him out of her mind and wrote her verses. She printed her feelings, her tears, and her laughter. Yes, there were a few moments of laughter with Humsa.

"Akka, do you read your poems to others?" asked Humsa.

"Yes, I did. I used to read to my family and my friend."

"Did you have a best friend?"

"Yes, my appa, and now, you."

The joy of being acknowledged as the best friend of someone so dear and special! The warmth diffused across Humsa's face, and she asked shyly if Buvana would read to her what she had just written down.

"Sure, Humsa!" Buvana cleared her throat and began to read.

All the lamps are lit.
Still can't fight the darkness.
But the dark clouds are welcome.
Helps me review what is forgotten.
Darkness does not shut my mind.
Imagination, boundless-
Thoughts, unbridled- look-
Look into the past- what could have been.

"Here, Humsa," said Buvana, after reading a few lines. "You can read the rest and tell me what you think about it."

Humsa took the notebook from Buvana and appeared baffled. "If only I could read, I would understand what you write day after day," said Humsa. "Akka, I can't read."

Buvana was certain that Humsa must have had some kind of schooling, at least for two, three years. "You went to school, didn't you, Humsa?" asked Buvana.

"No, Akka, they won't take me in their school because we are untouchables. You see, we still don't have municipal schools close to my home."

"Humsa, would you like me to show you how to read and write? Can I teach you?" Buvana asked encouragingly.

"You can teach me, Akka. I'll be a good student."

The rich, young tutor started instructing the poor, curious friend. Initially, Sethu's mother questioned Humsa for spending time over books and papers with Buvana when she should be finishing her chores. However, she didn't protest much once she thought about the situation at length. Her calculating mind convinced her that Buvana was not homesick when she concentrated on instructing Humsa. Anything to take Buvana's mind away from Brinda and its residents was a worthwhile effort in the cruel mother-in-law's estimation.

Eventually, Sethu allowed Buvana to write to her family. He dictated the message to her. The letter was screened, edited, revised, and dispatched. Buvana carefully obeyed his rules because Sethu's quick hand frequently contacted Buvana's cheek before his voice dropped insults. Humsa, who was steadily becoming Buvana's strong ally, explained the difficulty in posting a letter without Sethu's knowledge. The postmaster was in Sethu's pocket. There was no way Buvana could secretly send a message to anybody.

"Humsa, are you telling me that we can't think of anybody trustworthy in this entire town?" asked Buvana.

"No, Akka, that's not what I meant," replied Humsa. "Even my appa can take it. You know, he's not bright or brave. Your husband would hurt him if he found out."

"You're right, Humsa. Your appa shouldn't be involved in this. My husband will be very angry."

"And he'll hurt you, won't he?" Humsa whispered cautiously.

It was nice to have a storm-free week. Loads of laundry had to be washed and dried. While Humsa was collecting the garments from the clothesline, Buvana sat on the washing stone. Sethu's mother liked to maintain the distinction of classes, and she scowled at Buvana's eagerness to help Humsa. After making sure that the mother-in-law's eyes were not on her, Buvana folded vast stacks of clothing.

Sethu walked in from the garden gate, followed by a tall, dark man. Buvana had not seen this man before. Sethu went into the house, came back with an envelope, and the two men walked to the avenue again. A woman joined the men. Buvana recognized her. It was the same lady she had seen right here ... a while ago!

"Who is that man, Humsa?" asked Buvana. "Do you know who that lady is?"

Humsa looked up at Buvana for a moment before turning her face away.

"That lady, Humsa, who is she? Is she related to the family?" Buvana asked again.

"Akka," Humsa said slowly, making sure that they were alone before offering an explanation. "That man is the brother of that lady everybody is talking about. She is your husband's …" Humsa's voice sank very low, "she is his mistress. He has set her up in Market Street, in the house by the mill."

"Oh, that's the woman," Buvana said, blushing in shame and humiliation.

"Akka," Humsa said, almost in tears. "How could anybody give you to this man? It's like placing a delicate flower garland in a monkey's hands." She saw the pain in Buvana's eyes. Had she spoken too much? "Sorry, Buvana Akka. I didn't mean to humiliate you. My mother always scolds me for being dramatic!"

"No, you haven't humiliated me, Humsa," said Buvana, trying to sound impassive. "I'm glad you told me. Somebody has to, you know."

Buvana knew exactly what was wrong with her marriage. He had married her for her money, no, her father's money, and she was here to facilitate the prospect of a child, a male child. And the mother-in-law had the audacity to declare that she wanted to choose a girl from modest circumstances. Wicked family!

Sethu roared like a lion under the comfort of his home and seedy associates, but he was a mouse during certain occasions. Buvana discovered a few things about him that went against his superior manliness.

Several farmhands were brought in for extra help during a festival in the house. Some stalwart men were drawing buckets of water from the well for various needs. Sethu was prancing in the backyard, chewing tobacco and thundering at the farmhands. While thus strutting, he stumbled on a bucket that was left very close to the well. Hell broke loose. The farmhand, responsible for leaving the bucket unattended, was fired instantly.

Buvana, who was watching the entire scene from the kitchen window, ran to the backyard. Was it necessary to yell at these poor people just because the master had a slight accident? What fuss over something so trivial! Humsa explained the real reason for Sethu's shivering fit.

"Did you know, Buvana Akka," asked Humsa. "Your husband has been afraid of water ever since he was young?"

"Who told you that? Why is he afraid, Humsa?"

"Everybody knows that. I heard that when he was a child, he fell into that well and almost drowned. He could never learn to swim. You know, that's the reason he never walks near the river? I think he is afraid of water," whispered Humsa.

"Oh, I see." Buvana saw more than she had seen before. For some childishly wicked reason, she smiled at her dominating husband's paltry fears. She went to the hall to see how Sethu was doing after this interesting incident! She saw her mother-in-law cosseting her shivering son, surrounded by the doctor, aunts, and uncles. While the doctor was mixing a tonic to soothe the patient's nerves, the mother-in-law's glance fell briefly on Buvana.

"Look at her, Ponni," cried the mother-in-law. "She is no comfort at all to my poor son. After seeing what he has gone through, she just stands like one of these pillars."

"Don't we all know what you're going through, cousin?" Ponni asked.

"Stop gaping and try to find a way to comfort your husband," the mother-in-law yelled at Buvana. "Learn to do your duties! What did your mother ever teach you?"

Buvana moved away to hide her tears and shame. She could still hear the conversation in the hall.

"This is a second life for Sethu," said Ponni. "How narrowly he has escaped from the claws of death. Cousin, he was born under a lucky star!"

"He escaped from the claws of death? He just stumbled!" thought Buvana. She wondered under what star she was born. The more she thought about it, the further she disliked the idea of marriage, customs, and the foolhardy beliefs that completed the package.

Sethu didn't impose on Buvana's privacy for a few nights after his very unfortunate accident. In addition to having some privacy, Buvana noticed that her mother-in-law and her entourage were spending more time by Sethu's bed. The hall was empty that night. Why not try the front door? Buvana's feet quietly took her to the exit. Was the door locked? With an unsteady heartbeat, she tried the door after making sure that nobody was observing her covert activity. To her relief, the door opened. To her dismay, a pair of eyes stared at her. Those cruel eyes belonged to the gardener's wife! There were times when Buvana wondered if that lady was a woman or a demon. Buvana smiled nervously and frantically groped for an excuse.

"What do you want?" asked the woman, looking menacing.

"I … I was looking for my mother-in-law," replied Buvana.

The guard appeared to accept this excuse. How glad Buvana was that she could think of an excuse! After closing the door again, she walked back to her room.

Once in her bed, Buvana was thankful for not getting caught during her very tiny attempt at escape. It was a clear night. She gazed at the stars through the window. She thought about her insipid life under the blanket of marriage and the superficial protection, which the state of marriage was supposed to bring. A girl ought to choose what she wanted to do in life—if she could use her intelligence. Her society was pessimistic and the family was nervous to let a young lady sort through her priorities. Elders decided, destiny dictated, society conducted—a collaboration to plan a young lady's future happiness that was merely incidental. Her husband, who was supposed to take care of her, was a domineering, cruel monster. He had the audacity to claim that he was a MAN and the master of his house. He was not a man. She weighed the dictatorial authority of her husband and the restrained power of her father. Her father was a soft-spoken, considerate man. He lived his life quietly—as the head of his family and as the owner of a vast estate—without advertising his superiority either by voice or manner. He stayed in the shadow in a patriarchal society, and his subdued strength made him a better man. Buvana loved his quiet smiles, admired his passive strength, and respected his restrained authority.

◆ ◆ ◆

Buvana saw the house by the mill on a hot, sticky day in the month of May. Her mother-in-law was sitting by her inside the carriage on the way home from the temple. Mundy Street, the short route from the temple to the house, was blocked because a fruit vendor's cart had overturned in the middle of the narrow road. Consequently, Sethu's carriage took a detour through Market Street. It was as crowded as it could be. Vendors and hucksters were jockeying for the vantage spot to entice as many customers as possible. These attractions provided an exciting distraction. After all, Buvana didn't have many opportunities to see the town. The child in her made her forget the mother-in-law's unpleasant company and prompted her to glance quickly at the variety of entertainment offered by the astrologer, the one-legged performer, and the beggar, who was singing in a supreme baritone. The carriage stalled for several minutes to make way for another cart. Buvana saw her precisely at that moment.

Her husband's mistress was sitting in the veranda, decked in gaudy silks and heavy jewelry. What was the reddish stuff on her cheeks? Sethu, surrounded by his supporters, was sitting by her. She was laughing vulgarly at the men. Buvana couldn't help staring at her face. Thankfully, it was brief, and the carriage began to move. The embarrassment of the moment was so intense. Buvana looked down at her sweaty palms, and she raised her hands to hide the color in her hot cheeks. Why was she nervous? She was not at fault. Well, she was excessively ashamed of such a husband. A heavy silence filled the carriage.

"HE IS A MAN. If you give him a son, he'll stay home more often. I hope you prayed for a child at the temple, Buvana?" The mother-in-law's familiar voice was dropping familiar insults.

How typical! How convenient! How pathetic! Buvana had to produce a child as a bribe for his constancy! What a despicable solution! She had to share his bed to pull him away from a whore. The idea of having his child revolted her. Regardless of the disgusting situation, she was his wife, and there was nothing she could do about it.

This incident, while leaving a disgraceful ache in her heart, left her somewhat strong. Buvana got along a little better. She was not the inexperienced girl, the innocent girl, who walked into this hateful house as a new bride. Months of suffering had finally made her appear impassive during the day. The night was a different story. She tried to hide her feelings in her tears after sunset. The element of dislike she felt for her husband during the initial days of their relationship had developed into a strong hatred over a period of time. She feared him, she hated him, and she prayed for a day when he would disappear from her life. What wouldn't she do to be rid of his tobacco-coated breath, his offensive words when they slurred on a tumbler of arrack, his stifling presence, and his detestable touch?

Buvana was still not pregnant.

"Money can't compensate physical imperfection, can it?" asked Ponni.

"Ponni, the monsoon has filled all the wells, rivers, and ponds. Her womb is still empty," said the mother-in-law, angry and disappointed.

Buvana wondered what would be insufferable—being childless, a sign of failure as a woman, or having his child, a souvenir of his masculinity? And her compliance, as an obedient wife and a dutiful daughter-in-law, was significant in the eyes of Sethu's family and friends. There was no compromise. Humsa was her only source of comfort in that dismal house. Buvana never failed to cling to her for support.

The priest and his assistants were sitting around the holy fire in the temple on an auspicious day. He conducted a special prayer to invoke God's mercy and benevolence to fill Buvana's womb. Huge vessels of butter were clarified and baskets of flowers and fruits were collected for the ceremony. Enormous silver bowls were filled with colorful, flavored sweets for the offering during the elaborate prayer. Many sacrifices were made. Several poor people were fed. Buvana repeated ancient, holy chants after the priest to beg for heaven's mercy. When she prayed sincerely, she didn't beg for a child. She wanted freedom.

Buvana was giving the dishes a final rinse before taking them into the kitchen—a ritual instituted by Sethu's mother and her upper-caste peers. After Humsa scrubbed and cleaned the dishes, Buvana or another female member of the household had to pour water on them before taking them to the kitchen shelf. Humsa's hands were good enough to scrub, but they were not sanitized due to her inferior caste.

"Akka, follow me to the terrace in a few minutes," Humsa whispered, smiling nervously.

Buvana, puzzled by this unusual summon, went to the terrace.

"They're so bad, Akka, I just found out something," Humsa whispered again, panting for breath.

"What happened, Humsa?"

"I heard that your parents had come here last month. Your husband and his mother knew about their visit ahead of time. That's why your mother-in-law took you to the festival. Remember the festival you attended in the next village?"

Buvana had been wondering why her parents had not visited her. She received a letter from them once in a while. She had not seen them since her wedding day, and there was no reason for her parents to ignore her. In fact, her mother had written in the previous letter that they would be making a trip to Chinnoor within the month, but no news of their arrival had reached her so far. Humsa's latest information definitely explained a lot.

Buvana discovered later that this was not her family's first visit. According to the wicked mother-in-law's instructions, Buvana's family couldn't visit without announcing their arrival through a letter. Sethu and his mother had managed to keep Buvana away from home to keep her parents away from her sight. In addition, they had screened every letter Buvana had received before she read it. What an unprincipled and evil family! This devious scheme, however, was nothing compared to a distressing incident that portrayed another evil streak of the in-laws.

"Come down, Buvana," said the mother-in-law. "The doctor is here to take a look at your hand."

Buvana swallowed her tears and went to the hall where the doctor was sitting with a collection of medicines. He examined her wounded hand.

"How did you get hurt, little girl?" the doctor smiled and asked kindly.

"Oh, it was an accident, really," the mother-in-law answered on behalf of the little girl. "Her hand slipped and fell on the hot griddle. She's still learning to cook, poor thing. She didn't learn to cook properly before she got married."

Buvana didn't bother to hide her tears any longer. She was hurting—not from her stinging hand—from her mother-in-law's lies. Should she tell the doctor the real cause of the injury? Buvana had been suffering from one of her usual headaches that morning. When she went to the kitchen in response to her mother-in-law's summons, her pain was at its peak, and she failed to answer her superior's barking with her customary, respectful tone. The mother-in-law had been very angry. Buvana should have been alert because Ponni was also in the kitchen at that time. Ponni fueled the mother-in-law's nasty temper, and the two monstrous women pulled Buvana's tender hand and pressed it on the hot griddle. They made Buvana promise through her painful, screaming tears that she would always talk respectfully in that house.

Once the mother-in-law's perversion subsided, she had to find a cure for Buvana's hand. She couldn't let the servants notice the injured hand and speculate about the source of the injury. Accordingly, she concocted a story for the doctor.

Buvana wondered for a moment or two. Why not tell the doctor the real cause of the injury? He appeared to be a nice gentleman. Could he help her reach her father? Would he believe her version of the accident? The mother-in-law was standing just a foot away. The doctor was an established member of the community that was dominated by Sethu and his peers. Why would he believe the spontaneous complaint of a fairly new arrival? Buvana would only undergo another punishment if she spoke a word out of turn.

Buvana's hand healed in time under Humsa's gentle treatment. She took every precaution to guard every syllable that came out of her mouth.

While Buvana was sitting in the backyard, Humsa was throwing furtive glances around the garden.

"Buvana Akka," said Humsa, "I've to tell you something. Your mother-in-law was talking to Ponni about you and your family."

"What's new? What did she say, Humsa?"

"She said, 'Ponni, I'm a God-fearing woman, but these horoscope believers take it too seriously. You know what I did for my Sethu? I asked Easwaran to redesign our Sethu's horoscope to match Buvana's. A little adjustment is not bad, you know. Our ancestors said that one could say a thousand lies to conduct a marriage. All I'm responsible for is one.' Can you believe this, Buvana Akka?"

"She is a wicked woman, Humsa," said Buvana. "And she has the audacity to say that she fears God. I hope He is watching her and listening to her lies. Humsa, I have to alert my parents about my current situation. Is there another post office, one that is a few miles away from Chinnoor? It has to be in a place where the people wouldn't know my husband's family."

"Not unless we travel to the next village. I can find out. There is that depot in the railway station where they throw all those bags of letters into that dingy compartment."

"No, Humsa. Even if we can trust someone there, that person might be scared to help us because of my husband."

There must be a few kind people in that town. How could Buvana identify them? Her mother-in-law never allowed her to talk to anybody without her permission. Even if Buvana could approach someone for help, that person should be brave enough to stand Sethu's reproof. Was there such a person? During those few occasions when Buvana went out, her mother-in-law and Ponni performed sentry duty. She had steadily become a prisoner of tradition that concealed the ugliness of customs.

Buvana heard a familiar sound near her bedroom window and looked outside. Humsa was standing there. Buvana understood Humsa's signal and ran to the backyard. Humsa was very excited.

"Buvana Akka," Humsa whispered. "Remember my cousin's wedding I'm going to attend?"

"Yes. That's not until next week, right?"

"That's right. But my parents want to leave tomorrow. They want to spend a few days in my grandparents' house on the way. But, Buvana Akka," whispered Humsa. "I just found out that the wedding is in a village near Kanyakoil. Can I take a message to your parents? Why are you staring at me? It's too good to be true, I know. I'll be careful, Akka. You can trust me."

"Of course, I trust you, Humsa. Go to the terrace. I'll come there with a piece of paper and pen." Yes, it was too good to be true! Buvana had faith in Humsa. She trusted her young friend as much as she trusted her parents. The terrace was one place nobody bothered to look for her when she was not reprimanded for one mistake or the other. She ran to the terrace, scribbled a few lines, and gave it to Humsa before anybody discovered her stealthy activity.

Humsa was worried about leaving Buvana alone in that detestable house. She read her a list of instructions. "Buvana Akka, you'll be careful, won't you?"

Humsa asked doubtfully. "Please don't get into trouble when I'm gone. Remember what happened to your hand."

"I'll be careful, Humsa," Buvana promised.

Lately, Buvana seldom saw Sethu during the day. He came home only at night to breathe on her. He was still waiting for Buvana to bear his child. On one such night, he felt Buvana's reluctance that bordered on defiance. He was angry when she cringed at his touch.

"You silly beggar, how can you treat me like this?" Sethu shouted and glared at her. "I can have several women at my command. The only reason I come home to you at night is to get a son. Should I remind you not to shirk your duty?"

"I know about that woman," Buvana's voice spluttered. "I know she lives in the house by the mill." She regretted her impulsive outburst as soon as her words spilled out of her mouth.

"Oh, you know that? Good. Now listen, be thankful that I haven't brought her inside this house."

Buvana was banished to the terrace for a week. A punishment for her saucy reply! Her anguish was his strength. She wondered if Sethu or his mother would burn her hand again. Luckily, her hand escaped during this occasion. Buvana had forgotten Humsa's instructions already! Although Sethu was oppressively domineering, she shouldn't have talked back to him. For once, just once, her patience had receded to make room for her dignity. She was weary of being compliant and meek in his arms when he breathed on her, reeking of tobacco and arrack. How much she missed Humsa! Although Buvana never underestimated Humsa's support in that hateful household, she really understood and appreciated her value during her absence.

Buvana noticed that Sethu was in a particularly good mood. One of his elderly uncles left a few acres of prime orchards in Sethu's name. Sethu, who was essentially a spendthrift, was happy to acquire more money through that land. Now he had some extra income to throw at his mistress's feet. Recently, she had been a little annoyed because of his purse-pinched visits.

During one of Sethu's rare, cheerful moods, Buvana begged him to allow her to visit her parents.

"We've been married just for a few months. Your place is by me. Why can't you be contented with your status as a wife?" Sethu asked. "You don't have to cling to your mother anymore. Grow up. Didn't your parents teach you the duties of a married woman?"

"You're young. You should listen to our advice," said the mother-in-law, repeating her son's sentiments. "You're in our care. There's no need to leave your husband's home so soon, Buvana."

Buvana gave up. She was in their care! Buvana had never seen a family that was collectively evil. Many villagers feared Sethu and his mother, and those who didn't fit into their circle of friends, whispered about them in awe. They were exactly the people who might possibly help Buvana! Unfortunately, she had no access to their confidence, no means to their trust.

Chinnoor was known for its turmeric warehouses of which three belonged to Sethu. He was standing outside one of them with his friend. Sethu was on the verge of losing the warehouse to the financier. He needed a child to get a grip on Murthy's property on a permanent basis, and the useless Buvana was not pregnant yet.

There was not much family money left. Sethu's father died a few years ago. That old man depended on the judgment of his wife regarding every matter. No matter how hard she tried, Sethu's mother couldn't make a dishonest man out of his father. Therefore, she handled the business and kept him dedicated to his land. Farming was in his blood, and Sethu's father was the happiest when he stood in knee-deep gunk, gazing at the green, paddy fields.

By the time Sethu was eighteen, he had acquired the art of cheating in business dealings. His mother had taught him this skill. He wished he had the talent for spending less, especially on his mistresses. Managing his petticoat connections was getting quite cumbersome.

"Damn them!" said Sethu.

"What?" his friend asked.

"My mistresses," began Sethu. "They're not just happy with a house and a living expense any longer. One of them expects a bank balance to take care of her bastard in the future. What am I? A lending tree? I can't provide for the dirty bastards. Those bitches can throw them in the river."

"Why don't you ask them to do just that?" asked Sethu's helpful friend.

"I can't, you idiot," replied Sethu. How could he? He paid these women dearly to enjoy the privileges in their arms.

The dowry that Buvana brought in cash was already showing signs of exhaustion. Sethu had depleted almost all of it on his mistresses. Setting up a house separately for these questionable women was an expensive process!

"To top it all, that bitch in Market Street has hired a cook. What is she doing all day besides dressing vulgarly and prancing down the street?" Sethu asked his friend.

Sethu should be careful about how he dealt with his mistress. She had already fought with him a few times this month. Unfortunately, the latest argument had been an exhibition to the neighbors. Even Sethu's mother had cautioned him to keep his squabbles within the walls. Well, he could never think clearly when he was angry.

He wished he had more generous uncles on the road to heaven. How he wished he could marry once more to collect a considerable dowry! He could have any number of mistresses, but the law expected him to have only one wife. Strange!

◆ ◆ ◆

Humsa's sparkling appearance at her cousin's wedding received several compliments. Her ebony skin color made a striking contrast to the lotus-colored silk sari. Her long, oil-coated braid was secured with a colorful ribbon. Her family couldn't have afforded a genuine silk sari. It was a special gift from Buvana. Although the silk added grace to Humsa's slim frame, her tender heart couldn't rejoice in her unusual, elegant appearance. Buvana's letter was tucked inside the cloth pouch, tied to her waist. It felt like hot coal. The wedding ceremony was almost over, and she had decided to slip away for an hour after the feast. It shouldn't be difficult to locate Brinda. After all, it was supposed to be the most magnificent dwelling in Kanyakoil.

Humsa found Brinda. She stood outside the gate, a little apprehensive and unsure. She took a deep breath and wiped her sweaty palms with the delicate handkerchief Buvana had given her. Buvana had surprised Humsa with a couple of new saris, a few trinkets, and a beautiful handkerchief. When Humsa was reluctant to accept the gifts, Buvana had exclaimed that Humsa was like a sister to her. Was there a need to be shy?

Humsa looked at the endless land on one side and at the river on the other. She could even hear the bold, tiny waves kissing the shy pebbles on the sand, just like Buvana had written in one of her poems. Humsa got out of her dreamlike condition and walked forward with a determination that warranted her mission.

Murthy was relaxing in the veranda. A young lady opened the gate and walked toward him. While he was still wondering who she was, she enquired if this was the residence of Buvana's parents. She seemed more than relieved to be at the right place, and she hastily deposited a piece of paper in his hands.

"I'm coming from Chinnoor," whispered Humsa, nervously. "I'm a servant in Buvana Akka's house, her husband's house. I brought a note from your daughter."

Buvana had instructed Humsa earlier to introduce herself as Murthy's daughter's good friend. Humsa still couldn't collect sufficient confidence to do that. Habit! Perpetual habit! Years of subservient practice couldn't be washed away with the assistance of a kind human being.

Murthy was surprised to receive a note from his daughter. A few seconds satisfied his curiosity regarding the message. While Saroja was reading the note, he quickly dispatched a servant to fetch Kitta.

"Buvana Akka is very unhappy. You'll go to her right away, won't you?" Humsa asked.

"Yes, we will, Humsa. We're very thankful for your help. Here, please take this," said Saroja, persuading Humsa to accept a bundle of currency.

"No, thank you, I can't take this," said Humsa, taking a step back.

"Yes, you must, my dear. This is just a small token of our gratitude, the least we can think of at the moment," said Saroja, pressing the money in her hands. "I can't tell you how glad we are to see you with Buvana's note. Use this money to buy something you want, my dear."

"Thank you," said Humsa.

"We must thank you for bringing the message from Buvana," Saroja said kindly. "We'll always be grateful to you. Won't you please come in and have something to eat?"

"No, thank you," Humsa said politely. "I must leave before somebody recognizes me … somebody who might know my employer."

This explanation helped Saroja understand Humsa's furtive and nervous glances since she had arrived.

"Humsa," said Saroja, reluctant to let her go. "What happened to Buvana? We'll go to her right away. Can you tell us anything about her situation?"

"They … her husband and his mother are cruel, Madam. They are keeping her imprisoned. She is suffering in that house. You have to rescue her, you must go right away!" Humsa began to cry.

While Murthy and Saroja stared at Humsa in shock, she left after thanking them again for their generosity.

Kitta arrived within the hour. Saroja was relieved to see her brother.

"What is it?" Kitta asked. "What's wrong?"

"It's Buvana," Murthy said. "She has sent a note. I don't know what I read the first time. Please read it to me."

Kitta responded instantly to his brother-in-law's request.

"The note says,

'Dear Amma and Appa,

Please come and take me away from here. No time for details. Don't contact my husband or his mother by post. Come. It is urgent. Come quickly, as soon as you see this note.

Love,
Buvana'

Goodness! What's going on?" Kitta finished reading the note with a question.

"I don't know, Kitta," cried Murthy.

"Murthy, may I take Saroja to Chinnoor?" Kitta asked. "You're not well."

"I must go, Kitta, to get my daughter," Murthy replied quickly. "I've to see her as soon as I can."

"Murthy, listen to me," said Kitta. "I think I should go because if you go to get Buvana, you would get emotional. We don't know the exact situation there. The in-laws are not to suspect anything now, are they? Besides, your illness could be used as a reason to pull Buvana away from Chinnoor for a while. The in-laws have to let her visit her ailing father, don't you think? Let me see, we won't reach Chinnoor before sunset if we leave today. I can take Saroja to Chinnoor tomorrow morning. What do you think?"

Kitta's logic convinced Murthy. Before leaving for Chinnoor, Saroja scribbled a quick note to Thangam, who was currently busy with one of her nieces in Salem. Saroja saw Sivam, Murthy's foreman, hovering in the background. She handed him her note.

"Sivam," said Saroja. "Send a telegram to Thangam right now."

"Yes, of course," said Sivam. He ran with the note in his hand.

Thangam's presence here would soon be a necessity. While several other families could boast of half a dozen children, nieces, and nephews, Murthy's family could boast of only one; Buvana. Murthy's only sibling, Thangam, had no child, and Kitta, Saroja's only sibling, was not blessed with one either. Kitta's wife died during childbirth. He was an affectionate man, a rare soul, who loved his wife with a passion. He refused to marry again, and he decided to love Buvana as his own child. Well, Buvana was the apple of her uncle's eye and the dearest treasure in her aunt's heart. The recent note disturbed Kitta. He couldn't wait to see his niece.

Buvana came to the kitchen garden. She missed Humsa. Buvana was certain that her friend's mission had not failed because Sethu and his mother had not thundered at her regarding the stealthy note. Buvana would have been very thankful to receive a note from Humsa. Impossible wish! Humsa couldn't have communicated with Buvana during her absence, although she could read and write a little. Nothing could go past the rigid vigilance of Sethu and his villainous mother. Buvana was about to enter the house from the garden when she noticed someone near the kitchen. Her mother and uncle were standing a few feet away, just outside the kitchen door. She ran to them. Her mother-in-law entered the garden at that precise moment.

"Oh, Buvana, it seems your appa is not well," said her mother-in-law. "You may visit him for a week. Poor man! He must miss his only child." She turned to Saroja. "If only you had written a letter to let us know of your husband's health, I would've brought Buvana to Kanyakoil. I hope he feels better soon."

It was hard to detect the venom in the mother-in-law's tone when it was coated with honey. Buvana had a dozen questions to ask her mother, but she just gave her and her uncle a hasty hug, a hasty smile, and ran to her room to pack. What a liar the mother-in-law was! She would have escorted Buvana to Kanyakoil? Anyway, why would that matter anymore? Buvana's mother was here. The rest could be sorted out later. Buvana felt relieved when she realized that Sethu was not at home—not that he would have objected to Buvana's departure. His mother's word was final in that dismal house, and she had already granted Buvana permission to visit Brinda!

When Buvana came to the hall, her mother and uncle were just finishing coffee. They respectfully declined the host's polite invitation for an early supper. Kitta insisted that they should be leaving because they wished to reach home before dark.

When Buvana walked to the carriage, she saw Humsa at the end of the long gravel drive. Humsa must have arrived just now. Buvana's feet, naturally, took a couple of steps toward her dearest friend, but she quickly retreated. Her mother-in-law would never forgive Humsa if she suspected her of being the ultimate source of comfort and help to Buvana. If only Humsa knew what she meant in Buvana's life! As the carriage approached the gate, Buvana reached out to touch

Humsa's friendly hand and accepted her tears with a heart that was filled with love, misery, and gratitude.

The carriage picked up speed once it crossed the border of the town. The passengers were thinking about the most pressing questions. What were they to do about this disaster? How could Buvana be entangled in such a complicated alliance in the first place? This was not a marriage. It was a terrible, irrevocable error!

"How is appa feeling? Is he ill? Is it something serious?" Buvana asked anxiously.

"Appa is well. He's just a little weak," said Saroja. "He should recover quickly. Don't worry, dear. Besides, Thangam should be in Brinda soon. I sent her a telegram. She might be there when we reach. Are you comfortable, Buvana?"

"Yes, Amma, I am."

Each milestone brought Buvana a little closer to Brinda. They reached home just before sunset. The golden river welcomed the birds to dance on its palms. Buvana longed to touch the water. Just for a few moments, everything was forgotten—her husband, her mother-in-law, her imprisonment, the aching nights.

Murthy and Thangam met them at the gate. His eyes were misty. It was unnatural to see his daughter in such a state. What happened to her glorious eyes and brilliant smile? Thangam hugged Buvana before taking her inside the house. When the family gathered in the hall, Murthy invited Buvana to sit by him.

"What happened, my child?" Murthy asked.

Where was Buvana supposed to begin? How long was the night? She said a little. She said more.

"Buvana," said Murthy, in agony. "I'm so sorry for finding such a miserable marriage alliance. If only I had known, I wish I knew."

"No, Appa, you couldn't predict this," Buvana said affectionately. "Nobody could." She took his hand and smiled into his eyes. She had never seen him so distraught.

What a terrible mistake the family had made! How could they get Buvana out of the current misery? They must think of a good reason to keep their child closer to them on a permanent basis. Saroja and Murthy took their child to her room to rest peacefully during the night. This was a pleasure Buvana had not experienced since her marriage.

Buvana woke up to the call of sunrise. She looked around the room and saw a few, dear remnants of her childhood. She had managed to run away from her husband's house. She touched her bed, she felt the cool handloom sheet in her hand, and she picked up the sandalwood trinket box that had been on the table all her life. For the first time in many months, Buvana woke up with a smile on her lips. Relief filled her young heart when she bathed and prepared to welcome another day.

Buvana went to the hall. Her heart danced in joy when she found her father on the big swing. He invited her to sit by him. She felt the past rushing to her in a storm. How light her heart felt at this moment! The last few months disappeared. They didn't exist. She never left the security of Brinda and her parents.

One topic that the family redundantly discussed was the arrangement of Buvana's wedding. While her wedding plans were taking shape, Kitta had wondered at the rapid interest from Sethu's family to finalize the wedding arrangements. Murthy, on the other hand, had not been anxious. The family knew the matchmaker well. Would Swami mislead the family? Besides, this was the first time a man's horoscope perfectly matched Buvana's. At that point, Thangam didn't feel any anxiety about Sethu's alliance either. Since nothing seemed amiss, the family had decided to deposit Buvana in Sethu's hands.

"Saroja, Sethu's horoscope was perfect. The family seemed to be upright. How did we make such a mistake?" Murthy asked his wife.

Buvana, who was then sitting by her father, explained how Murthy's family was tricked into believing the validity of the horoscope. "Appa, the horoscope was fraudulent," Buvana told her father. "My mother-in-law had adjusted her son's horoscope to match mine."

"What? Even she wouldn't do such a nasty thing!" Murthy was shocked.

"But she did, Appa. Humsa told me." Buvana explained how Sethu's mother had changed his horoscope.

"Atrocious!" said Murthy. "If we had known the evil nature of their family, we wouldn't have given you to a villain like Sethu. But the deed is done."

The parents were curious about Humsa. After all, she had been the means of Buvana's safe return to her parents.

"Amma, I wish we could do something for Humsa," Buvana said sincerely. "I can't tell you in a day or two about her kindness. I would have …"

"We will, my dear," Saroja assured her daughter. "I'll find a way to thank Humsa."

Thangam took Buvana to the balcony to comfort her. Where was Buvana supposed to begin? Her misery began on her wedding night, but how was one to expose the aches and shame associated with such a union? Buvana made an effort. Her aunt listened. With every spoken word, an unspoken sigh halted her narrative.

"Buvana, don't cry, my dear," Thangam consoled her niece. "You're safe here. Stop crying."

"Thangam Athai, I wish I had your strength," Buvana sighed. "I've never seen you crying."

Buvana was more than relieved to have her aunt and her uncle by her side during her uncertain present, especially while the family was debating on her unpredictable future. Next to her parents, Thangam and Kitta were the dearest people in Buvana's world. Kitta was a staple at Brinda. He certainly filled a position that meant more than just a brother-in-law and uncle. Brinda couldn't exist without Kitta. Thangam! Buvana respected her aunt's wisdom, she envied her courage, and she cherished her affectionate nature. Thangam was a rare breed, a very different woman in that small sphere. She was a leader. Nobody knew the secret of her strength. It existed, it comforted many, and it offered hope to her family and friends.

On the third day of her visit, Buvana woke up feeling sick. Thangam ran to the kitchen to get tea. Saroja asked Sivam to fetch the doctor. The doctor, who had known Buvana since her birth, walked into her room with a friendly grin. After examining Buvana, he said that she was expecting a child.

Buvana was stunned. Her family was shocked. What news at such a time! A time to rejoice over the arrival of a precious grandchild was stained with the relationship of such a man. Buvana had no desire to feel better. The doctor visited everyday. He was worried that Buvana's condition was unusually complicated. Therefore, he prescribed a list of medicines and encouraged Buvana to take a lot of rest.

"Thangam, what shall I do?" Saroja took her sister-in-law's hand.

"Saroja, you don't have to say a thing. I'm here."

Buvana's in-laws were happy about the long-awaited good news. The mother-in-law sent a letter to grant Buvana a month's rest in her mother's attentive hands. Another unexpected letter arrived. It was from Humsa. They had to read Humsa's writing several times to understand the meaning. Nevertheless, the message was touching. She wrote a letter to Saroja to thank her for her kindness. Humsa was proud to announce that she bought a couple of workbooks, and she had used the money Saroja had given her to purchase the new items. She was going to practice her reading and writing, especially to keep her newly acquired literacy fresh in her mind. In her letter to Buvana, she wished her health and happiness during her freedom from her husband and during her rather delicate condition.

Delicate condition! How would it feel to carry the child of a loving husband, a man who was dear to her heart? Her mother had experienced that joy. Would Buvana love this child? Her baby was an unwanted addition. Her child would be a symbol of the miserable time she had spent in his clutches. This child was not conceived out of love. How she wished she had a different husband, a kind man, who would look at her, talk with her, take a walk along the river, sit by her when she watched the sun disappear into the earth at dusk. It was too late, just too late.

"Amma, would it be terrible of me to think ..." Buvana burst into tears. "I don't want this baby. I hate him. It's his child."

"I know, my dear. I know what you're feeling. Someday you'll understand. Not now, not tomorrow, but you'll be glad when the baby arrives."

"If only I can lose this child."

"Buvana, don't say such things," said Saroja, shocked. "Believe me. Your baby will bring you a lot of comfort."

Saroja held her sobbing daughter close to her. How young and innocent she appeared now! So much heartache and burden at such a tender age—to please a wicked man and his evil mother!

A month of rest didn't improve Buvana's health. Murthy wrote a very respectful letter to his son-in-law and his mother. He sincerely requested them to allow Buvana to recuperate under the love and care of her parents and the family doctor. Understandably, the anxious parents were on pins and needles until they knew the reaction to such a letter from the other end. There was no response to Murthy's request in the post. Sethu and his mother arrived without prior notice.

"It's not easy for me to travel anymore, you see," said the mother-in-law, complaining about the tediousness of her trip.

"We're sorry to hear that," said Murthy, smiling politely.

The tedium didn't ruin the mother-in-law's appetite during lunch. She sent several compliments to the kitchen. She enquired about the welfare of Murthy's family and his farms. She displayed extraordinary interest in the condition of the orchards and paddy fields that enveloped Brinda. When Murthy was able to deliver a positive report, she exchanged a greedy look with her son. After all, Sethu was going to reap the benefits of the vast property around Brinda!

Sethu sat in Buvana's room for a few minutes. Didn't he have anything to say to her? As he was leaving the room, he turned and looked at Buvana. "Let me know when you deliver my son," Sethu said in his dictatorial voice. "At that time you should return to my house." He didn't wait for her reply.

Sethu's mother had a long talk with the doctor, made sure that Buvana's feeble condition was genuine, and granted Buvana permission to stay with her parents until the delivery. "Well, I know our customs. A girl usually delivers her child in her parents' home," the mother-in-law said to Murthy and Saroja. "I would've sent her to the proper place, your home, after the seventh month. In Buvana's case … let her stay here through her pregnancy. What do you think, Sethu?" she turned to her son and asked.

Sethu was not opposed to this suggestion. Sethu and his mother were determined not to leave until Murthy's lawyer arrived with a solid plan for the allocation of the property. Sekaran had a specific list of the distribution of every piece of land, every bit of the orchards, and every tidbit in the cash box. Everything was accounted for. Such an attention to details was now necessary. The baby would be here soon.

"Sekaran, what does this mean?" Sethu's mother asked Murthy's lawyer regarding a particular section in the will. "I don't understand this. Why didn't somebody explain to me earlier?"

Sekaran began his nervous explanation. It was not easy. Murthy's father had left his will in such an ambiguous manner. There was a clause that allocated a portion of the inheritance to Murthy's grandson. If the family had a granddaughter, then the same allocation would be handed over to the next eligible male. This wrinkle in the will didn't mean that Buvana would be less rich if she delivered a female child. It simply meant that she would lose a portion of the property if she didn't have a son.

However, Sethu's family wanted everything. Buvana's mother-in-law, despite her calculating nature, had not paid attention to this particular clause at the time of the marriage settlement. She had been excessively careless! Now, at the prospect of an heir, she insisted on reading every line in the will to ensure her grandchild's future security. Murthy, who was never bothered by wills and such formalities, had not paid any attention at all to this particular article in his father's will. Now he was worried about the oversight of the in-laws.

Buvana had to produce a son to keep all of the property intact for future generations, especially if her husband was to benefit from the inheritance. A female child would inherit considerable property, including Brinda and a significant portion of the land, but Sethu wouldn't be able to touch it! Now, more than ever, Sethu was desperate to have a son.

The villagers were curious about Buvana's rather permanent stay in her parents' home so early in her condition.

"Why is Buvana already here?" Janaki, Kanyakoil's primary busybody, voiced her curiosity. "Shouldn't she stay with her husband until the seventh month?"

"The doctor has advised Buvana to stay under our constant care," Saroja explained to the impertinent lady.

This explanation should have been sufficient, but Janaki was not satisfied. She visited Brinda again under some insipid pretext, and on this particular afternoon, Thangam received her in the hall. Janaki restricted her visits to Brinda drastically.

Buvana's confinement turned into a blessing. She was surrounded by love, and she was glad that her husband never showed his face after his first visit. Her mother-in-law occasionally wrote to Buvana's parents to ensure the pregnant daughter-in-law's progress during her separation from her in-law's home. Buvana took several walks along the river with her mother or her aunt. Her father took her by her hand for a relaxed walk, just as he used to do when she was a little girl.

After returning from a long walk on a pleasant afternoon, Buvana went to her room to rest.

"Sekaran is waiting for you in the hall," Saroja said to Murthy. She asked a servant to get some coffee, murukku, and laddu for the guest.

Sekaran was here to discuss Buvana's future. What were they to do once the infant arrived?

"It is Sethu's child, Sekaran. Buvana ought to go back, but how?" Murthy asked his lawyer. He was reluctant to send his child, with her child, back to a home where she wouldn't be treated kindly.

"I know, Murthy. Don't worry. We'll find a way," replied Sekaran.

"But if Buvana decides to stay separated from her husband, she would face the criticism of the villagers. She would be the helpless victim of gossip. How can we watch her become the object of mockery?" asked Murthy.

"We need to think about this carefully, Murthy. As you know, Buvana's safety comes first," said Sekaran.

"Saroja, how I wish I had enquired more about Sethu's family before placing our innocent daughter in his hands," Murthy sighed sadly. "What I've done is criminal!"

"I know what you're feeling, but we talked to a few people. We heard only good things about his family. Some unseen, evil force must have manipulated us. You're not at fault," Saroja said to ease her husband's mind.

Whose fault was it? Buvana was not alone. Several young women were miserable in their married lives because their parents were reluctant to let them remain single. Marriage was a girl's salvation in Buvana's sphere. Naturally, most men took advantage of this principle and the insecurities that went with it. Further, the parents of such men used that principle as an opportunity to extract money from innocent brides and their helpless families. Well, whose fault was it?

While Murthy was reading the newspaper in the veranda, Sivam offered a deferential cough. He needed Murthy's advice on a pressing issue.

"What is it, Sivam?" Murthy asked his foreman.

"That farmhand has disappeared for more than two weeks. I allowed him to take a week for his wedding. What should I do? I need help."

Murthy, instead of offering advice, stared at him. Sivam was practically raised by Murthy's family. He had dedicated his days to the welfare of Brinda and the people it sheltered. Murthy was worried about him.

"Sivam, you can't remain a bachelor all your life," said Murthy. "Don't you want to get married?"

"How am I supposed to look for a bride?" asked Sivam, genuinely bewildered.

It had to be providence! Saroja, who was still thinking of a way to repay Humsa for her kindness to Buvana, suggested to Sivam that they should look for a girl beyond the borders of Kanyakoil. Sivam left the decision in Saroja's capable hands.

That was it. Here she was. Humsa was married to Sivam—a perfect match! Sivam brought his bride to Brinda to receive blessings from his master's family before taking her to his modest housing, annexed to the beautiful mansion. When Saroja invited the newlyweds to come to Brinda for lunch, Humsa looked stunned.

"Humsa," whispered Sivam, understanding his wife's confusion. "There is no room for caste discriminations here."

Saroja took Humsa to the prayer room. She offered her a silver tray—filled with saris, flowers, fruits, nuts, and money. A superior sense of elation carried Humsa to distant clouds—cool, misty, rain clouds. It was the monsoon of the Gods where the raindrops touched every head, regardless of religion, regardless of caste. What a wonderful beginning! It was a new life for the young bride in a delightful surrounding. Humsa was happy, and what a well-deserved happiness it was!

Brinda was decorated with flowers and lights again. Friends and family of Murthy and Saroja gathered in the great hall to celebrate Buvana's forthcoming delivery. Under normal circumstances, her baby shower would have been a remarkable festivity. Now, during a turbulent period of anxiety, it was not a welcome function, certainly not among inquisitive guests. But society expected it and customs demanded it! Janaki and her intimate crowd would have talked for hours if the Murthys had pushed this event aside. According to the doctor's instructions, Buvana was to be removed from her room only for a short period of time to make an appearance among the guests. Saroja and Murthy were thankful for that. It was time to receive caterers, florists, and extra help in the kitchen. The community would be astonished to see anything less than magnificent when it congregated in Brinda for a special celebration.

The mother-in-law brought a few of her family members and friends to bless Buvana. Thangam and Kitta, with the assistance of a couple of friends who were devoted to the welfare of Buvana, kept these intimidating guests away from the prying curiosity of Kanyakoil. Particularly, Janaki and company were kept away from the venomous mother-in-law. Sethu didn't come. Initially, Murthy had thought that his son-in-law refused to come as a result of his odious character.

"Saroja, our son-in-law was in a drunken brawl! Good God! How can a father send his daughter back to such a man?" Murthy asked his wife, shocked at the real reason.

"Where is Buvana's husband?" asked Janaki.

"Shouldn't he be here with his wife during this auspicious occasion?" asked another guest.

"Poor Sethu fell and hurt his ankle," replied Murthy. "His doctor has advised him not to travel for a month or two."

A week after the baby shower, Murthy asked the servants to prepare a room for a special visitor. His friend, Dr. Kannan, was appointed as the chief surgeon at the municipal hospital. He had acquired extensive experience in obstetrics and gynecology at one of the leading medical centers in Europe. Brinda was to be his home during the next few days. With an astute instinct that was quite natural to his profession, Kannan expressed an interest in Buvana's condition. During a private moment, he shared his concern with Murthy. He encouraged his friend to admit Buvana at the hospital for her delivery instead of calling the midwife to Brinda. Murthy booked a private room in the hospital.

Prayers continued. Murthy's family and friends developed a strong belief in miracles. Would Sethu mellow at the sight of his child, his own flesh and blood? On the threshold of fatherhood, his evil tendencies might make way for a little compassion. Would God answer their prayers? He had to. He must. If He didn't, what were they to do?

◆ ◆ ◆

The cool breeze of February made room for an excessively hot March when Buvana was getting ready to deliver her baby. Brinda was not prepared to welcome a baby on that sweaty evening, many hours after the earth had swallowed the sun.

The whitewashed corridors and metal cots looked impersonal and cold. However, if Dr. Kannan's prediction was right, it was essential to keep Buvana in the hospital. Humsa soaked soft pieces of cloth in cold water and pressed them on Buvana's forehead. Saroja was a nervous wreck. She burst into tears with every growing whimper from Buvana.

"Do you think Buvana will be all right, Thangam?" Saroja asked anxiously.

"Saroja, go to the corridor, imagine that it's the prayer room, and keep praying. It'll be all right. Buvana is young and healthy. Everything will be fine. Now run along and pray." Thangam sent Saroja out of the room and sat by her niece's bed.

Dr. Kannan's forecast was accurate. Even the family doctor had expressed his concerns regarding Buvana's precarious pregnancy. Buvana was in agonizing labor. The birthing room was quiet for a short period of time except for words of encouragement from Thangam and Humsa. The family was awake in anticipation, in worry, and in sheer fear of the welfare of a child, who was to bring her child into the world.

Buvana delivered around sunrise. The baby arrived with all the noise that was unusual for dawn. It was a girl! She didn't come alone. She dragged her mother's uterus with her. She had decided that her young mother had gone through enough misery for nine months. Also, she decided to be her mother's only child.

The family couldn't thank Dr. Kannan enough for his foresight that prompted him to have Buvana deliver in the hospital. A cold and horrifying thought plagued the family's peace of mind; could the young mother endure an intricate birthing process in the comforts of Brinda, under the sole supervision of a midwife? Could there be a doubt that Buvana and her baby were alive because of the timely medical attention provided by Dr. Kannan and his colleagues?

A cheerful nurse brought the infant to Buvana. The young, uncertain mother looked at the puffy bundle of flesh, with a chunk of brown-black hair. All the resentment she had harbored against an unwanted child disappeared at the sight of her newborn. Buvana held her daughter close to her heart. Her baby was a part of her—a little Buvana. She was the gift of sunrise. She decided to name her Aruna, the sunrise of Brinda. The grandparents also approved of this beautiful name, but they reminded Buvana to wait for the in-laws' endorsement before placing a stamp on that name permanently.

Murthy sent a telegram to Buvana's in-laws: "By God's grace, mother and child are in good health."

Buvana needed to stay in the hospital for at least a couple of weeks. Dr. Kannan monitored her treatment, which alleviated a lot of her family's stress. He also supervised her journey to Brinda after her release from the hospital. Sethu's family didn't come to welcome the new baby. It was his baby. Where was he? Where was his mother?

Next day brought Sethu's mother to Brinda. She was considerably disappointed because Buvana didn't deliver the much-expected grandson. Murthy and Saroja were waiting for Sethu to get out of the carriage at any moment. He didn't come. Why not? He was sulking. No son! Buvana's parents sat in the hall nervously. The strain of entertaining an unpleasant visitor, an unloved visitor, was evident in their polite but anxious expressions.

"Your telegram didn't mention the fact that my grandchild is a girl," Sethu's mother said, reprimanding Murthy and his wife. "This information came to me from another source."

Another source must mean a branch of grapevine.

"I'm sorry," Murthy apologized. "We should've mentioned that. You know, in all the tension and worry of seeing our Buvana through the trying time ..." Murthy replied, unable to end his babble.

"Well," the mother-in-law sighed a great deal, a little hope hanging on that sigh. "Buvana will probably deliver a boy next time."

Buvana's parents exchanged painful glances. What were they to do? They couldn't hide the unhappy truth any longer. Saroja cleared her throat and explained about Buvana's delivery in a nervous voice.

"Your daughter can't have another child?" Sethu's mother asked. "My son will never have a son!" She got up. Without a glance at her daughter-in-law or her grandchild, she walked out of the room, walked out of Brinda, got into the carriage, and left.

Sethu didn't come. He never saw his child. Instead, his lawyer arrived with a notice of annulment. Buvana was speechless, her parents were shocked, and their household was in agony.

"May I speak to my son-in-law, appeal to his better side? Please, can we do anything?" Murthy asked Sethu's lawyer.

Sethu's lawyer was not a man of cruel nature like his unworthy client. He felt the sorrow around Buvana and her family. But he was here for a purpose. He had a job to accomplish. "Mr. Murthy, it's painful, I know," he said. "I have two daughters. Your child is facing something that no young lady can bear. Sir, you must see that I'm helpless."

"Sir, can you exercise your influence on my son-in-law?" Murthy begged again.

"I have no influence," Sethu's lawyer said, looking cautiously at the door before lowering his voice. "I doubt if anybody has that power, except his mother. Anyway, in this case," his voice sank to a barely audible whisper, "I believe his mother is acting in his best interest."

What the lawyer didn't say but wished to mention was that Sethu's mother was the chief instigator of Buvana's misery and the major organizer of the recent developments. Murthy and Sekaran understood the lawyer's message.

Sethu wanted the annulment taken care of as soon as possible. Murthy and Saroja wondered why Sethu was in such a hurry to make their daughter nameless. His wish to hasten the separation indicated his need to cling to something. What was it?

Sethu's lawyer read the notice in a loud voice to Murthy in Sekaran's presence. He was supposed to do this to satisfy formalities.

"Mr. Murthy, my client's letter goes,

'To Murthy,

This is to inform you that I'm in the process of dissolving my relationship with your daughter. She is no longer my wife. Don't send her to Chinnoor. I don't want you to come here either. I am a very busy man. I have no time to talk to you. Send the papers with my lawyer.

Sethu'

Will you sign here to indicate that I have read this to you?" asked Sethu's lawyer.

Murthy signed. What else was he supposed to do?

Murthy went to the veranda to find his daughter. As a bonus, he found her with his little granddaughter. While he was wondering what he could say to make Buvana feel a little better, she burst into an animated speech, much against her personality.

"Appa, why do you want me to go back to that man?" Buvana asked unhappily. "How can you expect me to live with him, with my mother-in-law and her cruel family, when they hate my child?"

Murthy, a little surprised at his daughter's uncharacteristic outburst, tried to persuade her to understand his view of the current situation. "Buvana," Murthy began. "Our society respects a woman, who is a doormat in her husband's home, as long as she stays in that home. The same society spits on the doormat if she is no longer welcome by her husband. Please understand, my child. I don't want you to return to the same house where you were abused by your husband's family."

"You don't? What do you mean?"

"I won't let you go back to your husband's home, Buvana," Murthy replied quickly. "Nothing would tempt me to send you back there."

"What can we do? Appa, what should I do? What are you thinking of?" asked Buvana.

"What I have in mind is a compromise. I want to purchase a house or construct one close to Brinda, which would be yours and Sethu's. You would be expected to live in this house occasionally just to please our society. You and your baby would be under our family's constant supervision. All I'm planning to do is to beg my son-in-law to allow you to retain his name. Do you understand, my dear?"

Buvana thought about her father's plan. He was willing to do anything to retain his daughter's name and respect in a society that was not worthy of any thought.

"Appa, you've already spent a fortune on my wedding and the dowry. I can't remember what else," Buvana said pathetically. "Please don't spend more money. I feel so sorry."

"Buvana, please stop thinking about money. What am I going to do with it? I can't take it with me when my time comes to leave this world. What's the purpose of wealth if it can't bring happiness to one's child and family?"

"But, Appa, how can I ever return what you have done for me and …" Buvana was lost in her embarrassment.

"Buvana," said Murthy, taking her hand in his. "A child is not under obligation to her parents because they love her. You're a blessing to us. Your wish for our welfare and your love for us are just the things your mother and I expect from you. This is the last time you're going to worry about returning anything to us. Our relationship is not based on credits and debits. No more, child, all right? No more."

Buvana was touched. She knew that her infamous husband didn't have a better side. He would never listen to reason. Would he? She hoped that her father's magnanimity and good intentions were not utterly wasted on her wicked husband.

Murthy's magnanimous proposal and his good intentions to save his daughter's name became meaningless. Sethu gave a deaf ear! Sekaran had hoped to bring some good news to his client. He entered Brinda with a heavy heart and an empty pocket. Even the prospect of a new home and a considerable living allowance were not sufficient to tempt Sethu. News had arrived in Sekaran's direction in the form of gossip, conjecture, and speculations. He decided to take a different suggestion to Murthy.

"Murthy, I think that blackguard has found another woman," Sekaran said angrily. "His mother may want him to marry again to get a grandson. In that case, he can marry again … while he still maintains his status as Buvana's husband. This is not a new concept in some cases. If Sethu wishes to get a second wife to have a son, with Buvana's permission, would you consider it?"

"Well, what should we do?"

"Please don't be angry. I know it's an embarrassing option," Sekaran continued. "First of all, Sethu should agree to this. Buvana can sign an agreement. Sethu may marry another woman to have a son … without disclaiming Buvana as his wife."

Murthy was not angry. Sekaran was a kind man and a devoted friend of the family. Murthy, at this point, was groping for any proposal that might save his daughter from becoming husbandless and alone for the rest of her life. "No, I'm not angry. You're only thinking of a way to save Buvana from this disaster. Why don't we ask my daughter?" asked Murthy.

But it was a difficult alternative. How could a father ask a daughter such a ghastly question? Even the thought of suggesting such an idea was disgusting. Well, he had to do it. Murthy approached his daughter bravely.

Buvana, though initially shocked by such a suggestion, decided to consider it for one reason. "Appa, my daughter would have a father," Buvana sounded relieved. "At least for the sake of appearance, in the eyes of our society, Aruna could have a father. I'm willing to sign my consent for my husband's second wedding."

Sekaran got into his carriage. He was prepared to go on his knees and beg Sethu to consider the latest proposal from the Murthys. He didn't have much hope at this point. He was not only letting down a client. He was unable to help a friend in need, and the latter failure made him feel useless under the circumstances. He had known Buvana since she was born. He prayed and wished for a miracle all the way through his journey to Chinnoor.

Sekaran submitted Murthy's proposal to Sethu's lawyer.

"Can my client have some time to discuss this proposal with his mother?" asked Sethu's lawyer.

"Yes, of course," said Sekaran. When did Sethu make any decision without consulting his mother?

A servant came out of the house and asked Sekaran to wait in the veranda. Sethu's lawyer sat with him for a while, talking about the weather. Sekaran appreciated the lawyer's good manners. But the waiting was killing him. When was Sethu going to see him with his decision? Finally, after more than an hour, Sethu was ready to see Sekaran.

"Well, Mr. Sethu," began Sekaran.

Sethu glared at him, appeared bored and restless for a few moments, and laughed obnoxiously. "Sekaran, do you think I'm an idiot?" Sethu asked arrogantly. "Why are that luckless woman and her father still annoying me and my mother? If you come here again, I'll tell everybody that you are a prostitute's lawyer." He threw a final notice on Sekaran's face.

Sethu's lawyer winced. He was sitting through his client's monologue with a helpless expression. He was clearly ashamed of Sethu's disrespectful behavior. Unable to offer his apology for his client's shameful conduct in Sethu's presence, the sedate lawyer walked with Sekaran to the gate and offered a quick apology.

Sekaran returned to Kanyakoil, weary in mind and body. How was he going to tell his friend that there was no other option left to save Buvana's marriage? How was he going to approach Brinda again to talk about his failure? Murthy was disappointed when he saw Sekaran's dejected expression. Although Saroja was equally disappointed, she had the sense to see the futility of her husband's attempts.

"Saroja, the people—what must they think?" Murthy asked wearily. "Won't the society laugh at our daughter? What shall we do, Saroja?"

Saroja sat by him and took his hand in hers. "I know. That question has been nagging me too," agreed Saroja. "We're all that our daughter has. We can help her forget the unhappiness once in a while, can't we? Think of the baby. What that child has to face is something we can't even imagine. Together, we'll face whatever is ahead of us."

Murthy prepared to accept the hopeless situation. So did his daughter. At her tender age, Buvana prepared to be alone for the rest of her life, never to enjoy the kindness of a husband, and never to learn to love a man.

The carriage took Buvana and her family to Chinnoor. Sekaran had tried his best to conduct this disgraceful procedure without Buvana's presence. He came back disappointed. Sethu, with the support of his influential friends, vetoed Sekaran's request and insisted on having Buvana at the scene at any cost. His evil nature delighted in others' miseries. He characteristically looked forward to robbing a helpless woman's dignity and insulting a respected and decent family.

The 'mock court' had gathered around the majestic banyan tree in the outskirts of the town. The men assembled to display their importance. The women came to enjoy the show. A few gathered to show sympathy to a helpless young lady. Some whispered that Sethu wished to make a fortune at his wife's inability to give birth to a son. Some argued that a woman was useless unless she produced a son. Some speculated on Sethu's wish to make better fortune by marrying again.

The object of the whisperings was standing next to the leader of the assembly, stuffing a chunk of tobacco in his mouth. He made a perfect picture of wickedness. His unsteady gaze focused on Buvana. Where was his mother? She was sitting with her family and friends.

"Where is Buvana?" the town crier shouted.

All eyes were on Buvana. She walked obediently, humiliated and hurt by the cruelty of the community. The crowd sat still.

"Where is your child?" the leader of the assembly climbed on the platform and bawled.

Kitta took the baby from his sister's hands and brought her to Buvana. She held the infant close to her breast, afraid of losing her.

The meeting went through the familiar formality of rules. Rules! Buvana would no longer have a husband. An unprincipled family abducted a woman's pride and dignity under misrepresented rules and regulations. What a farce under the shroud of distorted tradition! Which culture could ignore such an audacity? Buvana felt nothing. The tears might come some day, but not today, not now. As she looked through the crowd of men and women, she saw her husband's mistress. Rules!

The leader read the note in a detached voice: "This woman, Buvana, wife of Sethu, daughter of Murthy, has failed in her marriage. She will lose her status of a wife and …"

Murthy had to make a substantial payment to Sethu's family for feeding Buvana. On the other hand, the villain didn't pay anything for the welfare of his child. As far as he was concerned, that child was never born, had nothing to do with his life, and didn't exist. It was the end of a nightmare and the beginning of a misery. Buvana had no ties to this town, or the people, or the family. Buvana's connection with her husband was over. She would no longer be imprisoned on the terrace. She wouldn't be abused physically or emotionally. The torture that she had experienced in her in-law's house was over. A different misery was born. Her dignity was on display, ready for auction. Her pride was sinking with every word from the crowd and with every glance from the throng of eyes.

The community that had welcomed the new bride with red water and yellow rice ignored her when she left her undeserving husband and his greedy mother. Not a single human being had the courage to question the deplorable actions of an unscrupulous family. Unfortunately, those who tried to gather some courage didn't have any influence—financially or socially—to question Sethu's atrocities regarding the innocent victim. That was what she was—a victim of male supremacy and greed, camouflaged under tradition!

Buvana returned to Brinda with her child. A part of her rejoiced because she need not share the life of a monster, but she wished for a better life for her daughter. Aruna was the outcome of a bitter union. The young mother prayed to God to look at her child with more mercy than He did in Buvana's case. Disillusioned and disgusted with what her life offered, Buvana began a new life as a mother. Motherhood was the only consolation she had in the middle of broken dreams and dissipated promises.

Sekaran had judged Sethu with precision and sagacity. News came via dependable sources that the infamous mother-in-law had chosen another bride, another victim, with considerable property.

"Sekaran, how did Sethu's family manage to get another victim?" asked Murthy.

"Murthy, I heard that this young woman has been unable to get a husband because of an unlucky incident," said Sekaran. "A few years ago, hours before her wedding ceremony, her fiancé died in an accident. No other family chose her for a daughter-in-law because her star must be under a bad spell! You know our society!"

"Sethu's mother doesn't mind choosing a girl-under-a-bad-spell?" Murthy asked incredulously.

"Well, my contact told me that Sethu's mother decided to ignore this young woman's misfortune," replied Sekaran. "She has money, Murthy. I'm sure Sethu's mother is hoping for a grandson."

Sethu married again—another wife, another victim, and another dowry. Buvana felt sorry for Sethu's new wife. News arrived that he found a new mistress. He established his new woman in the house by the mill on Market Street.

New wife! New mistress! A sudden, nameless shame engulfed Buvana. She felt like discarded slippers. She went to the balcony to hide her shame. The tears found her after weeks of separation from her husband—not because she had lost the position of a wife—because she had been his wife. Her tears indicated the travesty of a marriage and the shame of having shared the bed of a man, a remorseless man, who was happier with a whore. Those tears certainly acknowledged the helplessness of being a woman. Her parents came to the balcony to comfort her.

"Appa, can I please live in Salem with my daughter?" asked Buvana. "You know the property near your cousin's house?"

"Live alone, Buvana?" asked Murthy.

"What happened, my dear? Why?" asked Saroja.

"I'm a married woman," said Buvana. "Well, married and separated! I have a child. I can't live with my parents. I can support the baby with the dividends I receive from various corners, don't you think?"

Her parents wouldn't hear of it. No, that would only make more room for talk, not at all in favor of Buvana's reputation or her child's. And how could her parents get a wink of sleep if Buvana went away? Brinda was hers. Everything they owned was Buvana's. The widespread land and the whispering orchards belonged to their only child. They would have her live there for eternity.

An eternity in that society, especially among those neighbors, was not a comforting thought! But … by living with her parents, she was assured of unconditional love and security. She understood and accepted her dependence on her parents. She wouldn't be able to survive without her father's protection. As it stood, Buvana would be carrying a label. Living alone with her daughter, with no male protection, could make that uncomfortable label lethal for little Aruna.

How could a man abandon his child? After weeks of reviewing her miserable past from which she was waiting to escape and her uncertain future that she was afraid to meet, she still couldn't understand the mind of a human being that had no room for compassionate thoughts or merciful gestures. How could a father refuse to look at his innocent baby's face? And what would Buvana tell her daughter if she asked about her father? Buvana was prepared to live in isolation, but Aruna shouldn't do the same. Could her child look forward to a bright future? God, would Aruna have any future at all?

Buvana sat in the veranda with her baby. She looked at the horizon under the canopy of a thousand trees. The cool evening breeze rocked her memories. She remembered the time when her mother had walked with her along the moist banks. She had showed her how the sun kissed the earth at sunset. Little Aruna would walk with Buvana, taking in the fragrance of the flowers, dancing with the butterflies, and feeling the gritty sand on her bare feet. Buvana was a mother now! She was proud of her daughter. Aruna was hers to cherish for eternity. She would teach her to love, to smile, to feel the grainy sand slip through tiny fingers, and she would show her the beauty of sunrise. She held her baby close to her and enjoyed her first smile. She admired her sparkling eyes and impish dimple. Her baby would be the purpose of her sunrise, a birth to her mornings, and a lullaby to her nights.

Buvana took in everything—love, patience, forbearance, tears, and sighs—just like Mother Earth. Her days and nights chatted with the river that drenched the soil of Brinda. She would find peace during a sunrise, amber-coated and dappled with raindrops. It would be a beautiful sunrise. She began to wait for the perfect dawn.

PART II

This is my child

Aruna and her grandfather found the first-class compartment. The train station was packed with vendors, porters, and beggars.

"Are you comfortable, my dear? I'm so glad, Aruna. I can take you home permanently. Did I tell you how much we missed you when you were in college?" asked Murthy, smiling at his granddaughter.

Aruna returned his affectionate smile. Yes, she had heard that from her family because they loved her. She wouldn't hear that from the villagers because she didn't fit the robe of an appropriate, modest young woman. No wonder, Kanyakoil failed to tempt her to return to its community. The only attraction the village had was her home, Brinda, and its occupants.

Murthy's snoring matched the rickety rhythm of the train. Aruna looked at the rain and opened the window to breathe in the moist earth. The train rolled over the river that bordered her ancestral home, Brinda. She saw the kitchen garden and the gate in the distance. Aruna's delight in seeing her family was marred by her thoughts of the community. The turn of the century bragged about reforms. Did she see any? No. Aruna voiced her opinion too often, much to the displeasure of her grandfather. Murthy thought that Aruna had a mind of her own, just like her great aunt, Thangam. The theory that the two women were made of the same mold never ceased to amaze the family.

"Thatha, wake up. We are in Kanyakoil," shouted Aruna. It was almost dark when the train wheezed next to the platform.

The familiar potpourri of fragrances from the florist's stall, mixed with the steaming coffee in the vendor's hands, stirred a longing in Aruna's heart. She was home. The thought of home turned on the hunger pangs.

Sivam had brought the carriage to take them home. Brinda looked beautiful under the transparent shroud of twilight. When the carriage stopped at the courtyard, Humsa walked out of the house to receive them. Sivam took the horses to the stable after Murthy invited him to have supper with the family. Aruna noticed a small carriage near the veranda. Was there a visitor in the house?

"Aruna, how are you, dear?" asked Humsa.

"Hungry," replied Aruna.

Humsa smiled, but that smile lacked something.

"You're not happy to see me?" asked Aruna. "Are you worried that there might be trouble now that I've arrived?"

"Aruna, I'm delighted to see you," replied Humsa, affectionately hugging her. "It's just that we have a visitor. Get inside and you'll see. Did you have a nice journey, Aruna? I hope you're not too tired to face what's waiting for you in the hall."

Waiting for her in the hall? What was Humsa talking about?

The visitor was a gentleman. Murthy followed Aruna into the hall, looked at the man, and staggered. Aruna held his hand to steady him. The air was doused with an eerie calm that was unknown to Brinda.

"What are you doing here?" Murthy asked the stranger.

"I've come to acknowledge my daughter," replied the stranger, staring at Aruna. "Is that all right?"

It took Aruna just a few seconds to realize the identity of the man. She had never seen her father before. She had heard of him from her family and the villagers. Well, this was the man, the thoughtless man, who left his young wife and child at the outskirts of his town.

"My daughter lost her husband more than twenty years ago," Murthy shouted. "My granddaughter has no father. Get out of my home."

The man stood up. After a long look at Buvana, he walked out of the house.

"Who let him in?" Murthy asked, angered by Sethu's sudden appearance. "He'll not enter this house again, Saroja. How did this happen? How could you let him in?"

"He took us by surprise. Buvana was upstairs. I hardly recognized him," said Saroja. "His arrival after more than twenty years was shocking. Really, how could I be prepared for something like this?"

"Oh, Murthy, come on! It's not Saroja's fault," said Thangam, scolding her brother. She turned to Aruna. "How is my Aruna?" Thangam asked, embracing Aruna affectionately. "Your paatti sent me upstairs as soon as she saw Sethu at the door. Well, she was worried that I might kill him. I might. Actually, I'd like to."

Aruna walked to her grandmother. "Saroja Paatti, how are you?" asked Aruna.

Saroja embraced Aruna affectionately.

"Saroja, how long was he here?" Murthy asked.

"He came about half an hour ago," Saroja replied. "He said very little. He was waiting to see Aruna."

"I don't want him to enter the house without my presence. Don't let him in again, Saroja."

"I won't."

"Anyway, what did he want? Why did he come here? What did he say, Saroja?"

"He wants Buvana to forgive him," said Saroja, rather meditatively. "He wants to see his daughter settled in a good marriage."

"After all these years?" Thangam asked. "I can't believe it."

"I can't believe it. Sethu is a villain. He is cruel. When he threw my daughter out of his life, I had begged him to consider Buvana's plight and Aruna's future. He was immovable. He wants to secure Aruna's future! Humbug! He is a fraud. I'll do everything in my power to keep him away from Brinda. How can we believe his intentions now?" Murthy asked.

A few years ago, Murthy had sent a formal letter to the families in nearby towns to look for a husband for Aruna. He had lost faith in horoscopes! Not many responses came in Aruna's favor. People talked. They wondered about Aruna's father. Who was Buvana's husband? Where was he? Aruna appeared to belong to a respectable, distinguished, and wealthy family. Unfortunately, no family was willing to choose Aruna—a girl in a shadow.

Most families shared the sentiment that marriage was a terminal commitment. The chosen bride was to produce a crop of impeccable lineage, and they couldn't jeopardize the flow of flawless children by choosing a young woman like Aruna. Those who knew about Buvana and Sethu also knew about their separation, and they didn't hesitate to spread the word. Matrimony for Aruna seemed to be written on water!

Aruna decided not to get married at all after a visit from a bride-seeking family. This particular family didn't come in pursuit of a daughter-in-law. They were trying to replace their son's hysterical wife with a sensible lady, who would be assuming the responsibility of minding his four children. This fact became clear when Murthy carefully investigated the groom's past—a judicious step Murthy had failed to follow prior to Buvana's marriage.

"I hate this custom," exclaimed Aruna. "Men come here, check my status, and short of counting my teeth, they insult me in every possible manner. The farmers probably spend less time inspecting the cattle they wish to buy. I'd rather stay single."

Murthy was wary of marriage proposals after this incident. None of the prospective grooms had a decent education or a job worth mentioning. Murthy decided not to rush into choosing a husband for his granddaughter when his daughter was still suffering due to his earlier error in judgment. He was willing to wait for a decent alliance to knock on the door.

"Thatha, why are you still looking for a husband for me? Don't you know that men are scared of me? Leave them alone," said Aruna, smiling.

"Aruna, marriage is important in your life. It offers security, children, and many more advantages. Can you try to see my point?" Murthy asked Aruna.

"Thatha, security?" asked Aruna. "You must be joking! What benefit has my mother enjoyed from her marriage? She has seen none of the advantages, with the exception of a single child."

"That's her fate, child. Time, probably bad time! All marriages don't end in misery."

"No, you can't blame everything on fate."

"Aruna, don't think that all marriages are disasters! Mine was exceptionally unfortunate. Several couples stand by each other through happy and difficult times. My mother and father have been happy for years. Won't you consider for my sake?" Buvana asked her daughter.

"Can we talk about this later, Amma?" asked Aruna.

"As you wish," said Buvana. For the time being, Buvana's immediate worries were postponed by her daughter's return. Aruna's smile brought a lot of comfort and purpose in her mother's empty days.

Aruna took her worries to bed. The steady sound of the rain on the windowpane was out of tune with the sporadic thump of her wandering mind. She remembered the confused and horrific expressions at the presence of the strange man. How could he do this to her family? Aruna felt such an outrage. She wouldn't let anybody hurt her mother.

Further worries about her mother only increased Aruna's resentment toward the community.

"You were born defiant, Aruna," said Buvana, during breakfast. "I should have foreseen this from the day you were born."

"Somebody must fight, Amma," replied Aruna, with a further note of defiance. "You don't owe these people anything. Why are you afraid of our rigid society?"

"I'm not afraid, Aruna. Remember, quite a few people have been kind to us through all these years. Can you deny that?" Buvana asked.

"Kind! Well, perhaps, but they have no backbone."

It was useless to argue with Aruna. Her grandfather had exclaimed many times that if Aruna had been a man, she would have made an excellent lawyer. Buvana agreed with him. Aruna was the antithesis of her mother. While the daughter was ready to question the world, the mother was eager to hide from it. Yes, they were very different, but the love, trust, and understanding that subsisted between them were remarkably alike.

Nobody mistook Aruna for Buvana's daughter based on appearance, although there was a resemblance between the two. Aruna had inherited her mother's features. But her defiance and confidence made her tall stature appear severe and her angular face appear boyish. She preferred to pull her dense, long hair into a careless braid. She never noticed her slightly short and rounded nose or her seriously set lips in the mirror. She thought it was a waste of time.

Saroja took Aruna to the temple very early in the morning. They were accustomed to these sun-up visits because the temple was less crowded during the early hours. While Saroja found a shady spot under a banyan tree to talk to a friend, Aruna proceeded to the priest to make a request. There was a small building within the perimeters of Brinda that was currently empty. Murthy generously donated it to Aruna. The priest was to bless this building that was supposed to be used as a school for the children in the village.

"Saroja, you look cheerful now that Aruna is back for good," said a friend of the family. "Please tell Buvana that I particularly wished to know of her welfare."

Buvana stopped going to the temple as a result of a humiliating incident that occurred right after her separation from her husband. When Aruna was a couple of months old, Buvana had gone to the temple with the baby in her arms. Some of the villagers offered a greeting. Some avoided her eyes. A particularly orthodox family made every effort not to cross her path. The head of the family exclaimed that Buvana was a symbol of bad luck. She wouldn't bring good luck in the day's ventures! That was the wretched beginning of Buvana's reluctance to appear in public.

"Thangam, this is exactly what I was afraid of. See how our society punishes poor Buvana for Sethu's crime?" Saroja had said to Thangam.

"Society, Saroja, is a pit of muck," Thangam declared, voicing her anger in a way only she could. "Why should Buvana be afraid to appear in public? Why should she hide like a prostitute?"

"Thangam, you're so severe," said Saroja. "Your language! I know it's unfair. Time might help people forget the past."

Time did nothing. Buvana rarely showed her face in public after the humiliating incident. Her adventures outside the perimeters of Brinda were limited to visits to a few families that were dear to the Murthys in affection and loyalty.

"Has the post come, Thatha?" Aruna asked. "I'm waiting for Mary's letter. I wonder why she hasn't written yet."

"I think I see his cycle outside the gate. Here he is, Aruna."

The postman deposited a stack of letters in Murthy's hands and enquired after Aruna's welfare.

Aruna ran to her favorite spot on the sandy banks with the letter in her hand. Mary was waiting to see Aruna's school. She was eager to visit Brinda. Mary's visit was just what Aruna needed to make her school complete. The girls had undergone training together for a future in teaching. Aruna replied promptly to Mary, and she urged her to plan on a lengthy visit to Brinda. After asking a servant to post the letter, Aruna went to the veranda to talk to her mother.

"Here, Buvana Akka," said Humsa, holding a tray with a pitcher of lemon juice. "It's a sultry evening. Have something cold to drink."

Buvana was at this spot or on the balcony at this particular time of the day. She liked to watch the sun disappear behind the hills. She was never tired of it. Aruna took the tray from Humsa's hands.

"Amma, why did you marry that man?" Aruna asked.

Although Buvana was used to her daughter's frank outbursts, she didn't expect this. She turned her face away to stare at the half-hidden sun.

"You don't mind if I ask, do you? Why that man?" Aruna asked again.

"No, I don't mind," replied Buvana. "Well, I didn't prefer anyone in particular. You know how it is in our families and customs. I just trusted the elders' decisions and placed my future in the hands of destiny, I suppose."

"Amma, nobody knew what he was like?"

"Obviously, none of our acquaintances knew his nature. If our family had known, they wouldn't have given me to him," said Buvana, with a touch of shame. "Aruna," continued Buvana, after a few moments of silence, "the dependence on horoscopes in uniting a man and a girl is horrible. At that time, I was ashamed because many families rejected my horoscope. Apparently, I was born under an unlucky star. You see, I married him because his horoscope was the only one that matched mine, and I thought that it was something God had designed for me."

"I'm sorry," Aruna said to her shame-faced mother. "I know your mother-in-law cheated. Didn't she change her son's horoscope?"

"Yes, your memory is good. You see? It was not the hand of God that brought my cursed union with that man. It was that woman's," said Buvana, smiling. At times, she was past tears, anxiety, shame, and regrets. She was ready to laugh about her fate.

"And he married again. Amma, after seeing what happened to you, after their family treated you that way, how did that lady still marry him?"

"We were surprised, Aruna. But remember what paatti's friend once said? His second wife is strong, brave. She doesn't suffer like I did."

"I hope she made him suffer," said Aruna, in her usual fashion. "I hope she still makes him suffer."

At this frank wish, Buvana broke into one of her rare, undiluted laughter. "Well, why don't we talk about you now? I haven't seen your latest sketches. Are you hiding them from me?" Buvana asked.

"Would I hide anything from you? Let's go to my gallery, shall we?"

"You have a gallery, Aruna?"

"You know what I mean. Sivam found room for my new sketches. I didn't want you to see them until they found a home on the wall." Aruna took her mother to a bright room. The walls were filled with a tapestry of sketches.

"They are beautiful, my dear," Buvana exclaimed. "I especially like the one where the swan is taking a sip in the stream. What a talented daughter I have!"

"Oh, come on, Amma!" said Aruna, bashfully. "I wish I could write like you."

While the mother trapped her feelings in words, the daughter broke away from the same through her sketches.

Aruna woke up with an unusual sense of anxiety. It was the first day of her school. The building was ready at last. It was the first day of school! Why did this simple fact tumble in her mind again and again? Everything should be all right. The entire village knew about it. Besides, the village needed another school. What could go wrong?

Aruna waited with flowers and sweets to greet the children. They didn't come. Humsa and Sivam brought fragmented messages. The children wouldn't come because their parents were anxious about Aruna's influence. The vulnerable minds of their innocent children! After all, she didn't know her father. Abandoned by her husband, Buvana had raised a rather headstrong girl. Aruna must be headstrong because she went out of the safety of the village, like a man, to get advanced education! A young woman's place was at home. Aruna was not normal. She might teach the children to be independent and defiant. Her influence could have serious, harmful consequences! Unfortunately, the villagers could not appreciate the fact that Aruna was one of the first women in the state to reach beyond high school. The children didn't come. Wouldn't a child visit to receive the sweets and the flowers before they rotted and withered?

A lot of tongues were running lose.

"Aruna should close the school."

"Kanyakoil is a village of traditions. There is no room for rebellious women and their headstrong notions."

"A woman is running a school! What a silly idea! It's a man's job."

A medley of criticisms reached Brinda through reliable sources and unmitigated gossips. The little school would bear no meaning as long as Aruna presided over it. The position simply wouldn't fit her tainted frame. Well, Aruna had to show the villagers what she was made of. She was determined not to lose hope. However, on the brink of pessimism and nasty criticisms, how was she supposed to enroll any student from that community in her school?

Sethu came again. He waited in the veranda until Murthy talked to him. Aruna overheard fragments of the heated conversation between her grandfather and Sethu. Their voices picked up several notches. Murthy came to the hall, angry and tired. Sethu stormed out of the veranda.

"Apparently, Sethu visited with a proposal," said Murthy. "He feels sorry for what he did to Buvana, and he wants to make amends. He has the horoscope of a young man who would make Aruna a nice husband. He hopes to redeem himself in his wife's eyes by bringing the hope of matrimony in his daughter's life. Now, Saroja, what do you say to that?"

Murthy's personality didn't shine in sarcasm. His recital, however, informed and surprised the family. Aruna protested. Saroja exclaimed. Buvana was silent. Thangam, thankfully, was visiting a relative. Otherwise, she would be sharpening her cleaver now.

"I need to talk to Sekaran. Saroja, where is Kitta?" Murthy asked his wife.

"Kitta is in the mango orchard."

Murthy asked Sivam to fetch Kitta and Sekaran.

"The impertinence of that man!" exclaimed Aruna. "How can he assume that his cooperation is needed to facilitate my wedding? How can he propose something so drastic? What audacity!"

But Aruna's rage, supported by the confidence of her youth and personality, concealed the unhappy truth from her eyes; Sethu's cooperation—welcome or not, pleasant or unpleasant—would make a difference in her future.

A few hours after discussing Sethu's proposal with Kitta and Sekaran, Murthy became fairly calm. He saw some degree of practicality in the new development. Sethu knew the circumstances in Murthy's family. Most people would believe that unless Sethu formally acknowledged Aruna as his daughter, no man would be willing to marry her.

Sethu's assistance in getting a husband for Aruna meant a convoluted means to a hopefully happy end. Nevertheless, it was necessary. Hopeless or happy, a woman was nobody unless she was a gentleman's daughter, or a gentleman's wife, or at the least, a gentleman's widow. Sethu had come voluntarily with a change of attitude and personality. Should Buvana's family acknowledge his presence?

The decision to welcome Sethu might mean inviting severe consequences that would affect the happiness of many. Then again, could the situation get worse? Buvana's life was certainly not ordinary. Her daughter's was not smooth and happy. Until now, the family faced many problems to keep Buvana and Aruna reasonably happy. Therefore, considering Sethu's offer might not be as unsavory as it appeared initially. Murthy and his family didn't want wisdom to reach a solution regarding Sethu. They needed time. Buvana had been without a husband for over two decades. Her daughter had survived without her father's acknowledgment until now. The family could afford to wait a little longer, think about what was to be done, and take each step gingerly and wisely.

◆ ◆ ◆

On the brink of Murthy's property was a worthless piece of land. It shouldered a hill and useless vegetation. The pinnacle allowed a beautiful view of the river and the lush land that enveloped Brinda. Although there was occasional activity in the hill, the woods remained wild and unkempt to facilitate safety. It harbored drunkards and sundry criminals. Sethu was one of the frequent visitors. He sat on a rock, greedily staring at the rich land where his first wife and daughter lived. He knew he had been hasty in evicting Buvana. His second wife brought a reasonable amount of money and an intolerable quantity of courage. She gave him two sons and a fair amount of headache by trying to run his house. Sethu was not willing to relinquish his authority. He had to prove how effectively he could run others' lives.

The talk around town about how different his second wife was from Buvana was true. Sethu couldn't exercise his autonomy on this woman because she wouldn't let him. She was unusually brave and not at all gentle. What a contrast she made to Buvana! The methods that he implemented to walk over Buvana failed on his second wife because she had none of Buvana's gentle qualities. She was coarse, inelegant, fearless, and shrewd. There were times when Sethu was even a little afraid of her!

Sethu started to feel his deficiencies in management—in domestic circle and in business sphere—when his mother died. Sethu's mother was his sole and powerful ally, and she left him desperately helpless in her absence. His loose mouth and clumsy attitude made him less suitable for trade. He had none of his mother's shrewd management skills in his genes. His mother had pampered him until she died. He was not prepared to make important decisions without her acumen. He was a master at cheating in business transactions. He was also a master at spending recklessly. His 'cheating skills' didn't extend to management of resources. His second wife could have assisted him very well. How could he accept her help? Sethu was too much of a man to let his wife run his business. Things didn't look better at home either. His hypocrisy thinned his authority and made him appear foolish.

Sethu looked longingly at the orchards around Brinda from this vantage point. His mother bent a rule or two to get Buvana for Sethu. However, she didn't guide him in the right direction when Buvana didn't produce a son. She had encouraged him to get rid of Buvana and marry again, to get another woman to reproduce and to bring more wealth into the family. In that business, and in that business alone, Sethu felt that his mother had not used good judgment. He should have retained Buvana as his wife before marrying again. That had been Murthy's request, a humble suggestion made at the time when Buvana was separated from Sethu. Murthy did pay a heavy monetary compensation, but Sethu had spent it all. How did he manage to make such a mess of things, so much beyond remedy? In hindsight, Sethu wished he had not abandoned Buvana. If he had retained her as his first, useless wife, he could have tapped on Murthy's financial resources now without groveling and scheming. He certainly had made a gaping hole in his financial prospects! What was he to do?

His love for arrack and whores had left him purse-pinched and unhealthy. He was worried when he realized that his dissipated lifestyle had left him in a desperate state to make some money. His indolence depleted his financial resources. Sethu had mortgaged his house, land, and a good part of his orchards. His current wife's father was merciless. He had wisely allocated a good piece of land, including a house, in his daughter's name. Sethu couldn't claim any share in this land. His wife lived in that house with their two sons in reasonable comfort. Sethu lived with her occasionally, but he couldn't live in the kind of luxury he was used to. The property would eventually go to his sons. How horrible it would be if he had to depend on his sons' charity! He needed money. When could he get his hands on some?

Sethu's previous lawyer had warned him from time to time to watch his spending. When he advanced in years, Sethu hired a ruthless, young lawyer—not that this young man could make money grow in trees! He was sneaky and vile like his client, and Sethu got along with him very well. Sethu's desperation had led him toward Brinda again. Working out a way to get money was the easy part. But how was he going to approach Murthy?

ARUNA! Although Sethu had done nothing for his daughter since her birth, he frequently had news of her through the wagging tongues. She was doing fine, unlike her mother, unlike many women in the village. Strong-willed was how people described Aruna. But she couldn't find a husband—granted, not due to her fault. Sethu was extremely relieved to discover that he still held a certain power over Buvana's destiny and her child's! His acknowledgment of his daughter was required to get her married. In fact, it was necessary.

Sethu had made a couple of moves to contact Murthy and Buvana, but he had not been successful. He was still hopeful. He knew the power of matrimony without which a woman could do nothing in that ridiculous society. Aruna needed him to acknowledge her birth. Buvana had to count on his presence. Murthy would depend on his good nature.

"Sethu, Aruna needs you to call her your daughter even to be a damned teacher!" his lawyer had told him.

Unless Buvana's family welcomed Sethu into Brinda, Aruna had no future. Sethu felt a wicked sense of relief at the prospect of erasing his worries. Why didn't he think of this earlier? Didn't his society believe that marriage was a woman's salvation? A young woman's security, her dependence on a man, a good source of money—an evil triangle that led to matrimony! Men like Sethu thrived on this evil necessity.

Mary's train arrived punctually to meet the same weathered platform, the potpourri of aroma from the vendors' platters, and the busy crowd. Aruna waved to Mary and walked hurriedly to meet her at the door of her compartment. While she assisted Mary to get down, Sivam collected the luggage.

The carriage ride to Brinda was the most enjoyable that Mary had experienced in a long time. The cool breeze rocked the roomy carriage under the canopy of a thousand swaying trees.

"It is so beautiful here, Aruna!" said Mary.

There was so much information to exchange. Neither of the friends knew where to begin. They reached home soon. Mary tried to take it all in—a glimpse of the river from the veranda, the kindness of Aruna's family, and the fragrant garden. When the family sat down for lunch, all ears were eager for the latest news, which Mary was happy to relate. When Buvana, Thangam, and Saroja went to their own quarters to rest, Mary sat on the big swing in the majestic hall. Whenever she visited Brinda, she loved to sit here and gaze at the ceiling. It was a grand room that offered a clear view of the splendor around the house.

"Aruna, can you file these documents?" asked Murthy.

Aruna asked Mary to follow her. There it was; the beautiful, antique, teak desk. "Your favorite desk, Mary, remember?" asked Aruna, while finding a home for the papers in the appropriate drawers.

Mary acknowledged her friend's good memory. Yes, she had never seen any furniture so tastefully carved or finished. It was not a grand piece of work. There was something unique in its simplicity, something elegant in the modest curves, just like the people who lived in this gracious house.

Despite a delightful reception, Mary noticed a slight tension in the air. Aruna took Mary upstairs to the balcony to talk at leisure. While exchanging general news about their families, Mary observed Aruna's worried expression.

"Aruna, are you all right?" Mary asked anxiously.

"I'm well, Mary. Thanks. Something has happened. I'm glad you're here," said Aruna, smiling in relief. She was glad to unload her worries to someone reliable and close to her, someone other than her family. She told Mary about Sethu's visit to Brinda and his request for reconciliation.

Mary was listening quietly. She knew the family's history. After more than twenty years, to offer peace and to seek reconciliation—what were Sethu's intentions? "What can he mean by this sudden appearance and good will, Aruna?" Mary asked. "I can understand what your family must be going through. Do you think he has changed?"

"I don't know what he means by this sudden visit, Mary. I can't trust him. Men like him don't change, suddenly, after twenty years."

"True. But, Aruna, a change of mind or attitude doesn't require a lengthy period of analysis or an intense contemplation. Minds work mysteriously. At times, despicable characters do change and become decent. But, Aruna, I certainly understand your apprehension."

Aruna had written to Mary earlier about the hopelessness of her school. It was no mystery to either of them why no child walked into the school. If Aruna's family accepted Sethu's offer, the villagers might look at Buvana and Aruna with more tolerance. But what a price to pay for society's endorsement! Just as Sethu had heard from time to time about Buvana and Aruna, Aruna and her family had heard about Sethu and his misspent life.

"What're you going to do?" Mary asked.

"I can't guess what my mother wants to do. But I'll have nothing to do with him," replied Aruna. "He is meddling in our affairs. Our family doesn't have to tolerate this impertinence. I hate him, Mary. He is not going to hurt my mother again. I'm so glad you're here. You do realize, don't you, how comforting it is to see you?"

"I'm delighted to be here, Aruna. I'm really glad!"

"Enough about me and Brinda. Mary, what have you decided to do?"

"I've decided to accept my aunt's offer. I'm going to teach in her convent."

"And what about the other thing?" asked Aruna.

"My decision is firm regarding the other thing also, Aruna."

"I see, you've decided to be a nun!"

"Nothing has changed, Aruna," said Mary, smiling. "Over a period of time, you may begin to call me Sister Mary, that's all."

It was no wonder that Mary accepted a drastic change of attitude in Sethu as a natural process. Her heart made allowances for situations that were no less than miracles. Aruna's logical mind analyzed life critically. Mary's benevolent mind accepted life generously.

While the young ladies were discussing Sethu's sudden appearance, Saroja and Murthy were also talking about the same issue. Murthy was nervous. He wanted to discuss the matter again with his lawyer. In the mean time, his wife made an effort to steer his thoughts toward the welfare of his daughter and granddaughter.

"Think of Aruna," Saroja suggested.

"I'm thinking of Aruna, Saroja," Murthy replied, slightly annoyed. "How can we let Buvana face him after all these years?"

"I talked to her. Keeping Aruna in mind, she is willing to think about Sethu's proposal. Even Thangam thinks that there could be no harm in listening to his proposal in a rational manner."

"Let's talk to her," Murthy said, relieved. "Call Buvana. No, let's wait till the servants go to bed."

After the servants went to sleep, Murthy, Saroja, and Buvana had a long talk to explore the best possible way to handle Sethu—for Aruna's sake. The assistance of Thangam and Kitta acted like tonic. The family was ready. Unfortunately, the thought of Sethu was a thorn in a bowl of petals. But he could make a difference in Aruna's future. All that mattered at this moment was Aruna's future.

◆ ◆ ◆

As Aruna and Mary were returning from a long walk by the river, they saw Sethu's carriage again. He was persistent.

"Your father is here, Aruna," Mary whispered.

"Please don't say that, Mary," said Aruna, in a pleading tone.

"I'm sorry, Aruna," Mary apologized, "I should've remembered."

"Never mind, Mary. I refuse to think of him as my father. Nothing is going to change my mind."

"I understand, Aruna."

"Nothing would erase the shame I've carried in my heart for over two decades as a result of a heartless man's ruthless decisions," said Aruna, in a feverish tone. "Mary, I remember my mother's expression when I had asked her where my father was and when I could see him. My mother squirmed at the dreadful thought of describing the non-existence of that man. He doesn't deserve the status of my father."

"Aruna, what if your amma considers reconciliation and decides to accept your ... that man's offer?" Mary asked, encouraging her friend to consider the matter from a different angle.

"Oh, Mary, she wouldn't. After all these years, it's impossible!"

Aruna and Mary entered the house through the back door to avoid Sethu. They saw Humsa and Buvana in the garden.

Humsa was more worried about Buvana and her child now than she had been in the past.

"Humsa, what should I do?" Buvana asked her dearest friend. "I want to do what's right for my child. Should I let that man enter our lives?"

"Akka, you'll do the right thing," Humsa assured Buvana. "Let's listen to Sethu. You know what they say about him in the village? He has changed after his mother's death. That demon! I still think that she was the powerful instrument behind his wickedness. Besides, your father and mother won't let anybody hurt you. I'll kill that man if he even thinks of hurting you. It'll be all right. Don't worry."

Once supper was over, Mary went to her room to pack. Aruna got a gist of Sethu's visit from Saroja before following Mary.

"What news, Aruna?" asked Mary, in the middle of folding a sari.

"He came to repeat his wishes," replied Aruna. "He's not going to leave amma alone. He wants a second chance."

"Second chance?"

"Listen to this, Mary. He wants to know if the elders in my family would let him show affection to his daughter. And ... if that daughter would reciprocate his affection."

"Would you consider, Aruna?"

"Never!" Aruna exclaimed. "I don't trust that man."

After a life of dissipation and ruin, Sethu had no gentle recommendations to forward his wish. And to forgive such a man, without a trace of fondness, was impossible.

Mary returned to her town that morning. On the way home from the railway station, Humsa and Aruna tried to talk about unimportant memories to postpone imminent worries. Aruna looked at the rapidly receding greenery through the window.

"Look at that!" screamed Aruna.

"What is it?" asked Humsa.

"Stop the carriage," Aruna shouted, impatient to get out.

A small girl was standing under a crooked palm tree, immersed in tears and rain. Who was she? She was dressed in a tattered dress that was several sizes bigger for her frame. She couldn't be more than three or four. Aruna picked her up and walked to the carriage.

Within a few hours, Sivam brought a burly farmhand from the neighboring village.

"I know who this girl is," said the stranger. "She lost her father a few months after she was born. I think it was a mining accident! Her mother is suffering from tuberculosis. She is in the sanitarium in the next town. The girl wandered from her neighbor's house where she was sheltered temporarily. The mother has a request ..."

The man hesitated. Murthy encouraged him to go on.

"The mother wants to know if you can deliver the child to a particular orphanage in Salem. Can you?" asked the farmhand.

"What's your name?" Aruna asked the stranger.

"My name is Samuel," replied the man. "The child's name is Akila."

Every eye was on the little, homeless girl. After eating a satisfying lunch, she was sleeping on the bench in the veranda. She was out of imminent starvation, even death, which was the inevitable consequence in such cases.

Akila soon woke up and smiled congenially at the adults. They surrounded her new, safe world, but those adults were still anxious because they had a different worry to tackle. It was not an easy task to keep the public from the current events in Brinda. Bits and pieces of information seeped through the gates and trickled into eager tongues. The citizens had little to occupy their minds on a daily basis. Any news was food for gossip. News of Buvana and Aruna was always scandalous gossip. Why was Sethu visiting Kanyakoil often? What business did he have here? He didn't own any land around here. His frequent visits must have something to do with Buvana and her daughter. Sethu's visits kindled the general curiosity to a blazing flame.

Sekaran finished supper and opened the pile of papers he had brought with him from Murthy's home. A meeting between Murthy's family and Sethu was inevitable. Sethu's approaches had to come to an end—either positively or fruitlessly. Sekaran still couldn't understand Sethu's uncharacteristic, kind proposal of offering his name to Aruna. Really! What price did Sethu have in mind for such an offer? Miracles happened. But a miracle of this kind, from a man of Sethu's lot, justified Sekaran's doubts.

Sethu's visits became more frequent until Sekaran decided to take a firm step to stop his audacity. Sekaran asked Sethu to communicate through letters until the family made a decision. Sethu didn't disregard this request. He had a goal. If it meant cooperating with the old lawyer, he was willing to accommodate, despite his reluctance to submit to authority. He had become a little submissive. Lack of money, free-flowing money, could do that to a man.

Murthy soon received a message from Sethu. He couldn't believe the humble pitch of the letter.

Sethu wrote:

Dear Sir,

I hope my correspondence finds you and your dear family in the best of health. May I have a meeting with Buvana? I sincerely care about Buvana and Aruna. I am anxious to prove to you and your family that I am a reformed man. Can you find it in your respectable and patient nature to forgive me for my wicked actions against your daughter? I want to rectify my mistakes by helping my daughter. Although the society knows that Aruna is my child, I want to acknowledge our relationship in the presence of the elders of Kanyakoil and

Chinnoor. Would you make an opportunity for me to follow my repentance? I hope to hear a favorable reply from you at your convenience.

Sincerely,
Sethu

The tone of Sethu's letter didn't carry his characteristic flamboyance or arrogance. He sounded like a changed man. Did he really care about his first wife and child? While Sekaran continued to spend several hours with Murthy and Kitta, the ladies assembled in the hall to discuss Sethu's proposal. Later, the men joined the women to discuss Sethu's request.

"I'll have no part in this," said Aruna.

"Aruna, please listen to your family. Come on, I know that you're an intelligent girl. Please?" asked Sekaran.

It took the combined efforts of the family members to persuade Aruna to submit reluctantly. They all had one motive in mind—Aruna's future.

"Amma, how can you pay attention to that man, especially after he abandoned you?" asked Aruna.

"I'm not doing this to please him, Aruna," Buvana replied patiently. "Think about it. As long as the society thinks that you're unacknowledged by your father, my existence will have no influence in your welfare. My motive is utterly selfish. We need his acknowledgment—that you're his daughter. That's all"

"But I AM his daughter," said Aruna, in exasperation. "Everybody knows that."

"That's different, Aruna. He threw us out over twenty years ago. People have to realize that you have your father's support now."

"But what about you? What if he wants you to live with him?" Aruna asked, still in doubt.

"Goodness, I won't do that, Aruna," Buvana said convincingly. "Nothing will make me move away from Brinda when my parents need me. I've to be here to take care of them. I'll always take care of them. Anyhow, could I live with that man? No temptation would induce me to live with him as his wife. Don't worry."

Aruna felt a little relieved after this conversation.

Aruna was summoned to the hall where her grandparents were sitting. She knew what was coming. They reiterated what Buvana had explained to her earlier.

"Aruna, there's no harm in listening to Sethu, right?" asked Murthy. "I'm not getting any younger and after ..."

"I understand, Thatha, but,"

"Come and sit by me, Aruna," Saroja said, smiling at her. "Aruna, you're over twenty. You have a long life ahead of you. Let's see what Sethu suggests for your future's sake. We would do nothing to make you uncomfortable, Aruna. We're only thinking of your welfare."

Aruna sat between her grandparents and took their hands in hers. They were the most wonderful and loving people in the world. They had been her guardians since she was born. What wouldn't she do for them? What wouldn't she do to make them happy?

"Let's arrange something," Aruna said, smiling affectionately.

Sekaran said a quick prayer, one of many he had chanted since waking up. He got into his carriage. Now this reconciliation was initiated by the devil himself! Something didn't fit properly. Sekaran couldn't put his finger on the problem. Was it an occupational instinct? As a lawyer, he was tuned to hunt for discrepancies between appearance and reality. On the other hand, he might just be nervous like the rest of Murthy's family. This case meant more than the connection between a client and his lawyer. Murthy was like a brother to him. And he was justified in worrying about this meeting. Sethu had gutter shrewdness. Besides, a lifelong tutoring from battling with the authorities over his evil deeds had made him quite familiar with legal outcomes and consequences.

"Are you prepared to meet Sethu on your own, all alone, Buvana?" Sekaran asked her in the hall. "I'll be in the house when he comes to talk to you, all right? Take your time before you reply to him. And please talk to your father and me before you decide anything. Don't be hasty."

"I'll be fine," Buvana promised Sekaran. "You may not believe it, but I'm actually looking forward to this meeting. I want to show him that I'm not afraid of him. Trust me."

Buvana was prepared to meet Sethu, although she hardly knew him. She had shared his bed, eaten his harvest, lived through the filthy language, and endured his touch. But she didn't know him. Her situation was past praying for, but her daughter had a lot to look forward to. Buvana was willing to talk to this man and listen to his evil voice for Aruna's welfare. When Sekaran left the room, Thangam walked in.

"Buvana, be strong," said Thangam. "He can't harm you unless you let him. Be assertive. Remember that I'll be glad to stay a few feet behind you. There's no need for you to meet him alone."

"Thank you," said Buvana, smiling at her aunt. "I can meet him alone. I'll be careful."

"Buvana," said Thangam, taking Buvana's hand in hers. She had one of those rare, desperate expressions. "I won't say anything caustic in his presence and embarrass you."

"Embarrass me! Athai, how can you say that?" Buvana asked earnestly. "I'd like nothing better than having you with me when I meet him. But I've to do this. I want him to know that he doesn't frighten me now."

Thangam noticed the courage in her niece's delicate expression. This was not the Buvana she used to know. "That's the spirit, Buvana," Thangam said, quite relieved. "You'll be fine! God bless you, child."

◆ ◆ ◆

Saroja, Thangam, and Aruna decided to wait in the hall. Buvana was ready.

"Let me walk to the kitchen door with you, Buvana Akka," said Humsa.

Buvana entered the garden with Humsa. Sethu was sitting on the washing stone.

"Humsa, please go inside," whispered Buvana. "I can handle him. I've to do this now!"

"Akka," whispered Humsa. She was throwing furtive glances at the insidious yet important man. The days and nights on his terrace were more than mere memories. Humsa, by now, was holding Buvana's hand in a tight grip. "He is an evil man! I don't trust him. Let me stay with you, a few feet behind you. You must allow me to remain here. I just can't trust him."

At this moment, more than any other time, Buvana was sincerely thankful for Humsa's affection, warmth, regard, and undiminished loyalty. What had she done to deserve such unwavering kindness through years of trying moments? Buvana smiled gently at her dear friend and pushed her resolutely into the kitchen. "Humsa, I also don't trust this man," Buvana whispered again. "I'm not really alone. All of you are waiting in the house, just a few yards away. It's preposterous to think that he can harm me when my family is inside the house."

For once, Buvana was amazed at her own confidence and courage. Yes, that was what she lacked all her life, but now she was prepared to meet this man. Didn't he willfully bury her dignity? Her hatred prompted her to take a bold step. Buvana walked into the garden and ignored Sethu's smile. She leaned on the wall of the well, situated just a few feet away from the washing stone. The well was filled to the rim. She gingerly touched the cool water, hoping to quench her fear. Fear still lingered, playing 'hide and seek' with her fluctuating courage. She turned slowly and faced the man. He had gained considerable weight during the missing years. For some reason, she couldn't picture him as a portly man. She realized then that she was still afraid of him. No, there was no room for fear.

"How are you?" Sethu asked, smiling at her.

"You wanted to talk to me. What're you planning to do for Aruna?" asked Buvana.

"All in good time, Buvana. How're you doing?" Sethu asked again.

She didn't answer. He walked to her slowly. He looked around and smiled again.

"You look thinner than before, Buvana, but you still look beautiful," said Sethu, assessing her at length. "You look as pretty as you looked on our wedding day. How're you, my dear?"

His proximity allowed her to study his face. She noticed his sunken eyes and weathered skin. He looked several years older than he really was. Buvana threw a glance at the kitchen door. What did she expect to see there? Sethu continued to smile and enquired after her welfare. When would he stop exchanging niceties and get to business?

"What're you thinking of doing to help Aruna?" asked Buvana, impatiently.

"I'll get to that. After all, isn't that why I'm here?" asked Sethu.

He was doing it, something that he did with his evil eyes. When he did that, a dozen eyes pierced her skin. A sudden fear approached her. Should she seek either Humsa's company or her aunt's support? No, what a silly idea! She was no longer a child. She had to face this man for the sake of her child.

"Can you tell me what you have in mind for Aruna?" Buvana asked again.

"You've grown very well, Buvana, not the wispy girl I married a long time ago, now are you?"

"Yes, and?"

Sethu measured her with his eyes. "Be patient. I'm coming to the point. I've three things to propose. First, I'm planning to gather leaders from Kanyakoil and Chinnoor for a meeting where I'll formally name Aruna as my daughter. Don't you think that's the first and most proper thing to do?" he asked, smiling at her congenially.

Buvana merely nodded her head.

"Second, Aruna will marry my nephew."

"What?" asked Buvana, unbelievingly.

"The young man is the son of my wife's brother," replied Sethu. "He is in textile business. He also owns a fair amount of property near Mettupalayam."

"No, no, wait," said Buvana, desperately. "That doesn't matter. You're not here to discuss Aruna's marriage."

"What do you mean, Buvana?"

"I think we should leave Aruna out of this conversation, please," replied Buvana. She took a deep breath and prayed to God for fortitude. She wouldn't stand here, helpless, while he manipulated Aruna's future.

"Leave Aruna out of the conversation? Think about it. I'm doing all this to give her a name, to acknowledge her as my daughter. We can't leave her out of our conversation entirely, can we?" Sethu asked slowly, smiling a smooth smile that didn't reach his eyes.

"But?"

"Now, if you're acting defensive because of Sekaran's advice, let me remind you that we're both thinking of Aruna's welfare," said Sethu, even more slowly than before. "Remember, I'm coming down to help you and OUR daughter. Before you rush into your speech that you've rehearsed under Sekaran's supervision, don't forget that I'm here to do YOU a favor."

"I mean it," said Buvana, boldly. "If you bring Aruna's marriage or your nephew into our conversation, I must insist, I've to go back to the house." Buvana managed to look straight into his eyes. His eyes didn't evoke terror in her mind anymore.

Sethu stared at her. He had acquired some patience in the last few months. However, his newfound patience lacked endurance. He was not sure how long he could sustain his saintly appearance. He wondered at Buvana's courage in speaking up on behalf of her daughter's future. She never had any courage to defend her own dignity two decades ago. Had Buvana become defiant after all these years? She still had that insipid appearance, to be sure. Well, he could take care of her. How could she dictate terms to him?

"Well, then I've two things to propose, if you can listen?" asked Sethu, smiling again. Each inch of smile was dearly bought. It was totally against his nature to smile, to be pleasant, and to be kind. Well, he had to. On the other hand, did it matter any longer? He looked at the kitchen door. No face had looked out of the door or the window so far. He was convinced that no eyes were watching them. He had Buvana under his control. If he didn't capitalize on this situation, he was not worthy of being his mother's son.

"Please tell me what you're planning to do for my daughter?" asked Buvana, anxiously. She bit her tongue at the last two words, and a glance at Sethu's face confirmed her mistake. A habit that was formed over the duration of twenty years was not to be broken easily. Subconsciously or deliberately, Buvana didn't have a 'father' in mind for Aruna until now. But that father was right here, right now, and what was he going to do?

"So, after all the efforts I've taken to help you, she is your daughter, is she?" asked Sethu, menacingly.

"I meant to say our daughter," Buvana said nervously.

"Listen to me, Buvana," Sethu whispered, staring at her face. His attempts at appearing nice had made him impatient and weary. "Your father must write a will to make me the principal executor of all the property—land, money, and investments—that is to come to you after his death, which would eventually go to Aruna."

"This is outrageous," Buvana cried. His cold voice threatened her presence of mind. His demeanor confused her senses. Still, she found her voice. "My father and his property have nothing to do with your decision to call Aruna your daughter. You told us that you were a changed man, that you were repenting, and that you wanted to rectify your earlier mistake. We really believed and hoped that you had come to help our daughter."

"Now she is our daughter, is she? You women are all the same—clinging to a man when you need something from him. Do you think I care about your bastard? She has a superior attitude, hasn't she?" asked Sethu, mockingly. "Aruna can't do a thing unless I protect her and give her my name. She is a useless piece of trash without my acknowledgment and consideration. Buvana, listen. Your father's money, all of it, should be written in my care. If not, you can tell your daughter to wave goodbye to her future."

He was laughing—laughing at her, laughing at Brinda. Every time he mentioned Aruna's name, he sullied Buvana's soul.

"I won't do it," said Buvana, with extraordinary courage. "I just can't."

Buvana remembered Thangam's advice. She wouldn't let him intimidate her. She would have nothing to do with this monster any longer. She stepped aside to walk back to the house. She couldn't. He cornered her between the well and his body.

"Buvana, I'll gather the leaders of this village and my town. I'll tell everybody that Aruna isn't my daughter," Sethu whispered.

"You can't mean that. I can't believe you said something like that. Even you wouldn't be that cruel. She is your child. Everybody knows that. Don't you have any affection for your child?" asked Buvana, in a trembling voice.

He walked closer to her, picked up the rope that was tied to the roof of the well, and brushed it against her neck. "Buvana, listen. Everybody in Kanyakoil and Chinnoor would spit at you for giving birth to a bastard," Sethu said, laughing at her. "The entire community will know that you had a sordid relationship with a man. I'll tell the community that your daughter is a gift of that dirty union. That precious daughter of yours will never be able to show her face outside the gates of your sacred Brinda. Do you hear me? Your Aruna is a bastard."

"That's a lie. You know that's a lie," said Buvana, trying to push him away. "If you have any honor ..."

"Stop this nonsense. Honor! Lie! Utter nonsense! I'll bring a couple of men. They'll swear that you had an affair with a certain rogue who is dead now. Your daughter is the result of that illicit affair. Do you hear me? No money, your daughter and you might as well be hanging from this rope. Give me what I want. I'll make sure your daughter has a future, and you can retain your respect," he said, measuring her face closely, "or whatever is left of it."

Buvana felt his sneering breath. She sensed his insults. The monster held her dignity and her daughter's dignity in the middle of the road. The shame from two decades ago was to reappear with more brutal force. He was just inches away from her, still holding the rope in a tight grip. His other hand pinned Buvana against the wall of the well. She tried to speak. She couldn't. The sight of his eyes and the smell of his tobacco breath, so dangerously close to her, made her dizzy.

Sekaran, Murthy, and Kitta waited patiently in the veranda. Sethu's lawyer waited impatiently with them. He looked bored, annoyed, and had a permanent scowl on his face.

Humsa, while sitting in the hall, threw several glances at Aruna.

"I've to see if my amma is all right," Aruna said to Humsa.

"I'll go with you, Aruna," Humsa said encouragingly. "We can stand just inside the kitchen door. That way, we can keep an eye on Buvana. Come." Humsa requested Saroja and Thangam to remain in the hall before walking to the kitchen.

"Aruna's school is still empty. I can assure you that it shall remain so," Sethu said, laughing at Buvana again. "This disappointment is nothing. This is just the beginning of more disasters. I'm an evil man, Buvana. You can't escape from me.

I need money, a lot of it. I'll do anything to get it. Your daughter and your honorable parents will be ruined. Your Brinda will go to dust. I'll destroy your daughter."

Buvana jerked away from his grip. He reached for her arm, looking menacing and wicked. She pulled away from him again. Buvana didn't see that the kitchen door creaked open. Sethu didn't see it either. The rope fell from his hand. He tried to grab it. He extended his arm across the well to get a good hold of it again. Buvana saw his face when his upper body swayed across the well. She noticed something at that moment.

She saw just a glimpse—a shadow of pure fear in his eyes—fear in an evil man's eyes.

As his shoulders stooped over the well, something slipped from his breast pocket and fell by her feet. It was the snuffbox!

All she saw was his fear.

For a moment, for a brief instant, everything ceased. All that remained was the earth and its sighs, tears, and heart-wrenching screams. She was lost in a cloud of anguish. She saw the horror in his eyes.

All that mattered was his fear.

She held the sleeve of his shirt, pushed him with a strength she never knew she had, and saw him falling into the well. Even as she retrieved her hand with an undiscovered strength, he was heading toward the pit of the earth.

And Mother Earth was waiting. Whose voice was calling for the God of death? Could it be the call of fear? His arms were flailing when the cutting wind pushed him through the water. He was heading to the ravenous belly of Mother Earth. She was tired of waiting. It was time to appease her hunger, and all that remained was an echo of a time that was past praying for.

The softness and timidity in Buvana had turned into a monstrous wind, taking the tides of evil with it. Something snapped in her veins and turned into a thousand twigs. The bashful, warm light in her veins transformed into a blazing fire. She heard something—a call, a plea, and a tremor. She recognized nothing. She saw nobody. She was alone, powerful, and invincible like the rush of wind that carried rain clouds on its shoulders. In a few minutes, the quiet whisperings in her heart were abducted by thunder. She was alive, and she was flying on the chariot of wind. Buvana picked up the antique snuffbox from the moist ground and tucked it inside her blouse. It was a souvenir of her triumph over a wicked, cruel man—a memento of her victory. It was a milestone that registered her act of pushing an evil man to his death.

The kitchen door was wide open now. A babble of sounds followed a myriad of questions. Aruna ran to the well. Sivam and Humsa followed closely behind her. A minute later, Sethu's lawyer was also running in the direction of the well. They could still hear Sethu's voice. The screams receded when Mother Earth used all her strength to pull a venomous soul into her stomach.

"Where is Buvana?" asked Sekaran. "Is she all right? Get her out of that area before more people crowd around her. Move her indoors, now, right away!"

Panic! Commotion! Faces and voices! She saw nothing. She felt nothing.

◆ ◆ ◆

The news of Sethu's death spread like forest fire. The villagers couldn't stop talking about his mysterious death, over and over again, like a faulty record on a gramophone. The constant discussions analyzed the irony of Sethu's drowning incident in a well that was right in the middle of his previous wife's property. This was the very same house of the woman he had abandoned years ago!

Several voices expressed anxiety. Was it destiny? Was it heavenly intervention? Was it predetermined malice? Buvana was a wounded woman, wronged by a selfish man. Could her vengeance take such a drastic turn after two decades of separation? Impossible! On the other hand, she had lived like a recluse. Her mind, so disturbed, could have indulged in wild deeds! However, if Buvana had planned to kill Sethu, would she choose her own home to commit the crime, especially when many people knew of his presence in Brinda?

Several people had gathered on the previous day to rescue Sethu. It was too late. It was the most horrible day Brinda had seen. As the hours sank behind the dark clouds, every heartbeat reached the summit of fear. Murthy's decent family had to accept the presence of policemen, inquisitive spectators, and Sethu's family members. Murthy was speechless. Saroja was afraid to breathe. Sethu's sons arrived, along with a few able-bodied men, to take their father's corpse to Chinnoor. It took the effort of every good man and his brother to guard Buvana and her family from the wrath of Sethu's sons. Kitta sat outside Buvana's room. Nothing would induce him to move from that spot. In the middle of sighs and speculations, the entire village felt the pain.

The morning brought the constable again to the scene of the crime. A few unsavory friends of Sethu followed the constable. Sekaran had not left Brinda since the previous day. His position as Murthy's lawyer and his status as his client's best friend made his presence a necessity. While the family was having coffee, Mary arrived—in response to Aruna's telegram.

Some friends gathered to offer support to Murthy and Saroja. They felt relieved at Sethu's demise. However, they wished he didn't die in Murthy's home or … while he was with Buvana. But there were witnesses. Buvana couldn't have killed Sethu. Murthy, Saroja, Aruna, and the servants were inside the house. Moreover, Sethu's lawyer was there. Crime! What crime? Who committed it? Buvana! How could she? Why would she?

The families in Chinnoor talked for hours about Sethu's death. They remembered his childhood accident in a well. How strange that he met his end in a well! What would his mother say if she were alive? Why did Sethu visit his estranged wife's home to meet his death? The resonance of an eerie note was objectionable, but it was tempting at the same time. People talked. Voices whispered. News traveled fast. It always did when disaster struck a small, close-knit, tongue-wagging community.

"Poor Sethu! He was so unfortunate!"

"He deserved it! He was everything that was bad."

"What a way to die! His poor mother! Fortunate soul, she was gone before him!"

"She should have stayed alive to witness his cruel death. That's what every cruel man should face in the end! And she should have gone with him."

The citizens of Kanyakoil had a different drum to play.

"What an end to a lifetime of misery!"

"A good end, no doubt. But God can be more merciful to Murthy's family."

A few versions of Sethu's death circulated around Kanyakoil.

"Sethu was murdered. He was massacred. He was killed by Murthy's family and friends."

"Murthy might have hired a few men to end Sethu's life. After all, he must be tired of Sethu's intimidation."

"No, Sethu was murdered by his bitter enemies."

Every corner echoed varied reports of the disaster.

"How could this happen?" Sethu's lawyer voiced his anger to Murthy. "Why did your daughter insist on meeting my client alone? She had not been his wife for over twenty years. What did she want to say to him?"

"Your client wished to renew his relationship with my daughter," shouted Murthy, frustrated and angry.

Sekaran pulled Murthy away from Sethu's lawyer.

Even if Sethu's lawyer had not been present at the scene of the disaster when the irrevocable tragedy occurred, the fact that Sethu's body had floated in the well in Murthy's property was sufficient reason to require, even demand, an investigation. An inquest was inevitable. Buvana was not sorry that Sethu was dead. She was, however, very sorry for exposing her family to the criminal system and the ugliness it sheltered. Murthy's lawyer realized the seriousness of Sethu's death under questionable circumstances. He was a simple, country lawyer. He wrote to his friend in Madras to assist him.

Humsa walked upstairs with some snacks and juice. She found Buvana on the balcony with Thangam.

"Humsa, I should've listened to you," cried Buvana. "I admire your foresight. I wish I had let you or Thangam Athai stay with me when I was with him. See what all of you have to face now? I can't imagine the shame!" Buvana's tears knew no boundaries when her mind revisited the terrible incident.

"Akka, that's not something we must discuss ever again. It was meant to happen, and no matter who stayed with you, it would've happened. We're mere toys in the hands of destiny. What can we control?" Humsa asked, pouring a cup of juice for Buvana. She sat by her and took her hand. "Here, forget the tears, forget what is past, and drink this," said Humsa. "You know, a big, successful lawyer is arriving from Madras. Trust me, dear. It'll be all right."

"Stop worrying about the misfortune of your family, Buvana," said Thangam. "What shame are you talking about? Indignity caused by our wonderful society? What has the society done for you? Did any worthy human being, other than your own family, make the slightest effort to question Sethu when he threw you out of his house? The society should be ashamed of its lack of responsibility. Disgraceful! That's what it is. You have nothing to fear. Buvana, you have not one thing to be ashamed of!"

After living like a hermit for years, Buvana felt awkward and ashamed to appear in public. She cringed at the sight of the court. She wished to disappear when she saw her name and Brinda's printed in the newspaper. Her visits to the court terrified her! Although it was not a major trial, the inquest was still shameful! Without a doubt, this was the highest punishment in the eyes of a decent family.

Sekaran got the assistance he wished for. The high-priced lawyer arrived from Madras with his apprentice. His presence had a remarkable effect in the court and in the community. The grand lawyer met Sekaran's expectations. His talent matched his remarkable height. He dazzled everybody with his keen intelligence and sturdy eloquence. The lawyer soon earned the reputation of a celebrity. The market buzzed with the news of the inquest.

"Do you think Buvana will hang?" asked the blacksmith.

"If you don't succeed here, will you take the case to High Court?" asked Janaki.

Janaki was still very active!

The lawyer ignored the impertinent questions. "What a bunch of muddle-headed fools!" the lawyer whispered to his apprentice. "Why would there be a need to go to High Court when this incident is not pushed for a trial?" The famous lawyer could hardly hide his disdain. He was a renowned criminal lawyer of his time. "Poker face" suited his expression. He concentrated on Buvana and her speedy dismissal from the inquest.

The lack of trial, contrary to what the famous lawyer thought, was not the consequence of his intelligence alone. Sethu's wife was an exceptionally shrewd woman. She had trained her sons well. They might be cutthroats, but they were not stupid. During a trial, loads of Sethu's underhanded schemes would surely be exposed. His law-defying ways were no secret. Especially, his petticoat connections and his affinity to arrack stalls were quite notorious. However, the same law-defying episodes couldn't stand exposure in a court of law. Who could foretell what penalties such exposure would induce? There was much to be lost than just justice. Therefore, the family of the deceased, with significant counsel from Sethu's lawyer, wished to end the tragedy without a lengthy trial. Moreover, those relations—who were closely connected with Sethu—knew what directions his intentions were taking when he had planned on that meeting with Buvana. Therefore, his untimely death had to remain a terrible accident.

Buvana leaned on the crooked banyan tree. She retrieved the snuffbox from the velvet pouch. She remembered the day when her father had offered this trinket as a 'peace offering' just before the deadly wedding chain went round her neck. She placed this in her safe-deposit box—the secret compartment in the tree. Her blood vessels throbbed. Should she laugh or cry at this silly action? She was much older now, not the young girl who had found this secret spot to store her personal collections. However, while her mind ridiculed her for her insipid actions, her heart gave a deaf ear. This snuffbox symbolized her parents' shame on the day of her wedding! The shame was dead now … wasn't it?

Aruna found her mother near the river. Buvana's thin frame drooped like a spent flower under the sun. Aruna lifted her mother's face gently. What she saw in those eyes worried her. She saw no pain, no worry, no tears, nothing.

"Aruna, I've to show you something," said Buvana. "Come with me."

Buvana took her daughter to the keeper of her secrets. She showed her the treasures hidden in the tree. She was worried that Aruna might laugh at her for her childish secrecy. On the contrary, Aruna was spellbound. She saw a glimpse of a little girl in her mother. It was a young heart that was simple, innocent, and devoid of any wickedness that seemed to walk over her life.

"Aruna, do you think I should take these things into the house?" asked Buvana. "It seems foolish, doesn't it?"

"Amma, of course, it isn't foolish," said Aruna. "Let these things remain here. They're precious. You know, some day, many years from today, a little girl might find what you've left in this tree. That would be wonderful, don't you think?"

Aruna took Buvana's hand and walked back to the house. The daughter switched places with her mother. From this moment, Buvana was Aruna's to cherish and to protect. Her mother was her fragile treasure, found among the sand-coated pebbles. No word was exchanged between mother and child, but every unspoken word was understood between two souls that felt each other's pain, kindness, and love.

Aruna tucked her mother under the sheets and walked to the balcony. The view offered excellent prospects of the river—familiar and unknown. Their lives were in an indifferent world. How did this happen? Why did this happen? Her mother was not capable of murdering a person—willfully or otherwise. Buvana was an embodiment of compassion, love, timidity, and patience. There was no justification in this world for such an act by such a woman.

The mother's thoughts were running parallel to the daughter's. Murder! There was a time when Humsa, Thangam, and just about everybody wished to kill Sethu. After all that, Buvana committed the horrible crime! Did she really murder an evil man? Did she, without a sense of remorse, kill a human being? No, not she, not in this lifetime! It was an accident. It was just a terrible incident caused by the man's intimidation and actions. Sethu was hurting her, trying to strangle her with the rope, wasn't he? Good God, did she really shove him into the well or did he slip and fall? He must have slipped. He must have because if he had not, she must have pushed him to his death. Buvana lost the power to sleep. If she closed her eyes for a while, it was fretful and filled with tears. How could she live with the memory of those few moments when a power she couldn't comprehend dominated her senses?

Sekaran's counterpart from Madras was confident and efficient. He pulled the redundant interviews to a successful ending. No matter what perspective a person took regarding this case, the following indisputable facts gaped at the court: Sethu's notoriety as a wild villain and Buvana's reputation as a timid and decent woman. Although the memory of the tragic incident was still fresh, the final meeting of the inquest concluded uneventfully. Murthy and his family members were able to keep their heads above rising water, which was a lot to expect at this moment. The inquest was a nightmare that rattled the entire village. It was over! Murthy and Saroja were no longer afraid to breathe or welcome another day. The rich, famous lawyer received the most heartfelt thanks from Murthy's family before returning to Madras to attend to his pending cases.

"Murthy, I can't explain my relief in words," Sekaran exclaimed. "I have a list of temples I must visit to offer my thanks."

"I can't thank you enough, Sekaran. I'll thank you properly some other time. Where is my daughter?" asked Murthy.

A couple of Sethu's associates and relations were still angry. Sethu's mother would have liked to taste retribution if she had been alive. She would have eaten Murthy for a meal and would have devoured Kanyakoil for her dessert. Thanks to providence—merciful providence—she was dead. The rest of Sethu's family, although very distressed at his sudden demise, was not powerful enough to bring further shame to Buvana and her family. They cursed her audacity. They called her and her family evil names. They could do no more.

The questioning and analysis might be over, Buvana might be proved innocent, but she wouldn't be able to show her face in public ever again—not that she did before Sethu's death. The inquest was the culminating disaster in her life. Even those infrequent visits to her few friends' homes became nil. She had inaugurated her womanhood as an unwanted wife and had reached the status of a killer—with little hope of a happy existence during her motherhood. The court and the lawyers might have said things in her defense. Unfortunately, the society saw a murderer in her because Sethu died at her hands. Buvana was the society's black mark. She had been a stain in the society since she was sixteen. But a criminal! This was going to affect Aruna. What made it unbearable for Buvana was the fact that Aruna had no future because of the disaster in her mother's life. On the other hand, if Sethu had not died, he would have falsely labeled Aruna as a bastard. Aruna's future was blasted either way.

Buvana was sitting with Aruna on the balcony, with the little orphan, Akila, looking very happy on Aruna's lap. The homeless girl sat on her founder's lap as though she had discovered a perfect shelter. She had found comfort in Aruna's touch and had felt love in her smile. Her tender heart was happy. A young soul's dependence on Aruna seemed groundless and ironical when the lady herself was supposed to depend on society's approval. Only Buvana felt the irony in the scene that was gaping at the uselessness of Buvana's motherhood and her existence. Aruna might be an adult in the eyes of the world. But she was a child, in need of a father's love and protection, and she never enjoyed that blessing. Now all hopes were lost forever.

Brinda received the news of another tragedy. Akila's mother died in the sanitarium. Due to the disorderly circumstances caused by Sethu's death and the trying time following the tragedy, Murthy was not able to take Akila to the orphanage. Now the little girl needed a home.

"Amma, can our family adopt Akila? Won't you like that?" Aruna asked her mother.

"Aruna, I'd love to be this poor child's guardian," said Buvana. "Think about it. She deserves a better mother."

"Amma, I'm sorry. You have enough trouble with me!" said Aruna, understanding her mother's embarrassment.

"No, my child. You're always my sunrise. My life would mean nothing without you. I just wish you had a proper life, a nice husband, and ..."

"My own sunrise?" Aruna asked, finishing her mother's thought.

"Yes," Buvana sighed. "You'd make a very good mother."

"Thank you. I'm glad you think so. Amma, why don't I adopt this child? We both know that marriage is beyond my reach. I love this child. I can give her a good life."

"The world is not ready for it, Aruna."

"What's the world ready for, Amma? How long should we wait for the approval of a world that can't show compassion? Anyway, what are we waiting for?"

"Aruna, think. You're single. Do you think Akila will have any advantage if you adopt her?"

Although Aruna questioned her mother, she understood the impact of such an adoption. Akila would suffer ultimately. She would be mocked for her questionable birth—a spinster's child! And what was the point of adoption if it was to bring misery to a little life? She had to admit that her mother's advice made sense. Even Mary tried to caution her against adoption. After an impartial consideration, Aruna understood that defiance was not a solution to every problem, especially the kind of problem that involved the reputation of a female child.

Aruna looked at the orphan's small face. Her eyes no longer held a haunted, hollow look. Her cheeks had become puffy, her smile had a dazzle, and she smiled often with joy. A sparkly light—a little bashful and radiant—occupied the once vacant eyes. She was very fond of the people in Brinda. She was especially fond of the young lady, the kind lady, who found her drenched under a tree on a lonely road to nowhere. Akila often clung to the fringe of Aruna's sari; it was the cord of her life.

Aruna made up her mind. She held Akila close to her heart. Her school—which couldn't boast of a single class—became an orphanage. Akila was to be the first orphan to find shelter in that haven. Come hell or high water, this was a decision nobody would dare refute. Aruna was determined to make sure that no empty-headed citizen, seemingly upholding useless traditions, posed an obstacle to this dream that was to shelter Akila and her siblings. The paranoid parents—who were unwilling to let a single woman with questionable status teach their children—would probably ignore this new orphanage. Who was willing to worry or fuss about a group of homeless children? Yes, the children who were wanted by nobody, the children of an indifferent God, would belong to that shelter.

Children of an indifferent God! Buvana had told Aruna a long time ago that Aruna was a gift from heaven. Was God in an indifferent mood when he created Aruna? Was he dispassionate, tired, or a little reckless? Was she the child of a wayward God, sent to this earth in search of peace of mind, in need of a place in society?

Aruna had judged the villagers correctly. She faced no opposition! Now two boys and three girls filled Mercy House, the orphanage, with tiny steps and raindrop giggles. Samuel, the considerate gentleman who had informed Aruna of Akila's background earlier, was drawn to Brinda, to Aruna, and to little Akila. Aruna offered him a job. Sam was happy to make Mercy House his new home. Like magnanimous wind, Aruna's passion swept the village off its feet.

The unfortunate children found a home. Aruna saw her image in the children's eyes. It was not a perfect dawn when she woke up every morning, but it would come. She didn't expect to find happiness in life. She was not even sure of wishing for a normal existence. She was still trying to remove the distinguishable chaos from her indistinguishable, chaotic life. She had decided, a long time ago, not to look for something that went farther away as she groped for it. But Aruna wished for all the Akilas around her to find love and warmth in a harsh and unforgiving world. She decided to wait for the perfect dawn.

PART III

Children of an Indifferent God

Akila pulled her closet door. The wobbly frame, hanging on the rusty hinge, moaned as it creaked open. She stared at the scanty supply of garments. There were four saris, two without visible holes. Akila packed these along with some essentials before going to bed. In spite of her exhaustion at the end of a tiring day, she couldn't fall asleep. Her eyes darted from the window to the cracked walls. The patches on the wall gaped in the moonlight. This was the management's idea of repair! Akila sighed and longingly thought of a better life—a decent room, a comfortable bed, bright walls, and a few items in the closet that didn't require frequent darning.

Her mind, awake and restless, visited an irregular childhood in Kanyakoil. Surprisingly, she was looking forward to her visit to the same town early next morning. It was somewhat like going home. Mercy House was the only home she had known, in some ways, and Aruna had taken the place of a mother until Akila was able to stand on her own feet.

Standing on her feet! She had a decent education and a reasonably good job. It was a long journey that was impossible for many orphans, especially if they were girls. Most homeless girls, taken away from a protective shelter, ended up as servant maids. A few bold or desperate girls found financial comforts in prostitution. At times, a young, homeless lady settled for the position of a fourth or a fifth wife to facilitate the prospect of an heir. Some voluntarily found a permanent resting place in the bottom of the river. Akila was truly thankful for a life, more or less a decent life at that, despite finding her place at the poor end of the social ladder. Her poorly equipped room didn't appear so poverty-stricken now when she looked at it from a different perspective. Akila switched off the dim light and went to sleep.

Mary was sitting in the small room at the orphanage that was utilized as the office. The aged window displayed the neglected grounds. "Office" was probably an overstatement. It was just a big closet. Every available space was filled with filing cabinets and sundry, indispensable materials. Aruna managed the establishment well. Her attention to necessities had assisted her to avoid unnecessary frills. Mary's visit to Mercy House during this troubled time left her rather pensive. In the middle of pending bills and documents, Mary was chewing on the past.

Aruna was in a long-term feud with the society. She was intelligent, independent, and questioned authority. She was not supposed to! A greater part of the men wanted the women to be dependent on them. A greater part of the women were happy to oblige. A greater part of the society, under the blanket of tradition, was pleased to foster men's supremacy by keeping women's subordination under good regulation. It was a comfortable system. Aruna, however, wouldn't comply.

Aruna had tried her best to manage the estates around Brinda. It was a man's world. There could be no other opinion. She was struggling to maintain a land that was as unpredictable as the society that existed in it. Now, on the threshold of its thirtieth anniversary, Mercy House was in need of more room and more money. Donations were limited, but the needs of the children were not. Making ends meet was getting tough. Whenever she thought that she was going up an inch, she came down a foot! Aruna sold her grandfather's land, bit by bit, to raise money for the orphanage. What was she to do?

Aruna walked into the office.

"Well, I hope the meeting turned out as you expected, Aruna?" asked Mary.

"Mary, the loan has been sanctioned," replied Aruna, happily. "In addition to that, my lawyer has found another tenant for Brinda. Mary, there is relief in sight. Can you believe it?"

"Aruna, I knew your meeting would go well. I'm so glad."

Aruna didn't have the financial resources to run an orphanage that required continual maintenance on one end and growing demands on the other. She had Brinda! However, that huge property—seemingly stalwart and comforting—didn't offer moral support or financial consolation at the present time. There was a time when Brinda made her feel happy, secure, and alive. Where did those days go? Single and in her fifties, Aruna was alone, except for Mary, the children, and Akila.

"Akila is arriving tomorrow. I miss her, Mary," Aruna said. "I wish she could stay here. I wish I could afford it."

"Well, it'll be good to see her. There's something about you today, Aruna. Is something worrying you? Aruna, are you resting enough?" Mary asked, quite worried. "You look pale and thinner than usual. No, don't give me that look. I think you should see a doctor."

"Oh, Mary, nothing is wrong. I'm taking the vitamins Akila left with me during her last visit. Now let's talk about your plans for next year." Aruna changed the subject. She was always good at it.

Who was knocking on the door? It was Lionel Stevens, Mary's nephew. He was a young reporter with *The Express*, one of the nation's leading newspapers.

He wanted to write an article about Mercy House. He was a little early. Aruna gave him a warm welcome. After a few minutes of general enquiries, Lionel wished to see the orphanage.

"Mr. Stevens," said Aruna. "Mary and I were just about to go to the storeroom to take an inventory of the clothes that arrived yesterday. If you don't object, we can talk while we work."

"Oh, that would be perfectly fine. Miss Aruna, please call me Lionel."

"As you wish. Follow us, Lionel. What would you like to know first?"

"I'm not sure. Why don't you tell me about how the orphanage began?"

Aruna recited a concise history of Mercy House. She also offered a quick review of the current number of orphans in the center and a reasonable overview of the daily issues. Next, Aruna glanced at the various cartons of garments, which were precariously scattered around the room. "Look, Mary," said Aruna. "I'm so happy to see so much girls' clothing."

"My aunt said that the number of orphans here, especially girls, has increased significantly in the last few years. Is that right?" Lionel asked.

"Yes, we have more girls," said Aruna. "The high percentage is not a coincidence. A girl child is considered a burden, a liability. I'm very glad that most unwanted baby girls are dropped on the threshold of Mercy House. Some of them never see daylight."

"Really? What do you mean?" asked Lionel.

"Their lives last hardly a few minutes after birth. Their breathing stops as a result of choking on a few grains of paddy or wheat."

"No, it can't be! That's incredible," exclaimed Lionel. He was so shocked by this revelation that his pen stopped on its tracks.

"Incredible, yes, but it happens," said Aruna.

Although Lionel turned pale, he listened to Aruna's narrative for a while. But he was too young to stay collected at this very frank account. He requested the women to excuse him and left the room to fetch a drink of water.

"Mary, do you think I overwhelmed him with such stark facts?" asked Aruna.

"Overwhelmed him? Well, reporter or not, it's everyone's duty to learn the truth of the matter, especially when it concerns a child. He'll be all right," said Mary, turning her attention to the pile of garments. "Aruna, do you think you have enough clothes for the girls or should I send a few more from our convent? This is the last box of blouses and miscellaneous items."

"There's plenty, Mary. Thank you. Look at all the items we've received. I'm so glad. People have been very generous."

The bus growled to a halt at the crowded bus stop. Akila woke up reluctantly. The cool air always rocked her to sleep. While the conductor whisked her suitcase from the roof of the vehicle, Akila stepped out of the bus. She walked on the familiar dirt road. Nothing changed much in Kanyakoil. In the last few years, it had welcomed limited additions—a sprinkle of corner stores, a new post office, and magazine stands. A few remnants of war reminded the village of constant struggles. Dilapidated buildings and a long line of people with ration cards began to blend with elegant homes and thinning orchards. Akila was not surprised to find the bustle on Market Street. It was Wednesday and here was the usual crowd on market day. Around the butcher's stall, Akila saw the hearty smile of Samuel. He was the oldest, indispensable employee of Mercy House. The children loved him. It was Wednesday and Sam had come to buy meat. He rushed to Akila's side and insisted on carrying her suitcase.

"How are you, Akila? You look thin and tired!" Sam said.

"I always look thin and tired in your eyes. You should've become a doctor."

"No, me a doctor?" asked Sam. "Are you making fun of me? You're not eating well, that's the problem. But Humsa will take care of you. She scolds me for not taking my medicines, but she cares."

"Yes, she'll take care of me. She always does! How is everybody? All in good health, I hope?"

"Brinda is getting a tenant. That's nice, isn't it?" Sam asked Akila and chatted all the way to Mercy House.

Akila unpacked and went downstairs to the kitchen.

"Akila!" Humsa exclaimed delightedly and hugged her. "We've been waiting to see you. Have a seat. Let me make you a cup of lemon juice."

Akila thanked her and started to peel the mound of potatoes. Potatoes were essential to their daily menu. It was the cheapest vegetable and filler. Humsa used this filler to stretch the quantity of meat dishes. Meat was so expensive! Different, unimportant, and precious memories rushed to Akila. The kitchen had not changed a bit. It displayed the same wood stove, jaded cabinets, and scraps of utensils that were bought at second-hand price in the market. But this was the heart of the shelter. The stove, flanked by rusty shelves, offered comfort—like an old melody, like a weathered blanket.

When Akila went to the dining hall, a couple of children smiled shyly at her. She gladly returned the smile. She used to sit on that bench at one time, waiting for a miracle to happen. She expected a family to adopt her—to feel the softness of a mother's touch and the comfort of a father's smile. Over time, she found the miracle in Aruna—in her smile, in her affection, in her kindness. When the bell rang to call everybody's attention to the dining area, several feet marched to the assigned tables. At Aruna's invitation, Akila sat between Aruna and Mary.

"Akila, this is Lionel Stevens, a reporter from *The Express*," said Aruna. "He is here to write an article about the orphanage. He is Mary's nephew."

"*The Express* is contributing a sizable donation to benefit the children," Mary said, smiling at her nephew.

Akila enjoyed the meal. It tasted ten times better than what she ate at the nurse's hostel. It was amazing how Humsa could take food for a dozen, expand it to feed a small regiment, and still manage to make it tasty.

Akila sat on a cane chair with a cup of tea. It was a small stone porch, a part of Mercy House that awkwardly displayed its age. Aruna was busy with the newest arrival—a baby girl. The infant kept announcing its displeasure by crying loudly in the nursery. Mary and Lionel joined Akila.

"Sister, how is your family? Does your mother feel better? And how is your aunt?" Akila asked Mary.

"Everybody is keeping good health, Akila. My mother needs rest. We're making sure that she is getting a lot of it. She is with my younger brother now. Aunt Susan is taking it easy. I've threatened to leave her and go to another school if she doesn't listen to me!"

Akila laughed with Mary. They stopped laughing when they heard the crying of a very little baby.

"Fifteen," said Mary.

"Excuse me, Sister?"

"The mother of the baby, the baby who is crying right now, Akila," said Mary. "She is only fifteen and unmarried. They had to bring the baby here."

"Is she from around here?" Akila asked.

"No, my dear," said Mary. "The girl is not from this area."

Lionel appeared a little puzzled at this information.

"Lionel," Mary began to explain. "This baby's family lives several hundred kilometers from Kanyakoil. The pregnant girl would have temporarily lived in a remote part of the country, with a matronly, trustworthy friend or a reliable relative, until she delivered the baby. Her family would have forced her to wear a fake wedding chain or they would have persuaded her to pose as a young widow. If the young woman had a wife's role, her imaginary husband would have been on an extended business venture in Rangoon or Singapore. A family is willing to adopt this baby. They are waiting for the legal formalities to be over."

"Legal formalities, Auntie? It's a good idea to engage a lawyer to handle paperwork. That's the right way to go!" said Lionel, supporting such rules and regulations.

"Lionel, 'legal formalities' means more than paperwork," Mary continued to explain. "Generally, the family that wishes to adopt wants to remain anonymous. You see, most orthodox families decide to hide the news of adoption. Inability to bear children is considered an imperfection in a woman! As a result of this superstitious phobia, the non-biological mother and her family adopt through mediators secretly. As I said earlier, the biological mother delivers her baby clandestinely."

"Auntie, won't it be strange if a woman, who has not been pregnant, suddenly walks into the neighborhood with her baby?" asked Lionel.

"Well, Lionel, the non-biological mother supposedly visits her relations in a remote area for a few months before returning to her neighborhood with a bundle of joy."

"The adoption process is so complicated!" declared Lionel.

"If I adopt a child, I would let the entire world know about it. What a wonderful gift to give and acquire at the same time!" said Akila.

"Exactly, Miss Akila. I agree!" said Lionel.

"Who is moving to Brinda, Sister Mary?" asked Akila.

"It's the new collector and his family. They have rented it for two years, Akila."

"When are they moving in?"

"Next week, Akila."

"Where is Aunt Aruna? She didn't look well during dinner. Is she all right?" asked Akila.

"I'm all right, Akila," said Aruna, entering the porch. "Nothing's the matter with me. Just tired, that's all. I'm sorry. I'm neglecting you. How are you? Has it been very hectic at the hospital?" Aruna smiled warmly before sitting beside Akila.

"It's the same old routine, Aunt Aruna," said Akila, explaining her busy schedule in a light-hearted manner. "The hospital has a new x-ray machine. Some of the patients come just to see it!" Akila said, happy to see Aruna's smile. She ought to smile more, a lot more!

"Lionel, it has been very hectic, especially with the arrival of a very young baby. Sorry, I'm ignoring you. Is there anything I can get for you?" asked Aruna.

Lionel politely mentioned that it did not matter.

Akila and Mary knew that Aruna was more than tired. She was groping for a helping hand, stronger than Akila's or Mary's. Aruna went inside in response to a call from the nursery.

"I'll be right back, Lionel, Aruna needs my help," said Mary. She got up to follow her friend.

Akila promptly stood up to offer her share of assistance.

"Akila, stay here and get a little rest," said Mary. "I know how tiring your job is. Anyway, why don't you talk to Lionel?"

Akila obediently sat down. While she was thinking of an interesting topic, Lionel burst into a question.

"Miss Akila," Lionel said. "How do you know Miss Aruna? She seems really attached to you."

"She is," smiled Akila.

"I'm sorry. I hope you don't mind my question …" said Lionel, looking a little awkward.

"No, it's all right. I was the first orphan to find a home in this shelter. I lived here until I finished high school," said Akila, smiling to ease him out of his embarrassment.

Lionel didn't expect this. "I see," he said, recovering fast. "I heard that you're a nurse. Did you go to college at …?"

"I went to a vocational college and became a nurse. I found a job at St. Teresa's Hospital. It's not very far from here. Aunt Aruna made all that possible."

"No wonder, you're attached to Miss Aruna and the orphanage. Do you come here often?" Lionel asked.

"I do, whenever possible or whenever the orphanage needs my help."

"I'm sure that's greatly appreciated," said Lionel, looking at the grounds around the orphanage. "That's very nice of you. Aunt Mary talks so highly of you."

"I can't really offer much," said Akila, modestly. "What can I do other than allocate a little money from my meager wages? I come here to help whenever I get a break from work. It's not sufficient help. I know that, but it has to do for now. Until I'm in a position to offer more, there isn't much to do."

"I'm sure you're doing all you can right now."

"You know, Aunt Aruna is the dearest person in my life," said Akila, smiling at Lionel. "Her cause is my deepest concern."

"May I write about you in *The Express*? I'll not reveal your identity, of course. Can you tell me a little about how you arrived here as a child?" Lionel asked, once again opening his notebook.

"Sure. Well, I arrived here several years ago—more or less—in the same condition as that newborn in the nursery. I was then just a few years old, and Aunt Aruna found me stranded on the roadside. After I was established as an orphan in Mercy House, many homeless children came to the orphanage."

"Who else managed the orphanage at that time?" Lionel asked, writing diligently.

"As far as I can remember, Aunt Aruna always managed the establishment. I remember Buvana, Aunt Aruna's mother, who always supported her all the way. Her family was good to me. They loved the children! I'm so thankful for the safety the orphanage offered me during my childhood."

"Thank you for sharing part of your past with me, Miss Akila," said Lionel, sincerely. "I'm sorry to leave now. I wish I didn't have to catch the train tonight."

Aruna, Mary, and Akila shared coffee over Lionel's article in *The Express* a few days after his departure. The article was under the following title: Female Child—An Asset or A Liability?

"Not much originality, is there, Aruna?" Mary laughed.

"He is a young man, Mary," Aruna reminded her friend. "Let's give him some time before he can get more original."

"What has he written, Akila?" Mary asked.

Akila read the article in a clear voice to benefit her audience.

"Our society has become dispassionate regarding the loss of female children! Initially, some families turned into murderers at the sight of female children. Stray news in the air blamed this crime on poverty and illiteracy. Well, if that was the case, on what reason could reasonably educated individuals foist the blame of their crimes? Could it be the fear of allocating a big dowry for their daughters? Or were they worried about finding husbands for their daughters before they landed permanently on a shelf, doomed to be single?

The murders continue. Why? No family cherishes the idea of including a spinster in the family tree, and an unmarried daughter is a liability. Our society does not consider her fit to live alone! She has to be sheltered until she finds her way into the grave. In that situation, why not help her find her grave as soon as she is born, especially when she can feel no shame? No shame, yes, but do these calculating murderers realize that even a newborn feels the pain of death? Law overlooks these barbarians and the criminal activities. Who is to find a solution? There is no justice left in a world where the disappearance of a six-pound human being matters no longer. It just does not matter anymore."

"I must say that he has written well!" Mary exclaimed.

"There is also some information about the history of Mercy House," said Akila.

"What else does the article say, Akila?" asked Aruna.

"There is a small section about a lady. It says that she came to the orphanage as a little girl. Lionel hasn't mentioned her name, of course."

"Would that be you, Akila?" asked Mary.

"That is correct, Sister," replied Akila, smiling shyly.

"Akila, are you ready to inspect Brinda?" asked Humsa, walking into the kitchen.

Akila followed Humsa to Brinda. "We've done everything possible to make Brinda look nice," said Akila. "Hopefully, the tenant will like Brinda."

"He seems to be nice, Akila," said Humsa, picking up the last bit of mess in the big hall. "I met him when he came to see the house. His name is Mr. Raja. I heard that he is a very rich man."

"Really?" Akila asked anxiously. "I hope he isn't too rich. If he is, he may not find Brinda satisfactory. Do you think he'll really stay for a while?"

"I think he will, Akila."

"Well, I'm more worried about his wife. She must be a very wealthy woman! Would she like Brinda in the present condition? I know Aunt Aruna is counting on the rent money."

"Oh, you don't have to worry about that, Akila. Aruna told me that his wife died a few years ago. He has three sons, I think. They attend a boarding school in Ooty. They are coming here for the quarterly holidays," replied Humsa. "This is a huge house, Akila. I hope he doesn't feel lonely."

The new tenant arrived with a small army of servants, furniture, and resources. Mr. Raja's portfolio, according to the conversations between fences, went something like this:

"Did you know that he owns a car?"

"No, not a car. He has three cars. One of them is foreign-made. But he brought only one of his cars during this trip."

"But who cares about how many cars he has? Mr. Raja belongs to a backward caste. These social reforms! Anybody could get educated and pose as a collector. What a shame!"

This was a typical analysis. Categorically, Kanyakoil was not different from other towns. The citizens liked to maintain the distinction of classes and castes. If an upper-caste gentleman suffered a setback, then something was wrong in his star. If a lower-caste gentleman faced misery, he was getting what he deserved. In fact, that was why God had placed him in that deplorable category at the time of his birth. The collector had no business doing well in life. He should be poor, needy, uneducated, and take his place somewhere close to the bottom of the ranks. How could he be prosperous? It went against the order! Yes, the villagers knew a lot about the new, soft-spoken collector. Kanyakoil welcomed any news, any excitement. The arrival of Raja and his family generated significant interest in the mundane existence of an ordinary community.

When Akila went to the prayer hall, she was surprised to see the collector. He was attending the prayer with his children. It was nice to see a man of his stature attending a modest prayer that was initiated by homeless children! After prayer, the children walked to the dining hall for breakfast, and Akila saw the gentleman approaching Aruna.

"Akila, this is Mr. Raja," said Aruna.

Akila was impressed. His gentle manners and friendly disposition were very welcome. His sons displayed excellent manners. They were returning to school that afternoon. Akila gazed at the family with a sense of longing she thought she had overcome when she became an adult. How nice it would be to belong to such a happy family! That was a kind of happiness Akila would never know.

Aruna and Mary walked to the bus stand with Akila.

"What happened to that house?" Akila asked. "What did they do with it, Aunt Aruna?"

"What do you mean?" asked Aruna. "Which one, Akila?"

"You see that one, the second, two-storey house," Akila explained. "I can barely see the side of the house. It used to be covered in bougainvillea bushes. Now they have constructed a high wall and I can't see anything."

"Does it matter? Was it something special?" Mary asked Akila.

"Yes, Sister Mary, one of my friends lives there. You remember Vasanthi, don't you? She came to the orphanage when she was thirteen or fourteen. She stayed only for a few years. She is a maid in that house. She lives in the house … in the servant's quarters."

"The servant's quarters?" Mary asked.

"It's not bad, actually. They take care of her lodging and food. You see, Vasanthi never tried her best during her lessons when we were children."

"This happens to be a very proper assessment, Akila," said Aruna, smiling.

"Anyway, I try to see Vasanthi whenever I visit Kanyakoil. The owners normally don't let her have visitors inside the house, so I wait outside, near that wall, to chat with her. We used to call it The Bougainvillea Wall," said Akila. "I went to see Vasanthi yesterday. She was not home."

"Akila, there is a reason for that wall," Aruna explained. "Vasanthi told me when she came to see me. Her employers have new neighbors. They don't meet the caste standards! That wall is a symbol of intolerance! Vasanthi's employer, particularly the wife, doesn't want to see the lowly neighbors before her morning prayer."

"Really, Aunt Aruna?" Akila asked, outraged. "What a disgraceful insult! Her morning prayer! That's a joke. Which God would endorse or welcome such a prayer? That's the woman's excuse to maintain her superiority. If I ever have an opportunity, I'll teach that lady a lesson."

"Quite a few people do, Akila," said Aruna. "It's a disease that's not easy to eradicate."

The bus was ready to leave. Akila got in. As the noisy bus whizzed through the unruly roads, the familiar landmarks disappeared like a rapid flashback. The vehicle came to a full stop beside a queue of restless passengers at the nurse's hostel. Akila checked her mailbox. It was empty. In the entire world, there were only a few people who wished to write to her—Sister Mary, Aunt Aruna, Vasanthi, and her roommate, Selvi—because these were the only people she was close to. Selvi was usually punctual. Where was her letter? Maybe she was busy with her family. Understandable!

Joan Alex looked out of her room and smiled. She was an efficient supervisor. She was widely known among her colleagues and the nurses as Joanie, never as Mrs. Alex. Although Akila was a little fond of her, she avoided her because she was a habitual gossip. Akila walked down the narrow hallway and started to climb the steep stairs to the third floor. She was glad that her suitcase was light—thanks to indigent conditions and a meager closet.

Aruna finished the letter to the electric company. Her carefully chosen words requested a deferred payment. She was accustomed to begging a lot of individuals and institutions on behalf of Mercy House. Most accommodated her requests either generously or grudgingly, and she was thankful. Another check to write! How she wished she had more financial resources to lean on instead of begging for funds! The knock on the door halted her daydream.

"Come in," said Aruna.

"Aruna, Kali is here about milk money," said Humsa. "It has been overdue for more than three months. I had already sent him away a couple of times."

"Yes. I didn't forget. Here it is. Give this to him with my apologies."

Aruna looked at the bank statement. The manager of the bank was tolerant, but he was no saint. At times, Aruna wondered if she had drained too much of her grandfather's resources on Mercy House. Murthy had showered a vast amount of money on the orphanage. Without any warning, things began to turn unpleasant. His investments didn't bring brilliant returns, and he had no other resources to rely on apart from his land. Generations of people had a name for this. Bad time!

Aruna decided to divert her thoughts in a different direction and opened the file on the young boy from the nearby village. His file didn't contain any extraordinary information. The boy's father was a laborer. He had died as a result of an accident at a construction site. His mother offered him no protection. How old was he? Eight! He was probably ashamed of his background. No wonder, he refused to talk to anybody, and Humsa was worried that if he continued to decline food, he might starve to death.

Aruna found the young boy behind a cluster of hibiscus bushes in the backyard. "May I sit by you?" she asked. "You're Senthil, right? My name is Aruna. The children call me Aunt Aruna." She sat by him, a little apprehensive of his reluctance to speak. "Senthil, I'm so hungry. Everybody has eaten already. Will you eat with me?"

"Why did my appa die?" asked Senthil. "Now I have nobody."

Aruna understood that he was afraid to return from a dark but familiar past. This sudden question, although expected, took her by surprise. "I'm really sorry that your appa is no more," said Aruna, sincerely. "It may not sound like a good idea, but you could be happy here. I'll teach you a lot of nice things. Humsa makes very tasty food. You met Humsa earlier, didn't you? Sivam will show you how to help in the garden. See that man there? He is Sam. He'll take you to the market and the children will play with you."

The boy refused to look at her. Her pep talk didn't work.

"And we all will love you," said Aruna, earnestly. How could she convince him of the bright side of the orphanage? It had saved several lives. It took time, a lot of time, to hold the thought of trust. An unhappy child with a fragmented life! How could this child trust a stranger?

"I don't know you. How can I trust you?" Senthil asked, still looking away.

"Yes, you're right. You don't know me. But how will you know if you can trust me or not if you never give me a chance?" she asked.

A few minutes went in silence. It seemed like an eternity. Was this child going to believe her? Could he hold her in trust? He got up, took Aruna's hand in his, and walked to the dining hall. He smiled after a few days. He trusted Aruna and others after a few weeks. He found his brothers and sisters in Mercy House. He found rain after years of dreary, choking heat. He was home.

◆ ◆ ◆

Akila flopped on the bumpy bed, unevenly tucked inside the metal frame. It had been a long day. She was now scheduled to work in the emergency ward, and her unit was short-staffed because a couple of nurses were on sick leave. Selvi was still away on vacation with her family. Akila missed her roommate, although it was a luxury to be the sole occupant of the room for a few days. She collected her dirty clothes before walking to the end of the corridor to bathe and to wash her clothes. First, she carefully washed the dirty garments on the washing stone. She needed sufficient care to accomplish this chore because she didn't wish to enlarge the tiny hole in the blouse. She collected the washed clothing in a bucket. She filled water in another to finish her bath. She was almost at the end of her ritual when she heard a whimper somewhere close by. Was someone crying? Akila got dressed quickly and knocked on the next door.

"Is anybody here? Are you all right? Can you hear me?" Akila asked.

There was no answer. Whoever was inside didn't open the door, but the crying seemed to have stopped. Akila knocked vigorously again, but there was no answer. She could still hear movements inside. Then why wouldn't that person open the door or say something? The door was locked. Something was surely not right. Akila went downstairs to the supervisor's room.

"Follow me quickly, Joanie," said Akila, hurriedly. "I think someone is stuck in the bathroom and ..."

Joanie saw the anxiety in Akila's eyes. She yelled for the custodian before running after Akila. The cook saw the commotion and asked his assistants to follow him. The old-fashioned, heavy doors in the old buildings were quite stubborn. It took several hands to forcibly open the door. A woman was on the floor against the wall—with protruding eyes and a slightly distended stomach. Akila let out a gasp. It was Selvi.

It was after seven in the evening. The doctor confirmed Selvi's death. When did she return from her vacation? Did anybody know that she had come back? Akila certainly had not known anything. In fact, she was still waiting for a letter from her.

"Go ahead, Akila. Tell the doctor what you know," said Joanie.

"Doctor, I heard some sound in the bathroom," said Akila. "Sounded like someone was in distress, and I thought that the person couldn't get out. I ran downstairs to get help and ..."

Joanie finished what ensued afterwards. She took Akila to her own room and asked her to rest on the sofa. While the doctor left the premises for a short while, Joanie went to the porch to wait for him. How did the girl die? Was it her heart? That was impossible. How old was Selvi? Was she in her mid-twenties? Was she pregnant when she was still … unmarried? She couldn't be. Selvi was a good girl, not one of those fast young women. Joanie hurried to her desk to look for information about Selvi's family.

The supervisor sent a telegram to Selvi's parents: "Come immediately. Selvi is ill. Joan Alex."

The doctor was back. "Joanie, may I talk to that young lady, Akila, again?" he asked.

"Oh, yes. What happened, Dr. Arundel?" asked Joanie, curiously. "Did Selvi slip? I've been asking the servant to scrub the bathroom floors more frequently. Does she listen? No!"

"I don't know," Dr. Arundel replied in a flat voice. "I'll be able to provide details a little later. I must have more time. I would like to speak to her parents first."

"So this is how the business goes," thought Joanie. This incident in the nurse's hostel under her management was absolutely unpleasant. "Sad, sad business, to be sure," Joanie exclaimed and took the doctor to Akila.

When the doctor walked in with Joanie, Akila was sitting on the sofa, drinking tea and wiping her cheeks.

"I need to talk to her alone. May we have some privacy, please?" asked the doctor.

Joanie closed the door quietly. What should she tell the hospital authorities about Selvi? She ran a tight ship. There was no room for shameful affairs in her hostel. There was not a trace of any scandal in her eight years of service. Now this incident!

"Now tell me, Miss Akila. How long have you worked in this hospital?" Dr. Arundel asked.

Akila tried to assess the purpose of his visit. How much did he expect her to tell him?

"Where are you from?" Dr. Arundel asked another question.

"From Kanyakoil," replied Akila.

"My friend, Raja, just moved there," said Dr. Arundel. "He is the collector of Kanyakoil. All your family is there?"

"No, I don't have a family. I grew up in an orphanage. Actually, it's close to the house where your friend is living now. I met him just a few days ago."

Akila expected the usual, sympathetic reply when she mentioned her homeless past, but it didn't happen. She was rather relieved that the doctor took this piece of information without blinking his eyes.

"Now tell me something else," the doctor continued, "how well did you know Selvi?"

"When my old roommate left a couple of years ago, Selvi moved in," replied Akila, looking at him for a few seconds. She could infer nothing from his expression. "Doctor, what happened? How did Selvi die?"

"Selvi was young. There's no record of illness. We can't determine the reason for her death without a postmortem. We're waiting for her parents to arrive."

Akila saw no reason to reveal confidential information, but she had nobody else to turn to. Well, his position, in an ethical sense, required him to be confidential. "There's something I've to tell you," said Akila. She couldn't swallow the knot that was floating somewhere in her throat.

"Before or after the police comes?" asked the doctor, smiling gently at the apprehension in Akila's eyes. "Don't be alarmed," he continued, "the police will come."

"Doctor, we must think of Selvi's family! They are very orthodox people. A postmortem would mean a lot of scandal," said Akila. She was pleading without knowing what exactly she was defending.

The doctor patted Akila's hand and urged her to calm down. He was quite sure that Joanie had her inquisitive ears close to the door. "You look better. Can you walk with me to my office? It's in the next wing. Whatever you say will stay confidential," he whispered. He opened the door. Joanie looked inside to check on Akila. After the doctor offered a quick explanation to the supervisor, Akila followed him to his office.

Akila began her narrative. "Selvi met an engineer about a year ago. When they met, he was her patient. The chance acquaintance matured into love. Doctor, he proposed to her, which made her very happy at that time. Unfortunately, Selvi's parents were against her involvement with that man. Her father, in particular, was absolutely against this proposal."

"Why?"

"Selvi's family belongs to a high caste, and they would never approve of her marriage with a man from a very backward caste. In order to break Selvi's association with him, her father hurriedly arranged a marriage for her with an eligible young man from their caste. The wedding is … the wedding was supposed to take place sometime soon!"

He said nothing.

"Selvi tried to convince her parents to accept her man," Akila continued. "Her mother, although sympathetic, had no voice. She tried to persuade her husband to relent. Her entreaty didn't change his mind. Eventually, his hatred and prejudice goaded him to gather a lot of help from influential men in his community. He managed to push Selvi's man out of that town."

The doctor still didn't mention a word.

"Doctor," said Akila, nervously. "I think Selvi might have …"

"I know. When Selvi's parents arrive, I might call you again."

"Please do. I'll be glad to offer any help, just anything," Akila assured the doctor.

"Good! Did anybody else know that Selvi wanted to marry that man?" asked Dr. Arundel.

"No, Doctor. Selvi told me that apart from her immediate family, nobody else had any idea of her wish to marry that man."

"Have you seen that gentleman?"

"No, I have not. But Selvi showed me his photograph."

Akila looked at Selvi's bed. Selvi had taken Akila into her heart, into her life, to talk about her happiness in finding love and her sadness in losing it. But she never talked about her terminal decision. Akila still remembered her conversation with Selvi regarding her unhappy decision to quit her love—just on the day before Selvi went on vacation.

"Selvi," Akila had said. "You are over twenty, a major by age, and self-sufficient. Why can't you have a civil wedding? All you need is a marriage registrar."

"Akila," said Selvi, smiling at her friend's practical and bold advice. "I can go to the marriage registrar at any time. But you see, once I stealthily marry a man at the registrar's office, none of my father's friends would associate with my family. Most importantly, my sisters would never receive marriage proposals from decent families. How can I do this to my family? Akila, my love is hopeless."

"But, Selvi, how can you do this to him?" asked Akila. "He loves you. You love him. What about your future?"

"Akila, my father told me that he would commit suicide if I … if I pursued. What can a girl in my position do?"

"How can he say that?" Akila asked, aching for her friend. "That's emotional blackmail!"

Selvi had not responded to Akila's entreaty. Selvi abandoned marriage and happiness in order to maintain her family name and to secure her siblings' future prospects. Yet, at that moment, in her desperation, she never realized that the doctors might question the reason for her sudden death—and what a death it was! The means of Selvi's end could have ruined her family name forever. "Why didn't you say something, anything, just anything?" thought Akila, for the thousandth time.

Selvi's parents arrived. The mother was beyond control. Her precious daughter was dead—to please her husband's autonomy and to cement his dependence on the good opinion of a rigid society.

"If only I had known her decision, Akila. Oh, how I wish," said Selvi's mother. She didn't know where to begin her grief.

Akila sat with her and held her hand. Yes, they could wish. If only, what? It was too late. The family had thought more of 'an appropriate marriage' than the daughter's happiness or peace of mind. Selvi was supposed to marry appropriately and wisely for her safety and a lifetime of happiness. Now there was no Selvi to look forward to a lifetime of anything. Akila desperately wished to throw something at the cruel society. Didn't Selvi sacrifice her life to avoid leaving a black mark in that ridiculous society? Was it worth her tears, unhappiness, and beyond all hopes, her life?

Only four parties knew about the poison that killed Selvi—Dr. Arundel, Akila, Mr. Raja, and her parents. No other soul would be aware of the fatal truth. Selvi left two younger sisters and a younger brother behind her. The future of those siblings, especially the sisters', had to be taken into consideration. Their society, which considered caste as the most important fiber of the community, would eat that family alive and ruin all of its prospects if the real cause of Selvi's death became public knowledge. The fact that Selvi took her own life became an ambiguous question among those present at the time of her death. Dr. Arundel made sure that it went no farther. He certified Selvi's death using a medical term that Joanie wouldn't understand or be able to pronounce. Raja pulled a few strings to hush matters with the police. This was probably one of the few occasions when power, status, and authority worked toward protecting the prospects of a helpless and poor family.

Selvi's father had been the means of her death—indirectly or otherwise. **It was his crime and it was his punishment**. Akila felt outraged by the stark reality of this sordid business. Selvi's father must be punished. He should be forced to feel shame and mortification by announcing the real reason for Selvi's death to the public. But such an announcement would ruin the family and its young members forever. Akila was glad to be casteless and nameless. She was happy that she owed the unforgiving society nothing on behalf of caste.

Mr. Raja wished Dr. Arundel a very good day and placed the phone on its cradle. The unfortunate affair of that poor nurse, Selvi, had taken a huge portion of his time in the last few weeks. If the true cause of Selvi's death were to come out, the society would tear the family to pieces, causing a mass suicide. Such incidents happened—cruel, unbelievable, but true. This incident insisted on pushing his thoughts to his childhood. And he never disliked visiting his young years. Poverty and discrimination had this effect on a man. No matter how circumstances changed, no matter how wealthy and important a person became over time, the past always haunted like a chronic ailment. That was a good thing! The present shadow reminded a person of the past agony, and it hopefully kept him away from vanity and pride.

Akila heard her name announced in the intercom. A visitor was waiting for her. Who wished to see her here at the end of the day? Was it Aunt Aruna? She hoped nothing was amiss. But the visitor was a man she had not met before.

"Miss Akila?" the man enquired.

"Yes, and you are?" asked Akila.

He was Selvi's young man. He looked very different from the image Akila had seen in his photograph. His eyes and his unshed tears pulled an unknown string in her heart. Why was he here?

"Miss Akila, I'm moving to Bombay. I wanted to see you ... Selvi talked about you quite frequently," he said.

"She did?" asked Akila, in a barely audible voice. "She talked about you too."

"Can you tell me anything about how Selvi had ... or am I asking too much of you to tell me about her last day?" He looked away, at nowhere, at nothing.

How was she supposed to begin? Something shattered in Akila's heart. She could hardly imagine what he must have gone through since Selvi's death. She looked around and noticed a couple of nurses with whom she was barely familiar. Particularly, Joanie was nowhere in sight. She told him about his Selvi's last day.

He listened to her quietly. He thanked her earnestly. He walked away silently.

◆ ◆ ◆

Friday afternoon brought a lot of rain. When the bus stopped outside the rusty gates, the hostel looked hazy in the downpour. When Akila ran into the building, Joanie met her at the foyer with a piece of paper in her hand.

"Akila, how are you? You got a telegram," Joanie spoke hurriedly and gave the message to her.

Akila opened it impatiently and read the contents: "Come immediately. Aruna is ill. Humsa."

While Akila scribbled a note to her manager in the hospital, Joanie looked at the bus schedule.

"I see one that leaves right after six," said Joanie. "If you leave in a few minutes, you can make it, Akila. I'll give your note to your manager. I'll pray for your Aunt Aruna. She'll be all right. Don't worry now."

Akila thanked her before running upstairs to her room. She packed a few things and rushed to the bus stand to catch the 6:15-Express to Kanyakoil.

Samuel was at the bus stop without his hearty smile. He took the bag from Akila's hand. "Akila, it's good to see you," said Sam. "Miss Aruna is never ill. Mercy House just can't do without her. What are we to do?"

"I'm glad to see you, Uncle Sam. What are you doing here at this time? How did you know I was here?" Akila asked.

"Oh, that! I came to get the medicine from the pharmacy. I saw the bus and wondered if you had received the telegram."

Humsa greeted Akila at the front door with a hasty hug. Akila was relieved to see Sister Mary in the common room. She ran to her. When Mary took Akila to Aruna's room, the patient smiled gently.

"Sister, the doctor is here," Humsa whispered.

"Doctor, what's wrong with Aruna?" Mary asked the doctor outside Aruna's room.

"Sister, Aruna had chest pain during the last few days," the doctor began to explain. "She didn't call me. Later, Humsa called me, and I'm quite sure that Aruna had a heart attack. She is showing intermittent signs of recovery, but it's too early to tell the outcome of such an attack."

"What should we do?" asked Mary.

"I think you should take her to the city and let a cardiologist look at her condition. I'll send a telegram to Dr. Sathyam in Madras. In the mean time, would you please call me if you need anything?" the doctor asked. "Don't worry even if it's late in the night. Call me right away. Anyhow, I'll return in a few hours to check on her condition." He left right after assuring them of his assistance.

Akila walked into the common room with a cup of tea and offered it to Mary. "Sister, you should try to get some sleep now," said Akila. "I'm not tired at all. I'll relieve Humsa soon. She is sitting in Aunt Aruna's room now."

"It's all right, don't worry. Akila, I'm sorry to hear about your friend, Selvi. She was so young. Aruna and I were wondering what happened to that poor girl."

"Didn't Mr. Raja say anything?" asked Akila.

"No, he didn't," replied Mary.

In her letters to Mary and Aruna, Akila had not mentioned the real reason for Selvi's death. She was planning on telling them in person, but this was not the right time. Raja, who knew the details behind Selvi's sudden demise, had kept it confidential. As he had promised, he had left it to Akila to inform Aruna at a later time.

"It's all right, Sister. We can talk about it later," said Akila, eager to change the subject. "Aunt Aruna needs a lot of rest. Who'll be in charge of Mercy House when she is recuperating?"

"I know," whispered Mary. "The same thought has been worrying me. Aruna wanted to hire an assistant to manage the orphanage. She just couldn't afford it. A couple of women have been volunteering occasionally, but they can't work here permanently. We'll find someone."

Early next morning, Humsa asked Sivam to run to the doctor's home. The doctor arrived as quickly as he could to witness the dying embers of Aruna's life. The sunrise that brought Aruna to this world—with limited hopes and deferred dreams—decided to take her away to an unknown world.

Who was supposed to tell the children? Mary, of course, was the unanimous choice. A few children cried. Some wondered who would answer their endless doubts. A couple of very young children asked when Aunt Aruna would return from heaven.

Mary sat in Aruna's room and tried to recollect her dearest friend's last smile, last word. Yes, when would Aruna return from heaven? Why was God in such a rush? He could have spared her a little longer, a lot longer.

Arrangements had to be made to accommodate quite a few guests before the funeral. Raja generously opened his house for this occasion. This kind of magnanimity seemed to be second nature to him. Akila was hoping to see Vasanthi during this occasion. She didn't come. Where was she? Had she disappeared into the bougainvillea wall?

Aruna

Aruna—a gift of sunrise.

Cherished as the dearest friend, she shall live in our hearts forever.

Every wall in Mercy House, every flower in the garden, every sigh and smile around us have felt her touch, her hopes, her love.

Somewhere within all of us will be the memory of our dearest Aruna till the end of time.

God Bless

Mary's tribute was inscribed under the huge photograph of the deceased, which would remain to grace the common room of Mercy House for generations.

Vasanthi didn't attend Aruna's funeral. Instead, she sent a letter to Akila.

"Dear Akila,

How are you doing? It was grossly careless of me to leave town without telling you. It happened a while ago. I wanted to inform you. I just didn't know how to begin. And it feels strange to share the loss of dear Aunt Aruna in this manner ..."

Parts of the long letter comforted and surprised Akila at the same time. Vasanthi's racist employer, who couldn't tolerate her low-caste neighbor, had misjudged her son. He had fallen in love with Vasanthi, yes, the young woman who was no more than a servant in the household and one who was once an orphan. His mother didn't approve of his deplorable marriage. Marry a servant? Marry an orphan?

When the young man decided to elope with her, Vasanthi packed her bag and followed him. Her letter expressed her love for her husband. Akila could also sense a high degree of gratitude in her friend's tone. They were now married, but they could never return to Kanyakoil. In his mother's eyes, the union was an irrevocable damage. He was not her son anymore, and her daughter-in-law didn't exist. Vasanthi was a world apart from Selvi, who took her own life to please her caste-obsessed father. The world needed more Vasanthis. And the world should commend the young man, an unselfish man, who gave Vasanthi—a penniless woman with no dowry—a home, love, and security.

A week after the cremation, Aruna's elderly lawyer came to Mercy House to settle the property. Sekaran read Aruna's last testimonial in his elderly, firm voice. A scrap of land here was left to a distant relation, a bit of property there was left to a distant niece, and some insignificant commodities were left to sundry relations. A small amount of cash was left for the progress of Mercy House. The teak desk that had won Mary's fascination was left to her. Mary was touched. She had to leave the room momentarily to collect her composure.

Sekaran looked warily at the group of people. Aruna didn't have cousins. Who were these people? Her relations? Some of Aruna's family members, who had assembled in the pretext of being helpful, were waiting with whetted hearing! Where were these helpful souls when Aruna needed assistance? Most of these family members had not seen Aruna since her father's eventful death. Well, they were here with the capital question—who is inheriting the house?

Sekaran took a deep breath and continued to read. The whispers died. "Finally, the property in Kanyakoil, under the name, Brinda …"

Those thoughtful relations trickled away when they discovered that Brinda was left to a nameless, poor orphan.

"We should have known," said one of the relations. "Aruna never had any regard for her family. How could she give her ancestral property to a nameless woman?"

"Well, Murthy shouldn't have left it in Aruna's name," said another of the relations. "He was a good man, no doubt, but he had no luck in his daughter and grandchild!"

Akila couldn't believe that Aruna had left Brinda to her! What was she supposed to do with it?

"Why did Aunt Aruna leave Brinda to me, Sister?" asked Akila, during lunch.

"Akila, Aruna wished to leave a challenge with you."

"What do you mean, Sister?"

Mary looked pitifully at Akila's confused expression and smiled. "Really, Akila," said Mary. "You should know how Aruna held you in her thoughts, my dear. You were no less than a daughter to her. She left the property to you because she thought it would be in good hands. Stop worrying and we'll find a good use for Brinda. Now, let me ask you something. How do you feel about managing Mercy House?"

"I'll be glad to, Sister, but I don't have any experience," said Akila. "Besides, we have to think about my salary. If I continue to work in the hospital, I can at least contribute some money to maintain this place. What do you think? I'll do whatever you think is right."

Since the decision required some planning, the ladies put it aside for a later time. Right now, there were some immediate concerns to be addressed. Akila's superiors at the hospital granted her a month of family time. Mary, with Akila's assistance, struggled to find the best possible way to keep Mercy House alive. Aruna had excellent bookkeeping skills. Nothing in the accounts was a mystery. However, they had to consider the lack of funds! Where would the children go if the orphanage closed?

Raja knocked on the door.

"How are you, Mr. Raja?" asked Mary.

"I'm fine, thank you," replied Raja. "Is there anything I can do? May I assist you in any way?"

"Thank you," replied Mary, breathing a sigh of relief. His visits and his assistance were most welcome!

Akila's errand at the bank got over earlier than expected. She was not in the habit of managing a complicated account, or any account for that matter, and she was glad to have Mary's assistance. The employees at the bank stared at the pair. A get-rich-quick orphan lady and a nun-in-her-habit were here to settle business regarding a superior property. This stately house had belonged to a respectable family that had lived in that small town for generations. While Aruna's greedy relatives looked at Akila's luck with significant disfavor, the non-relations gawked with curiosity and envy.

"The entire community dislikes me, Sister," said Akila, on their way to the orphanage.

"Akila, things will look better," said Mary. "Sekaran has offered help. He has been the lawyer for Aruna's family since her grandfather's time. Don't worry. Besides, Mr. Raja has assured us of his help."

Akila pulled her eyes away from the endless, slushy paddy fields. The recent rain had filled the streams, which were happily running through the grassy borders. If only the plentiful rain filled the useless minds with discipline and a decent attitude! Well, that amounted to a lot of wishful thinking.

As it turned out, the visit to the bank was just the first step to more rigorous learning process. Who was to help Akila and Mary? Once again, Raja answered their questions. Aruna had described Raja as a benefactor of Mercy House in one of her letters to Akila. Mary knew that Aruna had held him in the highest regard. What more was needed to endorse him as a confidante and a trustworthy friend?

Raja's assistance allowed Mary to return to her convent for a few days. Some of her routine work that she had abandoned at the news of Aruna's illness definitely needed her attention. When she returned to Mercy House, she was glad to see certain improvements.

While Akila and Mary were delighted to have Raja's assistance, the curious neighbors looked at the situation with a lot of interest. Aruna's disappointed relations ignited the whispers once they knew which way the wind was blowing. Tongues were waiting to wag in that cursed town. What a vast amount of fence conversations the gentleman's help triggered!

"Aruna managed the orphanage without help, didn't she?" asked one of the neighbors. "Why can't Akila do the same? How hard is it to hire someone to manage Mercy House? Something must be going on between the wealthy Raja and Akila."

Samuel was the hapless bearer of this gossip. He had heard bits and pieces of information in the market. He promptly repeated it to Mary and Humsa. Such news didn't take long to reach Akila's ears.

"Sister, I feel terrible. What's all this nonsense?" Akila asked, thoroughly ashamed.

"Akila, don't pay attention to wicked insinuations," said Mary.

Raja was also aware of the talk in the community. He felt the narrow-minded gossips as intensely as Akila did, if not more.

◆ ◆ ◆

When Raja visited the orphanage again, Mary and Akila were sitting in the office.

"Sister Mary," said Raja. "May I talk to Miss Akila about a private matter under your supervision?"

Akila expected the generous patron to offer money, and she began to rehearse a grateful acknowledgment speech in her mind.

"Miss Akila, if you don't mind," began Raja, hesitantly. "I hope you accept my hand in marriage."

Akila, who was over thirty, had never aspired for a prosperous matrimony or any kind of union. In her tiny sphere, a young woman remained a spinster for life if she was not married before she hit twenty. A poor orphan, with no memory of class or caste, couldn't hope for a marriage. As these thoughts were running helter-skelter in her pleasantly confused mind, he continued to talk. Apparently, his wish took flight from three different reasons.

"My sons need a kind, motherly figure," said Raja. "My heart needs an unassuming, cheerful companion. Brinda and Mercy House are in need of financial aid."

Akila was stunned for a moment. The third reason for Raja's proposal arrested her attention. Brinda and Mercy House would be in good hands. The orphanage could go on. Aunt Aruna's Brinda wouldn't be sold to feed the orphans. An incredible sense of relief engulfed her.

"Akila," said Mary, holding her hand. "You don't need me anymore. I must take care of something in the nursery, all right?" Mary vacated the room with a parting smile at the gentleman.

"I hope I haven't hurt your feelings, Miss Akila," Raja said, resuming his proposal. His humble tone echoed the concern in his eyes. "I haven't forgotten that I'm a widower with three sons. I also understand that you might wish to marry a bachelor with no prior commitments."

"Mr. Raja," Akila said bashfully, worried that he had misconstrued her silence. "I'm honored and touched by your proposal. It's just that it's all so sudden and ..."

"I had originally intended to wait for an appropriate interval before approaching you with the marriage proposal, especially after Miss Aruna's recent tragedy," Raja said, interrupting her politely. "I decided not to wait, mainly to halt the general gossip in the community. Also, I wish to preserve Brinda and protect Mercy House from the position of your husband rather than as a benefactor. Will you please think about my offer?" asked Raja. He left with a lingering smile.

Earlier, Raja had touched Akila's gratitude by offering financial assistance to benefit Mercy House. Now, most unexpectedly, he pulled an unknown something from somewhere within her by offering a lifetime of security and happiness. Was this meant to happen? What was she supposed to do? She ran to Mary.

"Sister, what should I do?" Akila asked.

Mary smiled her approval. For the first time in many days, Akila saw relief in the compassionate eyes of her older friend. Akila and Mary talked for hours that night. Both found comfort in drawing the memory of Aruna into their conversation.

"Akila," said Mary. "Aruna and I were worried about your future. I'm still worried. How long will you work as a nurse and make wages just to keep body and soul together? Akila, Aruna would have approved of Mr. Raja. She thought he was a decent gentleman, unlike the majority of his contemporaries." Raja's polite demeanor, his generosity, his patience, his humility—was a night enough to praise his qualities?

"Sister, what about the orphanage?" asked Akila, dutifully.

"That was exactly what I was trying to tell you when your gentleman walked into the office a while ago," Mary said, happily noticing Akila's bashful expression.

"Did you find someone?"

"Yes, Akila. I received a letter from the convent in Madras," replied Mary. "She is a middle-aged lady. She has reasonable experience. You see, Akila, God always shows a way when something is meant to happen!"

The night before the most important day of her life, Akila packed her few belongings. Her possessions went neatly into a small suitcase. Were the new developments true? Or was she dreaming something fantastic? She was getting married to a nice, decent gentleman. Akila looked at the mirror. It seemed impossible. She was no beauty. She had always known that. She was even surprised that the lack of beauty never made her wish for it. A fashion expert would call her plain. Her chubby nose made her look immature and her large eyes seemed out of place on her small, gaunt face. Akila was too simple to realize that her unglamorous face, supported by her unassuming disposition, gave her features a charming, innocent appearance. Even if Akila had belonged to a reasonably wealthy family, her dark skin color would have been an obstacle in procuring a husband. Her family would have been forced to pay a heavy dowry to balance the lack of fair skin. But now, with no expectation whatsoever, a nice, kind man wished to marry her. Akila felt touched.

The wedding was designed to please a middle-aged gentleman, past a young man's fancies. It was planned to bring joy to a cautious lady, considered to be past her prime! No pomp was necessary and no fuss was required. The quiet marriage ceremony took place in the registrar's office. Ram, one of Raja's dearest friends, came from Singapore to attend the wedding. A couple of nurses, Joanie, and a few friends gathered for the informal reception in Brinda. Akila felt like an intruder in that huge, stately home. What had she done to deserve this?

Mary offered her warmest blessings to Akila and her husband. Nobody could be happier than Mary. This joyful event reinforced her conviction in one of the most compassionate, decent gentlemen of her limited acquaintance. The world could boast of at least one man, a decent man, who was not scheming on acquiring material gain through marriage. And God chose Akila to benefit from this selfless gesture. The guests trickled away, and the bride was left alone with her husband. Her husband! She looked at his dignified figure—his tall stature, well-trimmed mustache, grey-streaked side burns, friendly eyes, and his warm, childlike smile. Her husband! She felt guilty. Did she marry this man to save a building and a few homeless children? Was it so selfish of her? Her husband was a good man, a kind man. She had nothing to offer him—no wealth, no name, no dowry—nothing. Why did he marry her? The three reasons he had offered during his proposal randomly sprouted in her nervous mind.

Raja walked to his bride and took her hand. At that moment, Akila lost the guilt. She would be a good mother to his children, a wonderful companion to him, and an asset to his family. She would certainly shelter every homeless child who crossed her path. She would protect Brinda just as Aunt Aruna would have done. At this moment, she was immensely happy.

Akila opened her closet and gaped at the assorted materials. Her husband must have gone mad. He had told her that he ordered a few items to fill her closet. What she noticed was a small department store! There were enough saris and accessories to get her through this lifetime. No, there was enough to get her through the next. She was worried that a slap would land on her wrist if she handled the delicate silk.

"Are you ready, Akila?" asked Raja.

Akila was apprehensive about going to the temple. "Would there be a lot of people?" Akila asked doubtfully. "What if I say the wrong thing?"

"Akila, there is nothing to it. Relax," assured Raja. He encouraged his wife to wear a nice silk sari and heavy jewelry.

Akila was not used to this flamboyant display. Until now, her possessions had been a few inexpensive saris and a couple of earrings from the corner store. Understandably, she was very nervous about her metamorphosis from a poor spinster to a wealthy matron. Being the wife of a rich and important man required a lot of adjustments in her style and choices. Although Raja believed in visiting his humble beginning to stay away from vanity, he never missed an opportunity to display his wealth. His childish heart was glad that his excessive wealth got him respect—the respect that was stolen from him due to his low caste.

Akila went around the temple with the excitement of a child. "Look at that architecture! That is such a beautiful door. Can we go inside?" Akila asked.

"We can't go inside, Akila," replied Raja.

"Why not?"

"Because," said Raja, awkwardly. "We're not allowed to enter these areas."

"Why?"

"It's because I belong to a very low caste," Raja explained. His generous checks were needed when the temple funds dwindled to the bottom of the collection box. He was still not good enough to enter certain sections of the temple.

"What? Does it matter?" Akila asked, quite confused. "This is the temple."

"You poor thing," said Raja. "By marrying me, you're grouped with members of an inferior caste."

His explanation held a good degree of seriousness, mingled with a note of sarcasm, and Akila began to laugh. This introduction to a society—soaked in caste, class, and sundry community nonsense—hit Akila like a storm. Before her marriage, she had noticed her community's inhibitions, but she had not thought much of them when she was in the orphanage and when she was a woman-of-no-consequence in the nurse's hostel. She was, then, nobody. She was, now, somebody worthy of attention. Whenever she accompanied her husband, whether to a festival or a government function, she was treated with measured respect because she was the wife of a government official and the spouse of a rich man. She started to feel the strain of the society, especially from the women. They wouldn't let her forget that she was an orphan with no money, no name, and no connections, until she married a generous and important man.

Akila was not afraid of the women in Kanyakoil. They thought more about status and money. Unfortunately, their vanity devoured their courtesy. Akila's naivety might have added to her discomfort when she adjusted to her new life. It also gave her a sort of quiet, inner strength to take the whispered insults with a pinch of salt. She had the good sense to appreciate the position she had, and she was thankful for the resources to which she had access. She gave her time, her unlimited financial allowance, and her kindness. She took the town like a rainfall. In all her wildest dream, she had never expected to be a generous monsoon.

Akila was very happy, but she was beginning to feel the boredom of a highly comfortable and routine existence. Brinda was filled with servants. She had nothing to occupy her time. Raja asked her to read and relax. She was not used to this leisure. Was she missing her work?

"May I go to work?" asked Akila. "I mean, once in a while, on a part-time basis?"

"Akila, I don't think that's a wise decision, my dear. You see, 'working women' generally represent servants and menial laborers. I don't want you to work for a living when I can support you."

And he supported her in luxury. Akila, although disappointed, had to accept his decision. He was her husband! Akila's society taught the following tenet: marriage was a woman's salvation and the husband's wish was the heavenly commandment. While sulking over her boredom, Akila was glad to receive a letter or two. Mary's correspondence was exactly what it should be—considerate, loving, and dignified. Joanie's letter was anything but dignified. It was long-winded and intrusive. Akila blushed when she read the following lines: "Akila, love is a powerful element. Use it like a tool. You shall always have your husband wrapped around your little finger. Work on a fifty-fifty relationship!"

Akila found some humor in this letter. How could she take her correspondent seriously? Akila had not entered matrimony with any preconceived notions. On the brink of marriage, she had hardly known what the state of marriage entailed. Akila had married her man with simple expectations—a home, affection, warmth, and the hope of preserving Brinda and Mercy House. Raja fulfilled all of her expectations. But love? Joanie's suggestion of love confused her. That kind of love existed in novels and cinema theaters. Akila's simple mind was not romantic. There was no room for ardent love in her heart when gratitude for her partner's generosity occupied it. Her husband talked. She listened. He proffered opinions. She agreed. She smiled at his pleasure and frowned at his disappointment. Her respect for her spouse urged her to walk a couple of feet behind him whenever they went out together. Over a period of time, she became his shadow.

Yes, Akila was fond of her husband. It was just that certain annoying wrinkles irritated her. One was his lamentation regarding low caste that bordered on obsession. Akila believed that what couldn't be mended must be ignored. The other wrinkle was his passion for education. Akila valued education as much as the next person. But, at times, she wondered why it occupied Raja's thoughts every minute he was awake. Well, who was perfect? She knew she wasn't. And this wise analysis prompted her to ignore the annoyance.

Raja walked into the wedding hall with Akila. The cool, monsoon-licked breeze touched the fringe of Akila's heavy silk sari. She looked slightly awe-struck when she walked into this extravagant blitz. The hall held a few city people—some seemed sophisticated, some appeared ostentatious, and a few were a little welcoming. Raja's smile reassured her a little.

The bride's mother and father received Raja and his wife respectfully. Akila recognized the proud father from the newspapers. He was a very powerful politician with a colorful resume: corruption, house arrest, smuggling, and money laundering. This was another opportunity to launder money. A large amount of cash was going inside the bride's money chest for a rainy day. The Gods better be wrathful to send a torrential rain, and frequently too, so the bride could find opportunities to use the money. Akila couldn't help staring at the ornate decorations, silks, jewelry, and superfluous everything. This was still a new world to her—a wealthy, confusing, and superficial world.

As the Rajas followed other, very important guests to the dining hall, Akila noticed a corridor that branched out to another dining area. Why were some guests from this wedding sitting here? Were there too many guests that made it necessary for some to sit in a different area? But when Akila sat at one of the tables in the dining hall, she noticed that the hall was barely full. Raja explained the dining arrangements to her. Those people, sitting in the ancillary dining area, were from quite low castes. Traditionally, they didn't sit with the higher-caste people.

"Do they have to sit there?" asked Akila.

"Not always, not everybody does. It's something that goes without saying, you know?"

"But," Akila interjected, still not out of her childlike innocence. "You're low caste. I mean, we belong to a low caste also, don't we? Then, how come ..."

"My dear, years ago, I was with that unfortunate group," replied Raja. "Now I'm excluded from the list because of my position and wealth." His voice displayed no emotion when he made this statement, but his mind visited a time when he was the object of discrimination.

Akila, with her sensitive understanding, diverted the conversation to other topics. Raja was thankful.

While on the way home, Raja and Akila tried neutral topics unsuccessfully. Both minds were unsteady—with unanswered questions and unfulfilled sympathy. The conversation diverged to Raja's youth. When Akila wished to know how her husband's childhood drove him toward education and prosperity, Raja was delighted to open his heart.

"Akila, my father was a fisherman in a coastal village. We had beach property; a rickety hut, surrounded by salted, dried fish. My mother scrubbed and cleaned rich people's homes. They worked very hard."

"I know what you mean," said Akila, taking his hand in hers.

"Akila, there were days when I wondered whether I would eat and go to bed or sit painfully through a hungry night. Hunger is cruel. Nobody should go to sleep with that ailment. Sometimes, my father didn't return till late in the night because he was struggling with the waves. I felt miserable when I saw my mother crying. She was worried about his safety. I had a very rough, poverty-stricken life," Raja sighed.

"Yes, you did, but I'm glad you had a family. I'm also glad that you progressed so much in life. Look at you today, look how educated you are. What a career you have!" Akila said happily.

"Akila, I was very lucky. My mother was a maid in a rich merchant's house. He offered to sponsor my secondary education in a good boarding school. My poor mother didn't know how to react to the offer. She was happy about my good fortune. On the other hand, she was sad because she would be able to see me only once in a while. I wanted to be successful. Akila, I wanted to succeed in life more than I wanted food and water."

"Was your father willing to send you away?"

"We never found out, Akila. That's another incident I can't forget. He wasn't alive to see my progress."

"What happened?"

"A few fishermen brought my father's body to my house," his voice broke. "Apparently, the waves felt that it was a fair trade to confiscate his life as a payment for all the fish they had offered him over many years. I was only eleven then." How could Raja explain the pain he felt when he cremated the frame of his father? How could he describe the tears that sloshed his soul within his frame?

"Don't say anymore. It must be painful to think about such a past!" Akila said compassionately.

"That's all right. I can't tell you how relieved I am to talk about it. When I was worried about our family's future, my mother sat by me and offered the best advice. She asked me to study as though my life depended on the words in my textbooks. Her worst fear was that I might become a fisherman like my father. I promised my mother that I would do everything possible to have an education and a good, respectable life."

"What happened after that?" asked Akila.

"Occasionally, my benefactor's wife filled my hungry stomach with several kinds of nameless food. I didn't understand why she made me eat in the garden when her family ate inside the house. Akila, once I understood that my inferior caste was the reason for this exclusive seating, I avoided eating the wealthy lady's food."

"I'm so sorry," said Akila.

"I was also sorry, but that lady's discrimination motivated me to do well in life. My benefactor was generous and kind. My education would have been impossible without his sponsorship. He is solely responsible for my current financial situation. He showed me the key to success, Akila. Education! Education gave me freedom—freedom from poverty, freedom from indentured service, freedom from a low social status. That's why I would do anything to educate a child. There were times when I felt awkward about taking unlimited financial assistance from that generous man. How was I to repay his extraordinary kindness? He laughed at my concern and told me that I owed him nothing. He said that I could repay him when I grew up—by giving to the poor what I had received as a young boy."

"And you do, don't you? What would Mercy House do without your constant assistance? I'm happy for your happiness," Akila said, smiling in pride.

"Thank you," Raja said gratefully. "My sponsor had everything in life except children. He left a good portion of his property in my name. My life changed just as my mother had wished. And I held on to my education. Akila, it became the cord of my life."

Akila understood Raja's obsession regarding caste and education. His account moved her. It touched her and asserted her faith in a man, a remarkable man, who was worthy of her respect, affection, and regard.

Akila was determined to do something useful with her leisure. Her unassuming nature assisted her in enlisting some women to help her with worthwhile assignments to benefit the community. She was not shy to knock on a few doors. A few were willing to follow Akila's direction. The list didn't include that staunch matron, Vasanthi's former employer. The bougainvillea-covered home sheltered a cold, narrow-minded woman, and Akila's efforts might not be sufficient to change her attitude. It was all right. Akila was not on a worldwide mission.

As a result of small endeavors, there were fewer useless conversations between fences. This was significant progress for Kanyakoil. The contributions were not colossal, but the efforts and the congenial attitude of the women were. And when Akila hosted a gathering, her list of invitees included the important, the unimportant, the famous, and the unknown.

Akila's community service stopped abruptly. Raja wrote to Sister Mary to announce that his wife was pregnant.

"I can't tell you how delighted I am, Akila," said Raja, happily. "I hope we have a daughter. Akila, Ram wrote again. He really wants me to move to Singapore with our family. I'm not so sure. You know, at my age, to go into a new field and invest in business … what do you think?" Raja asked his wife.

"You know best," said Akila. She didn't want to be more than a few miles away from Mercy House and Brinda. Still … he knew best.

Akila delivered a baby girl. The delighted parents named her Tara. The proud father ordered baby products from an exclusive boutique in Madras, and he left the baby's nursery in charge of a costly interior designer. No part of the arrangement was left in a simple tone. The princess had arrived.

Raja's friend, Ram, came from Singapore to spend a few days with Raja's family. He brought his wife with him during this occasion. He had come to India on business, and he was delighted to see the new baby. And Raja delighted in the glory of his only female child. She was his angel. During dinner, Ram expressed his wish once again to take Raja as his business partner. Raja thought about it. He wasn't under financial worries. He wasn't tired of his career either. No, he wasn't eager to go to Singapore.

◆ ◆ ◆

Akila took her baby from the servant's hands. She felt a new love and pride. Motherhood was extraordinary. Baby Tara brought a lot of happiness in the once vacant life of her mother. Every action of the baby cemented the purpose in her mother's life. If Raja's affection and attention opened a blossom in her heart, her daughter's presence filled it with fragrance. Akila had always chased a dream before her marriage and motherhood. Now the dream was in her hands. Akila had never seen her father. She had a vague memory of her mother. In Tara, she saw a little life that reflected the joys of loving.

"Tara, would you like to receive Joanie?" Akila asked the baby and took her to the hall where the guest was waiting.

The baby's smile delighted the guest. Akila took Joanie to the veranda to enjoy the November breeze. Joanie loved to visit Brinda. She was in need of a cup of tea and some sympathy during this visit.

"Akila, I'll never be tired of sitting in your veranda," said Joanie, luxuriously. "I can almost hear the river from here."

"I'm glad you like it. How have you been?"

"You were always a good young lady, Akila," said Joanie, affectionately. "You still are. Some of the girls don't even spend a few moments to talk to me. This is the problem with this generation! The young women think they are too good to make time for the old."

Akila smiled. Joanie was a conscientious supervisor. She didn't understand that her mother-hen attitude irritated everybody. True, a lot of girls in the hostel avoided her. Poor soul! She wanted to help. Unfortunately, her natural curiosity camouflaged her good intentions. Selvi had once said that Joanie's inquisitive nature, bordering on impertinence, turned her advice to gibberish.

Joanie was lately in the habit of singing in praise of Akila. There was good reason for her heartfelt approbation. Mercy House had been the only world Akila had known until she became an adult. Now she thought about St. Teresa's hospital that had kept her fed and the nurse's hostel that had allowed her to live in modest independence until she got married. Joanie was thrilled when Akila approached her to form a team to execute whatever improvements she thought were necessary.

Joanie continued to praise Akila during lunch. "Now, that's charity! Not a bit of kind deed here and a slice of good work there. All our Akila thinks about is the welfare of others. Isn't that nice, my dear?" Joanie asked a nurse. "She's like an army of rain clouds, just what our community needs."

Mercy House was growing out of bounds. The present orphanage was converted to a temporary shelter called Helping Hands, and it was dedicated to homeless adults. A small addition was established to provide a home for women. Akila named this haven Selvi Nilayam, and it became a crisis center for women. About a couple of kilometers from Brinda, Raja built a new Mercy House. Akila remembered to share her good fortune with a good soul, an unselfish soul—Mary. Raja was glad to begin improvements in Sister Mary's convent. When Akila rejoiced in the welfare and progress around Mercy House, she thought longingly of her dear Aunt Aruna. If only she could see the prospects that were surrounding the orphanage! Akila's heart was filled with gratitude for her husband's kindness and pride for his generosity. Aruna was dearly missed, but her wish was fulfilled. Her children were in excellent hands.

Occasionally, a snide remark about Akila's past or Raja's newfound status reached Akila's ears or caught Raja's attention. Thankfully, this didn't occur often, and the collector and his wife ignored the insults. They thought of their good fortune, good friends, and their blessings.

Akila, from time to time, worried about raising her daughter in that narrow-minded environment. "Do you think we should accept Ram's offer and move to Singapore?" Akila voiced her concern to her husband. "Why don't we move from here?"

"Akila, I wouldn't worry about a few jealous people and their criticisms. If I feel any concern about Tara's future, I'll start packing that night. Don't worry," Raja comforted his wife.

Since her husband was more practical about dealing with such situations, Akila decided to forget her worries.

Akila sealed the lengthy letter she had just finished writing. Her daughter and the daughter's routine had occupied her moments. It was a very happy family. Raja's sons visited during the holidays, and the entire town talked about how blessed the Rajas were. Wealth and generosity never walked hand in hand as well as they did here. Akila was the mother of a young girl now, but she felt privileged to be the mother of four. Raja's sons were truly happy to receive Akila into their lives. She loved them. Particularly, the youngest boy, Anand, was very affectionate.

"Akila, you have visitors," said Raja, while she was finishing another letter.

"I'm coming. Are you ready to leave?" Akila asked.

"I'll be late from work, my dear. I have an afternoon meeting in Coimbatore. You know, some women are waiting patiently to see you. They're in the hall."

It was the new committee for—what was it for? Lately, her volunteer missions had been too many and too crowded. She went downstairs to greet her visitors.

After the women left, a gentleman arrived. Lionel Stevens was back with his pen and paper. He wished to write an article for *The Express* about the social developments in Kanyakoil! He appeared more mature during this visit. Akila welcomed him warmly. The main section of the article went something like this ...

"Kanyakoil, nestled among orchards and streams in the southeast regions of the country, is seeing mammoth improvements—socially and economically. Mr. Raja, the collector, and Mrs. Raja have nurtured the community.

Tara Trust has placed underprivileged women in shelters. In addition, it has established adult classes to teach skills to women to be self-sufficient. Many disadvantaged children have been placed in schools with secure meal plans. The Rajas' goal is to eradicate child labor.

Selvi Nilayam is a home for women. It has become a crisis center for women who need a shelter to survive. Domestic violence is no longer accepted as a parcel of marriage. It is not destiny that allows a woman to be physically and verbally abused. It is the unquestioned gumption and barbaric attitude of certain men. "Marriages are made in heaven. Take what is offered to you," wouldn't be a household mantra anymore. A woman in a dire crisis can find security, food, and compassion in Selvi Nilayam. Mrs. Raja wishes to help vulnerable women across the nation. These women die everyday as a result of being burned, strangled, or tossed into the waves because their parents can't afford to pay infinite installments of dowry!

The Rajas feel that the progress in Kanyakoil is in its infant stages. They hope that such modest developments would form a bridge to a seventh heaven. Kanyakoil should be proud for standing out as an exemplary town."

This new, happy life of Akila collapsed when her little daughter came home with tears in her eyes.

"What happened, Tara?" asked Akila. "Didn't you enjoy your friend's birthday party?"

"No, Amma," cried Tara. "Her grandmother made me sit in the veranda when the other children were playing inside the house."

"Why? What's the matter, Tara?"

"Because," explained Tara, through a fit of crying. "We are low caste, Amma."

How could that woman be so cruel? Akila comforted Tara and tucked her in her bed for a nap. When she came down, she was surprised to see the birthday girl's mother in the hall.

"Akila, I came to apologize," said her friend, in tears. "My mother-in-law showed up suddenly. I was in the kitchen when the children went to the hall to play. I didn't see that … Tara was left in the veranda. Please forgive me."

Akila appreciated her friend's good manners. She was kind. Unfortunately, she was under her formidable mother-in-law's control. Although Akila was extremely hurt by Tara's wounded dignity, she thanked her friend for her thoughtful apology.

When her father came home in the evening, Tara demanded his attention. "You're a big man, Appa. You're the collector, aren't you?" said Tara, crying again. "Make them stop saying bad things about our family. Tell them it's not true."

Raja took his daughter into his arms. Tara wanted him to do something he could not. Her wish sprouted from an innocent concept, a childish belief, that her father must be placed among high-caste gentlemen because of his position in the community. She equated status with caste. She was too young to realize that her childish heart misled her. Raja was willing to perform any feat to please his daughter, but how could he rewrite his birth? Although he knew that his inferior caste couldn't be wiped out, he had wished that its poisonous power wouldn't grip his dear daughter's dignity. An aborted wish! At least, his sons were kept away from the harmful bites of the caste system because they were in the boarding school for a good portion of the year. He wondered if he should send Tara to such a school. How could he? She was too young to be sent away.

"Akila," said Raja. "This isn't unexpected. I had wished ..."

"I know. I wished for the same thing too," said Akila, unhappily. "This is outrageous."

Understandably, this unhappy incident in Tara's young life triggered a sense of uncertainty in her parents' future plans. Such uncertainty also strengthened Akila's apprehension about raising her daughter in Kanyakoil where Akila's life as an orphan and her husband's backward caste would never be ignored.

"Akila, the people are not going to accept us," said Raja. "Tara would be scoffed and insulted for our shortcomings."

"There is no doubt. The past is going to ruin our daughter's happiness."

Raja made a decision. He sent a cable to Ram. After receiving a favorable reply from him, Raja sent his letter of resignation to his superiors. He was moving to Singapore with his family. His eldest son was already placed in a good college in Madras. He collected his younger sons from the boarding school. Raja was not one to run away from problems. His successful life, despite the obstacles in his youth, was a tribute to his endurance and determination. But this incident that hurt and humiliated his dear child triggered an enormous disgust in his powerful demeanor, and he decided to quit the suffocating community. Brinda! What were they supposed to do with it? Akila could have sold it, but she wouldn't, not in her lifetime. Raja asked his lawyer to lease it for a few years.

Mary arrived as soon as she heard the disturbing news. "Mr. Raja, could this sudden burst of criticism of your caste be a passing whim of a few people?" Mary asked, hoping it really was a passing whim of the society. "Many have been supportive to your family, haven't they?"

"I agree, Sister. Akila and I acknowledge the kindness of our friends. But we're weary of the talk," Raja said. "I can't let these people affect my daughter's future. Surely, you can understand that?"

"Yes, Mr. Raja, I understand."

Akila's farewell to Humsa and Sivam was not something she would wish to repeat. They were a part of an exceptional time in her life, an affectionate segment of her childhood. Akila had planned on taking care of this compassionate couple during their autumn years, and now ...

"Sivam, Humsa, the orphanage won't be closed," assured Raja. "I'll make sure of that. You can count on our support."

While Sivam concealed his grief behind his customary smile, Humsa found comfort in uncontrollable tears. "Akila, although I miss Aruna—and I'll always miss her—I've felt some consolation in seeing you, my dear. You've always been a shadow of my Aruna. Now …" Humsa couldn't continue her grief-stricken farewell.

"I promise. I'll visit all of you frequently," said Akila, holding Humsa's hand. "Believe me, I won't forget you."

Raja assured Sister Mary, Samuel, Sivam, and Humsa that he would stand by his wife's promise.

Joanie's unhappiness at the news was another story. No more tea and sympathy in that stately hall or in the cozy veranda! With many words of affection and several whispers of caution, she offered her farewell.

Akila had given her love and a precious part of her life to the village like unselfish monsoon. She had arrived like gentle rain, had grown to a torrential downpour, and now … she was sneaking away like a furtive drop of rain. She had nothing more to give. Encouraged by her happiness with her husband and her family, Akila had thought that she saw the dawn that was elusive to Buvana and Aruna. It was, after all, an illusion. Akila was glad that she had a glimpse of it—with blemishes and empty, gawky gaps—a tempting glimpse. Now it was Akila's turn to wait for the perfect dawn.

PART IV
Predestined Dreams

Tara's summer moments, at the end of her college days, were tied to a few 'select a bride' episodes that were deliberately arranged by her parents. Her ancestral home, Brinda, welcomed a few guests in honor of this unpleasant event.

"Tara," Akila stopped her daughter on her tracks early in the afternoon. "Go upstairs and get ready."

"Do I have to? Amma, how many times are you planning to display me?"

"Hush, Tara," said Akila. "What a mouth you have! Please get ready."

Same old scenery! Tara saw the silk sari and jewelry on the dresser. "Amma, this is a horrible custom! The prospective bride is displayed like a piece of property. A well-groomed idiot arrives with his entourage. The visitors eat till their stomachs burst, take a good look at the girl, and promise to send a letter in a week or two."

"Tara, you must understand …"

"If the deal is on," continued Tara, "the families meet again to draw a marriage settlement—a huge dowry in cash, land, and gold."

"Tara, are you finished? Why are you determined to drive me crazy?" asked Akila, quite frustrated. "How are we supposed to find a husband for you?"

"All right, Amma. If I feel humiliated again, I shall never get married. Well?" Tara asked her mother.

"Okay," said Akila.

Tara got ready. She could have written the outcome of this episode even before the guests arrived. The guests ate, laughed, and wondered why none of Akila's family was present when Raja's family members were actively involved. After a few moments of silence, Akila mentioned that she didn't have siblings because … The laughter stopped. After a feeble promise of a letter or a phone call, the guests left. There would be no letter. Her family should know that by now. Either Raja's low caste or Akila's homeless past nagged the family's peace of mind. Tara walked upstairs to avoid her parents.

When Tara finished high school in Singapore, her parents sent her to India, to a reputed women's college in Madras. By then, Raja was ready to return to India. He wanted to spend his autumn years in the land that had brought him prosperity and joy earlier. He moved to India with his wife. He decided to stay temporarily in Brinda. He had his eyes on an estate situated in the hilly village that was located an hour from Kanyakoil and wished to purchase it.

Raja and Akila had discussed the best way to find a young man for Tara. They decided on Kanyakoil for various reasons. This was a town that had more amenities than Raja's prospective estate. Further, they had a few friends here. Lastly, the tone of Brinda—it was in Akila's name. It was to be left for Tara in due course. It seemed to be a good choice. Tara didn't agree with her parents. She knew the circumstances under which her parents had planned their migration to Singapore. Because people talked! Then, why did her parents choose Brinda as a perfect place to settle their daughter's future? Raja and Akila were convinced that the society didn't preserve its idiosyncrasies from a couple of decades ago. They had maintained communication with a few good friends during the years they were away, and the correspondence conveyed the impression of a non-judgmental community. Further, they had seen a pleasant society during their visits to Kanyakoil.

The young housekeeper found Tara on the balcony.

"You're Bitsy, aren't you?" Tara asked, forgetting her humiliation. "I like your name. Is it short for …?"

"Yes, Miss, my name is Elizabeth. That's why it's Bitsy, Miss. I'm glad you like my name, Miss. I hope you also like me," Bitsy said, giggling.

That's what caught Tara's attention—Bitsy's effervescent disposition. Her chubby cheeks, sparkling eyes, and an ample frame completed a cheerful ensemble. "Well, I think I should like you on one condition," said Tara. "You must stop calling me Miss. I'm Tara."

"Okay, Miss. Oh, sorry, Tara, please come down for supper," Bitsy was giggling again, but her smile turned to a frown at the hurt look on Tara's face.

"I'm not hungry, Bitsy," said Tara. "I'm not going downstairs. I would like to go to bed."

Bitsy knew why. Tara must feel ashamed of the afternoon's incident. She felt sorry for Tara. But she couldn't force her to eat. She decided to report the situation to her mistress.

Tara felt bad about sending Bitsy away like that. She hardly knew her. Akila had recently hired Bitsy to manage domestic affairs in Brinda. Since Tara was attending college in Madras, she didn't meet Bitsy until she came to Kanyakoil.

Akila fixed a tray for Tara and went to her room. Raja followed her.

"Tara, I understand your humiliation," said Akila. "Please don't cry."

Tara's tears moved Raja. Was Kanyakoil a bad choice? Akila coerced Tara to eat a little.

"Does it matter—who raised my mother?" asked Tara, "and how long are we supposed to be chained to the useless, worthless bondage of castes?"

Her parents didn't reply.

"Appa, why did you bring us to India?" Tara asked her father. "Isn't it time to liberate our minds from useless beliefs and traditions?"

"Our only wish is to see you settled in a good marriage, a happy marriage, with a promise of prosperity," said Raja.

"See, your generation still thinks that marriage is a girl's salvation! Do you think those spineless men, who come to gawk at me and at Brinda, are going to offer me happiness?" Tara asked.

"Tara, you're talking in your father's presence!" Akila scolded her daughter.

Raja waved his hand to silence his wife.

"Tara," said Raja. "What do you propose as an alternative to the traditional 'girl seeing' system? I'm willing to consider your suggestions."

"Why can't I find a man?" asked Tara. She knew what her father's reply would be. Still, she just had to ask.

"Tara, be serious. You have to honor traditions and ..." began Raja.

"All right. In that case, please let me work," Tara pleaded, "please let me go to Madras and work for a while."

"A young lady in your status can't work for somebody," replied Raja, with a note of finality.

"Why can't I work?" Tara asked. "Then, why did you send me to college?"

"To get an education, a resource you could use in case of an emergency," said Raja. "Please don't argue."

"You worked, Amma, didn't you?" Tara looked at her mother for support. "You were a nurse."

"That was different, Tara. She had to survive," said Raja.

The father often replied on behalf of the mother. Tara thought that it was useless to talk anymore about this matter. Her mother never refuted her husband's opinion. However, Tara was determined not to give up.

"I sat through some insulting afternoons to please both of you," said Tara. "I need a break from this, at least for a short while."

The parents agreed to this suggestion.

Akila stretched her tired feet on the swing and gazed at the ceiling. Tara was right. She should go to work or get involved in something that her heart desired. Akila felt sorry for justifying her nursing career. Yes, it was her meal ticket until she got married. Her husband was perfectly right. Still, it hurt. She felt bitter. A strange pain started to nag her.

The huge photograph of Aruna, the founder of Mercy House, fascinated Tara. She liked to visit the orphanage. Here, she could laugh with the children and make some use of her time. She was bored at Brinda. She was tired of her mother's friends from the Rotary club and her father's friends' tireless debates on politicians and their latest atrocities. Whenever Tara entered the common room at Mercy House, Aruna's photograph arrested her attention. Every time Tara studied the face, she looked at something new.

Aruna must have had plenty of courage to live alone among an intimidating clan—a community with rigid traditions. Akila talked about Aruna very often. In fact, she had talked about old times that morning during breakfast. Tara, although initially intrigued, was irritated by her mother's view of Brinda and the society's reaction to an independent Aruna.

"Tara," Akila had started again. "Aunt Aruna gave me a decent life, education, and a means to support myself until I got married. She generously left Brinda to me, and she gave me the status of a daughter. When I was a young girl, she wanted to adopt me."

"Why didn't she?"

"Tara, Aunt Aruna didn't go through the adoption process because she was single. Think about the society. It wasn't a wise idea, Tara, especially for the child! It still isn't a good idea."

"Society!" exclaimed Tara, disgusted.

"Tara, Aunt Aruna treated me as her child and I couldn't have wished for a better mother. That's why I love Brinda. It's a part of Aunt Aruna. There was a time when Brinda was in danger of slipping into strangers' hands and the orphanage was about to collapse," Akila continued to reminisce. "But my marriage, your father's generosity, had kept Mercy House alive and had turned Brinda into a home again."

It was clear that Akila shared Aruna's sentiments. Tara was sometimes a little annoyed by her mother's perception of Brinda. It was not merely a building. It breathed, it cried, and it laughed. Akila's sentiments regarding Brinda were none of Tara's business. After all, she didn't grow up in that house or in that town. She didn't think much of anything in Kanyakoil. Well, Mercy House was an exception.

Tara took leave of the group of children at Mercy House and started to walk toward Brinda. Her mother's marriage was something she never understood.

Most marriages were arranged for convenience in her confined sphere. Her mother, however, had a different experience. Her father had asked her to marry him. But Tara didn't see a lot of love between her parents. She saw a sense of peace, mutual respect, friendly understanding. She also felt that her mother treated her husband with a great degree of reverence that was somehow out of tune in a husband-wife relationship. It was a kind of reverence that fostered a subservient attitude on her mother's part—not that her father encouraged this attitude, but he didn't seem to discourage it. Tara didn't want to be trapped in such a marriage.

What kind of marriage had destiny designed for her—happy, boring, spicy, or stuffy? The marriage search had been insulting until now! All young ladies, whose mothers were orphans at one time, didn't necessarily suffer premarital insults that Tara experienced. Well, those girls didn't have fathers and mothers who expected a high-budget marriage and an even higher-budget son-in-law. Raja didn't want an average man to marry his precious daughter! He was looking for stature, education, and a sizable bank balance in his future son-in-law. He neglected to consider the fact that such a young man, with commendable attributes, might have his own expectations. And what about such a young man's parents and their expectations?

When Tara returned from the orphanage, her mother met her in the veranda and ushered her to the backyard. "Tara," Akila said. "You'll never believe what happened. Where have you been, anyway? Always scampering about! You must get ready right now. Go to your room. Bitsy is there."

"Amma, get ready for what? What's going on?"

"A family has come to see you—not the usual kind—this young man shows a lot of promise," Akila smiled rather nervously. "Tara, he has a good job offer in his pocket. He is a young man from a nice family. The matchmaker says a lot of good things about him. Tara, remember your father said that this young man follows Gandhi's principles and … and wishes to marry against caste restrictions."

"Gandhi's principles? The matchmaker will say anything to make money. What does he know?" Tara asked, frustrated and angry. "Didn't I make a deal with you and appa that I'm not to be displayed as a showpiece? Didn't you agree to that deal?" Tara spoke in a loud voice. They were upstairs by now.

"Bitsy, get Tara ready," said Akila. She ran out of the room before Tara could protest.

"Tara, why don't you give this young man a chance?" Bitsy asked. "You'll never know if he is nice or not, whether he looks like a monkey or if he is handsome, until you see him and talk to him."

"Talk to him? They won't let me talk to him, Bitsy. It's not allowed before marriage."

When Tara went downstairs to perform her duty, she was surprised to find a pleasant family. His mother smiled. His father smiled agreeably at the entire arrangement. His sister, Seetha, invited her to sit by her. Tara looked at his face. He didn't look like a monkey. He smiled. She looked away because she was shy. Raja introduced his daughter to the guest of honor, Gopal.

"Why don't we let Gopal and Tara go to the veranda and talk a little?" Gopal's mother offered this suggestion.

Akila looked stunned. Raja looked shocked. The matchmaker looked confused. Tara didn't know where to look. This was an unprecedented suggestion.

"They are Delhi people. It's not unusual," the matchmaker whispered in Raja's ear.

After a brief consultation, Raja gave Tara permission to talk to Gopal in privacy.

"Miss … Tara," Gopal said, after a few moments of silence. "I'm pleased to meet you. I'm sorry that you have to sit through such customs."

Gopal was a handsome man with wavy hair, an aristocratic nose, and gentle eyes. He had a pleasant voice. He enchanted her with his measured speech. He wanted to know what she liked and disliked. How was she to tell about her life in a nutshell and discover all that was there to know about him in a few minutes? Their conversation stirred a pleasant melody. She didn't want it to end.

"I'm planning to accept my first assignment in Delhi. Would you be able to live in the north, so far away from your parents?" he asked.

Did he really want her opinion? She bit her tongue at her skepticism, but she couldn't help it. Habit! While her heart urged her to trust his sentiments, her mind cautioned her to be wary of his open-minded attitude. Tara made up her mind. She smiled in response to his generosity! She could find no words.

"I hope you offer me a favorable reply," he said, smiling congenially.

There was that smile again. She liked him. She could think of a day when she might grow fond of him. "You're a well-educated and sensible woman. Just open your mouth and ask him something!" prompted Tara's heart. She found her voice to ask him a couple of questions. The conversation turned to music, movies, and books.

"So, how is it going?" asked Seetha, interrupting the cool December breeze by walking into the veranda.

It was going well, of course. Unfortunately, the pleasant meeting must end. This unexpected joy, mixed with apprehension and suspense, drove Tara crazy. The visitors left with a promise of a phone call. Tara was certain that they would call. Her heart whispered that he would call. He did.

Gopal's father wrote a letter to Raja to ask if his son could visit Tara again.

Gopal and Tara had another opportunity to talk.

"Tara, I wanted to listen to your voice one more time," Gopal confessed.

Tara talked more during this occasion, but when she looked back, nothing she said made any sense to her. Gopal might have come to listen to Tara's voice again, but it wouldn't hurt his eyes to feast on her face. Tara was extraordinarily beautiful. Her classic features dazzled in a trendy, modern flair. She was wispy, delicate, and she carried herself like an elegant model. She held her hair in a sophisticated ponytail or a loose braid. Her fair skin enhanced the beautifully shaped eyebrows and the dark, almond-shaped eyes.

Bitsy came to the veranda. She apologized through her giggles and wondered if she could obtain a list of Gopal's favorite dishes.

Gopal walked with Tara along the banks of the river. The enchanted bride-to-be tried to ignore a few people, familiar faces, walking about twenty feet behind them. They were incidentally taking a stroll, and their leisurely walk had nothing to do with Tara and Gopal! And Tara was supposed to believe this? Was there really a need for chaperones? Well, she tried to focus on Gopal's words and his smiles. He brought a couple of albums and a few books for his fiancée. He remembered her favorite choices in music and reading. How thoughtful! He gave her a sizable diamond, set in a ring of dazzling gold, to seal their engagement. It was a very happy day!

Raja demanded a little of his future son-in-law's time. Although Gopal was against dowry and such degrading traditions, some formalities had to be addressed. Later, Raja bragged about his future son-in-law to his wife and daughter. Gopal had fulfilled Raja's expectations of a proper son-in-law—a handsome, educated, and cultured son-in-law. What about a wealthy son-in-law? Well, Gopal was reasonably rich, but not as wealthy as their dear Tara. Raja held the winning cards in financial matters, and this fact was essential in boosting his morale.

◆ ◆ ◆

Brinda was filled with guests. All of Raja's sons attended the wedding with their families to bless their little sister on the most auspicious day of her life. Tara was especially glad to see her brother, Anand, on this very happy day.

The guests were enthralled while touring the silver display, which was outshined by the gold collection. The ladies whispered that they had not seen some of the new shades of silk saris that were ordered from Kancheepuram. No wonder, they were specially designed for Tara. Although Gopal insisted on a simple ceremony, he was touched when he received a very expensive, imported car as a special gift from his loving in-laws.

The wedding party left by train the next morning. Raja had purchased two first-class tickets for his daughter and son-in-law to enjoy their honeymoon in London. They were to take a flight from Madras. As happy as Akila and Raja were to see their daughter's glorious wedding, they said their goodbyes with hearts heavier than the gold that was carefully packed in Tara's trunk!

Tara entered her in-law's home anxiously after her honeymoon. Her anxiety seemed groundless because Gopal's parents were very polite and easygoing. The entire family sat at the long dinner table and exchanged conversations with ease and friendliness. They were unlike the traditional families of Kanyakoil. Tara, although a little nervous, was a little happy.

The mother-in-law's friends sprouted from various clubs and neighborhoods to welcome the new bride. The Delhi socialites marveled at her beauty and praised her collection of clothing and jewelry. They invited her for tea and fought in line to be Tara's first hostess. Although Tara was touched by the attention, she felt the need for some air. She also wanted to spend some time alone with her husband.

It is common to find a hitch in a bride's new family. In Tara's case, it was Gopal's sister, Seetha. How could one describe her? Well, she was omnipresent. Gopal and his parents invited Seetha to live with them whenever her husband was away on business. Tara, out of careful upbringing and courtesy, tolerated her sister-in-law's interference that was gradually turning to impertinence. Seetha dominated everybody. She was her mother's guru. Gopal's father simply blended with the walls and the furniture. Gopal had no voice in his family. He looked at Tara in sympathy. Then ... why wouldn't he support her? When confronted by Tara, he declared that his hands were tied. Gopal was sensible, educated, and didn't lack common sense. Why did he look at his sister or mother to clarify every stupid question? He seemed incapable of making any decision on his own. In other words, the honeymoon was over.

Seetha had every reason to seek her parents' hospitality, but she had no right to be bossy. Tara needed her husband's support and cooperation at such times. She didn't receive any. She hardly knew her husband. Was she ever going to understand him? What did she mean to him? Did he wish to know her at all beyond the walls of this house and the confines of his family?

The first gathering at home opened Tara's eyes to her current, rather confusing and uncomfortable situation. A reception was arranged in honor of the married couple. A number of important guests were to attend, and Tara received her sister-in-law's instructions. Seetha suggested the choice of sari and jewelry.

"Tara, one more thing," Seetha continued to lecture. "Don't mention your caste, I mean … your father's caste. And if someone asks about your mother's family, tell them she is from Singapore. You do understand, don't you? We have a status to maintain."

Tara understood! If her mother supposedly came from Singapore, the guests wouldn't probe into her family's background. After all, how many people knew enough about Singapore and its families? Not many. On the other hand, 'Kanyakoil' could mean some damage to Akila's reputation. Seetha was extraordinarily inconsiderate. Why should Tara concoct such stories? What about her in-laws' magnanimity regarding castes and such discriminations? Weren't they supposed to be beyond such nonsense? What happened to Gandhi's principles now?

Tara longed for home. She never thought that she would miss Kanyakoil. Of all the things, she missed visiting Mercy House. She began to think affectionately of Kanyakoil and Brinda, nestled among dense orchards and welcoming streams.

Tara felt alone—all alone in a big city, filled with traffic, noise, and routine. She wished to get away from the confining flat for a few hours everyday. Why not find a job? Tara informed Gopal that she was going to apply for one. He, unexpectedly, took this information as her request for his permission!

"Go to work, Tara?" he shouted. "No. It wouldn't look nice if my wife worked like a commoner. Anyway, we're not poor, are we?"

"What do you mean by commoner?" Tara asked. "We're not royalty."

"Tara, be serious. Am I not a good provider? There is no need to work."

True. They were not in need of money. Tara received a significant allowance from her savings. This, in addition to her husband's salary, allowed them to live in very comfortable circumstances.

"Quite a few women from well-to-do families work these days, especially in a big city like Delhi, don't they?" asked Tara.

Gopal took a long look at his wife's downcast face. "Tara, my dear, are you unhappy?" Gopal asked, lifting her face to look into her eyes.

"No. I'm not unhappy," replied Tara. Just now, at this moment, she saw a glimpse of the young man, the considerate man, who spoke of sweet nothings in the flower-filled garden of Brinda. But that glimpse disappeared when the next few words trickled out of his mouth.

"All you need to do is dress beautifully, show your pretty face, and talk sensibly, whenever your presence is required in a gathering. Go out to work! What a crazy thought!" said Gopal.

Tara got used to becoming part of the furniture collection from that day—appropriate dress, polished face, cheery disposition, and mannequin display!

Tara was trying to get some beauty sleep for another evening party—her mother-in-law's suggestion! Her eyes focused on the painting on the opposite wall. It was a scene of dusky Brinda, shrouded in subdued moonlight, dressed by a sprinkle of stars. Seetha asked Tara not to reveal Aruna's identity if any of the friends enquired about the artist. What kind of secrecy were they supposed to hide? What were they ashamed of? What were Akila and her guardian, Aruna, supposed to be guilty of?

All in a night's dream ... gone in a day's dream.

Tara was a little unhappy in her marriage. Gopal's family, however, was very happy in the selection of the daughter-in-law. Tara's initial 'free spirit' seemed to disappear to make room for a more family-oriented woman. Tara was educated, but she didn't flaunt her intelligence. She was glamorous, but she appeared modestly beautiful. She listened more and spoke less. She was shaping very well into an ideal female member of the family.

Gopal's parents might not have picked Tara solely for her father's wealth. However, it had a great deal to do with the selection process of the daughter-in-law. Gopal's parents belonged to a modern society that frowned at caste-conscious families. It was quite fashionable to be more liberal about traditions. Gopal was a young, shrewd employee of the government. He had a very extensive career plan. Politically, it would work in his favor if he chose a wife from a low caste. It would certainly make him appear as a gentleman who followed Gandhi's principles on equality of castes. If Gopal had to compromise on caste, who said that he had to compromise on wealth also? Accordingly, Tara's resume looked very impressive when the matchmaker approached Gopal's family. Tara was a young woman of education, beauty, and considerable fortune. If she had belonged to an upper-caste family, her portfolio would have been perfectly complete. In that case, a young man with brighter prospects than Gopal's would have married Tara quite a while ago. The fact that she came from a low caste, supported by her advantageous attributes, made her a desirable choice in the eyes of Gopal's family.

Raja and Akila called Tara frequently to make sure that she was happy. Tara told them that she was happy. She had considerate in-laws, a comfortable home, and a carefree life. Was she happy? Gopal was kind. His family was courteous. But it didn't mean that Tara was captured in a joyous married life. Tara realized that she had seen a fleeting vision of a happy prospect in her future with Gopal. It was a mirage, merely a dream, something she mistook for reality. Undiluted happiness in married life happened by chance. Tara remembered, with a touch of shame, her conversation with her mother about marriages, equality, and happiness. Akila had said that she never wished for an equitable marriage. Her understanding of marriage was very different from Tara's. Akila knew that she was happy and she would always be. She had a good point. Who was Tara to force her mother to redesign her idea of matrimony? Perhaps, all said and done, happiness in marriage was a state of mind!

It was not a bad life. Seasons came and went. Seetha came and went. Guests came and went. Tara thought that Seetha came more than she went! That was Seetha. Her two boys, the only grandchildren of Gopal's parents, were especially welcome in that home.

Tara was still childless! When she couldn't bear a child after three years of marriage, her mother-in-law sighed a lot. One miscarriage followed another. Tara was sad, and Gopal's parents were disappointed. Did Tara's family have a deficiency? Several doctors—from homeopathy to gynecology—diagnosed Tara's condition. Gopal's mother took Tara to astrologers and palmists. A list of remedies came in Tara's way that included—but not limited to—herbal miracles, lucky Gods, fertility Goddesses, and popular temples.

"Why don't we adopt?" Tara asked Gopal. "We can give a needy child a home and love. How about a child from Mercy House? That would be my dearest desire."

"Tara, we can't adopt," said Gopal, angry at his wife's sudden, drastic solution to solve the baby issue. "We're not as desperate as that! Anyway, you're not so old that you have to worry about becoming pregnant, and even if you are, my family doesn't have the mentality to welcome an orphan. I'm going to withhold this information from Seetha and my parents. They'll be very sad to hear this."

This was the seventies. Still, inability to bear children was considered an imperfection in a woman! Another idiosyncrasy of their judgmental society! Well, he was honest about it. She was sad to hear it. Tara had one consolation at the end of this futile discussion. She was glad that Gopal was not going to run to his parents, crying over Tara's suggestion of adoption. The last thing she needed now was an awkward scene. And she would do anything to avoid Seetha's disapproval and droning lecture.

During the fourth year of marriage, Gopal's manager promoted him and sent him to Kenya. Tara was eager to go with her husband to a distant land. She hoped that the distance between her husband and his dominating family would allow him to be reasonably independent. She also hoped that a little private moment might bring him closer to her.

The new home was certainly charming. The lengthy verandas and breezy backyards spoke so well of a different air. Tara was right. Gopal changed a little. He listened to her. He was considerate. It was like a honeymoon—a few years after their marriage—nevertheless, a honeymoon! She had a conversation with him, and he seemed to care about her opinion on little nothings. Major decisions, however, were still his domain. That didn't upset Tara. She might handle major decisions over time. For now, she was content to feel his affection, sense his closeness, and cherish his smiles. They began to have a relationship after four years of marriage.

A new set of social connections began through The India Association. Unfortunately, Tara was not thrilled about the acquaintances. She had invitations for luncheons and tea, which she accepted with little enthusiasm. She reciprocated the invitations with even less enthusiasm. None of the women appealed to her. Was she getting cranky and picky? The women were conservative and boring. They expected Tara to be conservative and boring. She refused to be. She took long walks and buried her face in any book to avoid conservative and boring. But she couldn't entirely avoid the phone calls and luncheons.

Gopal, however, encouraged her to hold on to their new acquaintances. "Tara, some of the husbands hold very important positions in the community," said Gopal. "Some even have strong political affiliations in India. It's essential for me to maintain certain connections."

Tara had to oblige. She received an invitation from The International Women's Association. She was happy to meet Fiona Masterson, an educator from Oxford. She was here to establish curriculum in the local schools. While Tara enjoyed Fiona's company, Fiona enjoyed masala chai and onion pakoras in Tara's veranda. Fiona didn't summarily dismiss all Indian women as submissive and all Indian men as chauvinists. Her unassuming nature and sense of humor attracted Tara. Although Gopal didn't think much of Fiona, Tara was beginning to grow fond of her.

As the months crawled lethargically, Gopal's affectionate mood receded gradually. The 'Delhi Gopal' slowly crept into Tara's life again. What was happening to her relationship with her husband? The African experience taught Tara more than a different flavor and an interesting culture. She observed her husband. She understood him. She understood life. His congenial nature and change of attitude were real and unreal. Did that make any sense to her? It did … gradually. Initially, Tara thought that Gopal was affectionate when it pleased him. Not really. That was the kind of husband he was. According to his meager understanding about life and its little pleasures, he was at his kindest when he provided for his family, he did his duty when he stood by his wife as a dutiful husband, and he made his wife happy when he offered her the status of his wife. His family and his society taught him these ideologies. He lived by them.

Tara decided not to look for happiness in marriage anymore. She was glad to have intermittent moments of joy. There were several ways to escape from regrets. Distraction, any distraction! She looked forward to her visits to her parents' home. She visited Kanyakoil at least twice a year. She was getting attached to the groves and the banks. The river-drenched soil probably had this effect on her senses. Her parents' affection took her to Brinda and Bitsy's friendship kept her there. Bitsy was steadily becoming a sister Tara never had. And Fiona was more than eager to accompany Tara to Kanyakoil during a couple of her visits. It was her vacation paradise.

While sharing a cup of tea with Fiona on a breezy afternoon, Tara became sick. She was pregnant. Most importantly, this pregnancy lasted beyond the first trimester. Tara's doctor prescribed plenty of rest due to her shaky pregnancy record. Since Tara had suffered several miscarriages in the past, the family decided to get her through the next two trimesters by taking extraordinary care. Fiona visited almost everyday to keep Tara entertained. Help came in giggles and bubbly outbursts. Bitsy arrived with Akila. Tara couldn't be happier.

"Bitsy, having you around is equivalent to being fortified with a dose of tonic," said Tara. "I'm so glad you came with amma."

"I'm happy to be here, Tara. You're looking wonderful," said Bitsy.

A certified dietician monitored Tara's diet. Nothing was left to chance. No attention was unnecessary. Akila was excessively nervous, especially during her daughter's last trimester. Bitsy managed to stabilize Akila's sanity and kept Tara reasonably comfortable. Only Bitsy knew how to get Akila to relax when she worried about Tara's diet and medication. She even knew how to keep Gopal from nagging Tara. Really! Was there anything Bitsy couldn't do?

When Tara delivered her baby, the world looked better, the sun developed extra rays, and the heaven blessed the earth with raindrops. Gopal and Tara named their son Jayant and called him Jay.

"Tara," Akila said, proud and relieved. "There's only one thing in life that comes close to the glory of someone's child."

"What's that, Amma?" asked Tara.

"It's the blessing of a grandchild! Tara, you know how delighted I am that everything went well? I'm not sure if you noticed. I was so nervous that I almost upset Bitsy one day."

"You did? I never noticed! Bitsy, did you hear that?" Tara asked, smiling playfully at Bitsy.

Raja came into Tara's room to gloat over his daughter and his grandson. This was the proudest moment of his life since Tara's wedding day.

The baby grew like a weed. His smile occupied his grandparents' days, but Raja began to worry about Brinda and the orchards. It was in the capable hands of his assistant, Dev, who had walked into Brinda only a few months ago. Still, he wished to return to Kanyakoil. Although he basked in the baby's smile and in his daughter's love, he found his son-in-law's busy schedule a little irksome. Gopal was different from the young man, the pleasant gentleman, who had come to Brinda with a marriage proposal. He was still polite and very proper. But there was something out of harmony, a self-possessed importance in his behavior, that didn't improve his character. Raja was disappointed. He decided to return to India. His wife decided to stay a little longer to take care of Tara. Bitsy was in no hurry to go back. Anyway, Tara was not going to let her.

When Akila returned, the other set of grandparents arrived to see the baby. Tara was happy to see her mother-in-law as an independently functioning human being, free of Seetha's leash. What a difference the presence or the absence of a person made in one's condition!

◆ ◆ ◆

Jay was a robust child and demanded a lot of attention. Bitsy's supervision over his activities became essential, and Tara was sincerely glad to have her assistance.

"Where's Jay, Tara?" asked Fiona, while having tea with her on the balcony.

"He went to the park with Bitsy," replied Tara, looking at her friend's rather worried expression. "Fiona, what's wrong?"

"Is it obvious?" asked Fiona, laughing. "My African chapter has concluded."

"Fiona, I thought you would be here for at least another six or seven months. How can you leave me like this?"

"Tara, if I stay, my organization would expect me to linger during the whole school year. I don't mind really, but my mother is not well. I must go to her, you know?"

"Yes, you must. I'm sorry, Fiona. I'm selfish."

"No, not at all," smiled Fiona. "I'll miss you too."

Fiona turned to Jay who had just arrived from the park with Cadbury, his chocolate Labrador. She hugged him and gladly accepted his noisy greeting.

"I'll miss you, Jay," her voice turned soft.

Fiona was Jay's favorite aunt. He was unhappy to say his goodbyes. She promised him a 'mini Big Ben' and chocolates by post. His toddler anxiety was appeased by these simple compensations. Tara was not so easy to please. Fiona had filled the empty afternoons with sensible conversations and interesting anecdotes.

"Fiona, what'll I do without you at teatime?" Tara asked, genuinely worried about empty afternoons.

"Tara, come to Oxford," said Fiona. "Why don't you make a lengthy visit with Gopal and Jay?" Fiona understood her friend's spontaneous frown. "Okay, if Gopal is very busy, why don't you and Jay visit?"

"I'll see what I can do, Fiona. Thank you. Give your mother my regards. It'll never be the same without you."

While Tara was sulking after Fiona's departure, Seetha arrived with her family. This was all Tara needed to make her depression complete. But family was family! Tara had to steel herself for a few weeks of Seetha's undivided attention.

At least, Tara knew her sister-in-law's tastes. Seetha was fond of noisy and frequent parties. Tara invited every acquaintance and transferred the responsibility of entertaining Seetha to other hands. Thankfully, there were many attractions—safaris, guided tours, and nature walks—to keep Seetha engaged for several hours at a stretch. When Seetha was ready to leave, everybody, including Gopal, felt relieved.

Gopal saw Tara sulking more and more. Even Bitsy's effervescent attempts failed to cheer her. Did Tara really miss Fiona that much? He booked tickets for Tara and Jay to visit Fiona. Bitsy accompanied them, which naturally eased Gopal's mind about sending his wife alone with their son.

Fiona was delighted. Tara was very happy. Jay was thrilled to see Big Ben in full form. His adventures included double-decker buses, museums, and the immobile guard outside the queen's palace. His mother's adventures included leisurely walks along historical attractions and precious hours in the Masterson's English garden, accompanied by tiny sandwiches, scones, and tea. It was a wonderful vacation and a memorable relaxation during her rather puzzling married life. When she returned home, she told Gopal that he should have accompanied her. But she didn't mean a word of it.

Gopal and Tara were preparing to welcome their second child. Akila and Raja arrived to help their precious daughter and take care of their precious grandson. After a successful first trimester, Tara began to gain confidence in keeping this child intact. She hoped and prayed for an uneventful pregnancy, and she put everything else in her life on hold. Bitsy was there. Why should Tara or Akila worry about anything? The doctor arrived again with a list of instructions and restrictions.

Gopal's parents arrived after the baby girl was born. They were delighted because Tara had done her duty. She gave them a grandson and a granddaughter to brag about. Tara and Gopal named their daughter Niranjana, which condensed to Nina in just a few days.

Gopal walked into the house in the middle of a weekday—a habit that was quite unusual. He couldn't wait to tell the good news to his wife. The family was moving to Delhi.

The grandparents were delighted about the news. Their grandchildren would be closer to home! Tara was especially thrilled to return to Delhi because Seetha and her husband were moving to London for a couple of years. Perfect timing!

The family's return to India tempted Tara to make a long visit to Brinda. Raja never bought the estate in the hills, which he had planned on purchasing after his daughter's marriage. Brinda changed his mind, and he continued to stay in Kanyakoil.

This turned out to be a particularly pleasant visit for Bitsy! She found the love of her life during this vacation. Bitsy was over thirty. Until now, whenever Tara or Akila mentioned marriage, Bitsy summarily avoided the discussion or exclaimed, "Show me a man I could love." Although Tara was thankful for Bitsy's constant company and support, she worried about her future. Suddenly, a lightning named Dev—with a neat mustache, receding hair, and teasing eyes—struck Bitsy. This quiet gentleman, hired by Raja to take care of his property, snared her interest and sealed it in a proposal.

"Bitsy, he is such a nice gentleman. Are you happy about accepting his proposal?" Tara asked.

"Tara, I like him. But I'll agree to marry him on one condition. I'll not leave you and the children."

"Bitsy, what's this nonsense?" Tara asked, touched by Bitsy's devotion and unconditional love. "Stop thinking about me and the children. You need to think about your own life and needs."

But Bitsy was what she was—obstinate! She wouldn't change her mind. Earlier, while Tara had found a sister in Bitsy, Bitsy had found a sister and a home in Tara. How could she leave?

What surprised Tara more than anything else in this midsummer madness was the fact that Dev agreed to Bitsy's stipulation. Tara could never talk to Gopal in that manner and make such a demand! The charm of Bitsy's decisive attitude was that there was no pronounced authority in what she said or did. She simply got what she wanted. The addition of Dev to their entourage worked out well for Tara. She had been looking for an efficient administrator to manage her family's accounts. She found one.

Gopal's upscale promotion allowed the family to live in the most exclusive section of Delhi. Tara settled here with her children, Bitsy, and Dev. Gopal was rarely home because his career demanded his presence at work more often. Tara had grown accustomed to it. She didn't care, did she? Her children occupied her days that were already fragmented with rotary clubs, women's development leagues, young mothers' association, and a dozen other subsidiary charities. Besides, she had plenty of help from Bitsy and Dev. Still, she wanted her children to have more time with their father.

"You hardly have time with Nina and Jay. I'm sure they miss you. Do you have to accept so many responsibilities at work?" Tara asked Gopal. "Can you spend some time with them?"

"Tara, this house, chauffeur, cars, and all the comforts have not been given to us by a benefactor," Gopal replied, irritated. "I've worked very hard to earn what we enjoy today. Stop nagging me."

Tara never raised this issue again. Gopal was a needed yet dispensable part of the household. If he was determined to be detached, who could change him?

Tara received a pleasant phone call on a cool November afternoon. Fiona was coming to Delhi. Tara instantly invited her for dinner on the following Wednesday and shouted the good news to Jay.

"I've invited Fiona and her husband to have dinner with us on Wednesday. You'll join us, won't you?" Tara asked Gopal. "I checked your schedule. Looks like you're free."

"I may have a tennis date, Tara. I can't plan on being home."

"Couldn't you keep the evening free, if you haven't made a date already?" Tara asked again.

"Tara, I can't," Gopal said, a little annoyed. "It's very important for my career."

"But Fiona wished to introduce her husband to both of us," Tara said, quite disappointed.

"Fiona is not important, Tara. I'm telling you that it concerns my work. You don't expect me to neglect my work to accommodate her in my schedule? Go ahead and entertain them. You'll be fine."

Tara knew that she would be fine. She was used to her husband's detachment. But Fiona was dear to her heart. She didn't want her friend to feel slighted when she arrived with her husband. But Gopal didn't care. Fiona was not important—socially or politically—to attract his attention.

Fiona had not changed a bit. Her husband, Dr. John Woodward, was a swarthy, good-humored gentleman. The couple decided to spend a year or two in Delhi to benefit a non-profit organization. He looked exactly the way Fiona had described him in her letters to Tara.

"Dr. Woodward, I'm so happy to meet you," said Tara. "Welcome to Delhi. You know you can treat our home as yours."

"Well, only if you get rid of the 'Dr. Woodward'," said the guest. "I'm John to all our friends."

He was a perfect match for Fiona. He was pleasant, had a good sense of humor, and most importantly, he adored Fiona. Tara was very happy for her friend.

While Gopal's career progressed, his children had a glimpse of his face. Unfortunately, he had no share in their upbringing. This task fell mostly on the shoulders of Tara and Bitsy, with Dev's intermittent assistance. While Dev and Bitsy were becoming an essential part of Tara's life, Gopal was steadily walking away from it. Tara admired the special love between Bitsy and Dev. Bitsy went to her church on Sundays with Dev. Dev went to temple with Bitsy. Social and religious impediments didn't create a problem in their happiness. They were of one mind—an excellent match.

Seetha was unpleasantly surprised to see Fiona and Tara having tea on the terrace during one of her sudden visits. The fact that Fiona enjoyed Tara's close friendship—that was denied to her—irked Seetha. She had come to inform that she would be spending a year abroad. Seetha's husband had a job that required him to spend several long months away from the country. Seetha did return frequently, but she rarely stayed long in Delhi. Gopal's parents had settled down in a quiet town in the south, and Seetha found it necessary to take her boys to her parents' home whenever she returned to India from her trips abroad. Tara was thankful for small mercies.

"Tara, your dinner arrangement is impeccable," said one of the illustrious guests, trying not to burp.

Tara smiled and turned to her husband, who was talking to a minister across the table. Tara and Gopal were entertaining a few couples that evening. The guests were elite, wealthy, and boring. At least when they entertained, Gopal ate at home and ate with his wife. The house had become a hotel—devoid of unity, blind to feelings, and deaf to simple expectations. Her life was progressing toward another day, another sigh! Well, she got used to it.

Tara understood over time that tears ached and regrets stabbed when her mind was free, bored, and unoccupied. Well, Tara accepted more responsibilities to run away from her regrets. She had an active life, a little tiring at certain times. Her hectic life made her regrets hurt less, but they wouldn't vanish, no matter how hard she tried to numb her mind. How could they? Her marriage, though not a disaster, was not a happy relationship. What she had dreamed of years ago degenerated to meandering memories. It nagged her peace of mind whenever she had a few moments to recollect. So she ran from her memories. It was wise to ignore an absentminded past. Her love? His affection? They became dissipated dreams.

Tara and Gopal were acknowledged as a happy couple in parties and stately gatherings. She had everything a woman could ask for from a materialistic angle; she had a home many would envy, she had a loving family, and she was in the top of the list of benefactors in charity circles. Then … was she whining—ungrateful and greedy? What was lacking? What was missing? She wanted a husband who touched her heart. Matrimony was a matter of heart, wasn't it? A marriage was not limited to an occasional smile between spouses or a random visit to the theater. Despite all her efforts to maintain a loving relationship, the feelings between Tara and Gopal dwindled to reluctant attempts at good humor.

"Amma, look who is here?" Nina's voice floated in the air.

Tara's reverie was interrupted by cheerful laughter in the garden. She went to the window to see the reason for the distraction. She had spent too many moments on regrets! Nina was back from school. She had brought her friend again to play with her. She had a sizable social circle for a third-grader. Her little friend, Millie Bailey, arrived with a contagious smile and pigtails. Millie's family was from Washington D.C. Ed Bailey, Millie's father, was sent to Delhi on an appointment at the embassy. Millie was fascinated with this new land that welcomed her with fragrant flowers and fragrant food. Her mother, Sue, was a magnified image of her daughter. Her auburn hair floated on her shoulders like an everlasting sunset. While the mothers became better acquainted, the daughters flitted through culture and life. The Baileys and the Gopals became good friends.

◆ ◆ ◆

The family was in Kanyakoil for a long vacation. Unfortunately, Nina's best friend, Sandy, couldn't accompany her during this trip. What Nina loved most was the riverbank. Her favorite spot was on the east side, where a grove harbored a lopsided banyan tree. She loved to sit on the aged, curved trunk and gaze at the sky through the canopy of branches. Several kinds of birds built their homes among those stalwart twigs, and there was a perennial christening of baby birds. Nina chose this spot today to read the postcard Sandy had sent from London.

While Nina was sitting on the trunk, her skirt was caught on a sliver. When she tried to rescue the fine fabric, her hand landed on a smooth surface. She was thrilled to see that it was a small door that opened a compartment-like depression. Who would have thought of carving a box out of a curved surface on the trunk? She could hardly believe her eyes. How she wished for Sandy's presence at this moment! Nina dipped her fingers inside the compartment and retrieved a box, rusted and aged. She opened the latch carefully and lifted a weathered paper. What was written on it? It looked like a name, and was it Buvana? Did it say 1880 or 1890? The exact year was not clear. What was written underneath the name? Nina read with a lot of difficulty: "These things shall not be given as part of my dowry." The words were blurred and crinkly in quite a few spots. The wrinkled paper wouldn't allow her to understand the message completely. Although Nina spoke Tamil fluently, she was not very good at reading. Since she attended school in the north, her first language was Hindi, not Tamil. The only

Tamil she knew was what her mother and her grandmother taught her. Nina looked at the message again. Was she trespassing on somebody else's possessions? Really, this was her grandmother's property. This enlightenment gave her confidence and kindled her curiosity. What else was in the box? She saw a tiny polished wooden container with a few shells, a couple of bangles, and a brooch. There was something else. It looked like a jewelry container, a beautiful jewel-studded tin. She grabbed the contents and ran indoors with uncontainable excitement. Tara had never seen her daughter in such undiluted exhilaration.

"Amma, Paatti, look what I found?" Nina asked in utter excitement. "Look, I discovered a TREASURE. Can you imagine anything like this?"

Tara expected Nina to uncover a beautiful shell or a smooth pebble, which she often brought from her rendezvous by the river. When she scrutinized the contents in Nina's hands, she could hardly believe her eyes. When Nina began to describe the details of her adventure, her mother let out a gasp. Akila, who was inspecting the same contents, had to sit down.

"Paatti, who is Buvana? Do you know anything about her?" Nina asked. "You're not angry, are you? I couldn't stop once I realized that a compartment existed, and that too in a tree!" Nina sat by her grandmother and ruefully held her hand.

"Angry? Of course, not," Akila said and took a deep breath before explaining the identity of Buvana. "You know something, my Nina? I suppose this was meant to be. I really believe that Buvana expected a young girl like you to discover these things."

"Really? How fascinating!" exclaimed Nina.

"Nina, you can keep the things you found this afternoon," Akila said, sanctioning her approval. "These treasures belong to you."

"Oh, thank you, Paatti. But do you think I should leave these things where I found them? Another girl can discover a new treasure many years from now, don't you think?" asked Nina.

At this forthright, innocent question, Tara and Akila gave a shout of laughter, and the grandmother embraced her dearest granddaughter.

"Paatti, what's this thing, this container?" Nina asked. "Would someone store earrings or some other trinket in this box?"

Akila took the snuffbox from Nina's hand and explained that it was used to store a very spicy powder called snuff. Men took a pinch of this powder and inhaled.

"What?" Nina asked, astonished.

"Yes, they sniff to get a kick!"

Nina ran to the kitchen to show her treasures to Bitsy. Jay missed all the fun. He had gone fishing with Dev.

Nina and Akila returned from Mercy House to enjoy tea in the veranda. Akila had judged Nina's character accurately. On the surface, Nina appeared playful, but she was a very compassionate, serious, and mature young lady. She had a kind of quiet strength that operated independently. It accepted no interference from her playful attitude. Nina didn't twitch at the sight of gaping poverty in her secure and wealthy sphere. In fact, she insisted on accompanying Akila to Mercy House to offer help.

"Look who is here, Nina," Akila said delightedly, while finishing tea.

It was Anand. Nina ran to the car to greet him.

"How is my little niece?" Anand smiled at Nina.

"I'm not little. In fact, I'm quite grown up now," replied Nina. She narrated her recent adventure by the river. Anand admitted that he was impressed. Nina was very fond of her uncle. She liked him especially for his kindness and affection for Tara.

When the family returned to Delhi, Akila received a phone all.

"Paatti," said Nina, excitedly. "Amma found a good tutor to teach me Tamil. Just wait. I'll write a letter soon, a full page in Tamil."

Akila congratulated Nina. This was another quality that amazed Akila. Nina had that certain determination. She had so much of Aunt Aruna in her. There was no way her young granddaughter could have Aruna's blood running through her veins! Nina's ardent interest in broadening her knowledge in Tamil sprouted from Buvana's note, a message from the past. Interesting!

Tara and her children were in Brinda for the holidays. Everybody missed Raja. After he died the previous year, Akila insisted on staying in Brinda. Although Anand was frequently keeping an eye on her, Tara was worried about her mother, and Bitsy shared her concern.

As Nina grew older, Bitsy's love for Tara and her children intrigued her. Bitsy was an educated woman for a mere housekeeper. There were times when Nina wondered why Bitsy continued to stay with their family when she could have moved on to better prospects.

Bitsy brought tea to the table beside the swing. Nina loved that swing, which could easily hold half a dozen people. She loved to lean on her grandmother and take her gnarled hand in hers, listening to her fascinating stories, laughing with her. Akila was not feeling well that day. The doctor visited and whispered something to Tara, which made her cry quietly.

While Nina was sitting upstairs on the balcony, mesmerized by the amber sunset, her grandmother went to heaven. Gopal came from Delhi. Although Tara's two older brothers arrived promptly to offer condolence and support, it was Anand's arrival that brought immense relief to Tara. Anand was the closest to her in age and dearest to her heart. He performed the last rites at his stepmother's funeral. He was a perfect son in Akila's life, and he took care of every detail. Nina was surprised to see her father leaving within two days. Didn't her mother need him? Well, he was very busy. Tara understood. Others also understood!

Tara's nature didn't take comfort in explicit or unbridled passion. Her feelings experienced a calm disposition and found a quiet exit. Her emotions engulfed her in moderation, well under control. While Tara was struggling with the grief of losing her mother in her serene way, Bitsy spent more time with Nina and Jay. Jay was a responsible young man. He didn't give a moment's worry to his parents at any time, and during this time of grief, he was a pillar of support to his mother and sister.

Nina observed her mother and Bitsy. Tara patiently took care of the crucial moments that rolled by. Bitsy took care of various issues in the family to support Tara. Several questions resolutely sprouted in Nina's mind. For some reason, Bitsy's service to Tara's family arrested Nina's attention now more than before.

Bitsy invited Nina to sit by her on the balcony.

"Bitsy," said Nina. "I'm so glad that you never leave us."

Bitsy's shrewd eyes noticed Nina's desperate expression. She pulled the young girl closer and held her slender hands within her firm ones. "Nina, look at that sun going into the earth. Does it ever get tired of sinking into the same earth everyday?" asked Bitsy. "Your Bitsy is like that sun. You'll see me until there is nothing left in me, until all is taken away, and my Dev will be there too! I promise."

Nina burst into tears. A clamor of emotions surrounded her tender, aching heart. Each drop of tear showed her a door to a part of her future. Life was precious, but love was everlasting. Only love was enduring, like the sun sinking into the earth. Nina left Kanyakoil with a solid determination about one aspect of life; she would never compromise on love or the relationships that sprouted from that love.

Brinda was left to Tara. Tara didn't care about who inherited it now. Both her parents were gone! Anand promised to find a tenant to live in that grand house. Although Raja had left his affairs in a good condition, it was usually a hassle to settle inherited property under municipal regulations. Raja's family lawyer was elderly and very ill at the moment. Chandran, Gopal's lawyer, came from Delhi to settle the legal issues as smoothly as possible. Anand was with Tara through it all. How was she to repay this unwritten debt?

The family prepared for their return to Delhi for school and other uninteresting activities. Although Nina was a few years younger than her brother, she expressed a lot of interest in Jay's college admission process. After all, she had to make this move just a few years from now! Gopal dedicated his free time to fill various application forms. Nina didn't know that her father had some free time! Most of the sections required methodical, straightforward answers. However, there was a section that required a detailed description of the family's caste. This was tricky. Gopal belonged to a high caste. Tara came from a low caste. Gopal asked Tara to stress on her low-caste status to help Jay get into a good college.

"Now you wish to advertise my real caste?" Tara asked. "Your family isn't going to cringe at my caste now?"

Nina looked alternately at her father's discomfited expression and the unfathomable something in her mother's eyes. "Appa, why should the college be interested in a student's caste—good or bad? It's not any of their business, is it?" Nina asked her father.

"Nina, stay out of this," said Jay, a little exasperated. "This is for my college admission. You can worry about yours when the time comes."

Thankfully, the phone rang. It was one of Gopal's illustrious associates. As a politician, this gentleman could advance Jay's applications with no effort at all. Gopal smiled proudly and went to his study to talk to his friend. Consequently, Jay went to bed with a lighter heart. Nina had some idea about the connection between college admissions and caste restrictions. She wanted to know more and followed her mother for some serious explanations.

Tara, who had nothing to hide, decided to enlighten her daughter. "Nina, there was a time when people who were grouped under upper castes ruled all territories," Tara began to explain. "They prospered with education, land, and unlimited advantages. The individuals on the other end, who carried the label of very low caste, had to settle for indentured employment, with no hopes of reaching a higher standard of life. They received no consideration from the caste-conscious society. Most importantly, many of them had very limited education, if at all any. Essentially, the rich got richer and the poor got buried under poverty and misery."

"That's horrible, Amma," Nina declared.

"It is," Tara agreed. "Fortunately, the situation altered over a period of decades. A few political leaders fought for the rights of the outcasts. The government modified old rules and instituted a few new regulations. Currently, a young man from a low caste has a few seats reserved for him in the universities. Moreover, in order to claim one of these seats, he is not required to produce a brilliant transcript. All he needs is an official letter that testifies his inferior caste and certifies his deprived circumstances, and he has a seat in college. Most of the time, he can get into the college of his choice."

Nina's young, rebellious, and compassionate heart was delighted to hear this happy prospect. "That's good, isn't it, Amma?" Nina asked eagerly.

"You have to see the whole picture, Nina," said her mother. "While more and more young men and women from deprived or backward communities find opportunities for higher education, a large number of young people from higher caste or forward communities are struggling to find admission into good colleges. While a student in a backward community needs about a seventy percent academic average—I'm not sure about the exact percentage—a student from a forward community needs to produce a perfect transcript!"

"It's not fair that these young people should suffer because of what their upper-caste ancestors did!" Nina said, trying to make a point.

"Who said that life is fair?" asked Tara. "This is called reverse discrimination. Somehow, somewhere, all of us pay the price. My father was an outcast when he was a young boy. But his life became better when a generous and rich upper-caste gentleman took him under his wings. Now, there was an extraordinarily kind human being. When I was a child, my parents were practically driven out of Kanyakoil because some upper-caste families were envious of their successful existence. So you see, good or bad, right or wrong, there is no absolute. In fact, I know that some individuals from forward communities pay money to produce letters that falsely certify their backward status … just to obtain a good college enrollment."

"Then, what's your opinion about castes? Whose side are you on, Amma?" asked Nina. She had to see 'right' or 'wrong' in every situation.

"I support none," said Tara. "I believe that a child should receive a solid education, a higher education, based on merit and nothing else. I agree that children coming from deprived families need society's attention and support, plus a little boost. But we can't abandon one side to help the other."

As always, her mother's explanation made a lot of sense to Nina. Just as expected, Jay was accepted in a prestigious college. His academic record was good, but it was not extraordinary. This admission was undoubtedly bought with some assistance from his father's political friend and by some reinforcement provided by his mother's low-caste status.

Nina's growing pain was another story. Tara didn't know how to handle her. Nina was impatient and moody. Her fervor to change the society left her dissatisfied and restless. Nina had no patience for her society's mood swings when she was busy with her own mood swings, premenstrual syndrome, and pain relievers. Certain things had approval when some silly events induced society's censure. Who cared? She certainly didn't. Tara, however, was very careful about any decision her daughter made. Nina was tired of what people thought, what society deemed correct, and what her father considered appropriate.

Nina needed her parent's permission to go on a field trip. She ran to her mother for approval. After all, she was the parent who was visible in the house most of the time. Nina wanted her mother to stop the redundant chanting, "Let's ask your father before we decide what to do." Her father was one of the busiest men in Delhi. He was rarely home to take care of Nina's growing pains. Then, why would it matter whether he was consulted or not? Nina knew that her mother managed the household quite efficiently, and she decided to boost her mother's confidence.

"Why do you have to ask appa for this and that when you're capable of making decisions on your own?" Nina asked, assuming an innocent tone.

"Nina, a decision regarding a girl's absence from home requires a consultation between both parents," said Tara. "Besides, your father would be upset if he found out that you went on a trip for a week without consulting him."

"But, Amma, you wait for his approval for everything. Can't you make your own decision once?"

"I suppose I can."

"Okay, then why don't you make your own choices once in a while? If a woman could run our country, well, when are you going to change? When will women like you be liberated?"

"Oh, you sound like a representative of women's rights. Liberated! My situation isn't as bad as that," Tara said, hugging her daughter. "You know, running a country is easier than managing a family, my child. One day you'll understand."

Nina was not sure of her mother's theory. Her father was seldom home, but he expected things to be done his way. Tara was merely an executor of his will and command, and Nina hated this practice. But the following episode confirmed Tara's conviction in her domestic affairs, and the daughter understood why things were left as such.

Gopal was angry when Tara inadvertently changed one of his business dinner appointments to accommodate a family affair. "Tara, how could you do something so foolish?" Gopal asked, frustrated. "Why didn't you call and consult me? I have a meeting with Chandran. I'm waiting for his legal advice to take care of some business options."

And on another occasion, while Tara was waiting in the foyer to get Gopal's approval before he went to work, he offered an irritated lecture. "Tara, do you have to wait and ask me a dozen questions about every simple problem?" he sighed, exasperated. "You're an educated woman. Why don't you learn to make some decisions?"

Although Nina felt an intense urge to teach her father some manners, she understood the unexplainable between her mother and father.

◆ ◆ ◆

Seetha came to her brother's house more often than she ought to and more frequently than she was welcome. Her husband's job required him to settle down in Delhi rather permanently, much to Tara's dismay. Seetha wished to get Nina for her nephew from her husband's side. Matchmaking was Seetha's passion and mission. Whenever she hinted at her wish to unite Nina and the young man, Gopal became nervous.

"A marriage between relatives is not a good idea," said Gopal.

"Nonsense!" said Seetha, quite upset. "First of all, they're not related. And what's wrong with this alliance?"

Gopal was tired of arguing with his sister. He was never good at talking back to her. He decided to talk to Tara and Nina.

"An alliance between my daughter and Seetha's nephew is absolutely out of the question," Tara said to Gopal, quite at the end of her patience by this time.

"Nina," said Gopal. "Would you consider your aunt's proposal?"

"Never in this lifetime, Appa," said Nina. "Please tell Seetha Athai that it's impossible."

Gopal's fatherhood, until now, had been an indirect approval of checks, transfer of funds, and an intermittent frown at the choice of his daughter's clothes and his son's occasional extravagances. He had not been home long enough to get involved in a conversation with his family. He loved them, took care of their material needs absolutely, and expected his wife and children to accept his authority unconditionally.

"Have you tried to annex Nina's cooperation, Tara?" Gopal asked. "I'm the master of the house. What I say is final."

"I've done nothing," protested Tara. "Nina is in her second year of college. She is old enough to make up her mind. Besides, even my parents respected my opinion regarding my marriage. They left the final decision to me all those years ago."

Nina witnessed the beginning of the most heated argument between her parents. She quietly left the room to escape from a very awkward situation. Although Nina couldn't see them, she could hear their rising voices.

"My opinion is going to matter regarding this issue," said Tara, decisively. "My daughter wouldn't be forced to marry her cousin, blood relation or not. In fact, Nina wouldn't be forced to marry any young man."

"I'm not forcing her, Tara," Gopal said, frustrated. "You're making me look like a villain here. I'm merely asking Nina to consider this match. I know you never liked my sister, but she means well, and she is always thinking of our welfare. It won't hurt your pride to show a little gratitude."

"I owe your sister nothing, absolutely nothing," Tara said. "I want her to leave me and my daughter alone."

Gopal had never seen his wife in such an independent, reckless state in all the years they had been married. "Tara, what happened to you?" he asked. "I hardly know you."

"That's right. You don't know me," said Tara. "I disappeared a long time ago to make room for your ego, authority, and wishes. Control! That seems to be your life's ultimate wish!" Tara's heart was heavy, and she could hardly explain her emotions. Feelings—where were they? Yes, she existed only in her dreams. All he saw was her shadow.

When Tara walked out of the room, Gopal was speechless. He had already been insulted enough for one evening. He decided to let things cool down for a while.

Bitsy met Tara on the terrace. She disliked Seetha's dominance and impertinence. "Tara," said Bitsy. "That Seetha! It's one of her irritating adventures. It'll pass. Everything does in time."

Bitsy's position in that house was a little strange from Gopal's perspective. He appreciated everything Bitsy and Dev did for his family. He also understood that the couple's affection was always devoted to Tara and her children. Bitsy treated Gopal with unwavering respect. She was polite and dignified. It was as though she had a mask on her face in Gopal's presence. And that mask was removed when he was not present. Dev performed his duties and preferred to stay backstage. Gopal was too busy to analyze the mysteries of Bitsy, and he thought that he didn't care. For all the wealth he had, Gopal was not able to buy Bitsy's friendship or her husband's smiles. Bitsy and Dev were of no significance, and Gopal repeated this mantra frequently to ignore the couple's detachment to him.

Tara helped Nina pack. Nina was going to a university in the United States for graduate studies. It was not easy to organize moving arrangements for over two years in another country. One small consolation was that Nina wouldn't be far from the Baileys. Millie and Nina continued to keep in touch just as Sue and Tara had done. Sue promised her worried friend that Nina would be a very welcome addition in their home whenever she needed a home. And Chitra, Anand's daughter, wasn't far from the university.

Nina promised her parents to stay in touch with them every week. She was pleasantly surprised to see her father at home more often. He wanted to talk to Nina, he invited her to walk to the café at the end of the street, and he even convinced his wife to leave her charities for a while. He wanted to see her face! This was a new, pleasant beginning.

Tara smiled a lot, and Nina was happy to see this. She was happier to see her mother spending more time with her father. Was Nina making a mistake in going to America for her studies? Should she stay here and enjoy the renaissance of her parents' happiness? When Nina shared her doubts with her best friend, Sandy, she dismissed her worries with a vigorous shake of her head.

"Nina, no, what a silly idea!" Sandy exclaimed. "Your parents could probably use some privacy."

Nina was not right in thinking that her parents had revived their love for each other. They were more amicable, but love was farther than ever. Their independent lifestyles during a period of over thirty years had drawn them apart from each other, and it felt strange to seek quiet moments of bliss to bridge a wide, awkward gap. They took an evening walk together, each wondering when it would be over. They went to quaint restaurants, and the couple managed to make polite conversations, like old acquaintances at a reunion. They had a good life. It was a decent harvest. They just couldn't cherish the earthy core of love.

Nina's much-awaited days as an independent adult began with some pleasant experiences that included meeting interesting people in the campus, registering in a couple of novel activities, and exploring coffee shops. Her unpleasant experiences, on the other hand, consisted of laundry and food. She disliked the meals at the dormitory with a passion. Her conviction in sustaining her strength was revived only when her roommate, Kim Roberts, and a few other students redirected her taste buds to some reasonably priced restaurants. However, there was no relief in the laundry situation. She hated carrying a pillowcase, filled with dirty clothes, to the basement. This was just the beginning of an unsavory ordeal. Once she reached the windowless dungeon, she needed to find an empty washer and wait until the load was finished—because finding an empty dryer was another tricky situation.

Nina survived. She understood that this new land operated on self-help. It was a fulfilling experience. There were some very wealthy students, with unlimited allowance, who sent out laundry and ate at costly restaurants. Nina decided to live on the monthly stipend she earned for graduate work. Her father had deposited a significant amount in her account for emergency situations, and this sum was going to remain intact for such purposes.

Already, just after a couple of months of her independent survival, Nina was terribly homesick. She had an invitation from the Baileys to spend the Thanksgiving weekend with them. She was delighted to receive this phone call.

Nina liked autumn. She loved to walk on crunchy leaves and delicate twigs. She relished spicy cider on apple-picking days. One of the favorite times of the year in Nina's new life was the Thanksgiving holiday. She was sitting in the den by a roaring fire in Millie Bailey's home. The table was quite a sight. There was a huge turkey in the center, surrounded by an assortment of vegetables, relishes, and salads—all jockeying for a prime spot. And desserts were displayed on a separate table against the wall. Nina recognized the apple pie and trifle bowl, but there were a few more pies and puddings that she had not seen before.

"Nina, this is my favorite part of the Thanksgiving meal," said Millie, taking Nina's attention to an orange-colored dessert on the table. "This is pumpkin pie. We eat this with whipped cream. It's delicious."

Mr. Bailey handed Nina a glass of wine. She looked up at Susan Bailey, not sure of this recent promotion.

"Go ahead, Nina," Mrs. Bailey said, smiling encouragingly. "You're over twenty-one, aren't you?"

Yes, she was! Drinking a glass of wine might not necessarily make Nina feel mature, but her adult experience in a new land certainly did. In tune to his life-style, Gopal would give Nina a glass of wine or champagne in the privacy of their drawing room, among very close friends or family members. Nina wouldn't be caught drinking in a pub, under any circumstance, even after she arrived at the appropriate drinking age. He had one foot on traditional parenting and the other, slippery foot, on modern limits. Nina didn't wish to drink at will. She just wanted her father to trust her, understand her. After a rigid and sheltered youth, Nina struggled to ease into a single, independent, and responsible existence. She remembered her mother's advice. Tara had asked Nina to question her mind every time her heart told her to indulge in something new and strange. Lately, Nina was questioning her mind often!

Christmas followed Thanksgiving. Chitra, Anand's eldest daughter, lived in New Jersey. She invited Nina to spend the Christmas vacation with her family. Nina accepted the invitation delightedly because she was fond of Chitra. This was the beginning of her many visits to her cousin's home.

When Nina came home for the holidays at the end of her first year in graduate school, plenty of marriage proposals were waiting for her. There was someone else waiting—Leela, Jay's new wife. His bride was a very appropriate young lady, the daughter of a leading entrepreneur in Delhi. Gopal had played a major role in arranging this alliance. The wedding was arranged in a hurry because Leela's father was leaving the country on a long-term assignment. Jay, of course, wished for Nina's presence at his wedding, but the bride's family couldn't wait for her arrival.

The family was having breakfast on the terrace. When Gopal encouraged Nina to look at the proposals, she was ready with her answer. "I'm not going to look at them. Let me finish my studies. Besides, I want to concentrate on my internship now," said Nina, summarily dismissing the offers.

"All right, all right, we'll wait till you finish graduate school, Nina," said Gopal.

"So, Jay, are you seriously thinking about accepting the offer … where is it, Singapore?" asked Nina.

"He should. It'll be a good experience for him," replied Leela, on her husband's behalf.

Jay smiled. He hardly got a word in edgewise. His wife presided over most of the conversations. Nina decided to be happy for her brother, but she let out a long sigh at the thought of her sister-in-law. The situation was rather out of everybody's hands in such an arrangement. Leela was a perfect girl for the family. She brought money, status, and name. She belonged to a good caste. Nina looked at Leela. She was very fair, very tall, and very plain. Overall, she was not ugly.

Nina got a part-time summer internship with the writing staff of *The Express*. When she was not busy at work, Sandy visited Nina's home or the two girls went away with their other friends for an afternoon. Nina preferred to stay out of the house because she couldn't tolerate Leela.

"Nina, why does your friend, Sandy, have such a strange name? Is she Christian?" asked Leela. She didn't think much of Nina's friends because they were not sophisticated.

"It's a name. What's so strange about that? No, she is not Christian. She spent her childhood in London. Her name, Sanjushree, was rather long, I suppose. So it got shortened to Sandy, just like mine," Nina glared at her sister-in-law. "My name, Nina, is short for Niranjana."

Sandy was petite, had a soft, pleasing smile, and brilliant eyes. Her simple nature and remarkable sense of humor made her a comfortable companion. Sandy's simple and unassuming disposition irked Leela. According to her superior upbringing, Sandy wasn't important enough to be intimate with Nina's family. Unfortunately, Leela's sense of superiority prompted her to offer Nina unsolicited advice during supper.

"Nina, my dear, you should be careful about your friends. We belong to a very important family," said Leela. "You see, Nina, your future prospects shouldn't be affected by inferior associations."

"What are you talking about? Sandy's father is a businessman. Her family is educated and very decent. What's wrong with her?" Nina asked, quite irritated.

"Her father might be a businessman, but what kind of business is that? Clothing stores! Now think about it. What kind of influence does he have in the community? Nina, you simple girl, your friends don't meet the status of our family."

"So what? I …" Nina began.

"Dear Nina, you're so naïve," said Leela. Her voice escalated to a highly condescending pitch. "You need to grow up."

"Leela, I'm going to ask you to mind your own business," said Nina. "I'll not ask you again. I don't give a damn about your class-obsessed ideas. Take this as a warning. Never interfere in my affairs."

Jay was embarrassed. Tara was uncomfortable. Gopal, thankfully, was at his club. This was the beginning of Nina's frank reaction to Leela's overbearing behavior.

Leela's delicate and rather spoilt upbringing couldn't withstand Nina's insult. She packed her suitcases and ordered the chauffeur to drive her to her parents' home.

A week after Leela's departure, Jay was still embarrassed. How was he going to get his wife back? "Amma, please ask Nina to purse her lips when somebody important gives her advice," said Jay. "After all, Leela is only thinking of Nina's welfare, right?"

Tara rarely spoke harshly to her dutiful son, but she chose this occasion to speak frankly. "Jay," said Tara. "It's not Leela's business to choose friends for Nina. It's certainly not her place to tell Nina how to run her life."

Leela returned to her in-law's home after several apologies from Jay. However, the occasion that triggered Nina's outburst was not the first time Leela had been a pain in the neck. Leela didn't feel like royalty in that house. Her in-laws were kind to her, but her imperious nature didn't stir humility in their behavior. She didn't enjoy her husband's undivided attention either. Leela made up her mind.

"Jay," said Leela. "Why don't we move away for a while? Don't you want to get some experience elsewhere?"

"I'll think about it," said Jay. "For now, please try to get along with my family. Leela, should I accept the offer … in Singapore?"

Leela thought he should accept. They decided to move to Singapore for a lengthy period of time! Although Tara was sad, she saw the necessity for such a move. She had one consolation. Her friends in Singapore were willing to offer any assistance in Jay's new surroundings. Gopal saw the advantage of Jay's experience abroad and sent him away with his blessings.

It was time for Nina to return to the university. Gopal offered several words of caution on the way to the airport. Unfortunately, his advice, sprouting out of love and concern, poured into his daughter's ears like hot wax. Tara had already given her advice that morning. She was not in the habit of repeating her counsel, and Nina was thankful.

It was a beautiful, crisp day. Nina decided to walk back to the dormitory instead of taking the bus. Close to the entrance, she saw a middle-aged Indian couple and a youngish man. Had she seen them before? The group waved to her in a familiar manner. She was right. She had met them in Seetha's house. What were they doing here?

Apparently, the mother was the spokesperson of the family. Deliberately, with many a pause and a smile, she 'reintroduced' her son to Nina.

"Your father and I need to finish an errand," the mother said to the son. "Why don't you stay here and talk to Nina for a while?"

The father and mother moved away. Finish an errand? What kind of task were they thinking of doing here that they couldn't wait to do elsewhere? A few minutes convinced Nina of the imminent disaster. The young man was cruising through the last lap of his doctorate program. He was in search of a bride!

"Aunt Seetha talked highly of you to my parents," he babbled. "She thought that you would make a good bride. She encouraged us to meet you here."

While he was floating in his glory, Nina felt a sincere urge to slap him. Actually, he was not the source of her irritation. Was Nina ever safe from her aunt's officious interference? This stupid family could have called her or e-mailed before arriving on the spot in this fashion! Nina made sure, when the young man said goodbye, that she thwarted his hopes of 'reintroducing' himself during another occasion.

Nina called her parents that night. After a few failed attempts, she managed to get hold of the international line. "Amma, guess who came to see me and guess who sent them here?" Nina sounded angry.

"What happened, Nina?" asked Tara.

When Nina's anger abated a little, she explained the afternoon incident to her mother.

"Nina, I'm sorry that you had to go through such an uncomfortable visit from strangers. This won't happen again," said Tara, earnestly. "Another such visit won't occur."

Tara didn't like Seetha. She never liked her and she never would. She tried to avoid Seetha during various activities in the city, although she couldn't avoid her consistently. There was not much room to hide. Their families had the same circle of friends and similar, monotonous gatherings. Tara's detachment was part and parcel of her personality. Her friends accepted that parcel. Seetha couldn't deal with Tara's calm temperament and her indifference. In all the years as in-laws, Seetha could never break the barrier between them. Tara made sure that the barrier grew stronger by the day, and this irritated Seetha. She couldn't bully her sister-in-law, and she couldn't bully her niece either because Nina was becoming another Tara.

◆ ◆ ◆

Nina put the phone down with a sigh. She looked at the window, at the steadily falling snow. If only she could trap this picture—this transcendent feeling—permanently in her memory and take it home with her! She wished to work for a year before returning to Delhi. A long-term internship in America, right after graduation, would certainly forward her resume to a great length. Unfortunately, her father wouldn't hear of it. And her mother never made any decision without her husband's approval. At least, Nina had a few more months to enjoy before returning to Delhi.

Gopal called Nina that night. "Nina, you wish to stay for another year, don't you?" he asked.

"Yes, but you said …"

"Never mind what I said. I thought about it. If that's your wish, go ahead."

"Really? Thanks, Appa. What made you change your mind?" Nina asked suspiciously.

He didn't respond immediately. "Tara convinced me to consider your request," replied Gopal.

Winter crawled to spring and early summer. Nina got through her dissertation successfully and walked into a surprise party that her friends had orchestrated. The last two years held some of the most memorable moments in her life. Nina had an offer to work near the campus, but she accepted a job near Manhattan because it offered a tempting challenge and better prospects. The next few days were spent in goodbyes, shopping, packing, and farewell cocktails, accompanied by itsy-bitsy luncheons and dinners. Nina was ready for a real city life in New York City. She was especially happy because her roommate of over two years, Kim Roberts, was planning on accepting an internship in one of the leading broadcasting corporations, just a few blocks away. The friends decided to share boarding arrangements in the future also.

The phone rang. Nina was glad to hear her cousin's voice. Chitra invited Nina to spend a few days with her family before moving to New York City. Nina was glad to accept the invitation. Chitra encouraged Nina to bring her effervescent roommate along, and Kim was glad to oblige.

Tara moved the breakfast tray away. She had suffered from a nagging headache during the last few days, but she was feeling much better this morning. The shrill tone of the phone rattled her nerves.

"Amma, I have good news. Guess who is going to be a father?" Jay sounded delighted.

Tara congratulated him and Leela. There was so much she wanted to know. "Jay, when is Leela planning to come to India? Is she planning to come here for the delivery? Is she feeling well?"

"Amma, relax. She's fine. There's plenty of time to decide all that. I'll call you soon."

Tara ran to Bitsy to share the good news. Bitsy was delighted to hear it.

"Jay is going to be a father! JAY is going to be a father?" Bitsy asked.

Tara looked at the day's schedule. There was nothing urgent that needed her attention. Grandmother! It felt wonderful. Where was Gopal? She called his club. He was not there. Why didn't he pick up his car phone? Well, he could discover the good news whenever he came home. In the meantime, Tara basked in the thought of holding a baby again. Her present hope of future happiness was too intense to allow her to concentrate on her daily routine.

Bitsy's affection for little Jay made the good news seem incredible. Bitsy missed Jay terribly. She had contributed a lot during his growing years. Although he reciprocated her love, he wasn't able to demonstrate his affection as much as he wished to. Leela liked to maintain the distinction of classes. Bitsy was a servant. She would always remain one in Leela's eyes. Leela threw a few tantrums and made sure that Jay followed his wife's instructions.

The recent good news brought a minor inconvenience. Subha and her husband invited Gopal and Tara for a simple dinner. Tara couldn't decline. As much as she disliked Leela's mother, certain formalities had to be maintained. Leela was a replica of her mother. That should say it all. But an occasional dinner with the in-laws was inevitable. The men, however, got along very well because their personalities matched.

The dinner was anything but simple, and the evening was rapidly turning sour. Initially, Tara had expected Subha and her husband to celebrate the prospect of their grandchild with the other set of future grandparents. When Tara and Gopal arrived, Subha was bursting at the seams to share her joy. She did. Somehow, during the course of the evening, Tara's spirits began to deflate.

"Have you found a nice young man for Nina, Tara?" Subha enquired, when the guests were ready to leave.

"Not yet, Subha," said Tara. "Nina has to return from the States first. We'll see after that."

"How can you rest until Nina's future is settled?" asked Subha's husband. He and his wife were convinced that Tara and Gopal had to suspend everything in their lives until Nina was safely and expensively deposited in the hands of a rich, young man. Marriage was still a girl's salvation, and their society associated a girl's ultimate happiness with marriage.

"Tara, my cousin's friend is looking for a nice girl for her son. He is a doctor," offered Subha. "He has a flourishing practice in Bangalore." Subha always had a very prosperous young man in mind, whose mother was looking for a nice, family-oriented young lady.

"Subha, thanks, but not now," said Tara. In spite of her headache and irritation over a tiring evening, she smiled politely. "When Nina returns from her current obligations, there'll be plenty of time to look at some proposals."

Subha waved goodbye with the most congenial smile, but she sighed satisfactorily when Gopal's car went past the gate. "Poor Tara," said Subha. "She just doesn't have the luck with Nina that I have with our dearest Leela!"

Her husband agreed with her, of course. Gopal had a lot to face—with his impassionate wife and stubborn daughter.

Seetha arrived on the following day to congratulate Gopal and Tara regarding the prospective grandchild. While Bitsy was directing the maids in the kitchen to get supper ready, Anand made a surprise visit. Tara was delighted to see her brother. That was the best thing that happened to her during the absence of Nina and Jay.

"Hello Anand, how are you?" Seetha cooed. "We didn't expect you. Did Gopal and Tara miss your phone call?"

"I'm doing fine. Thanks, Seetha," Anand said and turned to his sister. "Tara, I tried but I couldn't reach you on the phone."

"There's no need to call, Anand," said Tara, affectionately. "This is like your home. You're welcome anytime." Tara hoped that this statement snubbed Seetha, although it took a lot to penetrate her thick skin.

"It's good to see you, Anand," smiled Gopal. He asked Anand to follow him to the bar and shared the good news of a prospective grandson. Gopal's glance darted to Tara more frequently today. She was dazzling in her smiles that she reserved for Nina, Jay, and Anand.

Tara wished to know how Anand's family was doing, and he was happy to relate the latest information about his three daughters—all married and settled in very comfortable circumstances. Gopal was a little jealous of his wife's undivided attention on Anand, and he was certainly envious of this simple but inevitable fact: Anand's daughters were happily settled in life. Why couldn't Nina be more like them? She had such a mind of her own, such a streak of stubborn determination. Well, she was a good girl, but she was too independent for her father's taste and peace of mind.

When Dev announced that supper was ready, Gopal was especially relieved. He was tired of letting his mind wander to issues that were well beyond his control. Tara and Anand had so much news to exchange. So Gopal had to entertain Seetha and her husband. As devoted as he was to his sister's affection, even Gopal was beginning to feel the strain of hearing Seetha's anecdotes through the entire evening.

Nina got out of the crowded bus. She picked up her mail before walking into her cramped apartment. She ran to answer the phone.

"How are you, Nina?" asked Jay. His kind voice made her wish for her home in Delhi.

Nina was happy to hear the good news. "You're going to be a father! I'm going to be an aunt!" shouted Nina.

"I know," said Jay. "Can you believe it?"

Jay had so much to tell his sister. Nina had a lot to talk about.

"Keep me informed, Jay," said Nina, reluctant to let the conversation end. "Tell Leela to take care. I miss you."

After wishing her brother well, Nina started to clean the kitchen. The original plan was to get all the girls to cook food. However, the roommates unanimously voted against more attempts by Nina. Getting dinner on the table was not her talent, and she gladly agreed to do other chores. Kim was an excellent cook. In fact, she could prepare some Indian curries better than some of Nina's Indian friends. Anyhow, dinner was not a big issue. For a very reasonable price, they could eat a variety of gourmet food from a worldwide platter. They were, after all, living in the most diverse city in the world. Occasionally, Nina felt homesick. She took the train to visit the Baileys. She hitched a ride in a friend's car to Chitra's home during long weekends. For a change, she was happy to act as a guide when a couple of her younger cousins visited New York City. This was a wonderful part of her life. Nina felt that it should be an essential part of every young person's college days—blithe and oblivious of a serious future.

Nina returned to Delhi for good. When she announced her wish to work for a living, her father was surprised and a little shocked.

"Nina, I had really hoped that you would marry and settle down once you returned to India. Why go to work? What would people think if I let my daughter work for a living?" Gopal asked his daughter. "What would my sister and her family think?"

"Appa, I spent a lot of time and invested loads of hard work to reach where I am today. What do you mean by questioning my wish to work?" Nina asked, determined not to retreat. "And I don't want to think of marriage now."

Gopal had no answer. He looked at his wife for help. Tara explained that quite a few young women from affluent families dabbled in careers these days, at least until they got married. Some of them continued to work even after getting married. He agreed. The modern times and its concessions! He was getting old.

Besides, his daughter was never easy to deal with. This was one more adjustment he had to learn to accept.

Nina was eager to begin her first assignment as a junior staff writer with *The Express*. Sandy had encouraged Nina to apply here because she was a junior editor with the same employer.

Sandy took Nina to a crowded restaurant at the end of her first day at work. Nina was waiting to see Sandy's young man. She had been away from the country for so long that she had missed this interesting addition in her best friend's life. A tall, lean gentleman—with a stylish mustache and a confident gait—walked into the restaurant.

"Nina, this is Jitender Singh," said Sandy, introducing her special friend. Her dainty figure made a cute contrast to his tall stature.

"Nina, I've heard so much about you. It's such a pleasure to meet you at last," he said, extending a friendly hand.

"Mr. Singh! I'm pleased to meet you too."

"Oh, please call me Jim," he smiled.

He worked for *The Eastern Globe,* which was a tough rival of *The Express*. Sandy's friend was working in the enemy territory! He liked to talk. His unassuming disposition encouraged the company to talk freely. Nina already liked him.

"Nina," said Gopal, while the family was having a quiet dinner on the terrace. "Have you thought about looking at some of the proposals? How about the young man in ..."

"Appa, I don't want to get married now," Nina said, not letting her father finish. "And I don't want to have my wedding arranged. I want to wait."

"Nina, many women work outside the house even after they get married, don't they?" Tara asked.

"Amma," replied Nina, still stubborn. "I'll marry sometime in the future, someone I eventually fall in love with. Not now, please."

"Nina, love and love marriages are not real. This just doesn't work in real life. You have a storybook fascination!" replied Gopal, on his wife's behalf. This was his exasperated assessment of the situation. But what could he do? He blamed it on the influence of the modern times and his daughter's free spirit. She was too old for reprimands and punishment. At such times, he took comfort in his club, in a cool cocktail or two.

"Nina, is there a young man I should know about?" Tara asked eagerly. Her own dream was still vivid in her memory. "Did you meet someone in America?

I'll talk to your father, you know, if you're worried about telling him. Well, is there someone?"

"No, Amma, I have no such young man in mind!" said Nina, studying her mother's eager expression. "Amma, just to please you, I wish I could think of a young man I could bring home."

"Oh, Nina, stop teasing me."

Nina ran to the phone. "How is it going, Sandy?" she asked.

"Nina, guess what? Jim proposed," said Sandy.

Nina screamed in excitement and shouted the good news to her mother.

Although Nina received some tempting job offers in other major cities, she decided to stick to her career in Delhi. That was a welcome decision to her friends and family. Nina's job forced her to work longer hours in the evenings. She returned late in the night to the exclusively residential neighborhood of her parents. This was becoming a hassle. Tara convinced Gopal to purchase a flat in the heart of Delhi, closer to Nina's office. Nina began to stay here during the week and spent the weekends in her parents' home. Tara requested Bitsy to keep an eye on Nina in the new flat. Bitsy gladly agreed to this proposal. Nothing would give her greater pleasure.

A few neighbors and friends didn't approve of Nina's independent apartment life. Gopal was certainly worried about his friends' disapproval. Tara was not. What was wrong with independence, anyway? The mother wanted to make sure that Nina's life didn't reflect Tara's.

Tara went to her dressing room to get ready for a dinner engagement. Gopal was waiting downstairs.

"That's a beautiful sari, Tara. New?" asked Gopal, eager to prove that he was interested in tiny, unimportant details—itsy-bitsy details that made women happy!

"No, it's not new, but thanks," smiled Tara.

Gopal had retired by now. He took an avid interest in what his wife did. What did she do? What didn't she do? Her unrelenting energy amazed him. Her passion for helping the needy overwhelmed him. He was a kind man, but he didn't have the charitable blood in his veins that seemed to flow freely in his wife's. He wanted to understand her passion for helping others. He followed her during her benevolent activities when he didn't spend time in his club.

Was Tara happy to have Gopal's company? She could never make him understand that she didn't want his borrowed time and granted smiles. She wanted a companion to laugh with her because past moments, present happiness, and future dreams warranted it—for the sake of laughing, dreaming!

A lifetime of hopes and promises meandered through a tinsel town. Broken promises and unfinished hopes dissipated to a doleful melody! Where did the days disappear? While Tara's life eternally searched for meaning, her nights fabricated new dreams and her days buried them. How could she justify the dissipated days? Expectedly but unfortunately, her days began with questions and ended with unanswered sighs.

Expectations peeped in, mingled with intermittent memories, and she was thankful for her memories, good and not so good, that allowed her to recall those dream-filled days. She altered sorrows to smiles. Like endless space, she touched many lives. Happiness! Doubts! Tears! The promise of a delightful married life that she imagined at the wake of her acquaintance with a young man disappeared within her, never to be visited. Disappointments ached. Such was life. Tara woke up and searched for a ray in the sun. She went to bed, trying to find her name in the folds of the moon. Would next day be complete? Would she see a perfect dawn? It was an elusive dream, an eternal sigh. She didn't see a perfect dawn. Was there one? Dawn came with blemishes and clumsy enticements. There was no perfect dawn.

PART V

Woman of a Different World

Nina pulled the hood of her raincoat over her head and tucked the folder under the waterproof material to keep the papers reasonably dry. The ominous downpour made the bleak, mossy walls of Dandiar jail appear cold and unrelenting. The dark mist sheltered dangerous religious fanatics, renegades, and fiends. Nina walked to the vehicle, cleverly camouflaged behind an unruly bush. Arun followed closely and urged her to slow down. Nina jumped in and dropped her rain-drenched jacket on the floor of the vehicle. She smiled at the driver and greeted the other two gentlemen. When Arun squeezed his damp frame in the backseat, Jim turned on the ignition.

"How was it? What was it like?" Jim asked.

"It was exactly what it was supposed to be, even more evil than I expected," replied Nina. "The supervisor was disappointed that *The Express* sent a woman to interview him." If there was sarcasm in her reply, her tone didn't reflect it. Such a response, however, invited a gurgle of laughter.

It was a stealthy interview, much against media ethics and civilian niceties. The interview was arranged through the cooperation of some select officials at Dandiar jail and a couple of veterans from *The Express*. Such secrecy was necessary due to the nature of the meeting. Lately, there was a controversy on Babies Born Behind Bars or Babies Born in Bondage. The tug-of-war between assorted women's rights movements and political gurus created enough tension, and the media had an abundant harvest of sensational printing! A wide variety of news, in turn, gave birth to a perfect formula that percolated sizzling dialogues between a very angry political circle and an outraged population. As usual, a few representatives of law enforcement sat on a pedestal and reaped financial benefits—while service or silence was traded for monetary compensation.

"Well, we're glad that you're out of that building. I was getting nervous, although you had Arun with you. Were you nervous at all?" Jim asked. He was the head of the investigative team. He maneuvered the vehicle expertly down the curving mountain roads of Mirzadun. The local chauffeur, appointed by *The Express,* was habitually in conflict with the village arrack vendor. Therefore, Jim, who didn't mind driving in strange places, became the designated driver during this business trip.

"Just a little nervous," replied Nina. "I'm going back there tomorrow."

"What do you mean?" asked Jim, taking his eyes away from the road for a few seconds. "We're not sanctioned for a second visit. Anyway, why do you want to go back?"

"I heard her voice, you know the woman who had written to me a month ago?"

"But then, why didn't you see her?" Jim was understandably perplexed.

"She probably couldn't reveal her identity. She was standing behind a door."

Although Jim recollected fragments of Nina's earlier reference to the letter, he requested her to explain in detail to inform the whole audience.

"I received a letter a month ago," Nina explained. "It was an anonymous note written in my mother tongue, Tamil. My correspondent was then about seven months pregnant. She had known my mother very well, and she thought that I was her only hope. She had to talk to somebody."

"A pregnant prisoner … waiting to deliver a captive baby! This is exactly what makes our team's mission here a necessity!" Jim exclaimed.

"You see, since she lost her benefactor, I was her only hope," said Nina. "She had included her prison identification number in the letter and that was it."

"Her benefactor?"

"My mother," said Nina.

"Did you try to contact the prisoner?"

"When we arrived here a few weeks ago, I called the jail officials to contact her. I was disappointed because there was no prisoner under that particular identification number."

"How did you manage to go to her cell today? I mean, that woman is not supposed to be in this jail, am I right? Anyway, it's not in our schedule," asked Jim, confused.

"I know. I was surprised too. I wanted to know where the maternity section was because that's what I'll be writing about," Nina explained. "The official took me through the building. That's when that woman talked to me through the iron bar, behind a dirty door, probably for a couple of minutes. They took her away. I think nobody expected her to say anything at that moment. In fact, I wonder how she knew of my visit today because she mentioned that she didn't receive my reply to her letter. Well, anyway, I heard someone's voice telling that woman that her doctor was waiting."

"What did she say before they took her away?"

"She asked me if I received her letter," Nina replied. "As I said earlier, she didn't get my reply. I still don't understand how she could see me through that door. How did she know that I was in the jail, precisely at that moment? I'm so confused about this incident. Do you think somebody arranged that … so she could talk to me for a few minutes?"

"Possible. But how are you going to enter the jail tomorrow? If they won't let you see her, if they are telling lies about her presence there, what makes you think that you can accomplish anything by visiting? Won't it be better to write to her?" Jim asked.

"My letters would serve no purpose. The jail officials are apparently reading that woman's correspondence. I'm making a visit on a personal basis, purely as a visitor. I'm not going again as a journalist. I don't know, maybe I can take them by surprise?" Nina's voice had its customary finality.

"Alone?" came the unanimous question.

"Yes," came the solitary and firm reply.

Nina's associates begged, coaxed, shouted, and screamed at her for being stupidly resolute. It never stopped her before and it wasn't going to stop her now. She was adamant.

"We won't let you take a taxi. I'll go with you. You can introduce me as your brother or friend. Nina, you can have one more chance to talk to your anonymous correspondent. But I don't think you should meet her alone. Well?" Jim asked.

Nina was thankful. Dandiar jail was a typical correctional facility, steeped in corruption and bureaucracy. While some of the atrocities made news, most of the dirt got buried inside the fence. It was definitely not a place for a woman to visit alone, especially if she planned on entering without the status of a reporter. Nina was intelligent enough to understand that her professional badge served as an exit ticket and got her admission into various facilities on a safe note, and without a badge, who knows?

Jim parked the vehicle in the portico of the guesthouse. After a nice hot supper, Nina went to her room. The heavy wool blanket warmed her tired bones in the raw, cold night of the northern hills. Her thoughts flew to the anonymous letter and the reference to Nina's mother. Benefactor! Nina could name any number of people who would acknowledge her mother as one. Since the untimely and gruesome demise of her parents a few months ago, Nina had often wondered if there was anything to look forward to in this world. When those two people boarded the plane, nobody anticipated it to explode to pieces. Here she was—an orphan on the threshold of thirty. Her thoughts rambled to the jail again, especially to the cell from where that young woman had talked to her. Nina remembered walking through a long corridor that seemed endless, before taking a turn into the maximum-security cells. The atmosphere was colder than the stone floor, and the expression on the jailor's face was more rigid than the iron bars. Why was this woman detained under such severe security? Was she really a dangerous criminal? Her anonymous note didn't reflect the tone of an evil mind. The correspondent's pleading tone and her desperate call for help told Nina that something was terribly wrong. Nina was determined to get to the bottom of this woman's affairs.

Nina's hand automatically groped for the switch on the alarm clock. After a quick shower and a hasty breakfast, she reached for the letter in the walnut box on the sideboard.

It wasn't there. Where was it? She rummaged through the chest of drawers and everywhere her hands could reach. The letter was missing. Did someone enter her room during the night? Who? Why? Besides the caretaker and his wife, a few servants entered the guesthouse on a daily basis. It would be impossible to trace the letter or find the culprit who was responsible for its loss.

The vehicle roared down the muddy roads toward Dandiar jail.

"Are you sure you left the letter in that room, Nina?" asked Jim.

"Yes, I'm certain."

"If the letter is missing, how are you going to remember the identification number of the prisoner you wish to see?"

"I know it. Here it is," said Nina, retrieving a small piece of paper from her purse.

"Nina, when was the last time you saw the letter?" asked Arun.

"Last night," Nina replied. "I left it in a box by the bed before I went to sleep."

An eerie silence filled the vehicle. Nobody said a word, but one desperate question plagued everybody's mind.

Nina and Jim went to the visitor's bureau. As they walked through a maze of booths, chai chat, and tobacco smoke, they were fortunate to stop by the appropriate window. The clerk took his time to assess Nina and Jim before muttering in an emotionless voice that visitors needed to apply a week ahead to see prisoners. After a brief discussion, Jim and Nina decided to use their professional identifications. As expected, their media badges got them inside a little quicker. Further, the money that Jim pressed into the clerk's hand under the table added an incentive to relax the rules. Bureaucratic misdemeanor was an understatement in a place that seduced corrupt officers and criminals. As soon as Jim and Nina signed their names in the register, a document was produced in which they had to explain the reason for their visit. Nina wrote the identification number of the prisoner and scribbled a short, generic explanation.

"Nina, don't forget to write that the prisoner spoke to you yesterday," Jim whispered.

When Nina was done, a clerk directed them to a small room and asked them to wait. Apparently, he had to take the document that Nina had just completed to the officer in charge. After what seemed like an endless interval, the clerk returned and asked the visitors to follow him.

Several eyes stared at Nina. She stood out—not just because she was a woman in a male-dominated environment—because she was an exceptionally beautiful woman. She tried her best to look casual and ordinary when she went on these assignments. But she couldn't effectively hide her soft, beautiful features. And she couldn't underplay her radiant eyes and gorgeous skin color. She preferred to think that she looked presentable. A certain unassuming quality and a brilliant smile enhanced her beauty.

The clerk stopped outside Inspector Pandey's office and knocked on the door.

The man, who was sitting behind a huge desk, stared at Jim and Nina. There was something unrelenting in his eyes—eyes of steel that never acknowledged a smile or a frown.

"Take a seat," said Pandey, staring at the visitors.

For some vague reason, Jim wished he had been successful in stopping Nina's visit to the jail today.

"I understand that you're here to visit Parvathi?" the inspector enquired in a flat tone, glancing at Nina's document.

Nina didn't want the inspector to know that she wasn't aware of her correspondent's name until now. "Yes, Sir," she replied, wiping her moist palms with a tissue.

"Why didn't you mention the prisoner's name in the document?" asked Pandey, staring at Nina.

"Oh, that," replied Nina, nervously. "Did I forget to write that down?"

"I'm sorry that your effort has been useless," said Inspector Pandey. "She is no more. Parvathi went into labor last night. The stillborn child took its mother's life with it." Inspector Pandey faced the visitors like a piece of stone—emotionless and cold.

Nina was beyond shock. This can't be. She had heard her voice just the day before! "May we pay our last respects to Parvathi?" Nina asked in a shaky voice.

"That's not possible. You must understand that Parvathi was a refugee. She had no family or friends ... who might wish to see her for the last time. There was no need to wait. The body has been cremated," replied Pandey, with no change in his deadpan expression.

"No, that can't be true. Her family …"

Jim squeezed Nina's hand to signal a warning. She glanced at his profile and kept quiet. She desperately tried to recall some of the details in the anonymous note. The prisoner had a family. She was anxious to talk to Nina—instead of a family member—because she believed that Nina would be the best person to help her in that particular situation.

"Did you make any attempt to meet Parvathi before now?" Pandey asked. His voice displayed no anxiety, no concern, and no curiosity. It was simply a bland question.

"Yes, I tried to call Parvathi," Nina replied, not sure of what she should say. "It was about a couple of weeks ago. But the clerk who talked to me said that there was no inmate under that particular identification number. That's why I was surprised when she … Parvathi spoke to me yesterday."

"Well, I'm sorry you couldn't see Parvathi when you called earlier," said Pandey, "we have some idiots working here. The clerk must have misunderstood your enquiry. Parvathi was here until yesterday and …"

The visitors walked quietly to the parking lot. There was not a soul around them, but as they returned to their vehicle, it felt as though a thousand eyes were watching them.

Pandey picked up the phone and commanded his assistant to come to his office. A tall, clean-shaven man walked in and closed the door behind him. Surprisingly, his huge, muscular frame made minimum noise as it entered the room. His physique that could effortlessly quell an opponent was not the only intimidating aspect of this man. His face, scarred on one side due to an encounter with a sharp razor during a violent brawl, displayed a cold determination that didn't encourage any man to cross his path. He stood attentively in front of his superior's desk.

"That woman, Parvathi—is it taken care of?" Pandey's voice was barely a whisper.

"Yes, Sir. All done."

"Any witnesses?" asked Pandey.

"Three, Sir. I was there and …" he mentioned the names of two other men who were devoted to Pandey's cause.

"Good. Keep up the good work."

Pandey's eyes were already on the file on his desk. The large man left the room as quietly as he entered.

"I've failed. She needed me and I couldn't do anything. How could this happen?" asked Nina. "That helpless woman is dead, overnight, as though she just vanished."

Comforting words surrounded Nina. She had tried. She had certainly taken a lot more effort than most people would have done in her place.

"I'll be back here sometime soon to work on the project. When I return, I'll look into the details of her death," said Nina. "There's something I'm not able to see that should be obvious. But I won't rest until I sort this out. That inspector! I'll break his teeth to get to the bottom of this!"

"There you go, Nina," one of her associates exclaimed. It was always refreshing to hear a zesty Nina.

The assignment at Dandiar was done. The train left on schedule that afternoon. Nina couldn't get Parvathi out of her mind. And she never would. It was a sad episode with no closure. Nina could never get over this misery. And her mother's face appeared in the backdrop slowly, gently. Tara was loved and respected by so many. She had been a friend of the unlucky Parvathi, but her mother had been a friend of many unfortunate individuals. And she was no more. Why did she die so early? She could have helped several other helpless people. Why did her parents die in such a horrific manner? Nina picked up a magazine. An inexplicable feeling kept fogging her vision.

The train arrived on time. Delhi was just a few hours away from Dandiar. Still, timely arrival was a rarity these days. Dev took her suitcases from the porter and opened the car door. It was nice to come home, in the middle of smog, vendors, noises, and an endless succession of sundry vehicles, all very dutifully following a nameless leader. Dev was an expert driver. He weaved skillfully through the Delhi traffic and narrated a list of events that happened in the few weeks she was away from home.

Home looked good. Bitsy handed a cup of chai to Dev and ordered him not to smudge the just-mopped floor with his street shoes. Bitsy continued where Dev had left off. She informed Nina about the current events in the flat above and the one next door.

Nina went to bed after a quick supper. What happened to the anonymous letter? Who had her reply to that letter? Who was behind this? A shiver ran through her veins.

A few weeks before the team from *The Express* visited the prison, Ahmed Asim dialed a private number known only to a few individuals. This man preferred to stay in neutral territory. He was an atheist. He got rid of certain men and women for the pure pleasure of earning money. Asim gave this assassin a peculiar assignment. He could have sent any of his dozen employees for this job. He didn't. For this particular mission, he didn't wish to reveal his religious association.

Asim was tired of waiting. How could he get rid of Inspector Pandey? Pandey aggravated him. He was a thorn in Asim's plans. Pandey represented a breed that had a price: money, a lot of money! Asim knew that Pandey had three flats in Delhi's suburbs, each registered under a different name. Only the house in Dandiar legally belonged to him. And this was just a fraction of Pandey's acquisitions. He was assured of a sizable allowance, neatly placed in various accounts. What was new? Pandey breathed easily and went to bed with no worries at all because of one comforting thought; he had the support of several corrupt politicians.

Pandey was one of many parasites that plagued the country. What made Pandey stand out in the list of Asim's enemies? He was a religious fanatic, definitely the hardcore variety. Pandey belonged to every association that proclaimed to keep Hinduism secure. That ancient religion would function so much better without the influence of a ruffian like Pandey. This religion, with its foundation firmly based on non-violence and compassion, would be terrified of Pandey and his association of militants. There was no fanatic worse than Pandey, was there?

Yes, there was one. Ahmed Asim! And he took pride in it. He hated Hindus with a vengeance. Every time he took the Koran in his hand, he felt a surge of emotion—not of piety, not of compassion, not of congenial feelings. His one and only thought was to uphold the superiority of Islam. And if his goal meant the downfall of other religions, let it be. If his passion meant the disappearance of certain individuals, let it be. Nothing mattered. Nothing—no child, no man—mattered beyond his religion.

Asim's family had conducted successful businesses in Dandiar for several generations. As a businessman, Asim couldn't avoid the path of Pandey. More importantly, these two men's cockeyed and opposing religious principles made them bitter enemies. Pandey knew what Asim did for a living, a comfortable living at that, just as the latter knew of the inspector's colorful career. Both men were looking for one slip, one mistake on the other's part, to put the enemy to public shame—the kind of ignominy where no important politician could offer help to extricate a friend from jail.

Earlier, Asim's clan was proud of smuggling alcohol, sandalwood, ivory, and gold. They also dabbled in narcotics. The new generation took a deep plunge into the field of weapons. Asim was in close contact with a couple of dealers on the other side of the border. This connection brought him significant profit and some fuel for explosions and disasters in the community. Lately, Dandiar jail had become a hub of nasty religious disasters. Irritating! Asim had some spies strategically stationed there. If one of Pandey's men sent a disciple of Asim to the hospital, one of Asim's servants sent that man to heaven. At times, the man's wife and children went with him.

Asim looked at the letter, written in Urdu and hand-delivered by a messenger in the strictest confidence because the post couldn't be trusted at the present time. He had to settle an issue before it got out of control. Interference from the police was getting more and more annoying. Some of them were in his payroll. Others, supposedly a little elusive, were not tempted by his bribery. There was a rumor that a tiny, close-knit, law enforcement unit was waiting to get the weeds of that society. The Asims and the Pandeys laughed obnoxiously at this group's sincere effort. Those poor officials were small fries! Honesty was an old-fashioned value and honor was a dead trait. Honesty! Honor! They must be joking!

◆ ◆ ◆

Anil Roy ruled this end of the journalism market with *The Express* in his pocket. He scowled at the end of the phone conversation with one of the unsavory executives. This bigwig was persuading Roy to underplay the noise about the jail stories or the Dandiar project. Roy must comply. Dirty politics! Besides, Roy had a family. He had heard rumors about a fanatic inspector at Dandiar and his equally mad opponent. Roy couldn't afford to make waves. Anyway, the Dandiar project was not worth losing his job.

Dev swerved the sleek vehicle into the new parking lot of Jawahar Office Park and wished Nina a good day. Nina took the lift to the sixth floor. She had a slight headache. She rummaged in her purse for a painkiller and took a cup of coffee before entering Roy's office. Arun was ready with his photographs, already processed and displayed on the table.

"Nina, you're back. It's good to see you," Sandy said, hugging her friend affectionately. "Jim told me. Are you all right?"

"I am, Sandy. Thanks."

As the associates were leaving, Roy requested Nina to stay a little longer. "You've done a good job, Nina. You've been working hard for several months now, haven't you?" Roy smiled affectionately.

"Thank you, Sir. I'm really excited about this project," said Nina. "I can't wait to see my work in print."

"That's what I wanted to talk to you about ..." his voice lingered.

Nina was beginning to sense something unpleasant. She had known Roy for several years. She could read him like a book. "Is something the matter?" Nina asked.

"They don't want you to be the writer for the Dandiar project."

"They? Who?"

He talked. She listened. She stormed out of his office.

Roy understood Nina's anger. Yes, dirty politics! He decided to remove Nina from the project because she was a shrewd and intelligent journalist. If she returned to Dandiar, she would dig into the dirt and shred the responsible parties to pieces. But *The Express* couldn't entirely retreat from the project at this point. That wouldn't be sensible. Roy decided to install Kumar in Nina's place because he had to send a moron to Dandiar for the sake of appearance. Roy had immense faith in Kumar's stupidity. Kumar would interview a few officials, collect useless information, and return with nothing worth mentioning. Roy was not proud of evicting Nina out of the project. Well, he would find something better for her.

"Sandy, do you have a few minutes?" Nina asked, stopping by Sandy's cubicle. "I'd like to talk to you."

They decided to have an early lunch. In the meantime, Nina went back to her office. She answered calls and took care of her mail. She looked at the day's schedule. She was meeting her family lawyer in the evening. Nina looked at the clock. She was hungry.

Sandy and Nina went to a small restaurant and ordered alu paratha and chai.

"What's going on, Nina?" Sandy asked.

"Roy, or whoever is behind this new assignment, is kicking me out of the Dandiar project," said Nina. "And the job goes to Kumar. Can you believe it? I need to transfer my hard work to that idiot."

It was an insult to call Kumar a writer. He was hired because of his father, who had been a writer for *The Express* for over forty years.

"Nina, you can't mean that. It's outrageous."

"Yes, Sandy, I'm supposed to withdraw because I'm a woman and it's a dangerous project for me. As the chief writer, I've to make a few more visits to Dandiar. They think I shouldn't. They want to give the job to Kumar!"

"Really? It wasn't dangerous when they sent you to the location to establish research?"

"Apparently, I'm not needed anymore, Sandy. Somebody wants me out of the way."

Sandy was furious. She hated Kumar, a spineless third-rate writer. It was no secret that he thrived on other employees' hard work. "Why Kumar? If they want to take the project away from a woman, why that idiot?" Sandy asked, genuinely confused.

"Politics, Sandy, just simple, politics. I'm so sick of it."

"I'm sorry, Nina. What're you going to do? Will you concentrate on your other projects now?"

"No, I'm going to quit," whispered Nina, staring at the smog-covered traffic.

"WHAT?" Sandy's voice went up several notches. "You're going to resign because of an idiot? What's wrong with you? Where's your spirit?" Sandy asked, frustrated and a little confused. Sandy expected Nina, of all the people she knew, to fight for what belonged to her.

"I'm tired of all the Kumars and the Roys in this business. I'm tired," sighed Nina. "I want to go somewhere and just disappear."

"You're scaring me, girl. Look here, Jim and I are always here for you. Now don't you ever forget that! Going somewhere? You're not going anywhere. You're having supper with us this evening, all right?" Sandy frequently ordered Nina to join her family for a quiet meal.

"Thanks, Sandy, but not today. I'm meeting the family lawyer regarding some property. I invited him to have supper with me."

Chandran arrived promptly at seven and rang the doorbell that chimed something classical. Dev opened the front door and politely welcomed the guest. While waiting for Nina, the lawyer looked appreciatively at the tastefully decorated flat. Must cost a bundle to afford such a place, but Nina managed. She was a well-paid journalist and a busy writer. She probably earned quite a bit through her freelance or paperback assignments. He wasn't quite sure how it worked. Besides, Gopal and Tara had left a vast fortune for their children.

Nina greeted Chandran with a certain degree of warmth he was used to since her childhood. Dev poured whisky for the guest and wine for Nina.

"So, how are you, my dear? Keeping good health, I hope?" Chandran enquired, luxuriously sipping his drink.

Nina smiled and exchanged proper niceties with Chandran.

"Nina, it has been a while. If I keep chatting, I might forget to settle the matter that brought me here tonight."

"What is it?" asked Nina. She noticed that he had grown more portly in the last few months. The sofa creaked as he adjusted his weight on it.

"It's about the property in Kanyakoil, which belonged to your mother's family. Now it's yours. There's also this building that's used as an orphanage. Your family has owned this property for several years, remember?" Chandran asked.

"Of course, I know exactly what you're talking about. My family has been using the property as a holiday home. I haven't visited Brinda recently. And I know the orphanage well. I've volunteered at Mercy House several times during my holidays. Well, what about the property?" asked Nina.

"I thought your parents wanted to lease it to someone when I talked to them last time. There are a few interested parties. Since the property is yours now, would you like to make a decision?" Chandran stared at Nina. She had a strange expression. Did she rapidly swallow a mouthful of wine?

"Don't lease it," Nina gasped. She took Chandran to the dining room.

"By all means, you can go to Brinda for a month now and then, but you can lease it to extravagant tourists at other times," he suggested, curious about Nina's sudden interest in retaining the property. "Time share is the buzz right now."

Dev served vegetable pulav, raita, and chips, and returned to the kitchen to get poori and masaal.

"I want to move there. I want to live in Brinda," said Nina, quite casually.

"Move to Kanyakoil, to that property?" asked the lawyer. It required a lot to distract his attention from food. This seemed to be one of the occasions. "What about your job, this apartment, and Delhi?"

"I've decided to leave my job. Anyway, I want to concentrate on freelance assignments now …" Nina spoke slowly. She was trying to assimilate the fact in her own mind.

"Leave *The Express*? I'll be damned! Do your uncle and aunt know about this?"

The question was inevitable. Still treating her like a child! Chandran did that often, especially when he was under the influence of her domineering aunt, Seetha. "No, they don't know," replied Nina. "I'll tell them later."

"And your brother?"

"No. I'll tell him later. I hope what I'm telling you will stay with you?" asked Nina. She was getting irritated. She didn't feel the least need to justify her decisions.

"Yes, of course, your information will stay with me," Chandran agreed. "It's just that we worry about you." He was fond of Nina, and he hoped she would become less defiant, marry a decent man, and let her family and friends live without worries. Nina's sudden news, however, didn't ruin his appetite. He sent a compliment to the kitchen and followed Nina to the drawing room for tea and dessert. "Nina, have you thought enough about your decision? I hope you're not going to move right away, are you?" asked Chandran.

"No, I'll be working for at least another month. I've decided to stay in Delhi for two to three months."

"That would certainly give me sufficient time to finish business before you move to Kanyakoil," said Chandran. He continued to talk about old times. When he got ready to leave, he assured her that he would be back in a week or two to discuss the final arrangements. He paused at the door and asked her to think again about her decision. "Nina, a young woman, living away from her friends and family—of course, you'll have Bitsy and Dev, still …"

"Should I remind you that it's the new millennium? Still treating me like a child!" Nina said, not bothering to hide her irritation.

He laughed and walked to the lift.

Bitsy and Dev received the news with a lot of ease that surprised and comforted Nina. Bitsy was generally under the impression that Nina was too strong-willed for her own good. Perhaps the quiet, retired life in the country would mellow her down and make her wish for a family of her own. Dev agreed with his wife. He started to look forward to happy hours in the gardens around Brinda. Bitsy and Dev went to bed that night with lighter hearts than they had experienced in several months.

While Nina's parents were alive, her father had occasionally suggested that they should sell Brinda that was in Tara's name. Tara wouldn't sell it. She had grown to view Brinda as a dear place to visit. It was more than a mere building, and she shared her mother's attachment to that property. Tara decided to leave Brinda in Nina's hands. The family owned other equally valuable properties, including the huge house in Delhi, which could be given to Jay and his family.

Nina was glad to inherit Brinda. She had spent several holidays in that beautiful home. Not surprisingly, she looked at it as her mother and grandmother had done. She had not spent much time there in the past few years because of her busy career. Now, suddenly, she couldn't stop thinking about the soothing effect of Brinda. The quiet whispering beauty and the modest grandeur had no equal. When she was young, she had spent several weeks in Kanyakoil, walking between paddy fields, listening to the streams. Chandran looked at Brinda and saw a 'time share' and vacation paradise! How typical! He meant well. He was one of her father's good friends. What vexed Nina was the fact that Seetha had a good influence over Chandran's opinion regarding Nina's future plans. She wasn't going to let Seetha influence her decision regarding Brinda or any other matter. It was amazing how fast news traveled even in a big city of this volume. A few friends of Nina's parents called to express concern at her sudden decision to move. A few were mildly curious. Some wondered if anything was amiss. Aunt Seetha! No media was more efficient than Seetha's mouth. How fast could she talk? Questions were inevitable, and Nina prepared to answer a barrage of enquiries.

Nina looked at the heavy traffic through the window in her office. A routine sight, no doubt, yet everything appeared new and different. She picked up the phone and dialed Roy's extension. Her boss answered promptly. Nina walked into Roy's spacious room and gave him her letter of resignation. He was naturally shocked by such an unceremonious announcement.

"You can't be serious about quitting!" said Roy.

"I am," said Nina.

Roy expected Nina to be upset about losing the Dandiar project to Kumar, but he certainly didn't anticipate anything as drastic as this. He tried one of his favorite tactics. "I'm not going to accept this letter, Nina," Roy said, assuming an indifferent air. "Why do you wish to resign? Do you have a better offer somewhere? It's that goat, the general manager at *The Eastern Globe*, isn't it? He's still mad that Jim left him to come to us!"

"No, Sir, I'm resigning because you can't trust me to do a man's job," replied Nina.

"What nonsense is this? You're the best in the business. Oh, it's the unmentionable project! I should've known. The decision has been made because it's not safe for a woman, Nina. Anyway, you can understand that it's certainly not my decision. My hands are tied, my dear. Please take a seat."

His hands were tied! Nina looked at him. She saw the shadow of a familiar and tiring trend. He was a master at getting work done, any work done, his way, for a successful finish! For the first time, Nina realized that she didn't want to become another Roy, and this resolution surprised her more than anything that had happened in the last few days. An unpleasant side of her boss, dormant so far, surfaced now. She felt the inevitable disgust of keeping one's head above water in this backstabbing profession. Why didn't she see this before? Why did it take so long to knock on her senses?

"Why is the assignment not safe now?" Nina asked. "I did all the research. I've worked day and night on getting this project to this level. This isn't fair. I'm leaving in a month." Nina was struggling to control her rising voice. She made every effort to stay calm. She refused to take a seat. Defiance would be the best way to get through this meeting. She was tired of old tricks and mundane habits. Anyway, she was the one affected by this miserable project. Why was he pouting like a child?

"Can we talk about this later?" Roy asked. "I'm sure you'll feel better once we discuss this issue over a nice dinner. How about tonight, Nina?"

"No, thank you," said Nina. She was out of his office even before he opened his mouth to protest.

Jim and Sandy met Nina outside her office. "Sandy told me last night, Nina. You can't be serious about leaving *The Express*? Are you really leaving Delhi?" asked Jim.

Nina realized then that she had a lot of explaining to do.

Seetha was happy to see her niece. In her opinion, Nina tramped around the country too often, for a woman. Seetha already knew about Nina's rather drastic moving arrangement, but she had not expected her little niece to go through it all the way. Too bad, Seetha should know that once Nina's mind was made up, it was set in stone. Well, Nina was here to confirm her plan, and she groped for a good beginning. It was a lot easier to explain her decision to her friends than to her hysterical aunt and her worried uncle. Seetha didn't mince matters. She read Nina a lecture—her niece's irresponsibility, her stubborn nature, how she neglected traditions.

"Why can't you marry a nice young man, Nina?" asked Seetha.

"I want to wait till I fall in love."

"That only happens in movies and novels," said Seetha. "Be sensible. If you can't see what's good for you, let the elders decide."

"Athai, I've thought about this. Marriage is not going to be my salvation!"

"Oh, Nina, listen. Why can't you marry a man first and fall in love with him later? Why not that young man, Kumar? He is from a good family. They have sizable property in the south. I know his mother. She asked me last week if I would talk to you about her son," said Seetha. "They have tea estates in Ooty."

"That family has estates in that area," said Nina's uncle.

"See, Nina, Kumar is significantly wealthy," said Seetha. "And he's your colleague. You must know him well."

"Unfortunately, I do know him well. He's an idiot. You don't really expect me to marry him, do you?" Nina asked.

"So are most men, Nina. So is your uncle! I married him, didn't I?"

Her uncle laughed nervously at this frank disclosure.

"Do you know that Kumar is a notorious playboy?" asked Nina.

"Oh, Nina, marriage will change him. You know boys!" replied Seetha.

Nina knew the hopelessness of any situation once her aunt was in charge. With a lot of reassurance regarding her careful decision, she tried to convince her aunt that she was, after all, going to live in a house that belonged to her mother, a house that was located in a quiet, small town. Nina didn't expect her uncle to interject at this moment with uncharacteristic courage.

"Seetha, how can Nina get into trouble in such a happy, simple surrounding? Anyway, she would always have Bitsy and Dev with her, wouldn't she? What harm can come her way in such a homely environment?" her uncle asked Seetha.

Nina had always valued her uncle's kindness. Now she thanked him for his timely support.

"You'll call us to keep us informed of your welfare, Nina, won't you? Why don't you spend a week with us before moving to Kanyakoil?" Nina's uncle asked.

"Thanks for the invitation, but I can't. Remember, I'm going to New York to attend my friend's wedding," replied Nina.

"That's right," said Seetha. "What's that friend's name again?"

"Kim. Kim Roberts," said Nina.

"Oh, yes, the famous journalist!" exclaimed Nina's uncle. "When are you leaving, Nina?"

"Tonight."

"Going abroad … spending all that money to attend a friend's wedding?" asked Seetha.

It was Nina's money! Was it Seetha's business? Well, old habits never die. Nina explained that she was attending a couple of business meetings during the wedding trip and went to the door before more questions appeared.

Dev dropped Nina at the airport. She was very excited about her friend's wedding, although the trip was going to be short. Nina was especially glad to get away from her recent disappointment at work.

New York City looked inviting. It had been her home for a year about eight years ago. It was a gorgeous wedding. Kim Roberts was a popular television figure in most households at dinnertime, and there was no surprise in seeing a milieu of photographers and reporters in the foyer of The Plaza. Nina recognized a couple of famous television anchors, and she was proud when they approached her to greet her. She had done some work for them from time to time, of course, with Kim's assistance.

Colin Hebert, Kim's husband, was pleasant. He was a renowned cardiologist. He was happy to exchange several niceties with Nina, his wife's special guest and friend from India. Nina enjoyed the luncheon and called for a taxi to go to the airport. She was looking forward to a weekend with the Baileys.

Sandy whistled at the pile of things Nina wished to get rid of at the auction before her move. "This is a nice painting," said Sandy. "You should have sold these things when Jim and I got married. I could have bought a lot of stuff at a decent bargain, Nina."

"You can still take anything you wish. You don't have to pay anything," Nina said amiably.

"Thank you, but no. We have accumulated too much already. Been married for years, as you know, and things just seem to multiply in the house. I guess that's a cumbersome annoyance that goes with marriage," Sandy said, smiling at her friend. "You know, you're still unmarried, Nina."

"Sandy! I always could count on you not to question me about THAT. You too?" Nina threw a faux wounded look in her friend's direction.

"I'm sorry. I couldn't help being nosy," Sandy said, looking apologetic. "I worry about you, Nina. Jim does too."

"I know, and don't be silly. You're not nosy. Perhaps … marriage is not for me. Do you think I'm strange?" Nina asked. "I've started to consider marriage more as an annoying necessity than as a mode of domestic happiness."

Sandy laughed at her friend's candid assessment. "Oh, Nina, an annoying necessity? It might be, sometimes. But the annoyance is quite comforting, and the sex isn't bad either."

Nina responded to her friend's impish wink with a wicked grin.

Nina and Sandy were not surprised to see some familiar faces at the auction. Stephanie's had a Victorian charm. It was a busy gathering place where the rich and the famous frequented to buy expensive knick-knacks. Some capital questions were imminent. True, but she was ready. She had rehearsed a good explanation: she was here to sell some contemporary furniture and art pieces from her flat because these particular items would be out of their sphere in Brinda. Her current task allowed her less time to indulge in chitchat, and the inquisitive women should be aware of that. Therefore, Nina managed to return home with minimum repetitions of "Why are you leaving? Why all of a sudden?"

Nina's flat was brimming with heads past counting. She owed her family and friends a farewell event. Cocktail glasses were moving about in profusion. Nina saw her uncle indulging in one too many, not at all mindful of the sharp glances his wife, Seetha, sent in his direction. With each swig, his voice went up a notch. Nina hoped for her uncle's sake that his wife wouldn't reprimand him in public.

Nina's eyes were momentarily on her aunt. She was sitting by one of her matronly friends. Nina couldn't control a spontaneous giggle at what she saw. There was her aunt, taking a social sip of some select wine. Aunt Seetha's proper upbringing didn't look at alcohol with a congenial eye. According to her upper-middle-class upbringing, women from respectable families were supposed to stay away from alcoholic temptations. However, her association and fascination with the upper-class-refined-folks nudged her to take a sip every now and then—discreetly, socially, advisedly! Seetha's friend, however, threw caution to the wind. She was boldly reaching for refills. When a few heads turned in their direction, Seetha shrewdly moved her friend to the front door and signaled to one of the servants to fetch the chauffeur. When the last guest left, Nina was glad to soak her tired feet in the hot tub.

◆ ◆ ◆

Nina walked out of the airport, slightly nervous and shaky. She was relieved to see Dev's warm smile. Bitsy and Dev had left Delhi a couple of weeks earlier to get Brinda ready. Nina had wished to travel together with them, but her wish was overruled. In certain matters, Bitsy's stubborn nature surpassed Nina's.

As the car went steadily through the tree-lined boulevard, Nina looked at the humble streams and the lush paddy fields. How fragile the fields appeared against the stark, blue hills! She poured a cup of tea from the thermos Bitsy had thoughtfully sent with Dev. Her heart whispered that she had made a wise decision. She was going to be happy and contented in the country. When Dev parked the car in front of the veranda, Bitsy welcomed Nina with a profusion of warmth that spoke of a renewal after a year's separation.

"Oh, Bitsy, how could I change in just a couple of weeks?" Nina asked. She accepted Bitsy's welcome and returned her embrace with ardent affection.

Brinda never appeared so outrageously big when Nina used to visit during the holidays. Did it seem enormous at the present time because it was now her home and was rather permanent? The usual fuss of unpacking and eating was over, and Nina was unwinding on the swing in the oversized drawing room. It was a huge swing, dented in many places, but it was charming and stately. She remembered sitting here, leaning on her grandmother's shoulder, listening to her fascinating stories.

"Isn't this wonderful, my dear Nina?" Bitsy asked. "So quiet and no traffic."

"Yes, Bitsy. It's wonderful to be here. But are you happy? Is Dev happy?"

"Of course, my dear, we are. I'll show you the vegetable garden in the morning. Oh, we have an assortment of vegetables and it's such a treat to cook with homegrown produce. You'll see the orchards at leisure, I'm sure." Next, Bitsy updated Nina about the mundane housekeeping news. She had hired a gardener to help Dev manage the outdoors and a daily maid to clean the house.

"Bitsy, please hire enough servants. I won't have you managing everything on your own. Are you listening?" Nina asked Bitsy in her usual fashion.

"Nina, stop worrying your head over these issues," replied Bitsy, authoritatively. "I've already hired a few hands. Remember, you decided to move to the country chiefly because you couldn't take the stress and tension of the big city, not to mention the hectic career. Learn to relax."

Nina couldn't fall asleep. Bitsy had done a beautiful job with this room. Muslin curtains and childhood souvenirs! The crisp cotton sheet and the handloom coverlet completed a cozy bed. But Nina's mind wandered to that woman's voice in the jail. How she wished she had a glimpse of her face! Nina had made a resolution that she would break Inspector Pandey's teeth for treating Parvathi's case callously. Lucky for him, those teeth would be intact now because Nina would never have a chance to go to Dandiar jail.

Nina looked at the array of photographs on the wall—her dear family. She loved that old picture of her favorite uncle, Anand. He was no more. She missed him. So much had happened in the last few months. She didn't regret her decision even a little bit. She was glad about leaving Delhi, glad to be on her own. When the Dandiar contract went to Kumar, she felt mortified. It was not her pride or her self-respect that couldn't stand the mortification. It was something within her that was nameless. She was definitely relieved to be out of the oppressive, career-jockeying lifestyle.

Nina had planned on sleeping late that morning, but she woke up sometime when dawn and night were at crossroads. She got out of the bed and walked to the balcony. What she saw took her breath away. The sun was rising, sneaking up on a dowdy, gray sky. She could stand here every morning and admire the orange streaks on the silvery water. Beautiful! She saw the image of a bicycle coming up the garden path. That must be the milkman. How serene the entire picture was! The morning breeze and the fuzzy clouds spoke volumes with the stooping branches, bending down to take a dip in the water. Goodness! She expected to be happy here, but her new home was turning her into a poet! She must invite

Sandy and Jim to come here during their next vacation. Their children would enjoy the visit. There was so much room to run around!

Bitsy brought coffee. "What would you like for breakfast, Nina?" she asked, leaving the tray on a wicker table.

Nina found Bitsy in the kitchen garden. "You're not going to the temple with us, Bitsy?" Nina asked.

"No, Nina, the contractor is coming today to undertake a couple of improvements in the kitchen. I'll stay home and wait for him," said Bitsy.

The priest greeted Nina with a friendly smile and enquired after her welfare. She was about to tell him that she had moved into her mother's family home, but he knew that already. Of course, everybody knew everything in this small town. She understood and smiled.

Nina walked toward the peepul tree. Dev had parked the car in its shade. Why was he muttering under his breath? What was the matter?

"I don't want people to leave things close to our car, Nina," Dev complained.

They found something placed near the car. Walking closer to the vehicle, they saw that it was a baby's carriage. Further inspection showed a baby inside. Where was the family? Surely, they must be looking for the child! Nina and Dev looked here and there. They saw nobody. That was very strange. The baby stretched its arms, yawned, and began to cry. Nina picked up the infant. It stopped crying instantly and stared at her face.

"Nina, you shouldn't have picked up the baby like that. What if the family is around here? What if they get upset?" Dev began to scold Nina.

"Dev, this baby was crying. Well, somebody has to pick it up. Do you expect this infant to wait patiently for its family to return?"

"Nina, just because the baby's carriage is close to our car, well, it doesn't mean that you attend to it right away. Think before you do something, child."

Nina asked him to be quiet. What else were they supposed to do? The child was obviously left there by mistake or on purpose. The baby started to whimper again. Dev looked in the carriage for a pacifier and found one, attached to a note. It was addressed to Nina.

In the middle of questions, suppositions, and speculations at the sight of an abandoned baby, the first business was to inform the police. Next, Bitsy made a list of essential baby products. The baby's mother had left some items in his carriage, enough for a few days, but the supply would deplete soon.

Where was the mother? Who was she? Why did she leave her child in that manner? Nina held the baby close to her. A week ago, the note surprised Nina more than the fact that the baby was left there. What a note to receive at such a time in her life! It indicated that the baby's mother was one of many who had been touched by the kindness of Nina's mother. She read it again.

Dear Miss Nina,

I am writing this letter to make a very strange request. I know how shocking it must be to find my child. Will you please take care of the baby until a family comes forward to adopt him? If he becomes difficult to manage, please take him to the orphanage. I'm requesting you to provide temporary care for my baby because you are Mrs. Gopal's daughter. Your mother told me that you are kind and that you accompanied her during many of her missions. Thank you for your kindness. God bless you. God bless my baby.

Sincerely,
Nikil's mother

Nina didn't think it was too much trouble to take care of the baby! However, every time she thought that the baby was her responsibility only until a family came forward to adopt him, something within her hurt.

Nina walked to the car with the baby in her arms. Bitsy followed with the infant bag. After sitting patiently for fifteen minutes in the waiting area, Nina rocked the restless baby in her arms. The nurse arrived with an apology and took them to a clean room. The baby smiled through the preliminary procedures, and the nurse said that he was the best baby.

"The doctor will be in shortly," said the nurse. She smiled at the baby and left. Bitsy followed the nurse to get a drink of water.

"Nina, how are you?" Dr. Menon entered the room and asked. He was a good friend of Nina's family.

"I'm fine, thank you. How are you, Dr. Menon?" Nina returned his smile.

"And you must be Nikil!" Dr. Menon smiled at the baby.

Nina had talked to Dr. Menon earlier to explain the situation regarding the foundling. At that time, the doctor had announced his decision to retire in a few months. His young partner would attend to the baby until a family came forward to adopt him.

"Have you heard anything from Children's Welfare Services, Nina?" Dr. Menon asked. "It's a long process, you know. Call me if you need any help."

"Dr. Menon, I've decided to adopt the baby," said Nina. She didn't realize that those were the words that were waiting to spill out of her mouth.

Bitsy walked in at that moment. She stared alternately at Nina and the doctor.

Dr. Menon tried to say something and cleared his throat. "You're going to adopt the baby?" he asked. "Well, well, you must've given this some thought, I'm sure."

"Yes, I have. I love this baby. I can give him a good life," Nina said earnestly.

"I'm sure you can. I'm also certain that you know the terminal nature of such a commitment. Good luck. You'll keep me posted, won't you?" asked the doctor.

Nikil cried when the needle poked his tender skin. While Bitsy took him to the porch to pacify him, Nina talked to the doctor a little longer before following him to the cashier's counter.

The short car ride appeared long. Bitsy was curious about Nina's sudden announcement regarding Nikil, but Nina didn't know how to begin. How could she explain her decision to Bitsy and Dev when she couldn't make a reasonable explanation in her own mind?

Nina left Nikil in his daybed before joining Dev and Bitsy in the drawing room. The visit to the doctor's office must have made the baby tired. He was fast asleep.

"Nina," began Bitsy. "Have you forgotten that you're unmarried? You have no concern at all about the society? What would it take to make you understand that adopting a baby is serious business?"

"Bitsy, this is the twenty-first century! I know at least two single women in Delhi who have adopted needy children. I have the financial means, I'm independent, I may never get married, and …"

"Oh, Nina!" exclaimed Bitsy, wincing as usual at the unsavory thought of Nina's reluctance to marry.

"Bitsy, Dev, I want to adopt this baby," said Nina, in a pleading tone. "I thought you both liked Nikil. I hope my decision won't be an extra burden! If it is …"

"We love the baby," Dev and Bitsy cried.

"How could you say such things, Nina?" asked Bitsy. "Surely, we want what you want. You're, after all, everything to us."

In the mean time, Nikil was crying fiercely for attention. Dev picked him up after announcing that it was his turn to pamper the little prince. That must have been the shortest nap in history.

Bitsy and Dev soon realized Nina's sincere intent in Nikil's case. Nina was level-headed, intelligent, and independent. She didn't have an impulsive bone in her body. If she was convinced that she was doing the right, sensible thing, it ought to be right and sensible!

Chandran had talked about a couple of professional acquaintances in Kanya-koil. Could one of his associates help her during the adoption process? Nina looked for her family lawyer's number and called him instantly.

"Nina, it's good to hear your voice," said Chandran. "What can I do for you?"

Nina explained the reason for her call.

"Adopt a baby? Really? Nina, I don't understand," he said.

"Will you pay attention to me and take me seriously?" Nina scolded him.

Chandran asked her roughly twenty questions in ten minutes. Every other question was, "Nina, do you know what you're doing?"

"Of course, I know what I'm doing," replied Nina, considerably irritated. "What I want you to remember is that I'm an adult."

Nina was sitting in her office, overlooking the kitchen garden. She had set up a separate room for her home-office to get her work done without distraction. As she was walking downstairs for tea, she saw Dev running to answer the phone. It was Aunt Seetha from Delhi! No, it can't be. She couldn't have discovered the famous story of adoption already?

"Nina, is it your ambition to drive your family up the wall? Chandran told me. Good God! What're you thinking about?" Seetha asked in a definite tone of despair.

Nina wondered if her aunt would ever understand how Nikil filled that little, empty something in her that was not easy to describe.

"If it's a baby you want," Seetha continued, "why don't you go about it the old-fashioned way? Get married, go on your honeymoon, get pregnant, and have a baby!"

"Athai, I'm not adopting this child because I'm eager to become a mother," Nina tried to explain. "It's just something that was meant to happen. We found each other."

"You're not a lesbian, are you?"

"What?" asked Nina.

"Well, I didn't mean to imply, but you know, you're not interested in men, and I just don't understand you or this sudden idea of your adoption business, Nina."

"I don't expect you to understand," said Nina.

"Nina, if you decide to go through this dreadful business, I'm washing my hands forever! I'll have nothing to do with you."

Nina fervently hoped that her aunt meant that. Seetha often made such promises, but she always came back to nag Nina!

Nina called the lawyer's office to make an appointment. She mentioned Chandran's name and managed to get an appointment with Mr. Sundaram within the week. Now it was time to answer her e-mail. Nina was happy to receive a mail from Sandy! She sounded happy at the news of the baby's arrival, but even she seemed to have her doubts.

Was it really such a big deal for a single woman to adopt and raise a baby? Why? Couldn't a woman hold enough love in her heart to delight a young life? When Nina held Nikil, she felt the softness of a thousand petals, the kindness of a thousand smiles, and all the love of a mother. She would give him affection, a wonderful life, endless bedtime stories, and much, much more. She didn't need a husband to recommend the society to certify her as an appropriate parent. Nina knew she would be a kind and good mother and that was sufficient to prompt her to make such an important decision. This child was meant for her. This love was meant to happen. She didn't know why. It existed in her heart and that was all that mattered!

Jay called Nina that evening to see how she had settled down in her new home. Really? That was the excuse he offered at the beginning of the conversation.

"Adopt a BABY!" Jay exclaimed. "Nina, what has gotten into your head this time? I know that you don't care about my sentiments, but please listen to me. Whatever happened to the traditional method of getting married and having a family?"

Nina listened to her brother patiently. If he knew that she wouldn't listen to his sentiments, why did he bother to lecture? This conversation was going nowhere. His association with his good wife was turning him into a suffocating and boring gentleman! Well, suffocating was probably a strong word.

"Jay, how did you discover the latest news so fast?"

"Seetha Athai called me, Nina. She was concerned, naturally."

Seetha wouldn't miss such a golden opportunity. Nina should have expected this phone call. Seetha liked Jay more than she liked Nina because he wasn't defiant or difficult. She approved of her nephew's very proper, responsible, family-oriented personality.

Jay calmed down considerably and promised to visit Nina in a month or so. She said that she would look forward to his visit and hoped that he wouldn't bring his insufferable wife along. Actually, she would love to see her brother. It was his wife she couldn't tolerate.

Customary to her nature, Bitsy recapped the day's events when Dev, Nina, and Bitsy gathered in the drawing room at the end of the day. "Nina, the contractor needs a month to finish the improvements in the kitchen. In the meantime, we can set up a temporary kitchen next to the washroom. What do you think about this?" asked Bitsy. "And Nina …"

Bitsy had only finished part of her recital when the doorbell rang. Dev opened the door and greeted a woman whom none of them had met before. She was young. Her demure eyes seemed to be constantly searching for something.

"Madam," the stranger said, nervously clearing her throat. "My name is Rohini. I've come about the job. I heard in my village that you needed a nurse for the baby."

Nina was surprised that help arrived so speedily. News, whether good or bad, did spread fast around these small towns. She smiled at the young woman and invited her to sit down.

"Madam," said Rohini. "I've brought a letter of recommendation from the director of the Women's Home in Chennai. Would you like to look at it?"

"From Chennai?" Nina asked. "I thought you were from around here."

"Yes, Madam. I belong to this area. But you see, I spent a couple of years in the pediatric ward at St. Anne's near Chennai. I was looking for employment locally to be close to my family … I mean, not far from it."

Nina read the letter. The director of the Women's Home had called Nina a week ago to let her know that she might be sending a young lady to work for her. So, here she was! She was young, was trained to look after infants, had a pleasant disposition, and was dependable. Nina looked at Rohini. She had round cheeks, beautiful eyes, and a ready smile.

"Rohini, when can you begin?" asked Nina.

"I can begin today, Madam."

Bitsy had been concerned about Nina's decision to hire a nurse, or a helper, or whatever position Nina had in mind. Bitsy had declared earlier that she needed no help! Nina, on the other hand, felt that Bitsy had a full plate already. It would be unfair to let Bitsy take care of the baby, in addition to the rest of her work. After seeing Rohini, both Bitsy and Nina felt reassured.

◆ ◆ ◆

Sometime around late afternoon on Tuesday, Nina received a call from the lawyer's office.

"I have some business in your neighborhood. May I come to your home to discuss the legal matter?" asked the lawyer. "This can save you a trip to my office."

Nina thanked him for his consideration.

"The lawyer is here," Bitsy announced and adjusted the blinds to filter the sunlight. "But here is another car, and who might that be? Are you expecting anybody else, Nina? But wait. These gentlemen seem to know each other."

Mr. Sundaram arrived promptly. Nina had met him briefly during one of her visits in the past. But she had never met the other gentleman. He was tall, had slightly unruly hair, a beard, and a mustache. Mr. Sundaram introduced the stranger as Dr. Tom Davis. Dr. Davis greeted Nina with a smile on his face and a twinkle in his eyes, and she was puzzled about his presence.

"So, what can I do for you?" asked Mr. Sundaram, sitting down on the sofa.

Dr. Davis sat by him. Bitsy deposited a tray with tea and vegetable puffs on the table, smiled at the company, and disappeared. The baby, napping in the daybed, was disturbed by the sound of the visitors and demanded instant attention. Nina picked him up and cradled him in her arms.

"What a cute baby! Your husband is going to join us, isn't he?" Mr. Sundaram enquired.

"I don't have one," said Nina.

The lawyer's eyes went from Nina to the baby. "Oh, I'm sorry," he said.

"Why? I'm not," said Nina, quite bewildered. She darted a glance at the doctor. He was shifting his position on the sofa, and that twinkle in his eyes was growing somewhat brighter. She had a strange feeling that he was enjoying this little conversation in which he had not taken part so far.

The lawyer was trying to find something appropriate to say, and a string of words just popped out of his mouth. "Mother—you—baby—alone," the lawyer babbled. "I didn't know that your husband had …"

"Mr. Sundaram, this baby was left in my care … that is until a family came forward to adopt him," said Nina, directly looking at the lawyer. "I wish to adopt him and I'm single."

It was apparent from the lawyer's expression that he had not come across such a sticky situation before.

Rohini picked up Nikil for his afternoon feeding. After she walked out of the room, the dumbfounded lawyer found his voice.

"Now, Mrs, sorry, Madam, do you want my assistance in the adoption process?" Mr. Sundaram asked. "This is why you want my assistance, I see."

"Yes, would you like to?" asked Nina, trying not to sound eager. If this lawyer didn't work out, there should be others.

Mr. Sundaram looked at her and at the doctor alternately. Nina, for want of a distraction, took a good look at the other gentleman. He was a little 'foreign looking,' with brown-black hair and rather light brown eyes. He couldn't be a product of India. Who was he? Why was he here? She decided to enquire him!

"Doctor, may I know the purpose of your visit?" Nina asked him. "Are you here with Mr. Sundaram?"

"No, I'm not with Mr. Sundaram. We just happened to arrive here at the same time. I'm sorry," said the doctor, his confusion matching Nina's. "I thought you were expecting me. Didn't Dr. Menon call you?"

"No, he didn't. Oh, wait. Actually, his secretary called me earlier to inform me that the doctor would be coming today. I thought that she was talking about Dr. Menon."

"I apologize for the confusion. Dr. Menon was sure that you expected to meet me here soon. Well, I'm Dr. Menon's partner. Anyhow, the reason for my visit today is ... I also serve as a sort of a representative or liaison for the orphanage and the adoption agency. I'll be handling the adoption of this baby and ... you'll be seeing a lot of me."

Nina saw Tom Davis a lot. Bitsy discovered a good deal about the doctor.

"Nina," said Bitsy. "Dr. Davis is thirty-something, a bachelor, a generous man, a favorite among the townspeople, wealthy, and very handsome."

Nina laughed at the flow of flamboyant description. "Bitsy, he is a wealthy, thirty-something bachelor, is he?" asked Nina. "How did he dodge the clutches of ambitious mothers and eligible daughters?"

"I saw Dr. Davis in church this morning, Nina. What a nice young man he is! He asked about you and the baby."

"Did he? That's nice, Bitsy."

"You sound like you don't think much of him, my dear Nina."

"Bitsy, I hardly know that man. I have no opinion of him," Nina said, smiling mischievously. "Should I caution Dev? Has he acquired a worthy competition?"

"Competition! You silly girl! Dr. Davis could be my son."

"Oh, Bitsy, I forgot to tell you. Guess what happened at the bank the other day?"

"What happened?" Bitsy asked anxiously.

"I met that big businessman, Balu. He knew Raja Thatha well, I think. He was talking about our family."

"That's nice."

"That's what I thought. Then he started to lecture about the adoption. I think he has a thing about women."

"You didn't open your mouth too much, did you?" Bitsy asked suspiciously.

"Don't worry. I didn't. I wanted to tell him to go to hell, but I just smiled and walked away."

"Good girl! If you want Nikil, you better watch your words!" said Bitsy.

It was a glorious, sunny day, and it promised nice weather. Nina decided to walk to the river. She liked to feel the gritty sand on her bare feet. As she was rolling up the hem of her jeans to keep it dry, she looked up and noticed a car coming on the driveway. Tom Davis got out and waved to Nina. He was walking in her direction the next minute.

"Dr. Davis, how are you?" Nina asked.

"I'm fine, thank you. How are you?"

"I'm doing well."

"I've a request," said Dr. Davis. "We'll be meeting often on Nikil's behalf. Please call me by my first name."

"Certainly, if you stop calling me Miss Gopal," smiled Nina.

"May I also make another suggestion? There's a festival in town. It's an annual affair that the townspeople diligently celebrate. You probably know about that already. Why don't you bring Nikil with you to the festival?"

Nina liked his suggestion. While she was thinking of a way to thank him, he extended the invitation to Bitsy and Dev. It didn't take long for Tom Davis to call Bitsy by her first name. Bitsy was always "Bitsy" even when Nina was a child. The name seemed to say it all: aunt, counselor, friend, and any other title a certain occasion may dictate. And Dev would have it no other way. He expected Nina's friends to call him by his first name.

"I'll be happy to come, and I'll bring Bitsy and Dev," said Nina, smiling politely.

"One other thing," he continued in his smooth voice, "you know the tendency of these people? A lot of them are very orthodox. Could you dress in a more traditional manner when you're among them for, what shall I call it, a social activity? Can you wear a sari?"

Nina saw him looking at her faded jeans and embroidered white shirt. She disliked the way his eyes twinkled whenever he disapproved of something or whenever he was amused by something. She wasn't sure which of the two categories she would fit into at the moment. However, she wanted him to know that his opinion didn't matter to her. "I see no reason to dress up at home. These clothes are comfortable. I know how to dress appropriately for formal occasions!" Nina sounded a little rude and hoped that he felt the rudeness. She started to walk to the house. "Anyway, why are you here?"

"Just to inform you about the festival. I tried to call you. Do you know your phone is not working?" asked Dr. Davis.

"Yes, we've known that, of course. We've been waiting for a technician to arrive since morning."

"Goodbye," said Dr. Davis. He waved to Bitsy and drove away.

Nina could see that Dr. Davis had become Bitsy's good friend. Madam Bitsy had a propensity to either charm people or scare them. Tom Davis was one of the lucky ones. Lately, Bitsy had started to rave about the good doctor. In fact, it was getting to be a rather monotonous situation. Dr. Davis! Dr. Davis seemed to be the subject of every other discussion. Wasn't there anything else the family could discuss?

Bitsy kept looking at the kitchen window. The afternoon milk was late. Nina, who was reading the newspaper in the kitchen garden, saw an elderly lady opening the garden gate. Her silver hair glistened in the afternoon sun. She smiled with a lot of cheer. After apologizing for coming late, she deposited her basket by the washing stone. Out came a couple of bags of milk, a packet of butter, and some eggs. Nina smiled at Valli. Wasn't she the legendary milk queen of the village? Bitsy had warned Nina not to let her mouth run in Valli's presence.

Valli measured Nina from head to toe, made a nice comment about her skin color, and admired her beautiful face. "My son, Ravi, is ill," Valli smiled. "So I decided to deliver the milk today. And I wonder why you want to adopt a baby without giving nature a chance."

Nina was accustomed to these appraisals and censures by now, and she was ready to laugh at this latest survey. A few men and women, who were acquainted with her grandparents, had already stopped her—at the temple, in the market, and just about everywhere—to question her about the adoption. Valli was not the first, and Nina realized that she wouldn't be the last. Valli was a typical representative of the traditional society! Instead of bristling at the old lady's impertinence, Nina tried a different route. "I know what you mean. But there's no decent bachelor in this small town. What am I to do?" asked Nina. "And why go through the nonsense of marriage, waiting, pregnancy, and finally … the baby, when I can have one without all the preliminary nonsense?"

Valli left without saying a word. Had Nina gone too far? Nina informed Bitsy about Valli and her advice.

"Nina, Valli could do a lot of harm," Bitsy cautioned her. "Please control your tongue next time."

Nina asked Bitsy to stop worrying about Valli and her meddling society.

Nina decided to show Dr. Davis how traditional she could appear. She pulled out a gorgeous sari of soft silk in sea green and chose a delicate pearl set that was designed for elegant yet simple occasions. When Nina came downstairs, she looked beautiful and elegant.

"Bitsy, Rohini, is Nikil ready?" Nina shouted from the drawing room.

"Nina, come here," Bitsy called from the nursery. "I think Nikil has a temperature."

Poor baby! Nina ran to the phone. As she was calling the doctor's office to leave a message for Dr. Menon or Dr. Davis, the doorbell rang. Dr. Davis was here!

"I just called your office," Nina said, quite surprised to see him. "Nikil is not well."

"I came to talk about something before you left. Well, it's a good thing I came. Is the baby with Bitsy?"

Nina's sari was not particularly rich or dazzling. It was quite suitable for the occasion. However, the cut of her blouse and the overall ensemble spoke of high fashion and sophistication. Tom pulled his eyes away from Nina and walked to Nikil's bedroom. The baby was sitting on Bitsy's lap with teary eyes and reddish cheeks. He smiled at the doctor for a moment. He soon cried when the thermometer poked his tiny ear. Rohini presented a list of Nikil's activities and wondered what was wrong with him.

Dr. Davis scribbled a prescription. "Nikil will be all right. I'll call in the evening. I'll be here tomorrow to check on him. In the mean time, will you call if you need me? This means that Nikil and you won't be going to the festival," he said to Nina at the door.

"That's right. We can't go now."

"Looks like you were ready to go."

"Yes, we were," replied Nina, unable to resist a mischievous smile. "Do you think the ladies would've approved of my appearance today? Is this traditional enough?" Nina darted a glance at his face to see his reaction.

"You look stunning!"

"Thank you," she said, trying not to blush.

"That's not a compliment," he said. "I asked you to appear traditional, not stunning."

Nina looked up, stunned. She saw the challenge in his eyes.

"Well," he continued, "you look like you're ready for one of your parties in Delhi."

"And what's wrong with that?" Nina asked, holding on to her patience that was on the decline.

"This is not Delhi."

"Tell me something," said Nina, not hiding her displeasure any longer. "Is fashion consulting one of your many talents?"

"Yes, in a manner of speaking. I own more than half the clothing mills in this area," said Tom. With that curt reply and a taunting smile, he walked away.

"He is the most overbearing, odious man I've ever seen," said Nina, once the doctor was almost out of earshot.

Bitsy, who had just walked into the drawing room at that moment, asked Nina why she was talking to herself.

"Because," said Nina, quite aggravated. "That Tom Davis is very annoying."

Bitsy displayed a sympathetic look to please Nina and walked away gingerly to hide her smile. She made a long list of instructions for the maid and a few alterations in the daily routine to accommodate a sick baby.

The phone was ringing. Nina answered it, and she was delighted to hear Sandy's voice.

"Oh, hello, Sandy! How are you?" asked Nina.

Sandy needed Nina's advice regarding an article. After a few minutes of shop talk, Nina, quite in tune to her playful character, explained the dressing scenario she had just experienced with Dr. Davis.

"Is he very unpleasant, Nina? What does he look like?"

"No, Dr. Davis is a nice man, I suppose. He doesn't look bad. Could use a shave and a haircut! Why do you want to know?"

"A woman's curiosity. What else?" Sandy laughed.

While Nina was placing the phone on its cradle, she saw Dr. Davis standing at the door. How much of the conversation had he overheard?

"I just realized that I had a sample of the medicine in the car. Here, you can use this for Nikil." He gave the packet to Nina and said goodbye again with his customary smile.

The maid announced Valli's visit from the kitchen. Since Bitsy was busy with the fussy Nikil, Nina went to the kitchen garden to receive her. Unexpectedly, Valli had come to please during this visit. She enquired about the baby and expressed an ardent wish to see him.

Bitsy, who was just bringing Nikil outdoors to distract his mind from the medicine, wondered if her earlier prediction was right. Was Valli here to make trouble? Nikil was crying in Bitsy's arms until a minute ago. What else was he supposed to do if someone shoved a teaspoon of disgusting stuff down his throat? He stopped crying and stared at Valli. She was standing in the garden with a big basket on her head.

"What a beautiful baby boy!" Valli exclaimed. She unloaded her burden on the ground, walked over to he baby, and smiled at Nikil.

To everybody's satisfaction, Nikil promoted her goodwill by blowing several bubbles and kisses.

Bitsy was still cautious. Nina, however, decided to give the old lady a second chance. From that day, Valli exchanged a few niceties with Nina when she saw her in the market, in the temple, or just about any place. She was making an effort at a decent conversation.

◆ ◆ ◆

Nina was reading the morning paper to a very elderly lady at Helping Hands, the senior home. Her gentle voice rocked the lady to sleep. She tucked the elderly inmate's frail frame under the sheets and walked out of her room. Nina usually volunteered at Helping Hands on Monday mornings and visited Mercy House on Wednesdays. She was getting familiar with the employees and volunteers. She waved to Veni, one of the regular volunteers, on her way out.

When Nina arrived from Delhi, she knew just a couple of people in this town. Now, at least a dozen faces were ready to smile. Simi, one of the volunteers, invited her for tea on Friday afternoon. Nina accepted the invitation gladly. As much as she enjoyed the solitude of a small town, she missed the lively conversations with Sandy and her other friends in Delhi.

Simi was a cheerful hostess. She loved to talk about her disasters in cooking and the mood swings of her children. Her son and daughter went to an excellent college preparatory school. Her husband, Vijay, was a lawyer. He had an impressive clientele in the city.

"I know," said Simi, smiling at Nina's amused expression. "My children go to school in the city, my husband works there, so why are we living here? Vijay and

I can't stand the noise and pollution. It's nice to come home to a quiet and clean suburb, don't you think?"

Nina agreed with her. Simi was unlike most women in that small town. She spoke her mind. Criticisms and opinions didn't bother her. She introduced Nina to her small circle of teatime friends, and the women met frequently to play cards or chat. Occasionally, Nina missed Delhi. Despite the crowd and the pollution, Delhi was very dear to her. The new set of friends relieved her from feeling homesick.

"Shall we go for a walk, baby?" Dev took Nikil from Bitsy's hands and placed him in his new carriage. Nikil looked like a prince. As Dev closed the gate behind him, he noticed a man on the other side of the road. Well, it was a common road and open to everybody. However, the way the man dashed away, as though he didn't want to be noticed by anyone, made Dev a little uneasy. This was not the first or only occasion he had noticed this strange occurrence. Dev decided to discuss this matter with Nina and Bitsy as soon as he returned home.

Nina, who was presently waving goodbye to Nikil, went inside to answer the phone. She had an invitation for tea and a game of bridge. She gladly accepted it.

Once the game started, Nina wondered if Simi had chosen the right afternoon for company. She was grossly distracted, more so than other days, and Nina asked her to pay attention. The culprit was the headache of college search.

"Nina, I'm sorry that I'm so stressed," apologized Simi. "It's just that I'm worried about placing my son in a good college. To be honest, I invited you for tea today to distract my mind from my worries."

"Simi, no need to apologize," said Nina. "I can imagine what you and Vijay must be going through."

"Vijay and I represent that inescapable middle class, Nina," said Simi. "We've more education and less money. Wish we had more inheritance and less education. And what are we going to do with our upper-caste status? Can't even dust furniture with it!"

"Simi, I know."

"I promise, Nina. Next time I won't talk so much and I won't be distracted," said Simi, smiling.

"Don't worry about it. Thanks for a nice afternoon," said Nina, politely. "I must say that your distraction really helped me think of a good content for my next article."

"What do you mean, Nina?" Simi asked, looking confused.

"Well, I'm supposed to write an article on college admissions and the disparity of the quota system based on castes. Everybody is talking about it. My editor wants me to write about it. Can I include your thoughts from this afternoon? Don't worry, Simi. Your name won't appear in the article."

"I'm not worried about that," Simi said and smiled.

When Nina returned from Simi's house, Bitsy was busy packing. She was visiting the next town with Dev to attend a wedding.

"Bitsy, are we supposed to know the bride or the groom?" asked Dev.

Bitsy bristled at this interrogation, and Nina had to intervene to calm her down.

"Dev, the mother of the groom was the housekeeper at our neighbor's house when we were in Delhi. That lady had become one of Bitsy's good friends. She used to visit frequently to have a cup of chai with Bitsy. Don't you remember her?" Nina asked.

"Yes, I remember her now. Talked too much! But I'm in no mood to go to a wedding, Nina. Crowds annoy me."

"Rohini, would you like to accompany Bitsy?" Nina turned to Rohini and asked. "You might enjoy a day away from home. Why don't you go?"

"Really? I'll be glad to, Madam," said Rohini.

Rohini had become a likable member of Brinda. Also, she was in the good books of the most formidable member of the household—Bitsy! Rohini's good management of trivial but nagging details allowed Bitsy to relax now and then.

"Oh, I would love to have Rohini's company. But, Nina, what about the baby? Who'll help you?" asked Bitsy.

"Bitsy, come on, I'm capable of managing Nikil for a short time! Besides, Dev is here. That young girl, who comes for daily help, can be of some use if I should need assistance, don't you think?"

Nina picked up Nikil and settled him in the carriage. She decided to walk to the river. Nikil's memory was remarkable. He raised his puffy hand to point out crows, a goat or two, and even a moo-moo cow.

"One day, Nikil," said Nina, "I'll show you the secret compartment in that big tree. You can hide your treasures there, which you can show to your children some day."

Nikil smiled at this crazy idea. He was in a good mood. He babbled incessantly during the stroll. Nina babbled back to humor him.

"It's getting warm. Let's go inside, Nikil. You can take a nice long nap. I've to work, all right?" Nina asked.

Although Nikil appeared cooperative, he lost interest in napping after reaching home. Nina sat at her desk, and Nikil sat comfortably on her lap. He liked to slam his chubby fingers on the keyboard when she was working. He clapped vigorously when letters appeared on the monitor. He liked this toy!

"Nina," Dev said, finding her upstairs. "I got a message from Dr. Davis just now. He wants me to meet him at Mercy House."

"Dev, why does Tom want to see you today?" asked Nina, doubtfully.

"No clue, Nina."

What time was it? Six! Nina picked up Nikil and walked downstairs to get baby's supper ready. "It's so strange to have the house to ourselves, isn't it Nikil?" asked Nina.

Nikil didn't babble because he was trying to shove his left fist into his mouth. The house was rather quiet. Bitsy and Rohini were supposed to arrive only late at night, and Dev had not returned from Mercy House yet! Why did Tom want Dev to meet him at Mercy House—not at his house, not at Brinda, but at the orphanage? And why was this bothering Nina at this moment? Lately, even tiny wrinkles irritated her. That didn't go well with her carefree nature.

"Madam, supper is ready on the kitchen counter," said the maid, meeting Nina at the foot of the stairs. "Can I get you anything before I go home?"

"No, thanks," Nina said kindly. "Go home before it gets dark."

Nina opened her eyes at the sound. Was it coming from the terrace? She must have dozed on the sofa in the drawing room. She looked at the clock, but she couldn't see clearly. She tried to read the time in the partial moonlight. Was it around nine? She reached for the table lamp. It didn't work. Were they out of electricity? Next, she reached for the candle, which Bitsy usually kept in the cabinet. There were more sounds. She was sure that they were coming from the terrace. She reached for the phone, but it was dead. She felt a little scared for a few seconds. She was certainly imagining things. Whatever knocked off the electricity must have messed up the phone lines. There must be a simple explanation.

"Dev, Dev, can you come here? Where are you?" shouted Nina.

Dev didn't respond. He should have come back a long time ago. Where was he? Her cell phone! As she went to the cabinet to get her phone, she saw something, a shadow near the window in the kitchen. She remembered that Dev had gone to the orphanage to meet the doctor. Could Tom and Dev still be there? Nina pressed the speed dial.

"Hello!" Tom said.

Nina never thought Tom's voice would be so utterly welcome to her. "Is Dev there? I'm alone at home. Something's wrong," said Nina. "I …"

The connection was lost. Should she run outside to call for some help or stay inside and wait for Dev? The shadow grew larger. There was surely someone in the kitchen. Nina picked up the baby from his daybed by the sofa and held him close to her. Thankfully, he didn't wake up. She desperately tried to stay calm and reached for a pair of scissors from Bitsy's sewing basket. Now she saw him. He was standing near the kitchen door, just outside the drawing room, with a knife in his hand.

"Give me the baby," he ordered.

Nina took a few steps backward and walked in the reverse direction toward the front door.

"Don't be foolish, lady. Do you think there is nobody outside that door?" the intruder asked. "Now give me that baby quietly or I'll kill you."

"Please stop. I'll give you money. See that cabinet?" asked Nina. "My purse is there. Just take anything you want. Please don't hurt. Please don't come near the baby."

He walked toward her unhurriedly and purposefully. It happened in a flash of a second. The front door burst open. Someone ran to the intruder and grabbed him by his neck. It looked like Tom Davis in the dull light. Another man followed him. Nina was screaming something even she could hardly understand. Then she realized that the other man was Tony, one of Tom's employees. They hauled the intruder out of the room. Sirens, police car, and a string of noises—it was over.

Dev arrived shortly after Dr. Davis. Bitsy arrived with Rohini in the middle of police sirens and noises. Seeing that Nina was in no condition to talk, Tom explained the situation to those who just arrived. Bitsy and Dev were shocked. Rohini's face was contorted with fear.

"Why did you call Dev to come and see you?" Nina asked Tom.

"I didn't call anybody. What are you talking about?" asked Tom.

It was Dev's turn to explain to the doctor about the phone call he had received earlier to meet him at Mercy House. "Dr. Davis, when I reached the orphanage, I was surprised that you were not there. But … there was another message from you."

"What was it, Dev?"

"Your message instructed me to go to the warehouse near the railway station. Doctor, you didn't call me?" asked Dev.

"I didn't," said Tom.

"You left Nina alone in this big house and went all the way to the warehouse?" Bitsy asked Dev.

"I understood from the message I got at Mercy House that you were already home, Bitsy. Do you really believe that I would leave Nina alone and go far away?" Dev asked, quite annoyed and confused.

The intruder had spoken to Nina in Hindi. The locals spoke Tamil. What did that mean? Was he from the north? How did he know that Nina was fluent in Hindi?

"How did the intruder get in, Doctor?" Bitsy wondered.

"Through the kitchen window, Bitsy," answered Tom.

Why did that man want the baby? Who was he? Most importantly, who called Dev to meet Dr. Davis? Possibly someone who had known the routine at Brinda? Nina looked at Rohini. Could she have …? Nina was not sure what to think. Although Rohini was at a wedding with Bitsy, she could have taken a few minutes to walk to a phone booth. No, that is silly. Nina was sure about what to think. Rohini ought to be innocent. Besides, if Rohini had anything to do with it, she shouldn't be staying in Brinda any longer.

Dr. Davis left after midnight. Sleep was impossible on such a night after such a disconcerting incident. Nina took Nikil to her own room. Bitsy insisted on sleeping on the sofa in Nina's bedroom. There was a knock on the door. Rohini was standing outside the room, holding a bundle of sheets and pillows in her hand.

"Madam, may I sleep in this room, just tonight? I'm so scared," Rohini asked, fear occupying her face.

"Of course. Come in, Rohini. You're always welcome," said Nina, inviting her kindly.

Prompted by such encouragement, Rohini dropped the bundle on the floor by the sofa. Nikil cooed in the darkness. That was the night's lullaby.

After a fitful sleep, the household gathered around the kitchen table in the morning. Bitsy deposited the newspaper and a cup of coffee on the table.

"Oh, Bitsy, how was the wedding?" Nina asked. "I didn't even get a chance to ask you last night."

"It was nice, Nina. It rained a little, but at least, it wasn't too hot. How was the weather here?" Bitsy returned to the table with a plate of biscuits. "Why did you wake up so early, Nina? Why don't you go back to bed and get some more rest?"

"Thanks, Bitsy, but I'm okay. Did you get any sleep at all?"

"As much as I could, Nina. I was in your room and there was no snoring of Dev, remember?"

"Good God!" Nina exclaimed.

"What is it? Nina, what is it?" Bitsy asked, startled by the alarm in Nina's voice.

"Listen to this," Nina started to read. "Abdul Hamid, an inmate at Kanyakoil jail, was found dead in his cell after he was arrested and taken there on a burglary charge. Bitsy, look at his picture. He was the one who broke into our house last night!"

"Are you sure you got a good look at his face?" Bitsy asked. "Remember, it was dark. We had no electricity for a while."

"That's right. But I'm almost sure. He was facing me when he threatened me. I could see a little because of the moonlight. Although the image was faint, I had an opportunity to look at him for a couple of minutes. Bitsy, I'm sure this was the man!"

"We must call Dr. Davis right now, Nina."

"Why must we?" Nina asked, pouting a little. "There's no need to bother him every time something happens." Their dependence on the good doctor's judgment was irritating Nina.

◆ ◆ ◆

"Nina, the doctor is here," Bitsy knocked on Nina's office door and announced.

"How are you?" asked Tom. "I came to see if you're doing all right."

"Thanks," Nina replied and wondered if he always went here and there to rescue the community from various disasters. "We're all doing well. You didn't have to come here. A phone call would have been enough."

"You don't want me to come here?" Tom asked.

She hated his abrupt approach. Her irritation, however, took a diversion at the sound of barking in the garden. What was going on?

"Nina, remember you were thinking of getting a dog? I brought a couple of Alsatians. I'll leave them here only if you want me to. Want to take a look?" Tom asked.

She followed him eagerly to the garden. The dogs were huge but appeared peaceful.

"Brownie is five. Tiger is six. They retired from the police department recently. They're very efficient. They'll protect you ..." he said and added hurriedly, "I mean all of you, especially the baby." The dogs wagged their tails when Tom mentioned their names and walked gently to Nina.

"Thanks, Tom. They appear docile. Are you sure they're brave enough to perform sentry duty?" asked Nina. She couldn't think of anything else to say.

"Yes, I'm sure. Don't let their appearances fool you. They're gentle, but they can be nasty if the situation demands it. Well ... I couldn't send them by phone."

Nina thanked him again, trying to look anywhere but at his teasing eyes.

"Nina, did you get a chance to read the morning paper?" asked Tom.

"Yes, and you?"

"I did. I know that the dead prisoner was the man who broke into Brinda last night."

How could Tom be so matter of fact about the disaster? That was his personality—a temperate, cool disposition.

"I always thought that you shouldn't have plunged into this baby business and ..." he whispered at the front door, looking at her face meditatively for a few seconds, "I still think so."

Tom was gone. He ought to be the most frustrating man. Who asked for his opinion? Nina was still fuming when the news bulletin arrested her attention. Kumar's picture was on the screen. Apparently, he was in an accident. The reporter mentioned that the victim was working on a project at the jail in Dandiar. Fortunately, he was still alive. Unfortunately, the photographer who accompanied him died instantly. The photographer's name was not revealed because his family was not aware of the tragedy yet. Nina swallowed the knot in her throat. Could it be Arun? He was like a child, so young. Nina felt a little silly. *The Express* employed dozens of photographers. Well, Nina was thinking of Arun because he had been part of the team during the initial stages of the Dandiar project. The reporter offered more information about Kumar. Some ruffians in a deserted alley attacked him during an assignment by the outskirts of—the name of the area wasn't familiar. Kumar was in critical condition at J.K. Hospital. Nina despised Kumar. Still, she wouldn't want anything terrible to affect him. She was distracted by the shrill sound of the phone.

"Sandy! I'm so glad to hear your voice," said Nina. "Did you hear about Kumar?"

"Nina, the rumor is that somebody doesn't want the reporters to dig into the jail project, especially about the delicate controversy on Babies Born in Bondage. I can't tell you how thoroughly glad I am now that you're totally out of that project," said Sandy. "According to the original plan, you would've been responsible for this particular project in the jail. Nina," Sandy continued, "I don't know how to say this. Arun is ... and he was barely twenty-three!"

It was horrible! Arun had joined *The Express* just a year or so ago. Nina wondered if she should mention anything about the prowler in Brinda and his attempt to abduct the baby. She decided not to. Sandy had enough worries for now.

Nina's mind was in a whirl. Why did the intruder want the baby instead of money or jewelry? And to top that worry, here was the Dandiar disaster! As if these worries were not sufficient to drive her crazy, there was Dr. Davis' parting sentiment that morning—she shouldn't have plunged into this baby business! What right did he have to tell her what she should undertake and what she shouldn't?

Sandy was on the phone again that night. "What's wrong, Nina?" Sandy asked. "Are you okay?"

"I'm okay, Sandy. I'm just a little irritated by this man."

"Would that be Dr. Davis, that gentleman you were talking about a while ago? Is he still bothering you?" asked Sandy.

"Yes, I've to tolerate his presence until the baby is legally mine."

Sandy apologized unconvincingly for being overly curious. Nina rapidly tried to change the subject.

Next morning, a reporter announced the state of Kumar's condition. He was out of danger. Nina was glad. Dev deposited a stack of post on Nina's lap. One was from Children's Welfare Services. She noticed that Tom Davis had received a copy of the same. He had not visited lately because he had left town to attend a wedding. She was happy about not having to see him at least for a short while! He disturbed her serenity. Well, she was too busy to analyze why he had such an effect on her peace of mind. Until the adoption was finalized, her dependence on Dr. Davis must continue.

As Nina was walking to the car outside Mercy House, she saw Veni near the gates. Veni was an aide in the nursery. She caught Nina's attention because she worked almost always around Nina's schedule. Veni had a sweet, honest smile that was irresistible.

"Hello, Veni, why are you standing there in the hot sun?" Nina asked.

"My husband can't pick me up today, Nina. I'm waiting for the bus."

"May I give you a lift, Veni?" Nina asked.

Dev smiled and held the car door open for Veni. After a few minutes of bashful deliberation, she got in and thanked both Dev and Nina.

"How are you, Veni? I see you here more often these days. Do you like working at Mercy House more than working at the senior center?"

"I'm glad to be at both places, Nina."

"It's certainly very nice of you to offer your time and help."

"Oh, Nina," said Veni. She disappeared behind her giggles and surfaced eventually. "Look who is talking? You seem to be at one of the centers all the time. They're so glad to have you."

"Thanks. But I've so much free time now. I'm proud to be here. My grandmother was the first orphan in Mercy House," Nina said, glancing at the shy passenger. "What brought you to the shelters, Veni?"

"I volunteered to help because I was tired of chatting with my neighbors. It's good to be here, isn't it?" Veni asked. "My husband didn't want me to leave home often, but I argued until he gave in. He is actually a nice man, Nina. He is only worried about his parents, you know, what they might say now that I go outside the house to work."

A woman was ready to rebel in this small town! Nina admired Veni's independence and promised her all the assistance she could offer. From that day, Veni grabbed every opportunity to talk to Nina. Nina was glad to listen to her.

"Nina, come down quickly. Look who is here?" Bitsy shouted.

Nina ran to the balcony to see the reason for Bitsy's excitement. Sandy and Jim! Nina took the stairs, two at a time, and ran to her friends' arms.

"We didn't call ahead, Nina. We wanted to surprise you. I hope it's okay?" asked Jim.

"Oh, of course, Jim," Nina said delightedly. Nina was engulfed in the laughter and noise caused by her friends' visit that she barely noticed the presence of Dr. Davis in the drawing room! He was talking, laughing, and blending with the party. What was he doing here?

Tom happened to be Jim's childhood friend, and the three of them had just returned from the wedding. The sly Sandy and Jim could have informed Nina of their association with Tom, at least a little earlier. So Sandy knew about Tom before. She had been teasing Nina all the time.

Rohini brought Nikil from the nursery. He thrilled everybody with his smile. Sandy held Nikil on her lap and fell into an easy conversation with him. He was happy that another adult was willing to listen to his babble.

Jim and Sandy decided to spend the night in Brinda, and Nina felt compelled to invite Tom for supper. He accepted her invitation gracefully and said that he would return in a couple of hours.

Jim went to the guest quarters to take a nap. This allowed Sandy and Nina to have a cozy chat. Nina took Sandy to the balcony that offered an excellent view of the river.

"Nina, do you know how heartily envious I am?" Sandy asked. "One could have such a serene life here."

"It's a big house, Sandy. Why don't you and Jim move in with the kids? Nikil will be thrilled to have instant cousins."

"Move to Brinda?" Sandy smiled at the invitation and promised many visits rather than a permanent move from Delhi. "Nina, why a baby boy? I would have expected you to adopt a girl, you know, with so many people being reluctant to have female children."

"I know exactly what you mean, but remember, Sandy, Nikil found me."

"Of course, he found you. God bless him! Nina," said Sandy.

"Yes, Sandy?"

"I can see that you love this baby so much. You realize that the adoption, I mean … the decision may not be in your favor. Can you handle the disappointment?" asked Sandy.

"I know, Sandy, I know. How can I ration my love for this baby at the present time in anticipation of my disappointment? He just brightens my days. He means so much to me. It's hard to explain. But I'm prepared to face whatever happens. I hope they don't take him away from me."

"I hope so too."

Sandy was Nina's closest friend. Therefore, Nina didn't mind when Sandy wondered about Nina's decision to remain single now when a baby was to become a part of her life. Both women knew that not many men would come forward to marry a woman who was already saddled with a child.

"Nina, what if you fall in love with a man and the baby becomes an issue? Why are you looking at me like that?" Sandy scolded Nina. "It could happen, you know."

"Sandy, when and if I find a man I could love, he would be delighted to love Nikil."

Sandy agreed that this made sense—if and when Nina found the right man!

Bitsy decided to outdo her previous talents. Some delicious items, favored by Sandy and Jim, were on the table. Dr. Davis' favorite dishes were also included in the menu. Jim and Sandy teased Bitsy about her special affection for Tom Davis. Had she acquired a new nephew? Nina discreetly kept quiet and watched the happy scene. She also ignored the frequent glances Tom threw in her direction and hoped that Sandy's eagle eyes didn't focus on the same.

Bitsy served dessert and tea in the veranda. The outdoor air completed the happy note of the company. Nina, hoping to turn everybody's attention away from her, asked Jim how he had met Tom during his childhood.

"Well, Tom, when did we first meet?" asked Jim.

"I met Jim in London. How old were we?" Tom asked, turning toward Jim. "Seven or eight? We met again in Philippines."

"And we always kept in touch," Jim smiled.

Sandy's eyes went to the dogs. She invited them to play with her. "They're very friendly, Nina. When did you get these lovely dogs?" Sandy asked.

A question like that required more than a simple answer. Everything, from the mysterious phone call to the housebreaker, came out in the open. Sandy and Jim were astonished. Why didn't Nina mention anything about it earlier? The fact that the intruder wanted the baby and not money or jewelry had been a matter of frequent discussions among Tom, Nina, and the police. Now the same question intrigued the guests. The intruder, having died the same night, left a mystery behind him. Why did he want the baby? Was he trying to sell babies for a living? Male children were in demand, but for a thief to walk in daringly into a household, where the residents were not unprotected, didn't sound feasible.

"But Nina was alone that evening," Tom reminded everybody, bringing the focus on Nina. "Someone must have observed the house. It was a planned attempt. She has to be very careful in the future."

"Tom, should I remind you about the excellent alarm system we installed after the incident, the addition of dogs, and the constant company of Bitsy, Dev, and the servants?" Nina asked, trying to hide her irritation.

"That's not quite sufficient," replied Tom.

Jim and Sandy exchanged glances.

"Well, do you have anything more to suggest for my domestic happiness, Tom?" Nina asked, not hiding her irritation.

"Yes," Tom replied without hesitation. "I think you should leave the baby with an unidentified, confidential guardian until the adoption is final."

"And you're certain that a similar attempt to abduct the baby won't be repeated?" Nina asked. She didn't care how aggravated and upset she sounded.

"No, I'm not certain about that. Nobody can be," said Tom. "All I'm saying is that it's worth trying. Please consider."

Jim walked away to answer his cell phone. Sandy followed him. Nina looked away. Tom was right. He made his point very well. She wished, oh, she wasn't even sure of what she wished anymore.

"Are you upset about my suggestion?" Tom's voice reached her ears as quietly as the gentle breeze that was playing with her hair.

"No. Should I be?" Nina asked, looking at his face. She saw a gentleness that she had come to recognize in this strange man who drove her up the wall one minute and made her wish he wouldn't leave her side the next.

"Well, you wish I wouldn't interfere in your affairs, don't you?" Tom asked, smiling gently.

Nina was glad that she didn't have to reply because Jim and Sandy returned to the veranda. She started to refill their teacups. When she reached for Tom's cup, he politely declined. He was expected at the hospital very early in the morning. He thanked her for a charming evening and left.

Sandy was reluctant to leave Nina behind—more or less alone—to face the uncertainty. On the other hand, she had never seen her dear friend so happy, so utterly belonging, as she did with the baby. Perhaps Nina knew what she was doing, much against the doubts of Tom Davis. Sandy chewed on Nina's stubborn assertion against the good doctor's worldly wisdom! She hoped that Dr. Davis' company had something to do with her dear Nina's current happiness.

Tom arrived next morning to take Jim and Sandy to the airport. He asked Nina if she would like to accompany them. Initially, Nina had wanted to take her friends to the airport, but Tom had approached Jim earlier. Nina felt it would be rather clumsy to go in a separate car. Sandy insisted on having Nina's company. Well, that settled it. Nina went to the airport in Tom's car.

Tony, Tom's employee, was snoozing in the back on their way home from the airport. Tom was attentive, uttered a lot of niceties, and tried to keep his eyes on the road. While Nina was thinking of something nice to talk about, Tom asked her if she had thought about his suggestion.

"Don't you ever give up?" Nina asked. "I must say that it's not your business to suggest such drastic alternatives. I can't think of anybody with whom I can leave the baby for a short period of time. Besides, I don't wish to leave him anywhere." She bit her tongue after her irritation found an exit. Did she give a hasty and biting reply?

"You can say it's none of my business, Nina," Tom said, not expressing any anger or irritation in his voice. "However, I must remind you that Nikil's welfare is as much my business as yours, if not more. And ... I don't give up."

Nina remembered his part in the adoption process. She should watch her temper a little better. "I'm sorry," said Nina. "I apologize for my sharp tongue."

"Don't worry about it," Tom continued to talk with that deplorable twinkle. "It must be very hard for you to take instructions from someone like me! I understand that you've been the mistress of your own life for a long time. You have a brother, am I right?" Tom asked.

"Yes," replied Nina. "But he can't control me. He is a nice brother."

"I see. Where is he? I suppose he has a family of his own?"

"He lives in Singapore with his wife and children."

"Let me guess, you don't get along with his family?" asked Tom.

"Yes, you're right. As I said, Jay is a nice brother. I just can't stand his wife. Anyhow, how did you guess that I don't get along with his family?"

"Well, a woman of your age, setting up your own home, all alone, and never mentioning her brother's family, and his family doesn't visit much."

"Don't you sound like one of the women in the crowd on market day?" asked Nina. Tom laughed with Nina at this frank analysis. "You're right. Jay's wife, Leela, is a woman from an appropriate family, someone with more fluff than common sense. My brother visits me as frequently as he can. I love him. I love his son and daughter. He was here last week, you know? I wish he had married a little more wisely. Well, he married her for his own pleasure rather than to please me. Leela visits rarely. I think she knows I don't like her. She thinks I'm much too independent for my own good!" Nina said, glancing at his profile.

"Perhaps, if I may ask, is that why you never married, Nina? Are you worried about losing your independence?"

"No, that's not the reason why I'm not married. I want to marry the right man, someone I could love for the rest of my life. I don't want to settle down just for the sake of ... you know what I mean?" Nina asked, looking at Tom's profile again. "And it's your turn to explain why you're still a bachelor."

"Of course. Well, I'm married to a cause. Besides, I don't think I can find a woman who'll be willing to marry me."

"Oh, don't be so hard on yourself. The way Bitsy draws your resume, you sound like a very eligible bachelor!"

"Don't listen to Bitsy," Tom said, smiling warmly. "I think she exaggerates."

"Bitsy exaggerates? You couldn't be more wrong. She speaks her mind exactly so, more than I do."

"Do you think a gullible girl might agree to marry me if I have a haircut and a shave?" Tom asked innocently.

"Oh, you're wicked!" said Nina, blushing. "I'm sorry." So ... he had overheard her phone conversation with Sandy!

"No need to be sorry," he said, smiling generously.

"You should never touch that mustache," suggested Nina.

"Why not?"

"It gives your face distinction, and ... you'll look like a plucked chicken if you remove it."

He burst into a kind of laughter that made him appear much like a schoolboy. "In that case, I shall never touch it," Tom promised.

"Well, what's your cause that keeps you single and safe?" Nina asked.

"Children, the welfare of children, homeless children."

Of course, it should have been obvious to Nina. She took a long look at his profile. What a simple man he was! Did he ever think of his needs? What did he like? What did he dislike? She had grown to like his smile. She had to admit that she didn't wish to see his frown. His passion for the welfare of the children touched her and humbled her. Nina tried hard to get out of this adolescent reverie. What was wrong with her today? She decided to change the subject. "Tom, if you don't mind, I wanted to ask you about something. I'm sure people wonder about your 'foreign' appearance. Where are your ancestors from?" she asked. As soon as her question came out, she wondered if she had sounded too inquisitive.

"I was wondering why you never asked me until now, Nina."

"I'm sorry," Nina apologized. "I didn't mean to pry."

"No, you're not prying," Tom said, smiling charitably. "My grandfather was a missionary from the United States. He was raised in Virginia. He lived a major part of his adult life in India, particularly around Kanyakumari, Nagapattinam, and Madras. My grandmother was from France. She met my granddad in Pondicherry during his travels. You can imagine the rest. The next generation married Indians, Australians, and so on. I have so many nationalities and religions in my veins." When he concluded and smiled, there was genuine humor in his expression.

"Where did you grow up?" Nina asked. She may not have another opportunity to make these enquiries. For some reason, she had to know. She just had to know whatever she could learn about Tom Davis.

"I grew up a little here and a little there—a few years in England, Philippines, and here, in India, not too far from Kanyakoil, and the United States."

"Is that where you went to college?" Nina asked.

"Yes. Seems like a long time ago."

They reached Brinda. Tony jumped out of the car to open the gates. Tom parked by the veranda and opened the car door for her.

"Tom," Nina smiled. "Thanks for the ride."

"No, no, that was nothing, Nina. I enjoyed our conversation."

Nina saw Bitsy standing in the veranda with the baby in her hands. Nikil squealed joyfully when he saw Nina. He was even more thrilled to see a car. He loved cars and the sounds they made. Tony gave Nina's purse to Bitsy before getting back in the car.

Brownie ran to Nina with a welcoming nuzzle. Tiger, the shy one, imitated whatever his friend did and engaged in a quick sniff of her purse. Nikil was thrilled to see the dogs and tried to jump on Brownie.

"Nina, I'm glad you're home. He thinks of everything, doesn't he?" asked Bitsy.

Nina looked at Bitsy questioningly.

"I'm talking about Dr. Davis, Nina," Bitsy explained. "He must've asked Tony to come back in the car to avoid gossip. This way, people won't talk."

"What nonsense is this, Bitsy? He was just offering me a lift. No more than a friendly gesture, that's all. What's there to talk about?" Nina asked, truly baffled.

Bitsy was not inclined to lecture in general, but she chose this occasion to explain to Nina how differently most country people looked at things, which might appear normal to folks in a big city. "Nina," Bitsy continued, "when an attractive, unmarried young lady goes out with a very eligible bachelor, it makes room for some very spicy conversation, yes, even during our modern times."

Nina had surmised from the conversation between Tom and Tony that the latter had come to town on an errand earlier and that he was simply going home with them. "Bitsy, I don't care about what our society thinks," declared Nina. "You can sing in praise of Lord Davis."

Tom parked the car in the portico of his bungalow that was nestled in the woods, just a couple of kilometers from Mercy House. He picked up the post from the lacquered tray in the foyer. A letter from Sylvia! He opened the envelope and read the contents with pleasure. Tom had lived without a family for over a decade. His parents had married quite late, and he was a late and only child! Not having grown up with siblings and with a few cousins scattered all over the world, his sphere included his work, his patients, Mercy House, and its subsidiary agencies. The children at Mercy House gave him a purpose in life. His good friends became his siblings. He frequently spent a weekend with one of his friends in the city, and he visited his dear cousin, Sylvia, who lived with her family in Chennai. Sylvia was not just one of Tom's cousins. She was his nearest and dearest relation. Surely, she held the status of his sister.

Next, Tom read the letter from the police inspector in Kanyakoil. The incident regarding the intruder was not at all what it appeared to be. That man was supposed to be linked to an association that took roots in a remote village beyond the northern borders. What brought him to the south? What was his business here? What was the reason for his interest in a baby, a poor orphan, who was with a family in a secluded town that was located so far away from where he lived? They would never discover the reason because the man was dead—his throat was cut. The newspapers printed plenty of hot information—political bureaucracy, corruption in jails, and the lawless state—to feed the curiosity of the public and to please the authorities. What was the bottom line? The killer or the organization was still unknown. This fact made Tom extremely uneasy.

"Sir, will you have dinner at home tonight?" Tony asked, after knocking on the door deferentially.

"Yes, I'll stay home tonight."

"Dr. Davis, Miss Sylvia called last night. Did I tell you about the phone call already? You were having dinner with your friends in Brinda."

"I remember, Tony. I'll call her. It's been quite a while since I saw Sylvia and her family."

Tony's thoughts took the same direction. In fact, Dr. Davis had not gone out of Kanyakoil since he visited that pretty lady, Nina, and the child she wished to adopt. However, Tony was not on informal terms with the doctor to question his intentions. Further, Tony's personality was rather quiet and reserved. He hoped that something fruitful would develop between Nina and Dr. Davis. He wished, he hoped, and he said a special prayer every Sunday morning.

"Dr. Davis, I was wondering. You haven't made a trip to the city to see any of your friends. Is everything all right?" asked Tony, getting rid of his customary, non-interfering personality for a short period. His eyes were far away, avoiding Tom's direct scrutiny.

"That's right, Tony. Nina and the baby have kept me very busy, you know?" Tom said, stealing a glance at the quiet Tony. "What do you think of Nina?"

"I ... think she is a very nice lady, Sir."

"Beautiful too, don't you think?"

"Yes, Dr. Davis. Let me see about dinner before it's late. May I?" Tony asked and ran out of the room without waiting for a reply.

Tom smiled, walked to the balcony, and looked at the river. He wondered how many uncertainties the water concealed in its depth. He thought of Nina and the baby. When Dr. Menon sent him to Brinda to establish his role in the adoption of Nikil, he knew that he was to meet a spinster, who had decided to quit the hectic lifestyle of a big city for a relaxed life in the country. But he didn't expect to see anybody like Nina. He thought Nina was not old enough or emotionally strong enough to face the challenges of a lengthy adoption process. What was she thinking? A beautiful woman and a wealthy one! Why the urge to assume motherhood without marriage? That question brought to his mind the conversation he had with Nina that afternoon. She seemed to know her mind, perhaps a little too well for her own benefit. He smiled at his lingering feelings regarding a woman, a stubborn woman, who walked into Kanyakoil only a few weeks ago. She certainly trespassed on his thoughts like a hurricane. She was not at all like any of the women he had known before. She was unassuming, down to earth, and a little too beautiful for his peace of mind. Nina had told him that afternoon that she wanted to marry a man she could love. She would wait until then. He had no doubt that with her beauty and wealth, she could have snared any man she had her eyes on. What was she waiting for? Tom had faced other beautiful women. In fact, he had seen several. It was not Nina's pretty face that threatened him to sway from his bachelor status. It was something about her stubborn nature, that vague little whatever in her mannerism that intrigued him. He admired her resolution and her certain defiance to saying "yes sir" to everything a man threw in her way. Did that little rebellious streak fascinate him? Tom smiled at his school-boyish fancy. Maybe a quick jogging would put things in perspective. With that purpose, he walked to his dressing room to change.

◆ ◆ ◆

Nina fed Nikil his supper with Rohini's assistance before placing him in her capable hands. She was sure that there was more food on Nikil's bib than inside his belly.

"Baby is teething, Madam!" Rohini offered her diagnosis.

Was Nikil teething already? Nikil's first tooth arrived with his first word "amma" or something similar to it. Brinda was alive with the thrilling news that Nikil said his first word. Nina was proud and made Nikil repeat "amma" several times. But Nina was not thrilled when she discovered that Nikil called everybody "amma." Her only hope was that he would soon get rid of this monotonous habit.

Nina tossed, turned, and stared at the swaying silhouettes on the wall. She couldn't fall asleep. It was a clear night. The moonlight, seeping through the blinds, was very bright. Nina walked to the window and adjusted the blinds to filter the light. She was about to return to bed when she heard it. It sounded like the creaky opening of a gate. Nina definitely heard the click of a latch. She looked down at the kitchen garden. A lady was standing by the washing stone, but she was not alone. A man was standing next to her! The couple appeared to be whispering. Brownie and Tiger were strolling around the man and the woman. What kind of guard dogs were they? The man walked away to open the garden gate and the lady strolled back toward the kitchen. Was it Rohini? Nina was pretty sure it was Rohini! That was why the dogs didn't bark to alert Brinda. They were perfectly comfortable with Rohini, who was one of the members of the household. What was she doing here in the middle of the night? More to the point, why was she stealthily talking to a man after the entire household had gone to bed? Nina had a good mind to walk downstairs and confront Rohini. But … what was she supposed to confront her about? Talking to somebody in the middle of the night was not necessarily wrong. However, why should that man come to talk to Rohini at such an odd time, outside the house? Nina decided to make further enquiries discreetly in the morning. There ought to be a sound reason for this nocturnal event. Rohini didn't seem to be such a woman. It disturbed Nina to even think of her in that manner.

Nina almost jumped out of her bed. Who was repeatedly tapping on the door? Bitsy was standing outside Nina's room, wringing her hands and looking extremely concerned. Nina glanced at the clock and realized that she had overslept.

"Bitsy, I couldn't sleep till very late in the night. Anyway, what's wrong?" Nina asked. "You look like you've seen a ghost."

"Nina, I wish I had, which would've been less disturbing than the news I just received. Nina, a few minutes ago, there was a phone call from a man. He asked us not to bother looking for Rohini. He told me that she wouldn't return to Brinda. Nina, he also asked me to assure you that Rohini is fine."

"Bitsy, didn't anybody wonder why Rohini didn't come out of her room for coffee or breakfast in the morning?" asked Nina.

"Nina, I thought that poor girl was sleeping," explained Bitsy. "You see, last night she went to bed with a terrible headache. I asked her not to wake up early. That's why none of us missed her. Good God! Where is she?"

Nina asked Bitsy if anybody else in Brinda was aware of Rohini's disappearance. Bitsy assured her that only Dev knew about it so far.

"Bitsy, this news must stay with the three of us as long as possible."

"I agree, Nina. What should we do?"

"Bitsy, where is Dev?"

"Dev is in the veranda with Nikil."

"Please ask him to come here. I'd like to talk to you and Dev at the same time. I've to tell you something, Bitsy."

Bitsy returned with Dev. Nina repeated what she saw in the kitchen garden in the night. It had to be Rohini! The daily maid went home at dusk. Apart from Bitsy and Nina, Rohini was the only other female resident in Brinda.

"Oh, Nina, remember?" Dev almost jumped from his chair. "Remember the man I saw around Brinda a few times? It must've been the same man who came last night. Every time I saw him, I could barely glance at his figure. I never saw his face. I wish I had. I'm sure he tried to avoid us. He has to be connected in this somehow. Don't you think, Bitsy?"

"That's right. I forgot about it. Who could he be?" Bitsy asked. "Nina, do you think it's possible? What should we tell everyone about Rohini? There will be questions."

"We'll tell the servants that Rohini had to visit her family for a short while. I wish I had done something about her secret meeting with that man last night right away! If I had not hesitated, perhaps, that poor girl would probably still be here. It had to be Rohini! The phone call verifies it. Don't you think?"

Dev and Bitsy didn't know what to think. Their conversation halted at the sound of the doorbell. Bitsy looked down from the balcony and saw the maid opening the door to let Dr. Davis in.

"The doctor is here!" Bitsy announced with obvious relief.

"Don't tell me he has the news already!" Nina said this with a little hope. As much as she valued her independence, she was glad to have Tom's assistance. She asked Dev to take the doctor to the library and ran to the bathroom to take a quick shower.

When Nina entered the library, her guest was having a cup of coffee. It was a beautiful room. It had the appearance of a retreat—with pastels on the wall, a few comfortable chairs, and a yoga mat near one of the windows. Nina took a cup of coffee from the tray and sat down. Apparently, the stranger who talked to Bitsy that morning had also called Tom Davis.

"Nina, did you have any idea about Rohini's past?" Tom asked.

"I didn't."

"Why did you hire a young lady from another town? Why not someone local?"

Nina was surely irritated by the string of questions. "Well," she said, "I wanted to hire somebody from the Women's Home, somebody who was obviously in need of support. Naturally, my intention was to assist a poor, needy woman." She continued to describe the purpose of the Women's Home, one among a few across the country.

"I know that these homes shelter women. What I would like to know is if you hired Rohini for a particular reason?" Tom asked in a rather serious tone.

"I had received a phone call and a letter of recommendation from the director of the Women's Home in Chennai, which encouraged me to hire Rohini," Nina explained with a touch of irritation. She looked at him defiantly, challenging him to question her decision. "Why? You don't approve?"

"It's your house, your life, and entirely your decision to hire and fire anybody. My only concern is the baby. In the future, would you consult me before adding a servant in the house or making any decision that might affect the baby directly?" After delivering his opinion, Tom abruptly left the room.

Bitsy knocked before entering the library. "Did Dr. Davis leave?" she asked.

"Yes, he left."

"What happened, Nina?"

"He huffed, he puffed, well, he didn't blow the house down!" said Nina, in her most sarcastic tone.

"What a shame!" said Bitsy. "I was going to bring breakfast for both of you." She stopped on her tracks at the dark look on Nina's face. She decided that it was wise to leave Nina alone for a while.

Nina was having a cup of tea in the cafeteria at Mercy House. Veni walked in and waved to her.

"Veni, you seem to be miles away. What's wrong, dear?" Nina asked.

Veni smiled shyly and recited the following information: "Nina, I want to do more than assist at the shelter, but I don't have the education to get a better position. I didn't graduate from high school because my parents forced me to marry when I was only fifteen. Now, a mother of three and still only in my mid-twenties, I'm eager to find a part of life that doesn't label me only as a wife and a mother."

Nina stared at Veni in amazement. How could anybody speak so fast and still convey reasonably comprehensible information? "Veni, do you know that you can still get a high school certificate? If you wish, I can help you get one."

For a second or two, Nina thought that Veni was going to deliver another 'bullet train' monologue, but Veni simply hugged her with joy.

"Really, Nina? When can you help me?" asked Veni.

"Right away, Veni," Nina assured her friend. "What are we waiting for?"

Nina and Veni chose Tuesday and Thursday afternoons for tutoring sessions. The following Tuesday, Veni arrived with three shy, anxious young ladies, who were also high school dropouts. It was an interesting hobby for Nina and the dawn of fulfillment for her young friends.

Brinda had an unexpected visitor. Seetha was waiting impatiently when Nina returned to the drawing room after an unsuccessful and exhausting attempt at getting the baby to take a nap. Nikil went to Bitsy's welcoming arms.

"Can I see the baby, Bitsy?" asked Seetha.

Bitsy brought the baby to Seetha and went to the kitchen to get supper ready.

"It's good to see you. What brings you here?" Nina asked her aunt.

"I was visiting my sister-in-law in Salem and simply didn't have the heart to return to Delhi without seeing you. I'm sorry I didn't call before arriving."

Nikil, restless and a little anxious about the stranger, jumped into Nina's arms.

"That's not a big deal. You'll stay for supper, won't you?" Nina enquired, mindful of her manners.

"Thanks. I will."

Nina was wondering if her aunt intended to stay in Brinda overnight. Should she ask her?

"Nina, could I stay here tonight instead of taking the last train to the city?" Seetha asked gingerly.

Nina was never one to shirk her duties. She invited Seetha to stay in Brinda and hoped that her visit would finish with just a few questions. The questions began!

"Nina, do you still hope that Nikil would be yours one day?" Seetha asked. "It's my duty to warn you that if you pursue this adoption when you're single, no marriage proposal will come your way."

Nina ignored the irritation and smiled. Her aunt, realizing that her lecture was sinking into deaf ears, changed the subject. There was always plenty to talk about.

Her narrative consisted of her grandchildren's achievements in top-notch primary schools, musical endeavors, and miscellaneous accomplishments in various activities. There was further news to be given in detail about Delhi, the latest fashions, and the most recent gossips. Next, she talked about bygone days. A long time ago, she had come with her brother, Gopal, to see his future bride, Tara, in this hall.

Dev carried Seetha's bags to the guest quarters. Well, the night was still young. The aunt would make time to pester the niece. After supper, Nina took her guest to the veranda.

"Whose car is that, Nina? Were you expecting somebody?" asked Seetha.

It was Tom Davis. He parked the car near the veranda and offered a cheery greeting. Nina introduced him to her aunt. She noticed how naturally Tom began a conversation with Seetha.

"Nina, I wanted to talk to you about something. May I have a few minutes?" Tom asked.

"Certainly, Tom" said Nina, following him to the front yard.

"I'm sorry for interrupting when your family is visiting. I should've called," Tom apologized. "I was on my way to the hospital. I decided to take a couple of minutes of your time without calling earlier."

"It's no interruption," Nina said, rolling her eyes expressively. "Believe me. I'm glad you're here."

"Oh, I see. If you're glad that I'm here, then things must be desperate."

Nina looked up at Tom's teasing analysis and moved her glance quickly to avoid his searching eyes.

"Nina, every family has a crazy aunt. Let the dogs roam freely inside the house. They'll protect you. What do you think?"

"She's not crazy like that, but I'll keep your advice in mind."

Brownie and Tiger came to investigate. It was just Dr. Davis. They sniffed a customary hello and went back to the gate.

"You said you wanted to talk about something?" Nina asked.

"Nina, Children's Welfare Services wants an interview with you on Wednesday, which allows only a short time for preparation. I've to be present at the meeting. You can be assured of my support. Is that a good day for you?" Tom asked.

"Wednesday is fine. Thank you for coming to Children's Welfare Services. Is there anything else?"

He cleared his throat and continued to talk after an awkward moment or two. "Nina, I hadn't meant to be bossy the other day when I had questioned you about hiring a servant, so to speak. I'm sure Rohini was a good choice. Please accept my apology."

"That's quite all right. Have you heard anything about Rohini?" asked Nina.

"No, I haven't. But I'm doing my best to trace her whereabouts."

Nina invited him to join her and her aunt for a cup of tea and dessert, but he politely declined. After another moment of silence, he was gone.

When Nina returned to the veranda, Bitsy was talking to Seetha. Dev deposited a tray with tea and dessert on a small table.

"Nina, does that doctor visit whenever he pleases?" Seetha asked, hardly hiding her curiosity.

Bitsy and Nina exchanged glances, pregnant with meaning. Time for further questions! Bitsy signaled to Dev to follow her into the house. If Nina's feelings were to be suffocated by her aunt's impertinence, she might at least undergo the misery without an audience!

As briefly as possible, Nina described Tom's role in the adoption process. Her aunt listened to her impatiently and interjected in her usual, thoughtless fashion.

"You're not going to marry him, are you? Nina, are you going to marry that doctor?" Seetha asked, paying no attention to manners.

"What a funny thing to ask, Athai?" Nina asked, not quite sure of what to say. "He is helping in the adoption process, that's all."

Seetha jabbered about religion, caste, and a lot of nonsense, which was sufficient to drive Nina crazy. Nina's good breeding supported her to hold a polite smile and tolerate the gibberish. Then it hit Nina like a hurricane. She realized that someone must have dropped a hint about Tom's frequent visits to Brinda. Seetha was here to appease her curiosity!

The gentle rain turned to a thunderous storm by afternoon. Nina sat in the library, rocking the baby to sleep. The lush garden seemed to come alive. Nikil raised his dimpled hand to wave at the raindrops. A few months ago, on a similar stormy day, she had listened to a woman's pleading voice. Nina's migration to Kanyakoil, so far away from Delhi, made those few months seem infinitely long. Life was simple here. It seemed to sprout from the palm of nature. Her life with the baby was a soothing melody that she had never imagined until now. She cherished his precious smiles, his noisy laughter, and his mischievous attempts at upsetting order. God bless him! Nina was glad to see her aunt's departure that morning. Seetha had declared that no man would be willing to marry Nina if she was involved in this adoption business. It didn't matter. Nothing mattered to

Nina at this moment except her baby. Nina held Nikil close to her heart. She would find her man—despite everything, despite her own defiance.

◆ ◆ ◆

Bitsy looked at the clock in the kitchen. It was past ten. Nina never slept this late unless she was ill. She went upstairs and found Nina with a severe headache and congestion. She ran to the medicine cabinet to get a thermometer, shoved it into Nina's mouth, and drew the blinds before ordering the patient to stay in bed for the rest of the day. Nina was too weak to argue with her. When Bitsy ran downstairs, the maid was dusting the furniture.

"Nina is not well. Squeeze a couple of juicy oranges, put the kettle on for a fresh pot of tea, and stop dawdling. Come on. Hurry UP!" Bitsy commanded the maid.

The maid ran to the kitchen to follow Bitsy's orders. Bitsy ran to the phone and called the doctor's office. Dr. Menon arrived soon.

"Where is my patient, Bitsy?" asked Dr. Menon, before going to Nina's room. "Bitsy, Nina has an infection," said Dr. Menon, when he returned downstairs. "Make her drink a lot of fluids. She can have some soup, and I want her to stay in bed for the rest of the day." Dr. Menon left some medicine in Bitsy's hands before leaving.

Bitsy issued a new list of orders. Dev was entirely in charge of the baby because Bitsy decided to take care of Nina. Dev was happy to have Nikil in his hands, and the baby decided to be extremely obliging in Uncle Dev's care.

Nikil was good, the maid followed orders, Dev didn't nag Bitsy, and everything went well. Bitsy and Dev were just finishing supper when the doorbell rang. Dev opened the door and greeted Dr. Davis.

"Dr. Menon asked me to see the patient. How is she doing?" Dr. Davis asked.

"Oh, not well, Dr. Davis," Bitsy replied. "She won't listen to me and she hasn't eaten much. At this rate, she's not going to get better at all."

"As bad as that?" Tom asked. "Take me to her."

Nina whined, although in a feeble voice. Why was the doctor examining her twice in one day? Tom gave Nina a shot to bring the fever down and to keep her quiet. He read a list of instructions to Bitsy before following her downstairs for a cup of tea. The topic of conversation happened to be Nina and her stubborn personality, especially in her feverish stage. While Bitsy and Dev enjoyed the subject of their discussion, Bitsy tried to assess Dr. Davis' attachment for the patient. What appeared in the doctor's expression and tone pleased Bitsy. Nikil's crying halted the conversation. He had been too good. It was time to be bad! Dev returned to the drawing room with the baby.

"May I see Nina once more, Bitsy?" asked Dr. Davis.

Nikil, who was very fond of the doctor, jumped into his arms.

"You want to see how the patient is doing?" Dr. Davis asked Nikil.

Nikil smiled, showing the beginning of another tooth.

"Doctor, we don't want the baby to get sick," Bitsy protested.

"Bitsy, Nikil has a robust constitution. Spending a few minutes in Nina's room won't hurt him. Besides, he is just recovering from the infection he had a week ago. Isn't he still on medication? Nina will feel a lot better if she sees the baby. You may follow me and take your Nikil shortly, all right?" asked Dr. Davis.

"All right," Bitsy replied. "I'll be upstairs in a few minutes."

Nina opened her eyes briefly and smiled at Nikil. While he gave Nina a flying kiss and wrestled in Tom's arms to jump on the bed, Tom pulled the sheet over Nina, tucked her in snugly, and wished her good night. She didn't answer. She was half asleep.

Dr. Davis was not prone to impulses. Did something possess him? He bent down and planted a kiss on Nina's forehead. "You won't tell her, will you, Nikil?" Tom asked.

"Amma!" said Nikil, uttering the only word he could pronounce so far.

"Traitor!" Tom smiled and turned toward the door.

"I won't tell her either, Doctor. Your secret is safe. Is that why you wanted to see the patient again?" Bitsy glared at him.

She was standing by the door like a guard of a rowdy pub, trying to look extraordinarily rigid. But the rigidity didn't reach her eyes. They were trying to match the twinkle in Tom's eyes. The doctor blushed, gave the baby to Bitsy, and walked away.

Wednesday was already on the doorstep.

"Everything will go well, my dear!" Bitsy assured Nina. "Anyway, Dr. Davis will be with you, won't he? That's what he told me the other day."

"Bitsy, please tell me that you didn't ask him to keep an eye on me," Nina said, gripped by an embarrassing thought. "I don't need him, all right?"

"No such thing. Would I do that?" asked Bitsy. She hugged Nina and kissed her. "God be with you, my Nina."

Dev drove Nina to Children's Welfare Services. She was nervous. Naturally, her apprehensions sprouted from the general attitude of her community.

Tom was walking out of Children's Welfare Services. Wasn't he going in the wrong direction? Nina couldn't help smiling at the stupidity of arriving in two cars when they were both here for the same purpose. Tony was not available to chaperone this time?

"Hello," Tom greeted Nina cheerfully. "I went inside to see your lawyer. He is supposed to wait for us in the foyer. He is late. Shall we wait here?"

"That's fine," said Nina. She sat on a bench.

Tom sat on another. "Have you recovered from your recent illness, Nina?" Tom asked.

"Yes, thanks," she said. Small talk! She felt silly about staring at the trees and the greenery around her when so much could be said.

"How long have you known Bitsy, Nina?" asked Tom.

"From the day I was born! She is one of the dearest people in the world to me. I love her and Dev very much."

"I can see that. They couldn't love you more. Bitsy will always be there to keep an eye on you, perhaps like a mother," he said, smiling. "Her eyes never leave you. Does she chaperone you more than you wish?"

"Yes, she would like to, although I'm not sixteen anymore," Nina replied. She was not going to miss this opportunity. "In fact, Bitsy thinks that you invited Tony to sit in the car when you gave me a ride from the airport after Jim and Sandy left. She said that you think of everything! I told her that there's no need for such insipid formalities, right?" Nina looked at him directly.

"Yes, I did," Tom replied in his forthright voice. "Tony followed us in a bus on the way to the airport and joined us after Jim and Sandy left."

Nina wasn't sure how to handle this. Did she start something that she wouldn't be able to finish? But she wasn't one to give up easily. "Why did you do that? Were you afraid … to be alone with me?" Nina asked.

"No, I wasn't afraid of you. I was worried about what these people might say."

"That's silly," said Nina. "What's wrong when a gentleman drives a lady in his car? You're a well-respected citizen of Kanyakoil. What can these people say? I'm not afraid of them."

"I'm not afraid," said Tom. "But we should pay attention to certain formalities if we expect to gain the approval of a town and its people, especially considering Nikil's situation."

Nina didn't get a chance to reply. They heard a car pulling into the parking lot. She smiled at Mr. Sundaram. After returning the smile rather nervously, the lawyer took Tom and Nina indoors. Soon, they were ushered into an airy room. The director was new at this center. Tom had not dealt with him before.

The director got up and invited them to take their seats. "Welcome, everybody. I'm Giri," he said, smiling generously. "I'm waiting for Dr. Davis. Would you be kind enough to wait patiently for a few minutes?"

"Sir," Tom looked at Giri instantly at this enquiry. "I'm Dr. Tom Davis."

"Oh, I thought that you were the lady's husband!" said Giri, looking at Nina.

What was going on? Giri looked from Nina to Tom. Tom looked embarrassed. The lawyer looked at the floor. Nina didn't know where to look.

"Madam, where is your husband?" Giri asked.

"I don't have a husband, Sir," Nina answered. The conversation was turning stale.

"Mr. Sundaram, why didn't you submit your client's complete history to Mr. Giri?" asked Tom.

The lawyer squirmed in his seat instead of offering a reply.

The meeting ended abruptly. Giri needed more time to think about this issue. Nina's case, as a single lady, posed a problem, which required some attention. The interview had to be rescheduled. There was no doubt about it.

Nina walked out of the office with Tom. Sundaram followed them.

"Miss Nina, I was worried about disclosing your spinster status to a very orthodox director. Will you please try to understand that the next time I'll do a better job?" Sundaram asked anxiously.

"There won't be a next time. You're fired!" Nina said, looking at the lawyer with blazing eyes.

The ride back to Brinda was miserable. The weight on her emotions deflated Nina's spirits, which were soaring that morning. She had thought earlier that her visit to the town was another milestone in her journey. Now, with an empty promise, her journey didn't even begin. Only when she tasted the salty tear rolling down her cheek, Nina realized that she was crying. She was a tough woman. It took a lot to make her cry. Was she crumbling under the pressures of an intricately crafted society that concealed many spider webs in the crevices?

"There, there, Nina. I'm here. Bitsy and I wouldn't stand for tears in your eyes. Nina, listen to me, child. There'll be a good end to the obstacles you're facing at present. You have to be brave and patient, just like you used to be in the past," Dev smiled encouragingly. "I never knew a teary Nina! We have to be strong. Bitsy and I are here for you. Remember that."

"Thanks, Dev."

Nina appreciated Dev's confidence, but she doubted her courage and patience, which were showing signs of retreat at the formidable pressures of the society. Was it worth the aggravation and pain? Yes, it was, for Nikil's sake, for that sweet child's sake.

When Nina entered the house, she didn't expect to see Simi and her husband, Vijay, watching the local news in the drawing room. Apparently, Bitsy had called them to stay with her until Nina and Dev returned.

"What's wrong, Bitsy? Are you all right?" asked Nina.

"Nina, there was another phone call," Bitsy replied. She sounded nervous. "Somebody called about the baby, and this time it was a warning. They don't want us to keep Nikil at Brinda, and we're supposed to take him to the orphanage."

Nina's fear accelerated, probably because of her recent, disappointing experience at Children's Welfare Services.

"Another phone call, Bitsy? What are we supposed to do?" Nina wondered.

"How was the meeting at Children's Welfare Services, Nina?" asked Simi.

"That lawyer has made such a mess of things, Simi," said Nina. She explained the reason for the postponed interview.

Simi, who was always in the habit of speaking spontaneously, asked Nina if she would let Vijay handle the legalities in Nikil's case. That was the best thing that came in Nina's way. She gladly accepted Vijay's legal help.

"Nina, I won't be able to work on the case for at least a week. I've to take care of our daughter's school issues. Is that all right?" Vijay asked.

"Vijay, please concentrate on your daughter before turning your attention to Nikil," said Nina. "I've waited this long. I can wait a little longer."

Simi and Vijay left soon.

"Bitsy, what has Nikil been up to? Was he a good boy?" asked Nina, taking Nikil from Bitsy's arms.

"Our Nikil is fine, but listen to this," said Bitsy. "Now he thinks that the postman is his amma!"

Nina tucked the baby in his bed and went to the drawing room where Bitsy joined her. So much had happened that day. She didn't understand where the adoption process stood at this point.

"Can I get you another cup of tea, Nina?" Bitsy asked.

"No, Bitsy. Thanks."

"You must've seen Dr. Davis this afternoon. How is he doing?" Bitsy asked. "You know, he was a very thoughtful doctor when you were ill. He really does his job so sincerely, above and beyond what is expected of him."

"Does he?" Nina asked mischievously. "I don't know how he does his job, but he certainly acts like a pillar of our community. You were right about your Dr. Davis."

"What do you mean?"

"Remember when Sandy and Jim were here? He did ask Tony to chaperone ME when we were returning from the airport. And I was beginning to think that he was a sensible man, free from orthodox inhibitions and old-fashioned formalities. He is just like the rest, Bitsy!"

"Nina, I thought YOU were sensible enough to know the difference between an old-fashioned formality and a well-meaning precaution. Think clearly before you go to bed. Good night," said Bitsy and went to her room.

Nina felt like an immature adolescent, and she was sensible enough to realize that she deserved it. When the phone rang, she methodically went to answer it. It was Tom!

"Nina, first of all, let me apologize for calling so late. I was concerned about the disappointing meeting this afternoon. How're you doing?" Tom asked.

"Thanks, I'm fine. How are you?" asked Nina. She appreciated his thoughtful nature. A sudden weakness enveloped her. She was glad that he was not standing in person, right in front of her. Then ... she would have been on the verge of finding a haven on his shoulder. His kind voice never failed to take her by surprise. As idiotic as it was, it stirred her emotions.

"I'm well," Tom replied. "I'd like to finish the conversation we started this afternoon."

"What are you talking about, Tom?"

"I'm talking about Tony's chaperoning incident! You understand me, don't you, Nina?"

"Yes, I understand, Tom, but I don't agree with you."

"That's why I like you," he said softly. "You don't say yes and amen to everything. Have a good night."

Nina's cheeks turned red. She was thankful that the conversation was over the phone. Under no circumstances would she let him see her blushing like a schoolgirl!

Nina decided to get some of the documents ready for Vijay before going to bed. She felt a strong sense of relief—thanks to Vijay's legal assistance. Her thoughts turned to his daughter's academics. Vijay should take care of his daughter's school issues first. What was the rush when she had secured his help?

The current situation regarding school and college admissions was beyond repair. Nina remembered her own experiences when she was a teenager. The present generation of upper-caste children was paying the price for their ancestors' racism. Well, this was more than paying a price. This was an example of corruption at its worst! On the other hand, as her mother had said, one way or the other, everybody paid the price.

◆ ◆ ◆

It was Nina's turn to be a student. Her lesson was in the kitchen. She was in the process of learning to cook a couple of dishes under Bitsy's supervision.

"Are you tired of Bitsy's food, Nina?" asked Dev.

"Oh, be quiet, will you? Nina needs to concentrate," Bitsy scolded Dev as usual.

"No, Dev, I love Bitsy's food," said Nina. "How can anybody get tired of it? I want to learn to cook because I'm going to be a mother."

While Nina was chopping potatoes and green beans, Dr. Davis entered the kitchen. He observed the scene and wondered if Bitsy was sick.

"No, our Nina wants to cook," Bitsy replied.

"Oh, Bitsy, you're going to be sick!" Tom declared.

Dev began to laugh and Bitsy pretended to scold him again. Nina threw a dishtowel at Tom. It fell on Brownie's face, who had just come in for a snack. Tiger, who often followed Brownie, grabbed the towel in his mouth, and the two dogs participated in a fantastic tug-of-war to win the coveted towel. Nina started to chase Tom with a long ladle and stopped only when he apologized breathlessly.

"I'm sorry, Nina. The temptation was too much to resist. You have so many talents. Do you have to learn to cook now?" Tom asked.

"Why? Is it because it's a woman's job? Does anybody ask you why you can't cook?" Nina asked in her routine fashion.

"No, but that's because most people know I'm a good cook," Tom said, after thinking for a moment. "I must prepare something for you soon."

"Another talent to add to your list of accomplishments!" Nina said and smiled good-humoredly. "I'll look forward to it."

"Sorry for arriving without prior announcement," Tom apologized. "I wanted to bring my sister to Brinda … to introduce her to you."

"You have a sister? I didn't know that."

"Well, actually, she is my cousin, but we grew up very close to each other. She lives in Chennai."

"When is she coming?" Nina asked.

"Actually, she came with me ... she is sitting in the car with her family at this moment," said Tom, smiling gingerly. "I shouldn't be asking you this, but is it all right to bring them in? They're on their way to the airport. If it's inconvenient, I can introduce her to you during her next visit."

"Please ask them to come in," said Nina.

When Tom went to his car, Nina ran to the kitchen to tell Bitsy and Dev that they had visitors. Her anxiety was so uncharacteristic that the older couple wondered about the excitement. What possessed their dear Nina?

Tom's cousin, Sylvia, didn't resemble him. But Nina noticed that she had his spontaneous smile when she was in a happy conversation and his hesitant frown when she was thinking about something. Her furtive glances and smiles were charming. Sylvia repeated her pleasure at meeting Nina at last.

"At last?" thought Nina.

Sylvia's husband, Victor, was busy with their young son. The daughter, who was about ten or twelve, sat next to her uncle. She was obviously enjoying his attention. The guests apologized again for an unceremonious visit.

"Please don't worry about that," Nina said, trying to make her guests feel at ease. "We're not busy at the moment. You're very welcome. But you must excuse my raggedy appearance. I'm learning to cook."

"Not at all. You look fine! I gave up cooking a long time ago. That's why my dear Victor found a very good cook. You know, Tom cooks very well," said Sylvia.

Nina could see that a good deal of affection and regard subsisted between Tom and Sylvia. Victor was an affectionate husband and father. A happy family! After talking and laughing for about half an hour, the guests prepared to leave. They had come in two vehicles. While Tony was packing the children in the first car, Sylvia stopped at the door to take Nina's hands in hers.

"Nina, I'm so glad to meet you finally," Sylvia said, smiling delightedly. "My brother speaks of you, only good things, of course."

Nina's glance flew to Tom's face at this. She couldn't understand his expression.

"Please visit us soon, Nina," said Sylvia, earnestly. "Anyway, you'll stay with us whenever you come to Chennai, won't you? You must."

After Victor repeated his wife's invitation, the couple walked away.

"Well, Nina, she insisted on seeing you. Now she is happy." Tom waved goodbye and joined his cousin and her husband.

Nina's thoughts were in a jumble. What could this mean? Sylvia was glad to meet her finally! And Nina must stay with them whenever she went to Chennai!

What did Tom tell his family about the stubborn, single woman, who had been giving him a tough time?

Bitsy went to the kitchen garden. "Late again?" Bitsy scolded Ravi for coming late. "How are we supposed to have coffee if you don't bring milk on time?"

"Haven't you heard?" asked Ravi. "There's a big commotion by the station. There's another accident. They found a man's corpse on the railway tracks."

"Good God, someone from our town?" asked Bitsy.

"I don't think so. Nobody knows where he is from," he said and lowered his voice dramatically. "Somebody in the crowd said that his throat was cut."

"Really? What's happening to our town?" exclaimed Bitsy.

"I know. Scary, isn't it? Anyway, I'll be back soon," said Ravi.

"Why? What are you up to?" Bitsy asked doubtfully.

"I'm going to be one of Miss Nina's students! Don't tell her. I'm going to surprise her."

The tutorial sessions were progressing at a good pace. On this sunny Thursday, Nina was totally surprised to see a couple of men in the library. Her small school was becoming co-ed! One of the men was Ravi, who supplied milk to Brinda. Did his mother, Valli, know about his tutorial visit? Ravi said that he knew all about the milk business, but his cousin, Veni, had inspired a desire in him to finish high school.

Nina was coming out of Mercy House when Tony approached her.

"I called Brinda," said Tony. "They told me that you were at the orphanage."

"What is it, Tony? Is something wrong?" Nina asked nervously.

"Madam, Dr. Davis will tell you," Tony replied very politely. "Can I take you to him? It's urgent."

Nina was not sure what to make of this. She called Bitsy to let her know that she would be away during the afternoon.

Tony didn't say a word. He drove the car to the outskirts of the town.

"Tony, where are we going?"

"I'm driving to the hospital—not the local one—the medical facility in the next town, Madam."

As the car approached the hospital, Nina felt queasy and anxious. "Tony, is somebody seriously hurt?" Nina asked, haunted by a nagging fear. "Please tell me."

"I don't know, Madam. I don't have the details. Here we are. We'll soon find out."

A few people were staring when Nina and Tony ran into the hospital. Tom met them by the lift on the third floor. Nina breathed a sigh of relief. For some strange reason, she had been worried that Tom was hurt. He was all right! Tom asked Nina to follow him to one of the rooms and asked Tony to wait outside.

"Nina, I know that I can count on your composure, right?" Tom asked, standing on the threshold of a sanitized chamber.

Good God! Was it the baby? It couldn't be the baby.

"Nina, don't worry," Tom assured her, reading the fear in her eyes. "It's not the baby. Nikil is safe at home with Bitsy and Dev."

Nina stepped into the room. She could barely see the face of the patient behind bandages and tubes. It was Rohini! What was wrong with her now? Rohini struggled to smile and reached for Nina's hand. Nina held her hand instinctively.

"I'm sorry," said Rohini.

"No, don't be, you'll be all right," whispered Nina. What else was she supposed to say?

"You'll take care of Nikil always, won't you?" asked Rohini, in a barely audible whisper.

At this, Nina looked at Tom. Did he know what was going on?

"Nina," Tom whispered. "She is the baby's mother."

"What?"

"Nina, Rohini is Nikil's mother," repeated Tom.

Nina sat on the chair next to the bed. She was, by no means, prepared for this bizarre turn of events. How incredible! Nina felt a hand on her shoulder. Tom was standing behind her.

"How long have you known that Rohini is Nikil's mother?" Nina asked Tom.

"Since this morning," replied Tom. "Nina, her real name is Parvathi."

Parvathi? Why a different name?

"Will you take care of my Nikil?" the patient looked at Nina and whispered.

"Certainly, dear, I promise," Nina replied, smiling gently at the patient. "You know I love him. He'll have a wonderful, happy life. I'll make sure of that."

"That's all I need to know," said Rohini, hoarsely. "Thank you, God bless."

"Nina, she's seriously hurt," Tom whispered outside the room. "There's not much hope left. Go home. I'll come to Brinda tonight and explain."

Nina was worried about Rohini's name. Tom said that she was Parvathi. Wasn't that the name of the mysterious woman who had written to Nina from the Dandiar jail? Although the letter was anonymous, the inspector had mentioned her name—purposely or inadvertently—and it was Parvathi! Didn't she die when she delivered a stillborn? Was that baby alive? What did this mean? Was there a connection? If there was, that baby ought to be Nikil. Nina was impatient to get home and hold that child before something happened to him. "Before something happened to him!" What a terrible thing to think of! What madness! There must be some connection between the intruder's wish to take the baby, all the phone calls, this woman's serious condition, and Nikil's future. All Nina wanted to do right now was to run home and hold her baby.

A few months ago, an important phone call reached Inspector Pandey's office. He woke up with a jerk at the shrill sound of the phone. He was tired to his bones. He had not gone home in over two days. The news he just received didn't make the situation better.

"Sir, he has gone to the south," the voice on the phone said. "We were able to trace as far as Chennai and no farther."

Pandey took the news calmly. His subordinates knew his quiet, evil strength. "Is the fugitive's family with him?" Pandey asked.

"His family, Sir, has vanished," replied the shaky voice. "Nobody knows where they possibly could be."

"Vanished? Nonsense! You'll find them, alive or dead. The next time you call me would be to let me know that I need to wait no longer. This is top priority. Are you listening? Find them."

"Yes, Sir, we will."

A week after this phone call, Dandiar and the surrounding districts woke up in shock at the following news. Three men were mysteriously found dead outside the perimeters of Dandiar jail. The nature of the assassination indicated that the tragedy was the general consequence of treason. The description of one of these men stated that he was built like a giant, with a nasty scar running along one side of his face, while the other two men were identified as ardent devotees of a fanatic cause.

Even as the still warm bodies of these three dead men were tossed on the moist grounds of the jail, Pandey picked up the phone and organized an emergency meeting with the committee members of his association. Something had to be done. That Parvathi was still alive, and how did the situation get this far? She was supposed to be killed before she delivered her child! What kind of idiots did his organization employ?

When Tom arrived after supper, the house was awake. Only the baby was asleep. Lucky for him, he was too young to be aware of the mystery that shrouded his precious life. Nina had informed Bitsy and Dev regarding that afternoon's strange incident. Therefore, they were as eager as Nina was, if not more, to listen to what Tom had to say. Tom asked Nina to take him upstairs to her room. The object of his attention was an antique desk. He pulled a pigeonhole and opened a recessed compartment. Nina watched him in wonder. How well he seemed to know where everything was!

"What are you looking for, Tom?" asked Nina.

"Nina, Parvathi told me what to look for and where to look for it," replied Tom. He pulled a stack of paper from the compartment. It was a letter written by Parvathi, and it was dated on the night of her disappearance from Brinda. "Let's go to the drawing room, Nina."

"Bitsy, do you want to read the letter first?" Nina asked in a shaky voice, handing the letter to Bitsy.

"Nina, do you want me to read the letter to you?" Bitsy asked.

"Yes, Bitsy, please," Nina said thankfully.

Bitsy began to read.

Dear Miss Nina,

I'm sorry to startle you with this letter. I meant to talk to you before leaving Brinda. I just didn't have the courage to face you in order to clarify several things. First of all, I apologize for misleading you about my name. Rohini is my nickname. I was named after my grandmother, Parvathi. Most people, including the director of the Women's Home in Madras, call me Rohini. My baby, Nikil, is the offspring of an unwelcome marriage between a Hindu woman and a Muslim man. Both families opposed the marriage. Miss Nina, my family disowned me. I haven't seen my mother since my wedding day. She comes from a very religious, Brahmin family. I don't remember my father. He died when I was very young. I was raised in my uncle's house where my helpless mother still lives.

My husband's name is Feroz. I met him at J.K. hospital in Delhi where I was a nurse. He worked there as an accountant. He was seen with a group, which was allegedly involved in a few disasters—train derailments, explosions, and unrest—in the heart of Delhi. Since then, he had been in trouble with the police. He was a victim, not a perpetrator. But the police didn't believe us. After we moved to Madras, Feroz found a job at one of the local banks. The police arrested Feroz on some charge and kept him imprisoned at Madras Central Jail and moved him to the jail at Dandiar on another charge. During that period, I was a nurse at St. Anne's where your mother was Director of Volunteer Services. Remember, your parents were moving to Madras for a few months? She was my only friend at a time when my family deserted me. She comforted me and offered help when I needed it most. I had to see my husband, and I was prepared to travel to the north to meet him. I was pregnant, and I wanted to see my husband very badly. I took leave of your mother before leaving Madras. That's the last time I saw her. She was the only human being, besides my husband, who looked at a person's character instead of religion and caste. She was a remarkable lady.

I received permission to see Feroz. A week after my visit, a police officer and two constables came to the apartment where I was staying with a couple of my husband's friends. They took me to the jail to see my husband. They said that he was hurt in a brawl. But when we reached there, they asked me to wait in a room with some food and tea. Miss Nina, when I woke up, I was also a prisoner. I was told that Feroz had a plan to escape through the help of some of his friends. They said that my fingerprints were on the letter that Feroz received, which described the plan for his escape. That was a lie. I had no part in any planning. They were probably afraid that I would help my husband escape. They put me behind bars.

A lady from the Welfare Services came to see me from time to time. She was sent to take care of me because of my delicate condition. She told me that Feroz was in an accident and died in the infirmary. The same night, I heard the news of the plane crash that took your dear mother and father. I was afraid, but I had to stop thinking of my welfare. I was pregnant and I didn't want my baby to be born behind bars. I was getting desperate. That was when I decided to write to you. Your mother talked about you very often. You're just like your mother—kind, generous, unselfish, and considerate. Please forgive me for all the trouble Nikil and I have caused you. I will call you to let you know about this letter, which I am going to hide in the desk in your room.

I apologize for leaving Brinda in such a manner when you have been kindness itself. It is against my nature to run away from the hands that fed me, clothed me, and sheltered me when I came to see my baby's face. But I need to go with my husband's cousin. He was the friend who got me out of the jail that night at the expense of his own safety and life. He got some very timely assistance from a few men in the jail. Miss Nina, these men were rumored to be members of a fanatical, religious organization, the one led by Inspector Pandey. I am so grateful for their help. One of them, a large man, arranged for me to wait behind that particular door in the jail when you were supposed to walk through that section. Unfortunately, the lady from the Welfare Services suddenly came, and I had to move away abruptly when I was talking to you. When the men rescued me, they told me that the inspector accidentally revealed my name to you. That is why I had to hide my name when I left my baby in your care. I didn't want the inspector to trace my baby to me. My rescuers were supposed to be an impediment to me, not a source of help. Those kind men were murdered after my escape. That inspector is a monster. Now my husband's cousin is helping me again to leave Brinda because he is worried that somebody or a group is looking for me. I seem to have enemies without faces, and I am running away from an unknown fear to secure the safety of my child.

I took a great risk by traveling quite late during my pregnancy. If I had stayed in Dandiar, Inspector Pandey would have killed me—just like that villain, Ahmed Asim, killed Feroz. Nikil was born in Madras. But I couldn't stay there for long. It was very risky. I eventually came to you. Especially after the incident, when that man tried to take Nikil away, it kills me to leave my baby like this. However, I am convinced that Nikil will be much safer if I disappear. I am the obstacle in his welfare, and that is the last thing I want in this world. It breaks my heart to leave my baby. But Nikil's safety is more important than my happiness. His life is the most precious gift. I will do anything to help him stay alive. Thank God, he is in good hands, and I know you will protect him. God bless you and my child. Please give my thanks to Bitsy and Dev for their kindness and convey my thanks to Dr. Davis for helping in Nikil's case. I won't return because my visit might harm the baby. But I hope to call you sometime soon. From somewhere far way, I will pray for Nikil's welfare and your health and prosperity.

Sincerely,
Your friend, Parvathi

There was absolute silence in the room for a few moments.

"How is she?" Nina asked. "Tom, how is Parvathi?"

"She is no more," said Tom.

In spite of all that had preceded this statement, Nina was flabbergasted. Parvathi was dead? She had left Brinda with the hope of contacting Nina sooner or later. Why didn't that helpless girl talk to her in person? Nina failed Parvathi twice—once in the jail and now, again, while she was looking for a sanctuary.

"Dr. Davis, how did she die? What happened to her?" Bitsy asked.

"She was killed, Bitsy."

"Killed? No! We all know the consequences of inter-religious marriages in orthodox families. Killed? What kind of fanatics are their family members?" Bitsy sounded utterly shocked.

"Family? No, Bitsy, she was not killed by her family or her husband's family."

"Dr. Davis, where is Parvathi's relative, the one who has been helping her?" Dev asked Tom.

"He was the man on the railway tracks, Dev," replied Tom. "They got him."

"It's unbelievable. What a nightmare!" exclaimed Nina.

"You must agree with me. I must insist, Nina," Tom said in an urgent tone. "We need to find another place for Nikil."

"Tom, how did you know that Parvathi was hurt?" Nina asked, curious about Tom's appearance at the hospital after Parvathi's injury.

"She was brought to the hospital after an accident," replied Tom. "She asked for my presence, and I went to her as soon as I received the call. She was hit by a motorcycle."

"Then, it could have been an accident. Don't you think, Tom?" Nina asked hopefully.

"Parvathi recognized the man and the woman, Nina. She remembered them from the jail."

An unknown chill seeped into the quiet drawing room.

A couple of days before Parvathi's accident, a much-awaited phone call reached Inspector Pandey's home. His wife woke him up to answer the call. He took the phone from her. Groggy or awake, he was a professional. He waited till his wife vacated the room to talk to his caller.

"Sir, we have located his wife," the voice on the phone sounded relieved. "We might have found the man who is assisting her. As you know, we already have information about his child. What should we do?"

"Leave the child alone for the moment," Pandey ordered. "Take care of the man and the lady. I want this to stop here."

The phone was ringing.

"Nina, have you forgotten all of us? It's not like you to disregard phone calls. Are you all right?" Sandy asked.

Nina groped for several apologies, but Sandy understood. She was concerned about Nina and the baby.

"Nina, did I tell you how glad Jim and I are that you lost the Dandiar project?" said Sandy. "Kumar's accident was severe. Nina, I can't tell you how glad I am that they took the Dandiar project away from your hands."

"Oh, Sandy, do you really believe that Kumar's accident was not just an accident? Some thugs could've attacked him for money. Did somebody really try to kill him?"

"Nina, I'm certain that some unknown individual or group doesn't want anybody to publish the articles about Dandiar jail," said Sandy. "Jim feels that the situation is more serious than just the apprehension of revealing certain embarrassing facts. Nobody is willing to undertake the project anymore. It is shelved for the time being. It might be shelved forever."

Nina told Sandy about Rohini. Sandy was shocked to hear the latest development, and she was more anxious to get Nina away from Kanyakoil. When Sandy heard further details about Rohini's identity and her bitter experience in the jail, she almost dropped the phone. Jim, who was sitting by Sandy at the time, took the phone from her. After all, he had been with Nina when she had received news of Parvathi's death.

"Nina, did you really see her in the hospital?" asked Jim.

"Yes, Jim. I wish I had known about Parvathi's troubles a little earlier. I could have done something to help her." Nina was crying. She didn't bother to control her tears. She was glad to unload her worries to Jim and Sandy. It was uncanny how incidents from various corners converged to one place—the jail in the north.

"I'm coming to get you and the baby, Nina," said Sandy, firmly. "I'm serious."

Nina assured Sandy that she would always keep her and Jim in mind if the current situation went from bad to worse. But she couldn't leave Brinda at this point when several questions stood unanswered. "Besides, I can't take Nikil from Kanyakoil without an authorization from Children's Welfare Services," said Nina. "That's not easy to obtain, Sandy."

"Then, I think you should listen to Tom, Nina. Please don't delay. I'm very nervous. Is there an individual or a family you can think of? Can someone take care of Nikil for a short time?" asked Sandy.

"You and Jim. Who else?" asked Nina.

"Oh, we would love to. Will it work?" asked Sandy.

"I don't think so, Sandy. Thanks. They won't let me send him that far. I'm sure we'll find some other solution."

Who was going to take care of Nikil? Simi and Vijay wanted to take care of him. It wouldn't work because their home was not a confidential or an unidentified location—regarding Nikil's safety. Well, who was going to take care of that poor child? And how was Nina going to endure the separation?

◆ ◆ ◆

Nina was surprised to get a call from her old boss, Roy. She was actually relieved to hear his voice.

"Are you ready to come back to Delhi, young lady?" asked Roy. "I hope you're not angry with *The Express* or me. I've a couple of projects. I wouldn't dream of giving them to anybody but you."

"It's nice of you to ask, thank you," Nina replied politely. "I'm settled quite well in my ancestral home. My life is full. Going back to Delhi? No, I don't think so. And no, I'm not angry." Nina was honest. Her anger had died a while ago.

"I guess you haven't changed much, Nina?" Roy laughed. "I beg you to think about my offer, Nina. Please expect a call from me soon."

"I'll be glad to receive your call," said Nina.

Roy placed the phone on its cradle and looked at the window. The Delhi smog made the crowded city appear milky. He couldn't get rid of this terrible feeling. He was partially responsible for taking the special project away from Nina, which consequently provoked her to quit *The Express*. To add insult to injury, he had to give the job to Kumar. It was too late to think about it. That project was dead. He had to get Nina back and make her feel better. He had to admit that he hoped to feel a little better in the process. His guilty conscience made him restless.

Roy made another phone call to Kumar's home. He felt miserable because he had chosen Kumar as a namesake journalist for the Dandiar project. How could he anticipate such a life-threatening disaster?

The tutorials continued despite the pending adoption and other disturbing circumstances. They offered a welcome distraction from worries. Nina came into the library to begin her lessons for the day and was pleasantly surprised to see Valli. She was sitting among the eager students! Her son, Ravi, appeared a little insecure of her presence here because Valli's tongue-on-wheels was an acknowledged fact in that small town.

"I never went to school, Nina," Valli said sheepishly.

"You didn't?" asked Nina. "Then, how in the world do you keep all your milk accounts distinctly in order?"

"I do the math in my head. My mother taught me," replied the old lady, smiling at Nina's amazement.

Formal school or no school—Nina admired the intelligence and inherent resourcefulness of the simple men and women of Valli's generation. When the students were vacating the library, Veni was still hovering near the door.

"Nina, may I talk to you about something?" asked Veni. "I won't take more than a few minutes."

"Of course, you can. You look worried. What's wrong, Veni?" Nina asked, concerned about Veni's doleful expression.

"Nina, did you hear about that young woman, the one who died in the hospital?" Veni whispered.

"What do you mean? What young lady, Veni?" Nina was obviously stalling. Was Veni referring to Parvathi ... or Rohini, by which name she was known in this town? The neighbors, who were naturally curious about her absence, were told that Rohini decided to stay with her grandmother and had found a job close to her home. Her mysterious death was not public news yet. At least, the newspapers had no clue regarding her real identity because her injury happened in the next town where she was a stranger.

"This is someone I've known for a long time. Nina, she went to school with me," replied Veni, on the verge of tears. "You know how my parents stopped me from going to school before I graduated? This girl was smart. She even went to college. And she died ... it's her family's fault. I ..." Veni had tears in her eyes by now.

"I'm sorry, Veni. Of course, you're talking about the incident in the paper. Doesn't she, I mean, didn't she live near High Street? Bitsy told me something about that. Wasn't she ill? If she was your classmate, she must be quite young."

"Ill? No. No! She was pregnant," Veni blew her nose loudly and continued. "The family wanted to see if she was having a boy. Well, she already has two daughters, you see. So they took her to the doctor to do the ... the test."

"Ultrasound? Amniocentesis?" asked Nina, helpfully.

"Yes, yes, that's what it was. Her husband, or his family, or whoever it was, forced her to have an abortion. And Nina, he is an engineer. The husband is educated. Can you believe it? Where was his brain? Nina, she didn't ..." said Veni.

Nina had a long, soothing talk with Veni before dropping her at her house.

Nina sent her article to the editor and stretched her tired limbs. She had developed a whopping headache after her conversation with Veni. Bitsy, seeing that Nina was restlessly in pain, forced her to go to her room and take a nap. Nina was exhausted. She decided to listen to Bitsy. Was there a time when she didn't listen to her? When Bitsy woke her up in the evening and reminded her of Dr. Davis' visit, Nina tried to get out of her bed in a hurry.

"I packed a tray," Bitsy said, pushing Nina back on the bed. "I don't want you to strain after the miserable headache. Are you all right now, Nina?"

"Bitsy, you and Dev shouldn't be walking up and down with a tray of food."

"Nina, stop worrying about me and Dev. You know I can't stand that," Bitsy said, looking at Nina's pathetic expression. "I meant to ask you earlier. Is Veni okay? Dev told me that she looked upset."

"Yes, Bitsy. You were at the dentist's when Veni was here. Can you believe this?" asked Nina, repeating the disturbing news about Veni's friend.

Aruna's soul was probably awake at this moment. Things had not improved much since her time. Then, it was a grain of paddy that took the life of a newborn female child. When Nina was young, she had heard fragments of such atrocities from her grandmother.

"Isn't it awful, Bitsy? Now, thanks to advanced medical technology, one can prevent the birth of an unwanted female child rather than killing it at birth."

"As though that fact is supposed to offer some consolation," Bitsy sighed. "It's disgraceful, all the same."

"Yes, Bitsy, it is."

Tom and Vijay arrived after supper to discuss a temporary home for Nikil. Nina took the gentlemen to the library. After the recent developments, she was more than willing to listen to any option. Tom wanted to take Nikil to Kottoor. The director of the establishment was a good friend of his mother's—a generous, trustworthy lady—who was aware of Nikil's situation. Vijay also saw the advantage of placing Nikil in a location that was totally unknown to Kanyakoil.

"I have given this location plenty of thought. I wouldn't send Nikil away unless I'm certain about the excellent care he would receive. Nina, you trust me, don't you?" Tom asked.

"I do, Tom," replied Nina.

"Nina, once you decide to leave the baby under the care of another shelter, you can't stay in contact with anybody over there until it's safe to bring him here. Can you do that?" asked Tom, with a note of finality.

"Yes, I can do that, but," said Nina, "what makes that place safer than here? I'm going crazy because I can't understand why Nikil is in danger until he is somebody's child … until a piece of paper announces his parent's name."

"I think somebody has an objection to Nikil's adoption," Tom explained.

"Because I'm a single woman?" Nina asked.

"No, that's a nagging issue that bothers those who have nothing else to do in their lives. I think that Nikil's paternal family wants to adopt him."

"Is that family responsible for the anonymous phone calls we've been receiving?" asked Nina.

"Oh, no. That's still a mystery. There couldn't be a connection between the phone calls and that family. They want to adopt Nikil. I don't think they mean to cause trouble."

"Then why don't they come forward?" Nina asked. "Do you think they'll take the baby away from me? I mean, by force?" Nina turned pale.

Tom saw the worry in Nina's eyes again. "No, I won't let them, Nina," said Tom, in an extraordinarily soothing voice.

It was not a promise. It was a simple statement. That was enough to allay her fears for the time being. Besides, Nina had the letter in a safe place, that letter which authorized Nina as the guardian until Nikil was adopted. The baby's mother authorized it. However, in the middle of religious inhibitions, what power did such a letter hold?

The following Saturday was chosen for Nikil's transfer from Nina's home to the new, unknown place. After Tom and Vijay left, Nikil relaxed on Nina's lap. She was reading him a goodnight story. He had developed a new habit—when somebody read to him, he repeated the sounds, slapped the pages with his chubby hands, and said "Amma." Everything was still amma to him. Nina smiled and promised not to keep him away from Brinda for a long time. He uttered a bubbly "Amma" and returned her smile.

"Good boy!" said Nina. She hugged and kissed his double chin. As she walked to his bed to tuck him in, he saw Parvathi's photograph. She was holding Nikil in her arms. It was a picture taken in the garden. He pointed to the photograph and said "Amma" with his dimpled smile.

"You know, Nikil, for once, you're right!" said Nina, unable to control a flood of tears.

Inspector Pandey snuffed his cigarette and took a last swig of the arrack from the milky glass. He glanced at the entrance of the arrack shop. The grubby door was flanked by a couple of his disciples, who never left his sight for more than a few minutes. One of these men signaled to Pandey. The inspector left the shop without paying for his drink.

A scruffy man was standing under a street lamp, a few yards away from the arrack shop. When Pandey entered the street, faithfully followed by his men, the man smiled at the inspector. "My sister wants to speak to you," the man spoke animatedly.

Pandey asked him to lower his voice and crossed the street. As the group walked toward the other end of the street, Pandey saw her by a window. She smiled and waved before disappearing behind the curtains.

The man took Pandey and his men to a rickety tea stall. It seemed to precariously hold its own with the aid of a thatched roof and bamboo pillars. Behind this stall was a small house—that woman's office. While her brother ran the tea stall, she ran a lucrative business in her small home. All her clients were men, and she made a significant sum every night. She had started her career as a skilled pickpocket, blossomed into a talented forger, and developed into an actress. Pandey had been a regular in her 'office' during the past several months.

She was proud of her recent performances. She had acted as a representative of Welfare Services at Dandiar jail, which allowed her to talk to Parvathi. She was the thief who took the anonymous letter from the guesthouse in Dandiar. She was the anonymous caller who summoned Dev to meet Dr. Davis on the night the intruder walked into Brinda. She was on the motorcycle with a man when the vehicle hit Parvathi. Since Pandey was a very important person, she had allocated a special room for him, which she often kept aside for politicians, businessmen, and fraudulent officials. Her questionable career never got her into trouble until now. After all, she had Pandey in her hands, and she had the support of other officials. She had earned quite a bit of praise from Inspector Pandey for some very devious work in tracing Parvathi, her allies, and any other thorn in the path of his vendetta. Pandey looked at her through the rings of cigarette smoke. She asked him, while putting away the cash he just shoved in her hand, if he had any other job for her.

"No. Everything is complete in that troubled area," he replied. His voice held its usual arrogance.

"What about the baby?" she asked, quite disappointed.

"That orphan can go to hell as far as I'm concerned," he said. "It doesn't interest me anymore."

"But I don't understand. Months ago, you were passionate about the disappearance of Feroz, Parvathi, and …"

"That was then," he said, not letting her finish. "Now that Feroz and Parvathi are dead, I've lost interest in the baby. It's not going to enter my path, all right? Anyway, it's time to go home." Pandey's tone indicated that this topic was over.

Yes, that was always the case. They all had to return to their little wives. He picked up his shirt and walked to the door. Something told her that his visits to the tea stall would dwindle. It didn't matter. There will be other men and other assignments.

The skilled assassin, who was also an atheist, received an important phone call. Even Ahmed Asim, Pandey's chief enemy, respected this neutral force. His name or nickname was "Neutral." Nobody knew his real name or his original identity. For a change, this call that this assassin received was not from a group of terrorists. It was from a law-abiding police officer.

This officer was not only a clever man. He also possessed a rather crafty mind. His superiors were relieved that his intelligence didn't take a criminal turn. He had the good sense to realize that regardless of the efficiency of his unit and its established courage, the Asims and the Pandeys were not to be caught through regular methods. They could only be arrested on an irregular, offbeat routine. If an arrangement had to be made to accomplish this feat, it could only be through Neutral's help. It was a good thing that the hired gun worked for one thing only: money. Religion, politics, race, and sundry impediments didn't stand in his way. The officer typed a detailed plan and subsequent procedures, made a couple of phone calls, and asked his chauffeur to get the car ready. He had some very important meetings to attend and some urgent issues to settle. The prospect of his success was marred only by this nagging thought: he and his colleagues had to resort to the support, although indirectly, of a despicable, parasitic man—a cruel, ruthless assassin! Well, if that was meant to be, there was nothing anybody could do to change it. At times, one had to befriend a cunning fox to capture a wicked hyena. With this reassuring thought, he stuffed the sealed envelope in his briefcase, uttered a sincere prayer, and hoped to send Asim and Pandey to hell.

The mercenary smiled. What a strange phone call! His unlisted number could never be traced to his current residence or identity. Still, it was quite uncommon to get such a request from such a caller. If he had initially thought that the call was strange, the assignment was more intriguing! He didn't care as long as he got paid. The call that the assassin received was not to take a life. It was to stall the action. At first, the mercenary felt astonished. Was he getting old? Did the terror-seeking fanatics lose faith in him? Well, according to the caller's assertions, the group that wished to engage his services had unwavering faith in his efficiency. The job that was offered to the mercenary was of a different nature. For a phenomenal payment, all he had to do was pinpoint a couple of groups' irreparable errors, of course, backed by reasonable evidence. For the first time in his life, he was to add to his already overflowing bank balance without the assistance of his trigger or the unpleasant red flood. In addition to the temptation of money, the assassin was to obtain this comfort: the officers would overlook some of the previous atrocities committed by the trigger-happy man—that is if such atrocities could be connected to his talent. Anyway, it felt good to have the consideration of the police, regardless of its worth.

◆ ◆ ◆

The afternoon nap revived Nina reasonably well. After tossing and turning for a while, she let her eyes rest on the antique desk. Parvathi had chosen this furniture to hide her letter! What else could be hiding there? A surge of excitement filled the stillness of the night. Nina walked to the desk and pulled the pigeonhole where Parvathi's letter had been kept. She reached inside the compartment. Her hand touched no hidden article. As she was about to give up, her little finger touched something that felt like paper. She pulled it out very carefully. She had to strain her eyes to read the words on the cover. The letters were faded, but they were still legible. It was written in Tamil, and the writer had signed … "Buvana." The collection of writing looked like a journal. Where had Nina heard that name before? There was something scribbled beneath the name. Did it say Brinda? How incredible to find something written right under this roof! Nina took Buvana's work to her bed and opened the first page. They were beautiful poems and reflections of a lady. Sleep was impossible on a night like this. Nina flipped the pages. When was this written? She went back to the first page.

'September 15, 18 …
'Now that I am thirteen …'

Was it 1893 or 1899? Was it from that long ago? Nina felt guilty. She wondered if it was a diary. But it was written over a century ago. Besides, it was too precious to be ignored. It was the writing of a young girl—an innocent look at the world through non-tinted lens. Her writing reflected a time spent around the river, the same river Nina saw everyday of her life.

March 13, a few months after my wedding, jailed on the terrace of my husband's home, fearful of crying—I want my mother …

God, give me wings to fly home-
God, give me strength to swallow my tears-
Wipe my sorrow, banish my fears-
Send me a rainbow to make my carriage-
Or take me to you.

A few months after her wedding! Was she married at the age of fourteen, fifteen? Nina could feel the young bride's tears, a drop at a time, from a distant shadow. She skipped a few pages.

May 16, 1897
Distant sounds have no curfew-
Nearby smiles have no boundaries-
Hidden tears and borrowed smiles-
Pretend—Run—I need wings to fly away-

My baby, Aruna-
The sunshine in the palms of a petal-
Without a father, holding the fire of society-
My laughter, in the hands of destiny-

Nina's eyes rested on the name, Aruna. That was it. Buvana was the mother of that lady whose picture was in Mercy House. Aruna had raised Nina's grandmother, Akila! Nina went to the cupboard and pulled out a box that contained a few trinkets. She had discovered these a long time ago during her rendezvous by the river. She was just a child then. She still had the note that went with the box, a short note written by a girl called Buvana. Then … there could be no doubt about it. The same person must have written this journal!

Nina woke up, not quite sure of where she was. She looked around her and realized that she was in her own room, surrounded by familiar things. Buvana's journal had taken her to a distant time, a journey on clouds where she heard whispers and tears. She couldn't get that journal out of her mind. She showed it to Bitsy during breakfast. Bitsy remembered certain occasions when Akila had talked about Aruna and Aruna's mother, Buvana.

"You've seen her portrait, haven't you, Nina?" asked Bitsy.

"Which one, Bitsy?"

Bitsy asked Nina to follow her to the drawing room. On the wall near the stairs was a portrait of a lady with a shy smile and unsure eyes. Nina read the inscription: *My Mother, Buvana.* Aruna was the artist. "Nina, that's Buvana. Didn't your grandmother talk about her?" Bitsy asked.

"Yes, she did. Somehow, I didn't pay much attention to this portrait. Aruna must have been very talented. Are there more of her work, Bitsy?"

"Yes, some scenes of the village and the hills, which were done when she was young, I think. They are on the walls of the orphanage. I heard that she didn't spend any time on art once she reached adulthood. Mercy House became her life and her mission until she died."

Bitsy sat by Nina on the foot of the stairs. "It'll be all right, my dear," Bitsy whispered. "It'll be all right. I promise."

Nina felt a sense of relief. As long as Bitsy believed in something, it was sure to be all right.

On Friday, while Nina was sifting through her bank accounts, Bitsy entered the office after a quick knock on the door. "Nina, Dr. Davis is here," Bitsy announced.

What was he doing here around noon? He was not supposed to arrive until that evening when they were scheduled to go over the final plans for Nikil's stay at the new location. Nina met Tom in the library. He looked tired. She certainly appreciated all that he was doing. Would she be able to repay his timely and unwavering help in some manner? He was standing near the window, looking at the silhouette of the mountains. He turned suddenly when Nina entered the room, but he didn't have his customary smile. What was wrong?

"Tom, you're here early, aren't you? Are you eager to take Nikil away from me?" Nina asked.

"No, I'm not eager to take Nikil. How are you?" Tom replied and sat on the chair by the window. "There's a new development. Nikil's great uncle, from his father's side, wants to take the baby into his family."

"What? You can't be serious!" Nina's voice displayed a little fear and a little doubt.

"Would I come to you with some information that is not concrete?" asked Tom.

"But the letter," Nina replied, confused and worried. "Tom, it must have some influence regarding Nikil. The wishes of the baby's mother can't be ignored."

"Nina, according to the letter, you are the guardian until somebody decides to adopt Nikil."

"Okay. I want to adopt him, don't I? Nikil was left in my care. I HAVE HIS MOTHER'S LETTER."

"Nina, how much influence would a letter carry against the traditions of the baby's families, especially two families with different religious principles?" asked Tom. "My advice is to reconsider your original idea of adopting Nikil, considering all the obstacles in the way, the baby's future, and your safety."

"My safety? I'm not worried about it, all right?" Nina sounded upset.

"You should be. You should give this adoption serious thought."

"Serious thought! How can you talk like this? How can you talk as though I … I'm buying something on an impulse?" asked Nina.

"I'm talking from experience. I've dealt with similar situations. Think again about what you're doing, please."

"Experience! Well, how many children have you raised?" Nina was angry by now. Her gratitude for Tom's help receded due to the frustration of explaining her dearest wish in life to Tom and others on a regular basis.

"I've helped raise more than thirty girls and twelve boys, out of which, ten girls have been sent to college, two are married," Tom replied, making a proper list for Nina's benefit. "Five boys are situated in self-supportive careers. All I'm trying to do here is offer some advice. Please think again."

Through all this, Tom never raised his voice. That fact irritated Nina more than his impertinent advice. She tried a different angle to cut him to size. "To rethink my decision at this point! Anyway, what makes you think that I need your advice?" asked Nina.

"Well, you don't get along with your brother's family or your aunt. If you had a father or a husband …"

"Stop! STOP right now!" shouted Nina. "None of the people would be able to influence me once my mind is made up. I'll not let anybody bully me. You're not my brother. You're not my father. You're not—heaven forbid—my husband. Even if you were, do you really think you can make me change my mind about something I strongly believe in?"

"No, I know you well enough by now to be thankful that I'm not your husband!" Tom shouted. "You're determined to be pigheaded. My only concern is this child. Whether you like it or not, I'm responsible for his safety and welfare. You can worry about your own safety, but for Nikil's sake, I've to question your damned beliefs, and I don't care what you think of me." He stormed out of the room.

Nina wanted Tom to get out of her life forever. The burden of facing so much censure from a meddling society made her extraordinarily weary. In addition, the thought of her separation from the baby was something she couldn't face. She went to her room and had a good cry. Even Bitsy failed to revive Nina's jangled nerves. Nina's only hope was that things would be miraculously resolved soon. Then she would never look at that overbearing Tom Davis again.

Bitsy packed Nikil's suitcase. She remembered to include his favorite toy and blanket. The tears were ready. Bitsy saw Nikil's attempt to get out of the playpen. He was getting good at crawling. He was determined. He yelled "Amma" and hoped Bitsy would take pity on him.

Tom arrived in the evening to take Nikil to his new, temporary shelter. Only three parties knew of Nikil's destination: a counselor from Children's Welfare

Services, Dr. Davis, and Nina, including Bitsy and Dev, of course. They were gone, Nikil was gone, and they couldn't determine for how long.

Bitsy found Dev in the kitchen. "Dev, what are you doing? How can you cry like a baby when our Nina needs us?" asked Bitsy.

Bitsy's reproach worked like a tonic. Dev packed a tray with some tea and snacks and followed Bitsy to Nina's room. Dev and Bitsy convinced Nina to get out of the bed and go to the balcony to get some fresh air. Dev deposited the tray on the wicker table and smiled.

"Nina, starvation and tears are going to be useless in bringing the baby back to us. You need to be strong to welcome Nikil when he is ready to come back, right?" Bitsy's pep talk started a fresh flow of tears. She saw how useless Dev was going to be in the current situation and sent him downstairs. "Nina, what is it?" Bitsy asked softly. "Is something bothering you … besides Nikil's absence?"

"I hate that doctor, you know, Bitsy? I hope he never comes back here. Listen to me, if he ever comes here again, you talk to him and tell me what he wants, okay? I don't wish to see his face or hear his voice again."

"I will, Nina," said Bitsy. She didn't bother to ask for the details that led to Nina's absolute and sudden aversion. She thought she knew. She promised Nina that she would be right back and went downstairs to attend to her husband. Dev was such a baby—kind, innocent, and mild-mannered—unlike most of his peers. She should have known that he would go to pieces at their separation from Nikil. Bitsy sat by her husband and encouraged him to appeal to his God. "Dev," said Bitsy, "it's a good thing that we have two helpers in heaven between the two of us. Let them pull their resources and send that beloved child to us."

The weekend went by uneventfully, making way for an unexpected Monday. Nina decided to immerse herself in her articles. Thankfully, various deadlines offered a welcome distraction from her worries. While Nina was working upstairs, Brinda had the most unanticipated visitor. A swarthy gentleman of about sixty knocked on the door. His bushy eyebrows and shaggy beard gave him an unkempt appearance. A few able-bodied men stood respectfully behind him.

"I'm Hussein. I'm Feroz's uncle. I've come to see Nikil. Where is he?" asked the gentleman.

This was the relative who was eager to take Nikil away from Nina! She requested him to take a seat. He waited till Nina was seated before sitting down. He looked intimidating, but he had a mild voice. He declined refreshments and respectfully expressed his wish to see Nikil.

"He is not here, Sir," Nina said, cautiously choosing her words.

"Not here?" asked Hussein, doubtfully. "Where is he?"

Nina was beginning to feel very nervous. He couldn't harm her, not right here in her house, but his associates looked menacing enough to cause doubts in her mind. "Sir, Nikil has been taken to a different home, a foster home, and he'll remain there until his adoption process is finalized," said Nina.

"Why wasn't I informed?" asked Hussein, with a touch of annoyance. "Who is responsible for this?"

While Nina was wondering whether to offer Tom's name or not, the gentleman got up, brought his hands together in greeting, and walked out of the room.

Nina called Vijay and informed him about Hussein. He agreed with Tom's sentiments. Who didn't agree with his sentiments? That was Nina's constant wonder and irritation.

Bitsy offered Nina a cup of tea after supper and encouraged her to relax in the drawing room. A week had gone by without Nikil. It was miserable to remember his angelic face when they couldn't see him, hold him, or talk to him. Nina would have given anything to hear his voice at this moment. Bitsy turned on the television. Nina almost dropped the tea on the floor. A man was being arrested regarding some serious misdemeanor. He looked familiar. The man, Pandey, who was being arrested, was an officer in Dandiar jail. Pandey! He was the stern officer who had told Nina and Jim that the pregnant prisoner died during her delivery when he had planned something devilish. Another man's arrest followed, but he had his back to the camera. His name was Ahmed Asim. He represented a powerful group of Muslims, had his hands in many disasters, and he was Pandey's religious opponent. The two men had used their personal, religious feud on their society, and the result was the loss of many lives. Dev joined them to see what the commotion was all about. Nina and Bitsy explained the news to him.

"Bitsy, I can't believe this," Nina said incredulously. "I wonder how many lives have been traded for these fiends' monstrous goals."

The list definitely included Nikil's mother, father, and Arun, the young photographer. Unfortunately, Arun had accompanied Kumar on that fatal night near Dandiar! Arun and many other innocent people were dead because of the horrendous acts of a few men, fanatical men, who buried their senses in religious convictions.

The phone rang. It was Vijay.

"Nina, Hussein didn't waste any time. He has submitted a special request to the adoption services to consider him as a guardian in Nikil's case. I have booked the following Monday for the second hearing at Children's Welfare Services. Are you available on Monday?" Vijay asked.

"Yes, I am. Thank you, Vijay."

"Nina," continued Vijay. "Tom will be present. There is no need to worry. Would you like Simi to accompany you? She'll be glad to come."

"No, thank you, Vijay. Simi has to take care of the children. Besides, the session at Children's Welfare Services might take a long time. Don't worry. I'll be fine."

Nina was impatient to call Sandy and Jim. Incidentally, they were just watching the news. Jim also recognized Inspector Pandey. It was incredible. Pandey had several counts of unrest under his belt. The charges were heavy. He was chiefly blamed for initiating many domestic disputes among Hindu/Muslim communities.

Sandy and Nina talked for a long time. Sandy was eager to know how Nikil's case was progressing and encouraged Nina to be optimistic. Nina, in spite of the distance between them, felt reassured by Sandy's comforting voice.

Hussein's family had spent a few years in Kanyakoil when he was a child. He still had business contacts in the south—especially in Kanyakoil—where he purchased the famous southern handloom for his stores in Delhi. He was a guest in his contractor's house. Balu was an exceptional businessman and an excellent host! Here, the guest was treated with considerable respect. Hussein had earned the reputation of a ruthless businessman in a tough business district in Delhi. He had temporarily left his business in the capable hands of his son.

Hussein was still disappointed because his nephew married a Hindu girl! Unfortunately, there was a child from that marriage, reminding the society of a mixed union, conducted in bad taste. Hussein had to thank his other nephew for informing him—by a slip of tongue, of course—about Feroz's baby. This nephew had diligently tried to help Feroz earlier, and he had given his life in protecting Parvathi. After all his struggles, he had to sacrifice his life on the railway tracks! Hussein had seen Parvathi from a distance. Feroz had not listened to Hussein. He had ignored his uncle's suggestion to get his young wife to convert to their religion. How could they raise a child—with one foot in Hinduism and another in Islam?

"Now the child is an orphan as a result of religious fanatics and political fiends," thought Hussein, angrily. He hated fanatics more than he hated politicians. All that the Hindu girl left behind her was an elderly mother who could barely take care of her own needs—economically and physically—and the latest information told him that she didn't have long to live. Hussein believed that only Allah knew how long one was going to live! A few years ago, Hussein's brother and his family were massacred, leaving young Feroz behind to face the harsh reality. Now the heavens took him also. Hussein decided that it was up to him to protect the infant, although he was old. Then, he heard a rumor that a young Hindu woman was eager to adopt the child! Upon his arrival at Kanyakoil, the rumor became an insolent truth! What would this young journalist know about raising a child, alone, without a man's protection? Well, that silly Parvathi had left the baby, along with a letter, in her care. What did that prove? Nothing! Hussein shared his sentiments with his host. Balu agreed with him. In Balu's patriarchal, traditional circle, there was no room for the adoption of a child by a single woman. Hussein decided to come to Kanyakoil to talk to the young female journalist. Nonsense! What was done was done. Now this child needed a proper home and a strong religious supervision.

The officer, appointed by Children's Welfare Services, appeared rather aloof. He welcomed Nina and Vijay in a monotonous tone and read Nina's biography in a loud, authoritative voice. Nina's courage began to sink. Thankfully, the officer didn't talk about Nina's spinster status for which she should remember to thank Vijay at a later time.

Nina glanced at the people in the room. Hussein concealed his expression behind his beard and glasses. Nina was thankful for this. She endured the formalities calmly. She might have a few enemies. However, she didn't want her own apprehension to be one of them. She just had to be strong on behalf of Nikil.

"Do you still wish to adopt this child, Madam?" the officer asked.

"Yes, Sir, I do," Nina said, aware of many eyes on her.

"You do realize that this child is a product of two religions, which strongly stand against each other. What do you say to that? How are you planning to raise him?" the officer asked, making no effort to hide his judicial curiosity.

"Sir, I am aware of that fact. The baby's mother left a letter in which she requested me to care for him until ..." Nina had no chance to complete what she wished to say.

"You went ahead with your wish of adopting him even after realizing the baby's background and his family's wishes. Can you deny that?" asked the officer, glancing at Hussein.

Was she here to adopt a child or ... was she here to follow a painful, religious protocol? When was her society going to consider Nikil as a child ... instead of a religious accident?

"Sir, when I saw this child, I saw a young human being. I didn't notice a Hindu, a Muslim, or a Christian. I saw a human being!" said Nina.

A week from the current Wednesday was chosen for the final hearing. Nina left the formidable atmosphere with uncertain questions and worries. Vijay left for home directly, and Dev drove her home. Tom, after a brief nod toward Nina, followed Vijay. For the first time since her heated argument with Tom, Nina wished she had not been so harsh to him on that particular day—the day before Nikil was taken away from her. She had come to realize how much Tom's assurance had comforted her every now and then. She wouldn't have been so angry if he had not provoked her. Well, she didn't need him any longer. In fact, once Nikil came back to her, she had no reason to look at Tom except when the baby needed a doctor. Yes, she didn't need him. She decided to ignore that little something which began to hurt inside at the thought of never seeing Tom. She must be hurting because she missed Nikil. That was it! She needed the doctor to offer counsel regarding her precious baby. Otherwise, Tom Davis didn't matter.

Nina received an unpleasant call.

"Nina," Seetha began. "Did you forget that your parents died in a plane crash that was triggered by the hatred and violence of Muslim rebels?"

"Athai," Nina said sadly, "why are you talking about that disaster now?"

"You still want to adopt this child. Do you realize what blood runs in him?" Seetha asked in her domineering tone. "Chandran told me. That baby is related to that businessman in Delhi. What's his name—Hussein, is it? He is notorious. His family appears in the news constantly. Nina, remember what blood runs in Nikil. That child will turn wild when he is older. Aren't you worried about that?"

"Nikil is an innocent, young human being," Nina shouted. "Every child who has Muslim blood in the veins doesn't necessarily become violent and every child who doesn't have the same blood is not essentially a saint."

"Nina, if you don't pay respect to my age and my relationship, what shall I do? Your father was my brother and blood is thicker ..."

Nina had heard and suffered enough! She dropped the phone and went about her business.

On Tuesday, Valli, Veni, and the other students were assembled in Brinda for a different reason. Lately, Nina's concern about Nikil had become their worry.

"Nina," said Valli, speaking for the group. "How is Nikil? We miss him too. We hope he is doing well."

Nina couldn't believe what she was hearing. These people, especially Valli, represented the society, which had partially been an impediment in her adoption procedure because she was a single woman! And here they were, hoping things would turn out in her favor.

"Thank you for your concern," Nina said sincerely. "But I'm not able to disclose Nikil's whereabouts."

"Oh, no," cried Valli. "You shouldn't worry about it. After all, Nikil's safety is of primary importance! We'll pray for him and you, Nina."

Tuesday night ought to be long. In anticipation of Nina's nerves, Bitsy decided to sleep on the sofa in Nina's room. Staring at the dancing shadows, Bitsy reminded Nina of her visits to Brinda during her childhood. Her soothing voice rocked Nina to sleep.

◆ ◆ ◆

Despite her anxiety and apprehensions, Nina woke up reasonably rested. Sandy and Jim called to wish her luck. Nina instantly felt energized. She was pleasantly surprised to receive another phone call. It was from her brother.

"Nina, I wish you all the best," Jay said kindly. "Everything will go well, Nina."

"Thank you, Jay. I'm glad you called," said Nina, touched. "I'll call you as soon as I hear something, all right?"

"Was it Jay?" Bitsy asked delightedly and smiled. "I'm going with you, Nina."

"Of course, you have to go with me. What would I do without you, Bitsy?" asked Nina, with obvious relief. She needed all the help she could gather.

Vijay followed in his own car with Tom. Nina talked briefly to Vijay when Tom was looking away. She had no wish to exchange words with the doctor.

The meeting began punctually. The officer read his decision without unnecessary preliminaries:

"In view of the baby's blood relation, Hussein,"

Nina's confidence was receding at this announcement.

"And keeping in mind, a personality who is held in respect among his community,"

This didn't help Nina recover her confidence.

"The decision of adoption and custody would be deferred until …"

That certainly didn't mean that Hussein would be the guardian. It simply meant that the decision would be announced later. Nina was disappointed and wondered how long Nikil had to wait to belong to a family.

Nina got up and walked out of the oppressive atmosphere. What she saw outside was incredible. The whole town seemed to have assembled outside the building. Clearly, Veni had orchestrated the crowd, assisted by her husband and Ravi. Even Valli was standing in the front row. She smiled, displaying the betel nut-coated teeth, and she took Nina's trembling hand in her weathered hands to express her support. Nina's eyes darted from one face to the other. She didn't know all of their names, but she remembered seeing the faces in the community. Nina felt touched. The unknown something that had been floating in her heart pulled away with a snap, but she was relieved. She waved to her supporters and got into her car.

Dev drove quietly and Bitsy held Nina's hand. What could be said at a time like this? Nina wondered if she had behaved badly by walking out of the meeting. If she had continued to stare at the pompous faces another minute, she would have screamed. THAT would have been unforgivable in the eyes of the rigid system! She was tired of this exhibition, especially when she was the main attraction of the event.

"Mr. Vijay and Dr. Davis seem to be following us, Bitsy," Dev announced.

"Are they?" asked Bitsy. "They probably wish to discuss something. Who knows?"

Bitsy made sure that the gentlemen were settled in the drawing room before fetching something to drink.

"Vijay, thanks for all you've done so far, although," Nina said, collecting her steady voice in a few moments. "Thank you."

"Nina, it's not over, okay? Please don't give up. It's not out of our hands. The final decision is yet to happen, right?" asked Vijay, trying to comfort her. He left after a quick cup of tea.

Nina expected Tom to follow Vijay out of the house because he had come in Vijay's car. However, he disappointed her by still sitting on the sofa. What was he doing here? 'Clumsy' was an understatement in such a situation. He just sat there and stared at the window. Why couldn't he get on with it and leave her alone as soon as possible?

"Nina," said Tom. "I'm sorry about the way things went today. It means that you have to wait longer."

"Thanks. It's not easy to wait indefinitely, but there's no other choice. How much more time do you think they'll need to make a decision?" Nina asked, trying to steady her faltering courage.

"It can take anywhere from a month to a few months. I've made sure that it doesn't take more than a couple of weeks."

Nina's desperate expression transformed to immense relief. How did he manage to do this? Did she want to know? All she wanted was Nikil. God willing, if everything went well, she could discover at a later time how Tom managed to do what he seemed to do so well.

"Nina, there'll be no more disturbances in your house. Nikil and you are safe. It's over."

"What?"

"The persons, the groups that were responsible for a lot of unrest, are behind bars," Tom explained. "You should be all right. Still … we might as well let Nikil stay in a different location until the adoption decision is declared, don't you agree?"

"You mean the police official and that other man who were arrested recently in Dandiar?" Nina asked. Was there anything Tom didn't know?

"Yes. I'm glad that we don't have to discuss the Dandiar stories now. We'll certainly talk about them later. Even if the interest is revived on the project, you're not going to have anything to do with it, are you? I mean … considering the safety or lack of …"

"Why not? If I feel like it, I shall. I'm not afraid," Nina said, not letting him finish. She simply couldn't get rid of the devil on her toes.

"You should be a little afraid for Nikil's sake."

How could she forget? He was, clearly, worried about Nikil and Nikil only. She wanted to tell him to go to hell. She didn't. She decided to control her tongue unlike the other day. However, she couldn't resist delivering a few cutting words. "If Nikil should be mine," said Nina, "I'll know exactly what to do and how to act."

"Yes, of course. Well, thank you for your time," said Tom. His level, cool voice indicated that she didn't have the pleasure of insulting him.

"Excuse me, Nina," said Bitsy, looking into the drawing room. "Tony has come to pick up Dr. Davis."

After Tom left, Nina felt the deficiency in her manners. She could have thanked him decently for his extraordinary efforts regarding Nikil's adoption, especially during the last couple of weeks. Nina wondered at Tom's memory. A while ago, she had casually talked about the reason behind her decision to quit

The Express. He still remembered, and he somehow stood in her life, managing the wrinkles and the tears. She wanted to thank him. How?

The much-awaited letter arrived. Nina couldn't open it. Finally, Bitsy opened it with a resolution that she had mastered over many years. Bitsy and Dev felt the pain, perhaps as much as Nina did. It was a good thing that Nikil was away. Otherwise, the misery would have increased several folds.

Vijay called. He was apologetic, although it was not his fault. Well, he had tried his best. Nina took it well or as composedly as she could, at least while Vijay was still on the phone.

"Nina, shall I come over?" asked Vijay. "I promise you. We can file a resubmission, anything I can do to help. They'll not give Nikil to his new guardian so soon. There are still some legal formalities to be observed."

"Thank you, Vijay. I'll think about it."

"Nina, never forget that Simi and I are always here."

Simi took the phone from Vijay and repeated his sentiments.

Nina thanked them for that one lingering assurance, gave the phone to Bitsy, and walked to the river. Wherever she went, tears followed. Everything seemed devoid of happiness since Nikil went away. Nina was walking up the footpath from the river. Somehow, the path seemed to be long-winded. What was she doing here? Where was she going? Did life have a purpose? If it did, why was it taken away from her? Her aching heart called her baby's name a thousand times. Her stinging eyes dropped a thousand tears. Whose fault was it? Who was responsible for taking Nikil away from her?

Bitsy gave the phone to Nina when she returned. It was Roy.

"Have you thought about my offer, Nina?" Roy asked. "Your answer is all that is needed. Are you coming back to us? Come on, tell me that you're returning to Delhi."

Tom arrived in the afternoon. Bitsy took him to the drawing room without her usual enthusiasm.

"Bitsy, may I see Nina?" Tom asked.

"She is not home, Doctor," replied Bitsy. "She is finalizing our travel plan."

"Travel plan? What travel plan, Bitsy?"

"Nina is anxious to take care of things right away, you know?" said Bitsy. She had an eye on Dr. Davis' face when she informed him of Nina's whereabouts.

"Where are you going?" Tom asked.

"We're moving to Delhi," Bitsy sighed. "You see, with things turning out this way, it's very hard for Nina. Actually, it's sad for all of us."

"And she didn't tell me," said Tom. "She never mentioned it, not that I need to know. When are you leaving, Bitsy?"

"Sometime soon, Doctor. I'm sure we shall leave sometime soon," Bitsy said, stopping Tom at the door by holding his hand. "Thanks for all you've done."

"Tears in your eyes, Bitsy? Unbelievable!" Tom wiped Bitsy's weathered cheeks. "Take care, Bitsy. I know you'll take care of Nina. Give my regards to Dev. God bless."

Hussein was sitting in Balu's veranda after a very satisfactory meal of mutton biryani, an assortment of vegetables, and sweet dishes. For a perfect ending, he was chewing on betel leaves, scented with flavored nuts and fennel. The country air, seasoned with the fragrance from the orchards, made the evening perfect. The serenity was momentarily interrupted by noises from the street.

"What's going on out there?" Balu, Hussein's attentive host, asked one of his servants.

"Sir, some people are standing outside the gate. They want to see Mr. Hussein," said the servant, meekly.

"How many?" asked Balu.

"A lot, Sir," replied the servant.

Balu asked his men to get some weapons to tackle the crowd. While he was assembling a small army, the servant gave a note to Hussein. It was an appeal, respectfully penned to request a few minutes of his time. Hussein asked the servant to let the people in. He was surprised to see a group of men and women, with sober faces and earnest expressions, walking quietly toward him. What were women doing here—leaving the shelter of their homes and walking equally with men?

Balu recognized some of the visitors. Young Ravi was in the Dairy Farmer's Association. A small fry! He also knew Veni. Her father used to be his turmeric vendor before Veni's burly husband took over that business. Even Valli was here! What was she doing here among other old crows? This promised to be quite entertaining! Balu rested his thin frame on a chair behind Hussein and got ready to enjoy the show. Hussein greeted the visitors with just a hint of a smile and waited anxiously for what was to come.

They had come to appeal to Hussein's kindness. They had a story to tell. Veni was the narrator.

"A child was left in the world without a home. She took him into her home and into her heart. She wanted nothing in return except an appeal to the society to allow her to protect the child, to educate him, to give him a beautiful life, and to earn the status of his mother.

This child has become her mission and the meaning of her life. She can't understand the evil around her, the kind of evil that raises its head in the middle of culture, traditions, and convictions. She sees the virtue in her friends and walks over the superstitions in the community. She embraces friends, regardless of their status, wealth, and religious beliefs. She is a remarkable human being.

She read to us that we allow religion to make us hate and not to love one another. She is independent, a position strengthened by intelligence, kindness, fairness, honesty, and love. She is fire, with an ardent flame. She has it in her to be a kind mother, a good parent, and a careful guardian. This child can find none better.

Can she call him her son? This is an appeal from us—a group of friends who have discovered the values of turning a rigid society into a loving community. And we learned these ideals from the lady who is living by those values. Now it is in the hands of a kind and generous gentleman, Mr. Hussein ..."

Tom was waiting in his drawing room. Although he held a book in his hands, his eyes were not on the words. His restless mind was far away, searching for a glimpse of hope and love. When will his search be over? He missed her and the baby! If this was not meant to happen, then what was? For the first time in his life, when he gave up his search for an ardent love and true happiness, here they were, hidden behind a curtain of uncertainty.

He opened the front door and smiled. He was glad to let in Veni, her husband, and a few other townspeople, who had come here straight from Balu's house. They had performed a feat, a courageous and unprecedented act on behalf of a kind, generous, and selfless lady. Now they came here to thank the considerate doctor for encouraging them to take such a big step.

◆ ◆ ◆

Nina had an appointment at the bank around noon. She was quite surprised to see Vijay and Simi in the parking lot.

"Nina, please join us for lunch," said Simi, characteristically issuing a spontaneous invitation.

Since Nina was at the end of her errands, she gladly accepted the invitation.

"Where have you been, Nina?" Simi asked. "We called home. Bitsy said you would be out all morning. Vijay had the afternoon off and we wished to come and see you. You're not leaving Kanyakoil right away, are you?"

"I'm sorry I wasn't home when you called. I forgot to take my cell phone with me. That's why Bitsy couldn't reach me. We'll leave as soon as we can."

The *Tiffin Room* was not crowded. Vijay requested the host for a table in the air-conditioned room.

"Isn't this strange?" asked Simi. "You're moving and Tom Davis is moving to ..." Simi turned to her husband. "Where is he going, Vijay?"

"I'm not sure," he said, "I think he has decided to accept that contract at ... what's that hospital in Chennai?"

Nina lost interest in the menu and froze at this information. Tom never said a word. Why would he? His interest in visiting Brinda or seeing her was over. There was no Nikil. She didn't care. Why would she care? It didn't matter where he went, as long as it was somewhere far away from her. Nina swallowed the lunch with as much grace as she could gather under the circumstances and thanked her friends for inviting her. "I've to go home. Would you be spending the rest of the afternoon here, Simi?" Nina asked.

"Yes, Nina, we have a shopping list. Is Dev coming to pick you up? Can we give you a ride home, Nina? It'll be our pleasure, my dear."

"Thank you for the offer, Simi. Yes, Dev is picking me up later."

"Nina, why don't you spend a week with us before leaving? We'll miss you, but you know that."

Nina hugged her friend and promised to spend some time with her before her departure.

Nina read Bitsy's list and made sure she purchased everything she needed. She was done with her errands earlier than expected, and Dev was not supposed to pick her up for another hour. The weather was unseasonably cool for this time of the year—a perfect day to take a long walk. Nina walked into a store. The storekeeper was one of her students.

"May I leave my packages here?" Nina asked. "I can come in the car later to collect them."

"Absolutely, Miss Nina," replied the storekeeper. "Can I get you anything to drink?"

"No thanks. I just need to use your phone to call Dev. I left my cell phone at home." Nina called home and requested Dev to pick her up at the temple in about an hour.

The temple was just a kilometer away, and Nina walked through the throng of market day. In spite of a small supermarket, a couple of beauty salons, and other modern amenities, the town still clung to the traditional bartering in the dusty stalls among chickens and goats. The river was full. Her eyes took in the silvery water and the sand. The familiar smoky smell from the vendor's grill, the rhythmic waves, the birds, fiercely squawking the arrival of the fresh-water fish—she will miss this. But life in Brinda would be painful. Every corner echoed Nikil's laughter, his toothless smile, and his bubbly babble. It would be impossible to breathe in the days toward empty dusks. Bitsy and Dev agreed with her. Getting out of Kanyakoil was the sensible thing to do. Then again, when did Bitsy and Dev disagree with her? Was Nina being selfish? Bitsy and Dev had settled down in comfort and peace. They enjoyed the country air. Dev and his garden—won't he miss that in the cramped apartment in Delhi? Nina had suggested that Dev and Bitsy should relax a little longer in Kanyakoil. Further, there was no need for them to follow Nina right away. But … Nina saw the pain in Bitsy's eyes. Bitsy would go wherever Nina went, like the sun sinking into the earth. That was exactly what she had promised her when Nina was very young, and Bitsy was the sort to always keep her promise.

Nina was close to the temple. There it was—the peepul tree where she had found Nikil for the first time. She walked on the gravel to the entrance of the temple. What was she praying here for? Where was God hiding when she prayed ardently to grant her the love of a child? Well, she continued to pray for Nikil's welfare. Nina walked back to the tree and sat in the shade. An unknown weariness engulfed her. She buried her face in her hands.

"I think you must look up at the sky to appeal to God."

Nina raised her head to see where the voice came from. Hussein was standing in front of her! He requested her to sit down when he saw her getting up. What was he doing here?

"Mr. Hussein?" Nina said, surprised. "I thought you had already left with …"

"The lady in your house told me that I might find you here. Do you have a few minutes?" Hussein looked directly at Nina.

"Yes, of course," said Nina, trying not to sound nervous. Understandably, she was a little nervous. Was he looking for her? Bitsy sent him to the temple? Interesting! Why was he here?

"Did you know that I lived in this town?" Hussein asked Nina. "I was just a boy. I used to swim in the river, the same one that borders your home. During one of those times, my limbs got tired. I collapsed on the sand, and I was taken to the orphanage. That's right. A few people took me to Mercy House! They thought I was a homeless boy! Miss Aruna was a wonderful lady. She fed me, filled my young heart with smiles, and sent me away with a handful of sweets."

Nina brightened when he mentioned Aruna's name. He smiled gently and sat down a few feet away from her. He took a wrinkled paper from his shirt pocket that looked like a photograph. He placed it in Nina's hands. It was a picture of Parvathi and Feroz, with colorful garlands and brilliant smiles. Nina's heart skipped a beat or two. This must be their wedding picture! She was sad and utterly bewildered.

"If I can count the number of family members and friends I've lost in the hatred," he said. "It's just hatred, you see? Young lives, old tears—God doesn't plan for the bloodshed that man so willingly jumps into. The world needs love and kindness so badly."

"Sir, I …"

"I never approved of Feroz's marriage," Hussein said rather blandly. "If only I had known how severely those two young people would be battered. I should've known."

Nina was scared of the naked rage in his eyes. Thankfully, it disappeared just as quickly as it appeared.

"If only I had known," Hussein continued, "I would've taken them to my home. They were already in my heart."

"I'm sorry," said Nina. "I would've gladly helped Parvathi and any of her relations if … if only she had talked to me once, just once!" Nina looked away to hide the tears.

"You, young lady, can take care of fifty Parvathis," Hussein smiled. "When God made you, he took kindness, determination, love, and the most compassionate heart, and he multiplied the portions many times."

Nina felt the attachment of a father in his tone. Prompted by such comforting thoughts, she took a stab at a streak of spirit. She spoke up. It was now or never. "Still, you don't think I can take care of a baby, Mr. Hussein?" Nina asked.

"Perhaps, Miss, God fortified you with persistence a hundred times?"

Nina wasn't sure how to treat this comment. She was relieved to notice an abundance of kindness in his expression when he smiled.

"But that's what got you where you are today," Hussein said, smiling again. "I feel honored to know you, a very special, remarkable human being. God bless you!" He got up.

"Thank you. Sir, your photograph?" Nina asked.

"No, that should stay with you," replied Hussein. "That's where it belongs."

Dev parked the car by the veranda. The monsoon that began a couple of days ago didn't want to retreat. Dev got out of the car and opened the umbrella for Nina, but it collapsed in the wind. Nina rushed to the veranda.

"Appa!"

What was that? Nina heard it again.

"Appa!"

It couldn't be! Was it Nikil's voice? It was Nikil! The precious baby was sitting under a bench with a mischievous smile.

"Nina, where did the baby come from?" Dev asked. "I must ask Bitsy. Where is she?" Dev was never as confused as he was now.

Bitsy came to the veranda. She pulled Dev into the house, announced that Nina had visitors, and walked away.

Nina took a deep breath. She picked up Nikil and hugged him. "Oh, what are you doing here all alone? Where did you come from, Nikil?" Nina asked. The raindrops, slowly trickling down from her wet hair, fought with her imminent tears. "Who brought you here?"

"Appa," said Nikil, not willing to give up.

Nina was not sure whether to laugh or to cry. "No, my sweetheart. I'm not appa. You don't have a father."

"Yes, he does, only if you approve, Nina."

Tom? He was standing behind one of the huge pillars. Nina looked alternately at his face and at Nikil's. Tom was smiling as though standing there at that moment was the most natural thing to do.

"You didn't leave?" Nina asked. That was all she could say. She pretended to be busy, wiping her face and wringing out the water from the fringe of her shawl. There was an internal tremor she had never experienced before.

Tom smiled and took a few steps toward Nina. He took Nikil from her, told him that he had important business to settle with his mother, called Dev, and deposited the baby in his hands. "You didn't leave either," replied Tom, smiling at her.

"Nikil is here. What happened?" asked Nina. "Tom, did you do something? You did, didn't you?"

"Yes, Nina, along with several others." Tom took Nina's hand and walked to the front door and opened it.

The community that strived to find faults with her earlier was there. The same men and women had gone through a tremendous, unprecedented effort to bring a child to her today. They were assembled in the drawing room of a single woman, supposedly not qualified to raise a child on her own. They were waiting here to see the joy in her eyes. Nina brought her hands together to thank them. She could say her thanks all her life to express her complete gratitude and still come out incomplete. Tom closed the door. The relief after seeing Nikil again, the mere surprise of hearing his voice, the touching affection of the community, and Tom's presence, his assurance, his affection—the deferred tears broke loose.

Tom pulled her close to him and let her cry. She needed to. She had to. "Nina, cry all you want. But this is the last day you're going to cry as long as I'm alive. I'm going to make sure of that, all right?" Tom lifted her chin and whispered in her ears. "You got what you wanted, Nina. Now help me get what I want."

"Let me go, what if somebody sees us?" asked Nina.

"Who is going to see us? The entire population is sitting in your drawing room! First, promise me that you'll get me what I want."

Nina was speechless. She discovered a stroke of happiness for the first time in her life that she thought never existed. "What do you want?" Nina stammered.

"You and Nikil. Will you marry me?"

Although Nina was used to his abrupt tactics, she didn't know how to handle this question. Thankfully, he continued to talk.

"When I thought you left," said Tom, "something within me died! And if you had left, all of me would have perished. Nina, you must realize by now that I love you."

Now Nina was totally lost, but she wasn't going to let him discover that. "You want to marry me to take care of Nikil, don't you?" Nina looked into his eyes defiantly, but she quickly averted her own at the unmistakable glint in his.

"What's this nonsense?" he asked, lifting her chin again. "If I had to marry a woman just to take care of a child who needed a home, I should have been married at least a few dozen times by now."

True! Nina wished she had not teased him with that. But she was swept off her feet. How could she think clearly? She had been in search of her dear child. She didn't expect to gain motherhood and the love of an utterly wonderful man at the same time. A man who lived for others' welfare, a man whose calling was to bring happiness around him with no strings attached, loved her. And she had an entire lifetime to return that love, along the river, under the canopy of rain-drenched orchards.

"Now, my dearest Nina," Tom said impatiently, "stop being silly and tell me you'll marry me. Our friends are not leaving your drawing room until you say yes."

"Well, in that case, I must say yes."

Nina blushed and tried to free herself when she heard footsteps behind her. The rain stopped out of respect for those souls, unselfish souls, who were waiting to come out to see a blue sky that would guide them during a safe journey to their homes. Veni and her associates trickled into the veranda to congratulate the clever doctor and the kind journalist. It was the blessing of a thousand stars. A storm of laughter and noise gradually disappeared when the friends left Brinda.

"Okay, now tell me you love me. I've been waiting a long time to hear this from your lips. I'm a stubborn man, although not as stubborn as you are."

"Oh, yes? Well, I love you, but I probably shouldn't because you were planning to go away. How do you think I felt when I heard about it?"

"What's good for one is good for the other, my dearest Nina! I was planning to leave only because you were. How could I live here after losing you? How could I walk by the river when I could see just your shadow?" Tom asked and paused at the softness in her eyes. "What made you change your mind? You decided to stay here!"

"Well, I thought I lost you too after losing Nikil, and I wished to disappear from here. But there was something that needed me here. These people—Veni and Valli and others—I felt touched by how they let me into their lives, how they let me make a difference. They needed me, and I felt I could try to make up for Nikil and you in their laughter and happiness. And why didn't you leave?"

"I didn't leave because I was hoping to convince you to be mine. Now, no more tears, darling. I can't stand to see tears in your eyes." He took her face in his hands and began to kiss her. He was interrupted. Someone was eager to blow bubbles in his ear. It was his son … well, soon to be one. Dev had Nikil on his back. Bitsy was standing by him.

"Dr. Davis, move away. Dev and I don't want to wait for hours to congratulate our dearest Nina on acquiring a couple of blessings; a son and a husband!"

"What about me, Bitsy?" asked Tom. "No hugs and congratulations for me? Has Bitsy already forgotten me?" Tom asked, appealing to Dev.

Tom's twinkle was no match to the wicked twinkle in Bitsy's eyes when she hugged and blessed him with a heart filled with love and joy.

Song of the Dawn

What ensued afterwards established a society that broke several inhibitions. The townspeople conducted a wedding between a catholic gentleman and a Hindu lady. Tom and Nina got married in the presence of Sylvia and Victor, Vijay and Simi, Fiona and John Woodward, the counselor from Children's Welfare Services, Mr. Hussein, and several important pillars of the society. Kim Roberts and

Dr. Colin Hebert arrived from New York City, and the Baileys arrived without Millie. She was expecting her second child! Veni and her friends were surprised to see Balu among the guests. Balu! A humble, new step for a patriarchal businessman! One couldn't describe the pride and love with which Dev and Bitsy gave away the bride. This happy event didn't occur until Nina signed the adoption papers that endorsed her as Nikil's mother. Tom insisted on seeing Nina as Nikil's mother before he married her—not to defy the system, but to prove a point and to establish Nina's intentions. Jim, Tom's best man, was to become one of little Nikil's favorite uncles, and his wife, Sandy, was to be his proud aunt. Victor and Sylvia greeted the guests as Nikil's devoted godparents. Nobody raised an eyebrow at the bride or the groom. Veni and her associates wouldn't tolerate that.

Seetha sent an excuse instead of attending the wedding. She also stopped her sons from making a trip. Nina's cousin, Chitra, represented Anand's family. Jay arrived without his haughty wife. Nina breathed a sigh of relief. Bitsy was thrilled to shower her love on her little Jay—thanks to Leela's absence.

The married couple received a kiss from a child who was half-Hindu and half-Muslim until a few days ago. He became Nikil Davis. With that new name, he embraced three religions with his chubby arms at a very tender age! For the first time in Kanyakoil, a spinster adopted a child and married a gentleman—not because she had to—because her heart desired it. Brinda echoed the laughter, music, and heartbeat of many at the wake of a revolution that took the little town like a raging storm.

A new woman, a very different woman, emerged.

> Resilient earth fed her forbearance.
> Raging wind blew away her fears.
> Merciful water drenched her purpose.
> Complacent ether gave her tolerance.
> Blazing fire ignited her focus.

She lived a beautiful life, holding her husband's hand and cherishing her son's smiles. Nina saw the sunrise everyday of her life. It was a perfect dawn, flanked by amber clouds and rain-drenched horizons. Tom saw heaven in his son's eyes and felt love in his wife's whispers. Nikil saw the sun kissing the earth from his mother's lap. He asked for the moon from his father's arms. It was a perfect dawn that spread sunshine in the lives of Nina, Tom, and their baby. It was a beautiful dawn that filled the lives of Bitsy and Dev with joy and peace. And what an extraordinary dawn it was that welcomed Veni and her fellow revolutionaries with open minds, undiluted happiness, and the monsoon of the Gods!